Undeniable

By K. M.

All characters are fictional. Any resemblance to persons living or dead is coincidental and quite unintentional.

ISBN 0-9754922-5-X

First Printing 2004

Cover art and design by Samantha E. Ruskin

Photo by Joy Argento

Published by:

Dare 2 Dream Publishing

A Division of Limitless Corporation

Lexington, South Carolina 29073

Find us on the World Wide Web

http://www.limitlessd2d.net

Printed in the United States and the UK by

Lightning Source, Inc.

This book is dedicated to all those who have offered me their kind words and thoughts of encouragement. I can never fully express my gratitude.

Undeniable

K M

Chapter 1

This simply wasn't going like she had planned. It should have been a mere formality. Just walk in, mention unforeseen circumstances, get an extension of time. That's it. Done all the time. Five minutes later, walk out. No problem. No big deal. Nope. I rest my case. Let's all go home. Right?

Wrong.

Why can't anything that's supposed to be easy, be easy?

"Ms. Harrison?" Judge Hancock ventured a quirked eyebrow as he sat perched at his bench in his hearing chambers. "Your client has had over sixty days to respond to these interrogatories, with one extension of time already granted. I'm not persuaded to give you any more time on this. Discovery rules are here for a reason, Ms. Harrison, as I'm sure you already know."

Jessica Harrison was a newly made junior partner in the firm of Roberts & McDaniel, Orlando's largest and, most people would say, most prestigious law firm. To say that becoming a partner in only six years' time was remarkable would be quite the understatement. With the proliferation of law students graduating out of ever increasing law schools, adding to the abundance of already practicing attorneys, eight years to make partnership was now the standard. And billable hours helped. A lot. Those billable hours had contributed mightily toward her fast track partnership status.

"Your Honor, my client has been and still is out of the country. He was scheduled to return in time to prepare our response, but was unexpectedly detained. I am assured that he will be returning before the end of the month. This was totally unforeseen. Your Honor knows that counsel cannot just fabricate responses to interrogatories when such answers must be sworn to by the client." *I'm grasping at straws here.*

"That's enough, Ms. Harrison." Judge Hancock's hand went up in front of him as he peered over the rim of his glasses and turned his attention toward the opposing counsel. "Mr. Jacobs, I take your point. You are entitled to your discovery responses in a timely manner." Glancing momentarily at Jessica, the judge then directed his next comments to both counsel. "Mr. Jacobs, your motion to compel is granted. Ms, Harrison, get in touch with your client. Find him, fax him, phone him, e-mail him, whatever. You've got ten days. That's it. No more. If those responses are not served on opposing counsel by then, I will hold both you and your client in contempt of this Court. That is all." And with that, the judge abruptly stood up, muttering something unintelligible under his breath, and swiftly exited his chambers.

Jessica stood in place a moment before exiting the courtroom. *Damn, I need a drink.* The truth of the matter was, she had no earthly idea where on God's green earth her client was. *We might have to withdraw from this case if we can't find the little bastard. Shit.* The firm would not want to lose this client. He was an eccentric, yes. But deep pockets and lots of litigation make one happy law firm and one happy senior partner, both of which held her future, or so she thought, in their figurative hands.

****

"Look, Harry, we've got to find him. I'm sure as hell not going to fork over any contempt of court fines because no one can find this guy." Jessica's voice was raised in exasperation.

Harry Roberts, senior partner of the litigation department for the firm and mentor to Jessica Harrison, listened patiently as she continued.

"I'm serious here. I've got two trials in the next three months and a warehouse full of documents waiting to be reviewed. I need help here, not another headache. Assign this to someone else. Someone else can find time to track down this guy. Take me off the case. I've got too much else going on right now." Jessica's somewhat agitated voice became calm once again. "You know I'm right, Harry."

Harry pondered her plea for a brief moment. She was one of the firm's most gifted attorneys, always working late, coming up with brilliant legal arguments. She was completely dedicated to the firm, and rarely asked for anything. "I get your point, Jess." Harry looked out of the wide floor to ceiling windows in his large, partner sized, well appointed office. Harry Roberts was one of the very few people who referred to Jessica by a shortened version of her name. It somehow seemed to him to suit her tall, nearly six foot frame. "Okay, what if we do this. Paul will deal with our elusive client. And I think you maybe right. You need more help. I'll assign you one of the new associates and get you some paralegal assistance. Happy now?" Harry let go a small grin and turned to Jess expectantly.

"Thanks. I knew you'd see it my way," she said a bit too triumphantly. *That was just too easy. He's got something up his sleeve. I wonder what I'll owe him later.*

"You're welcome. Oh, and Jess?" He looked directly at her. "Win those trials, will you?"

Jess quirked an eyebrow and then winked. "You know I'll do my best." She looked intently at Harry and turned her attention to her victory. "So which associate do I get?" She met his eyes mischievously. "I promise I won't torture whoever it is mercilessly. After all, we'll be going to New Orleans for a particularly stimulating document review. Surely, no one could pass that up," she said with a devilish grin.

In the litigation world, it was a well-known fact of life that very often, in standard litigation cases, volumes of documents had to be reviewed. It was also a well-known fact of life that no one, absolutely no one, in a run for the hills screaming for your life mentality, wanted in any way, shape or form to spend countless hours holed up somewhere reviewing documents. Lots and lots of documents. Lots and lots of boring documents. It was, quite frankly, inhumane and beyond torture, just to put it mildly.

"Well, let's see. How about Robin Wilson. I was impressed by how dedicated she seemed when the recruiting committee met with her. I'm sure she can take whatever you dish out." He winked. "Let me go talk to her this afternoon, then you two can meet and strategize." Harry glanced at his watch. "I've got to get going. Come see me later if you need to." Running late for a lunch appointment, Harry raced out the door leaving a very relieved junior partner to contemplate her victory, albeit small in the grand scheme of things, but significant enough to put a satisfied smile on her face.

As Jess headed back to her office, she tried to picture in her mind just who this Robin Wilson person was. *I remember her, I think. Back at the welcome social for the new associates last week. I didn't get to talk with her, though. I got there late. Should have tried to meet everyone. Damn.*

Jess entered her newly furnished office, sat down at the cherry wood desk, and dialed the phone. "Paul? Hi, it's Jessica. You free for lunch? I need to go over a case with you about a client who's dropped off the face of the earth. You are one very lucky man, my friend." Her voice held a decidedly amused tone as she spoke into the phone.

******

"Okay." A sigh. "I'm done. Finally." Robin Wilson said to herself as she placed the last framed diploma on the wall of her new office. It had taken over two days between meetings, new associate gatherings, and new work assignments for her to finally unpack her things and set up her very own office. The office had a wonderful lakefront view from the 16th floor office suite. Robin was fresh out of law school and more than a little nervous at starting her career at the prestigious law firm of Roberts & McDaniel. She smiled to herself and booted up her computer to check her e-mail. She brushed her fingers through her short blonde hair and blew out a breath. *Now comes the hard part. They were impressed enough with me to hire me, now I just have to prove them right.*

Her musings were interrupted by a short knock on her partially open door. Harry Roberts stood in the doorway with a pleasant grin on his face. "Robin, how's it going?" His boisterous voice came in from the doorway. "You got a minute? There's something I wanted to talk to you about." He took a seat in front of the desk and sat back in a relaxed posture as he spoke. "I'm going to assign you to work with one of our junior partners, Jessica Harrison. She has several cases coming up for trial in the next few months. I've asked her to come see you about what she needs to get done. I'll give you a little heads up, though." He hesitated slightly. "I think there's a document review involved in there somewhere."

A mental groan. *Oh, great. A document review. Great. Terrific. Why couldn't I have gotten at least a little break here?* "Sure, Harry whatever Ms. Harrison needs, I'll be happy to assist," Robin answered. "I'm looking forward to working with her."

"She's one of our top litigators and I think working with her will benefit you. It's really something to see her in action," he said a bit wistfully. "She has a reputation for winning the big ones." He glanced approvingly around her office. "So, I see you're getting settled. How's everything else going for you? You getting enough work?"

"Oh, yes. I've already gotten several research assignments and I'm scheduled to sit in on a deposition tomorrow with Paul Franklin. And I've finally gotten my office together, so I'm ready to go."

Harry stood up and headed for the door. Looking back at her, he spoke in a sincere tone which she somehow found quite reassuring. "Good. And Robin, if you need anything, I want you to come see me. Okay?"

"I will. Thank you, sir." As Harry retreated out into the hallway, Robin sat back and thought about this new work assignment. *Jessica Harrison. Jessica Harrison.* She rested her chin against her hand. *I don't think I remember meeting her. She wasn't at the welcome social last week, was she? God, I hope I can get along with her.* She sighed. *A document review. Damn. This is really going to be torture.* Another sigh. *Okay, lets check those e-mails.*

When she was finished, she glanced at her watch and found it was already after 5:00. Shutting down her computer, Robin mentally checked off everything she had to do that evening, not the least of which was unpacking what would soon be the contents of her new apartment. *Moving is such a bitch.* With that not too pleasant thought, she grabbed her briefcase and made her way home.

****

It was already late morning when Robin took a break from her research, got a cup of coffee, and returned to her office. She was feeling a bit tired as the result of staying up late the previous night unpacking several, but not all, of the many boxes now cluttering up her new apartment. *These cases are not directly on point. I need more to go on.* A brief knock on her door brought her attention from her case law. A tall form stood in the doorway. Robin couldn't help but notice the woman's dark, almost black hair and very blue eyes.

"Hi, Robin. I'm Jessica Harrison. I don't believe we've met." Jess extended her hand to the new associate.

Robin shook her hand gently. "Ms. Harrison. Good to meet you."

"Listen, I wanted to talk to you about something." Jess stepped further into the office and took a seat opposite Robin's desk. "Nice view." She motioned toward the expansive windows overlooking the lake and fountain.

Robin turned to look out the same window, noting the way the late morning sunlight glistened off the gently rippling water. "Yes, it's really very nice."

Jess turned her attention to the reason she stopped by to see the new associate in the first place. "Did Harry speak with you about working on some cases with me?"

"Yes, he did. What do you need help with?"

Jess regarded the new associate. She was petite with short blonde hair and green eyes. *Sea green eyes,* her mind mentally supplied. It wasn't often that she noticed such things about people she'd just met, but there was something about the new associate that caused her to do just that. It was barely a conscious thought, and if she had thought about it more fully, she would have considered it highly inappropriate. Nevertheless, it was something that caught her attention and left her with a subtle, vague impression.

Drawing herself back to the conversation, Jess sat back in the chair and explained. "I have a couple of cases set for trial in the next few months and we've got a lot of discovery to complete at the moment, and then trial preparation further on down the road. I have a document review scheduled next week that I really need help with right now." Jess gave the new associate a wry smile and a slightly quirked eyebrow. She knew full well what most new associates would be thinking right about now, and she just couldn't resist testing the waters, so to speak. She stared intently across the desk. "The document review should be an extremely good opportunity for you and very challenging as well. Think you might be interested?"

Is she teasing me? Robin couldn't be sure. "Um…of course I'm interested, Ms. Harrison. I'll be happy to help in anyway I can." Robin was a bit flustered, and she was sure it showed.

"Please, call me Jessica or Jess, if you'd like." Jess debated with herself whether to tease the new associate just a little bit further. *Why not have a little bit of fun?* "Our client's principal office is in New Orleans and that is where the document review will take place." Again, she looked intently at the new associate. "I think it'll be quite an exciting time. Don't you agree?"

She can't be serious. Documents, exciting? Not likely. Robin wasn't sure how she felt about being teased like this, especially by someone she had just met. But this was a partner with whom she would be working closely, and she really did need to get along with her, so... "Uh, yes, I quite agree. I can't think of anything else I'd rather do," she said rather seriously.

At this, something between a curious and bemused expression crossed the junior partner's face. Clearly, this was not the reaction she'd expected and not the reaction she usually received. Blue eyes questioningly regarded the new associate. "You can't think of *anything* else you'd rather do than go to a document review?"

Gotcha. The new associate smiled sweetly. "Well, actually, what I meant was I can't think of anything else I'd rather do than go to New Orleans." Robin couldn't help the full grin which spread across her face and the barest twinkle in her eye when the junior partner simply nodded her head slowly in understanding and smiled weakly.

Touché. "I guess I deserved that. I think. Perhaps, if the document review goes well, there might be some time to see some of the city while we're there. But we'll have to see how it goes, first." With that, Jess stood up and walked toward the door. "Alright then, I want to fill you in on the strategy we're looking at and then you can spend some time reviewing the complaint and discovery requests which are due at the end of this month. I'll need your help in drafting our responses after we've seen the documents." She stopped and checked her watch. "If you're free for lunch today, we could grab a bite to eat and discuss the issues of the case further."

"Yes, I'm free."

"Good. Let's meet at the elevators in 15 minutes and we'll head out."

Jess made her way down the corridor toward her office, thinking to herself. *That new associate surprised you, Jess. She's not like all the rest. You might just be in for more than you know.* She left that thought to ponder for another time.

****

They sat at a small table near a window in the far corner of the sandwich shop which was just around the corner from the law firm's office building. Standard lunch fare for Jess when she had time to eat, which for her was not often.

"So, you're new to Orlando, aren't you?" Jess asked between bites of her Ham and Swiss sandwich. "What made you want to come to this town?"

"Well," Robin began, "I found the offer from Roberts & McDaniel, well...quite frankly, hard to pass up. This is such a prestigious law firm and I thought I would do well to start my career here. Plus it was a very generous offer." She grinned.

"Yes, I know." Jess grinned back and nodded. Not one for much in the way of small talk, she surprisingly found it quite easy to carry on a conversation with the blonde new associate. "So, where in town did you move?"

Robin looked up into blue eyes and spoke. "The east side, away from a lot of the traffic, near the community college." She took a bite. "I'm still unpacking, though. I never knew I had so much stuff. I'll probably be unpacking for months, maybe even years." She managed a small laugh. Robin was enjoying the relaxed nature of the conversation. It seemed that just maybe she might get along with the junior partner after all. She turned her attention back to her lunch companion. "Um...where do you live? I mean, what area of town?"

Jess regarded the new associate for a moment. "As a matter of fact, I live very close to the community college. I used to teach a legal ethics course out there a couple of years ago. I think you made a good choice in picking that area. The traffic's bad but not as bad as most of the other parts of town. I really think you'll like living out there." Glancing out the window in front of her, Jess thought about this for a moment. *We live on the same side of town.* She didn't stop to consider, however, just why it was she thought that piece of information was particularly significant.

As they finished their lunch, Robin shook her head and gave a small chuckle. "You know, we never did discuss the case."

Jess frowned a little. "Whoops. Sorry about that. My fault. Listen, I'll have my secretary make the necessary airline and hotel reservations for New Orleans. I'll fill you in more about the case on the plane. Is it okay if we leave Sunday evening? I'd like to start fresh on Monday. I expect we'll probably be there all week. We may even have to go back again later if we don't finish."

"Yeah, I'm okay with that," Robin nodded. "Let me know if you have anything you need me to do before we leave." Without further discussion, they stepped out into the bright mid-October sunlight, the fall wind a bit blustery but rather pleasantly warm, and headed back to work.

For Jess, the rest of the day was one where she was better off having never gone to the office in the first place. One crisis after another and a little issue of questionable malpractice by one particular third year associate, to which her reaction was better not mentioned in polite conversation, meant that Jess left the office rather late that evening, even by her standards, very much exhausted and more than a little cranky.

Once home, Jess popped a frozen dinner in the microwave oven, changed into her more comfortable t-shirt and shorts, and after having eaten, stretched her long frame out fully onto the plush living room sofa. She flipped on the television, idly changing from station to station, not really taking notice of the images as they appeared briefly on the screen. Other than the muted sounds of the television, her senses barely registered anything else as she closed her eyes and let her mind drift slowly over the events of the day. In reality, what should have been a bitch of a day, was, in fact, just that. The day from hell. But there was something about the day, in spite of everything that had happened, in spite of the stupidity she had to contend with, and the ever-increasing demands that plagued her time, and in spite of the shear exhaustion she felt, that lingered in her mind.

Robin.

That one simple thought, yet not quite analyzed, eased through her consciousness and carried her far from the troubles of the day. Within a few moments, she had drifted off asleep, as that one simple thought made its way quietly through her subconscious mind, enveloping her gently in calming sea green waters.

****

Sunday.

They boarded their flight to New Orleans and settled into their assigned coach class seats.

"Have you ever been to New Orleans before?" Jess asked as she pulled a paperback book out of her briefcase.

"No, but I have heard quite a bit about it. Both the historical and the...ah...you know, the more 'colorful' aspects," she said and grinned sheepishly.

Jess chuckled. "Well, we'll certainly have to make sure you get a chance to experience the 'full flavor' of the city while we're there," she said with a hint of something Robin couldn't quite decipher. "The French Quarter can prove to be quite an educational experience, in more ways than one." Jess leaned over closer toward Robin and spoke conspiratorially. "I, myself, have found the French Quarter *quite* interesting on occasion." She waggled a dark eyebrow.

Robin nearly choked. *She's teasing me again.* She was finding out quite quickly that the junior partner had a propensity to try and catch people off guard. It worked well in her legal practice, and although it should have bothered Robin, she curiously found it rather enjoyable.

As the plane taxied and prepared for take-off, Jess sat back in her seat, adjusted her seat belt, and glanced over at Robin just in time to see her tense ever so slightly as she stared intently out the small double paned window.

"You don't like flying?"

Robin startled just a little and turned her head from the window toward the junior partner. "I'm okay with the up in the air part." She laughed slightly in embarrassment. "It's just the getting up and getting down parts that make me a little nervous. It's silly, I know."

"Not really," Jess said sympathetically. "When we level out, we can get a glass of wine or something. It might help you relax a little."

"Yeah, that sounds like a good idea. I might do that." Robin took a deep breath and turned her attention to the book in Jess's hand. "So, what are you reading?"

Jess showed her the book cover.

"Danielle Steele? You're reading Danielle Steele?" Robin laughed.

"Yes. What's so funny about that?" Jess was enjoying the light banter. "I'll have you know that Danielle Steele is one of my favorite authors," she teased.

Robin shook her head. "It's just that I never figured you would be the type of person to read that stuff."

"Well, to tell you the truth, I rarely have the time to read. My mother left this book at my house the last time she was visiting. I thought I'd bring it along to kill some time." Jess smiled then decided to come clean. "Actually, I've never really read one of these books before. Wasn't sure I'd like it." She looked up and over to where Robin was sitting and then grinned mischievously. "If you would rather, we could always read the legal briefs I brought instead." She quirked a dark eyebrow.

Robin shook her head emphatically. "No, no, that's quite alright. You go right ahead and read your little book. I'm sure it will be quite to your liking."

Jess focused her attention down to the open pages, and without looking up, asked softly, "So what type of person do you figure me to be?" All kidding aside, it was a serious question. Why it mattered what the new associate thought of her was another question altogether best left for another time.

Robin turned her head hesitantly, not sure she'd heard what she thought she'd heard. She really didn't know what to say to that. It's not like she had known the junior partner for very long. Only a few days. Although if she were to admit it to herself, there was something about the junior partner that was oddly familiar. It was something she couldn't quite put her finger on, but she knew it was true just the same. So, being honest, she said the only thing she could. "I figure you to be a good person."

There was a long silence and Robin didn't think the junior partner was going to say any more. Without further conversation, Robin sat back in her seat and stared out the window again as the plane rose higher above the clouds.

"Thanks," came a soft reply.

Robin looked over toward Jess and smiled, and even though Jess hadn't looked up from her book, Robin knew she was deeply affected by the answer she'd given. There seemed to be much more to the junior partner than Robin had first thought. And that was intriguing in and of itself.

The remainder of the flight somehow seemed to pass quite quickly, both women lost in their own contemplations and both feeling a sense of quiet comfort neither had ever experienced before. It was a feeling that was, quite simply, good.

****

Monday was filled will meetings and employee interviews and files and documents and just about everything imaginable one needed to build a strong legal defense. The client, RSJ Industries, kept meticulous records, and the latter part of the day was filled with surveying the documentation housed at the client's warehouse facility. It had been a long and tedious day, at best.

They had arrived in New Orleans late Sunday evening, and after having checked into their hotel, agreed to call it a night, each ordering room service and intent on getting a good night's rest before tackling the busy week ahead. Meeting for breakfast over beignets and coffee the next morning, Jess laid out for Robin the plans for the week and the work ups she had prepared on each of RSJ's employees and their involvement with the case.

Upon arrival at RSJ, they had been met by Phil Jacobs, Vice-President of Legal Affairs for RSJ Industries, and after brief introductions, were given liberal access to the necessary employees and documentation. As the day progressed, it became apparent that there was much less to be accomplished than Jess had originally thought. From surveying the warehouse records and talking with the company's employees, it was looking as though they might indeed be able to accomplish their goals by the end of the work week.

As 5:00 approached, Phil Jacobs made his way into the dusty warehouse area where Jess and Robin were still surveying the remaining boxes of documentation.

"Hi, you guys. Sorry to have left you two to fend for yourselves all day long. Have you found everything you need to get started?"

"Yes we have. Thanks Phil," Jess said. She stood up and closed the box of documents she was looking at and motioned for Robin to do the same. "We're quite impressed with your diligent recordkeeping here. Believe it or not, that goes a long way toward making a great case for trial. Since it's already after 5:00, we'll get out of your way so your employees can go home. As it stands right now, we'll need to be here the rest of this week, and barring anything unforeseen, it looks like we'll be able to get what we need by Friday. I want to thank you again for your cooperation with this matter. I know it can be a bit disruptive to have people plodding through your offices asking questions and such. But believe me when I tell you that it will make a difference in the long run."

"Sure, no problem," Phil replied. "Anything you need Jess, you just ask. Robin, I hope you like your first stay here in New Orleans. Let me escort you ladies out and on the way, I can give you some recommendations for dinner, if you'd like. I know of some great Cajun and Creole restaurants."

At the mention of food, Robin perked her head up and grinned. "Boy, that would be great. I'm starting to get really hungry." Robin patted her stomach for emphasis.

Jess looked over as Robin said this and smiled widely. *She is adorable.* She reflected on that thought for a moment. *I'm not sure I want to know why I just thought that...but she is definitely adorable.*

****

"So, you're originally from Detroit. What made you want to move all the way to Florida?" Jess looked across the dimly lit table at Robin and took a bite of her shrimp jambalaya. On Phil's recommendation, they had found a nice little restaurant nestled in the heart of the French Quarter just off Bourbon Street. They were seated in a lovely courtyard, pleasantly enjoying the sound of the Dixieland jazz filtering through the night air as they ate their dinner.

Robin took a sip of water and thought about how much she should reveal about the reasons she decided to get as far away from Detroit as possible. It was hard to think about, and she didn't much want to dwell on it.

She sighed. "I wanted to get a fresh start on my life, with nothing to remind me of some of the things back there. I thought Florida sounded kind of exciting. I'd never been to the South before, and the offer from Roberts & McDaniel was very generous. It seemed like the right decision to make at the time. Even though it's only been a couple of weeks, I feel like I did make the right decision."

Jess nodded, thinking there was more to the story than Robin was letting on, but let it go at that. "I think you'll like Florida." She grinned. "There's no snow, for one thing."

"Yeah, though it is pretty sometimes, as long as you're not shoveling it." Robin laughed. "So, what about you, have you always lived in Orlando or did you live somewhere else?"

The glow from the candlelight on the tabletops gave an ethereal quality to the courtyard surroundings, the flickering light almost mesmerizing. Jess poked her fork around on her plate and looked across the table to see intent green eyes staring back at her. "Well, I grew up in Tampa, went to undergraduate and law school at Florida State and then began my career at Roberts & McDaniel. I've been in Orlando for the past six years."

"And you like it, right? Is your family still in Tampa?"

"My mother and brother live over there, my father now lives in New York. They were divorced when I was ten-years-old. I don't really see my father anymore." Jess looked back down at her plate effectively ending the discussion.

"I'm sorry," Robin said. "I didn't mean to pry."

"No, it's alright, really. That's all in the past anyway. I'm much more interested in you." *Damn. Did I just say that?.* "What I mean is, I'm much more interested in how you're finding working at Roberts & McDaniel and how you're getting along. It must be kind of hard not knowing anyone in town."

With a small smile, Robin replied. "Well, I do know you, right?" *Do I? You seem so familiar.* Robin stared up at the starless sky and took a breath. The jazz music in the background surrounded her with a sense of peace she hadn't known in a long time, and she realized that this was indeed where she wanted to be. Even though she was far away from Detroit and her family, and even though she was in a strange city, at that moment she knew she felt completely at home for the first time in her life. And It was a tremendous feeling. She just wished she could put the more painful things out of her mind.

Jess saw Robin's face suddenly take on a subtle troubled expression. "Listen, Robin, if talking about Detroit is hard for you, I won't mention it again, okay?"

"No, please. It's okay." Robin smiled weakly. She did need to talk to someone about it. She lifted her hand across the table and placed two fingers on top of Jess's arm, then removed them and let her fingers rest on the linen tablecloth beneath them. "Let me tell you about something." She took a deep breath then spoke softly. "My boyfriend up there, David...we...um…we went together for many years. I loved him and I thought we could have a life together. After I graduated from law school, he told me that he would rather I not pursue my law career, and that after we were married, I should stay at home and raise the kids. I was upset because this was not what we had planned." She took another breath and continued. "Anyway, we had a huge fight about it and he stormed out of the house." Robin closed her eyes and swallowed hard. "Later that evening, I learned he had been involved a car accident after he had left." She turned her head, staring unseeingly into the night sky, her eyes shining with tears that threatened to fall. "He died on the way to the hospital." Her voice broke as she said this, as she continued to look across the expanse of the darkened courtyard, feeling her composure threaten to crumble before her. In a shaky voice she continued. "I…I felt it was my fault it happened, that if I hadn't been so selfish, he never would have been so angry when he left. I said some horrible things..." Robin looked away again and closed her eyes to the tears she knew were coming.

Oh God. Jess momentarily didn't know what to say. What could she possibly say? Almost on instinct and without really thinking, she reached over and grasped Robin's hand in her own. It was a simple gesture, but one which lent a calming and quiet strength. "Robin. I'm so sorry. I am so *very* sorry." She paused to collect her own thoughts, then gazed tenderly into green eyes and whispered, "It wasn't your fault. You know that, right? You're not to blame for what happened. You must believe that."

Robin nodded, unable to speak, her voice still raw with emotion. She looked across the table at Jess, sensing a warm compassion residing in the depths of blue gazing back at her, easing her heart somewhat of the burden and guilt she had been carrying for too long. They sat there silently together, hands still linked, surrounded by the night air and the sounds of the waning jazz above the breeze, giving and taking comfort in each other's presence, and oblivious to all around them save for the strength of an undeniable connection each felt deep within.

After some time had passed, Jess gently released Robin's hand and looked with concerned eyes across the table, giving a small smile. "Feel up to taking a walk around?"

"I would love to, but I guess I'm really just kind of tired right now. Could I take a rain check? Maybe tomorrow evening we could walk around a little and take in some more of the French Quarter." Robin's face brightened just a bit. "I'm really enjoying the jazz music and I love looking at the style of the buildings with the ornate railings and flickering lanterns. It reminds me of another era in time." She looked at Jess apologetically. "But right now, would you mind if we just went back to the hotel?"

Jess nodded in understanding. "No, I don't mind at all. We have a busy day tomorrow and it's getting rather late anyway. I'll get the check and then we'll head on back."

They left the restaurant and walked back to the hotel, neither saying much to each other. They entered the hotel lobby and stepped into the elevator, riding up to the floor where their rooms were located. They walked down the hall directly to their rooms, which were across from each other, and stopped, each at their own doors. Robin turned to face Jess after placing her key in the lock.

"Jess, I..." Robin began. "I just wanted to thank you for listening to me tonight. It felt good to talk about it." She sighed. "I'm sorry to have put such a damper on the evening, though." She looked down at her feet, feeling the embarrassment of having become emotional with someone whom she hardly knew.

Jess stepped closer and brought her hand up to Robin's shoulder, giving it a gentle squeeze, and then ducked her head down to look intently into sea green eyes. The warmth of that touch was enough to settle the turmoil raging in the young blonde's heart. Jess spoke softly. "You don't need to apologize for that. I am always here if you need to talk. Remember that, okay?" She removed her hand and turned to open the door to her own room. Then, tuning back once again to face the associate, she gave her a reassuring smile. "And, Robin...you did not put a damper on the evening. You are very good company." As she stepped into her room, Jess called back behind her. "Let's meet for breakfast in the morning at 7:00, okay?"

Robin gave a small smile. "That would be great. Goodnight, Jess."

"Goodnight," Jess replied then closed the door behind her. *Goodnight, sweet Robin.*

****

The next day went much like the first and by day's end, both Jess and Robin were exhausted. Reviewing documents can be very strenuous work, tedious and mentally fatiguing, and at times more that a little frustrating.

When the day finally came to a close, they returned to the hotel to change and get ready for a little sightseeing. They had planned to take a horse and carriage ride through the streets of the French Quarter while there was still some daylight left. Once dressed casually for the evening, Robin and Jess wandered down to Jackson Square where the horse-drawn carriages awaited eager passengers.

"It's a little chilly tonight." Robin mused. "I'm glad I packed a sweater." She was wearing khaki pants and a green and white pull-over sweater. "I almost didn't bring anything warm since I thought the South was always pretty mild. I guess I have a lot to learn, huh?" She shook her head at herself and glanced at Jess.

"Well, not every part of the South is like Florida. In Florida you're lucky to get a day to even wear a sweater, but most of the rest of the South gets its share of cold days. Sometimes I wish we had more of them in Florida." Jess wore blue jeans and a light blue, tailored long-sleeved brushed cotton shirt.

They arrived at Jackson Square and boarded one of the carriages, relaxing in silence as the driver took off to explore the side streets and less traveled areas of the French Quarter. Robin marveled at the rich history of the city and the wonderful culture and architectural styles as the guide gave a particularly thorough explanation of various points of interest. She could hear the sound of jazz permeate through the evening air as the spicy aromas of Creole and Cajun cooking made their way through her nostrils to awaken her stomach.

"That smells wonderful. I wonder where it's coming from." Robin grinned and glanced over to where Jess was seated. "I think we're definitely going to have to find a place to eat when this ride is over."

Jess chuckled. "You call the shots tonight. Wherever you want to eat is fine with me." Jess sat back and enjoyed the night air, listening to the clip clop of the horses' hooves on the uneven street as they turned their way onto Esplanade. If truth be told, she was enjoying the carriage ride more than she let on, and Robin's wonder at everything they saw. *Who said a document review had to be all work and no play?*

Jess took a moment to reflect on things. She hadn't really been happy in a very long time. *Not since James.* She closed her eyes. It seemed like a lifetime ago. Since then, she had tried to focus all her energies on her work, on making partner, and being a successful attorney. There was just no time for anything or anyone else. Or maybe she just didn't want to make the time. *Not again.* Now, though, it felt so good to enjoy someone else's company. She hadn't realized how much she missed that.

"Hey, Jess," Robin said softly and lightly touched Jess's arm. "Are you alright?"

Jess was brought back from her thoughts. "Yes, thanks. Just thinking." Robin's fingers still rested lightly on her arm, and Jess tried not to think about the shiver that ran up her spine at the contact. She could feel the warmth of those fingers burning through her shirt sleeve, chasing the cold vestiges of loneliness away, and bringing a lightness to her heart she never thought she'd know again.

Clearing her throat, Jess looked up ahead. "I see we're almost back. So where would you like to eat tonight?" She gave Robin a wide smile. "I swore I could hear your stomach growling the whole way back."

Robin gave her a playful swat as the carriage pulled up to the park and came to a stop. They climbed down and paid the driver. "How about some gumbo? I'm starving."

"Alright, then. You're in charge. Lead on." Jess moved her arm in a sweeping motion, following after the blonde as she led them toward their destination. Jess hung back a bit, watching the blonde sashay up the avenue. *Oh yes, she is most definitely adorable.*

****

The remainder of the week actually flew by. One would have thought quite the contrary. That a week of reviewing documents would seem to drag on in endless boredom. But to their surprise, the week was coming to a close rather quickly.

They had made a routine of meeting at the Café du Monde every morning for a small breakfast. Robin absolutely loved the beignets and wonderful chicory coffee. The open air tables of the riverside café beckoned passersby to sit and enjoy the quaint atmosphere and quiet charm of the French Quarter. The early morning shadows would cast intriguing long patterns on the ground as the sun made its way up the horizon, with the backdrop of the mighty Mississippi River meandering slowly alongside in timeless splendor. Occasionally, a tanker or barge would lumber its way up stream, heading for ports unknown waiting to unload its precious cargo. It was truly beautiful and Robin's favorite part of the day, well worth getting up early to see it.

On Friday morning, the two attorneys strolled down from their hotel as usual to the Café du Monde before heading over to RSJ Industries to complete their work.

"I can't believe it's our last day already." Robin sighed. "The week went by so quickly. I'm definitely going to have to rethink my opinion of document reviews from now on." She rested her chin on her hand and gave Jess a wistful smile. "I wish I could have spent more time exploring the French Quarter, though. There's so much here to see."

Jess cocked her head slightly and deadpanned. "Well, if you had really wanted to spend more time exploring Bourbon Street you should have said something sooner." She arched a dark eyebrow and waited.

Robin looked up with a momentarily stunned expression on her face, opening and closing her mouth several times before she could speak. Certain parts of Bourbon Street were famous, or infamous as the case may be, for their more, shall we say, risqué establishments. Not that she had personally experienced any of them, mind you. And one of the few times they had actually been on Bourbon Street, a bouncer from one of those said establishments kept kicking the door open as they passed by to give them a little peek or two inside.

"That is not what I meant and you know it." She gave Jess a playful slap and continued. "I meant that someday I'd like to spend some time exploring the southern plantations or taking a paddle wheel riverboat cruise or window shopping for antiques." She took in a deep breath and watched a river barge slowly make its way north, idly wondering where it was headed. "I like this city." She looked down at her now empty coffee cup. "And I absolutely adore the café au lait they have here. I'm gonna go order another cup. You want one?"

"Sure, but I'll get it. Stay here. I'll be right back." Jess stood and weaved her way to the front of the building, disappearing behind the small serving area.

Robin took the opportunity to consider the events of the past week. For one thing, she felt quite relieved to be getting along well with the junior partner. *She's becoming a friend, too. I need that.* But it was more than simple friendship. To Robin, it felt like there was a connection that ran deeper, something she couldn't quite grasp in her conscious mind, but which had seemed to possessively grab hold of her entire being, refusing against all odds to let go. It was undeniably so. As undeniable as the air she breathed. And as strange as it sounded, she didn't want the week to end. Not yet.

When Jess returned with the steaming hot beverages, she sat them down carefully on the table and gazed toward the river for a moment. "Um…listen, Robin, I was thinking that if you really wanted to spend some more time in New Orleans and you didn't have anything major planned for Saturday, we could reschedule our flight and spend another day here. I mean just to kick around some, and you could do some of the things you wanted to do."

Green eyes flew open wide with excitement and Robin gave a Jess a huge smile. "Do you think we could really do that?"

"Sure. Of course, we couldn't charge the client for an extra night in the hotel, but I'm sure we could work something out." She pondered this for a moment. "We could each pay for our separate rooms for another night, or we could just keep one of them and share. Unless you wouldn't be comfortable with that." Jess took a sip of her coffee. "What do you think?"

Robin considered this. "Well, I suppose we could keep just one room, if it's available, and share. She furrowed her brow. "But both our rooms have just one king sized bed…you know…to sleep." She looked questioningly at Jess and then took a sip of her café au lait.

Jess pursed her lips for a moment, appearing deeply in thought. She then looked directly at Robin, an amused glint in her eye. "That's alright." A beat. "I trust you."

Robin's eyes grew very wide, and she nearly blew out the coffee still in her mouth. *Oh my God. Did she mean…?* She finally swallowed and looked over to see Jess trying very hard to suppress a quite satisfied grin. "You always do that to me, you brat." Robin laughed, shaking her head. "And I never see it coming. I think you're corrupting me."

Jess couldn't hold back the full grin any longer. "Why, Miss Scarlet, whatever do you mean?" She gave Robin her best southern accent imitation.

"You know perfectly well." Robin chucked and took another sip of her coffee. After a few moments, she glanced shyly at Jess. "I guess it would be okay to keep one room for the night." Then more boldly. "You seem very trustworthy to me, too."

Jess smiled brightly. "Good, glad that's settled." *Trustworthy. Oh, boy. I am in so much trouble.*

****

Phil stepped inside the warehouse just as Jess and Robin were finishing the last of their document review. They had gathered enough documentation to put together a crucial timeline of events in order aide in preparation of the case for eventual trial.

"I see you ladies are about finished. If there is anything else you think of when you get back to Orlando, please give me a call and I'll see what I can do."

"Thanks, Phil," Jess replied. "You and your people have been very helpful."

Robin closed the lid on the last box of documents she was working on and returned it to the shelf before joining Jess and Phil near the front of the warehouse.

"So, when is your flight?"

"Actually, both Robin and I have decided to stay in town for another day. We thought we'd get in a little sightseeing tomorrow before heading back." Jess looked over to where Robin approached.

"That's a great idea. There's certainly plenty to do in this town. Might I suggest the riverboat dinner cruise. You still might be able to get tickets for tonight if you're interested."

Robin's eyes lit up, first at the mention of dinner, and second at the mention of the riverboat cruise. It was something she had really wanted do during their stay in New Orleans, the aura of the Mississippi River having grown on and fascinated her during the past week, but it had appeared as though they just wouldn't have enough time.

"Thanks, Phil. We'll check it out." Jess picked up her briefcase and nodded toward Robin in an indication that it was time to leave. "We'll call you if we need anything else."

Phil escorted them out into the lobby area. "You ladies have a safe trip back."

They left RSJ Industries and walked outside into the early evening sunlight. The gentle breeze and the crisp fall air rustled through the city as the faint sounds of jazz could be heard in the distance, a lively melody infusing its way throughout the slowing awakening French Quarter.

"Would you mind if we went down to the riverside to see if there are any tickets left for the riverboat tonight?" Robin asked as they headed toward the hotel.

"Well, the concierge at the hotel this morning told me that they usually sell out pretty early in the day."

Robin shuffled her feet in slight disappointment. "Oh, well, maybe some other time, then." She glanced over at Jess. "What? What are you grinning about?"

Jess looked like a Cheshire cat. "Nothing. Nothing at all."

"Tell me. Come on. Tell me."

"No."

"Please?" She peered at Jess with puppy dog eyes.

"Jeez, aren't you the nosy one?" Jess gestured in mock exasperation. "Can't a girl have any secrets?"

"No. Tell me."

Jess feigned an aggrieved expression. "Fine." She stopped, reached into her briefcase and pulled out an envelope. "Here."

Robin took the envelope and looked inside. A radiant smile came across her face, and Jess's heart nearly melted at the sight.

"Oh, Jess! You got tickets to the riverboat. But...when did you...how?" She looked at Jess slightly confused.

Jess shrugged as if it were no big deal. "This morning. I got them before we headed over to RSJ while you were still getting ready."

Robin shook her head in amazement. "Thank you," she said, the smile now fully covering her face.

"You're welcome." Jess looked sideways out of the corner of her eye. "Now, lets get back to the hotel and get ready, shall we?" As they continued walking, Jess thought for a moment and mentally complimented herself. *You done good, Jess. Very good.*

****

"Of all the places you've traveled to, which is your favorite?" Robin sipped her glass of Chardonnay and looked across the table into sparkling blue eyes.

They had boarded the paddle wheel riverboat shortly after dusk and were now seated in the dining cabin just below the uppermost deck. The riverboat had begun to make its way upstream, the large paddles churning through the water behind its stern. Through the large glass windows of the dining cabin, the flickering lights of the riverside piers and docks shimmered off the gently rolling waves as the riverboat gracefully forged its way up river.

"Not that I've been to very many places, but my absolute favorite place in the United States is San Francisco. The hills and the bay are truly a breathtaking sight. Have you been there?" Jess gently stirred her martini and plopped a ripe olive into her mouth.

"I've been to L.A. but never to San Francisco. Someday I would like to go there. I've heard many wonderful things about it." Robin raised a blonde eyebrow. "You wouldn't happen to have any document reviews scheduled for San Francisco in the near future, would you?"

Jess laughed lightly. "Oh, so now you're a fan of document reviews, huh? I'll have to remember that. But no, right now, I'm fresh out. Sorry."

Robin glanced at the menu in front of her. "Too bad." She joked. "So, tell me, do you take all the new associates you work with on such exciting travels?"

"Nah, only the ones I like." *Damn.* It was out of her mouth before she could think of what she was saying. *Whatever you're doing, Jess, cut it out.* She quickly recovered. "Some of the associates we had…well, we sent them to document reviews in one God forsaken town or another, and we haven't heard from them since. Quite a shame, too." Jess shook her head for a moment in mock regret, then smiled. "Just kidding. It's really the luck of the draw. You just happened to get New Orleans." *And me.*

And you. Robin fingered the linen napkin on her lap. "Have I thanked you yet for getting these riverboat tickets?"

"Only about a dozen times. And you're welcome. Again." Jess peered at the menu trying to make up her mind on what to order.

Robin knew she had to ask, and stared out the window for a long moment trying to gather her courage. "Can I ask you a question? I don't want you to take this the wrong way, though."

"Okaaaay. Shoot."

"Um…all this." Robin gestured with her hands. "All the fun stuff we've done while we've been here. Well, I don't think it's standard practice that when you're out of town on business, in between doing your work, that the partner traveling with you makes it a top priority to make sure you have fun, too." She sighed and shook her head. "I'm not really saying this very well, am I?" She took a deep breath. "What I mean is, I mentioned some things the other night that, well…were probably not appropriate in a business setting, and…well…I just didn't mean for you to have to feel you were obligated to try to make me feel better…you know…by keeping me entertained." Robin stared down at the menu, afraid to look up at the junior partner.

Jess straightened up and sat completely still for a very long moment, her face taking on an expressionless mask. *What…the…hell? She thinks I'm only being nice to her because I feel sorry for her? Shit.* After another long moment, Jess deliberately and very slowly put her menu down on the table and folded her hands together in front of her. She chose her next words very carefully.

"Robin, I want you to listen to me." Jess looked over to the associate seriously and spoke in an even, businesslike tone. "I admit that I don't usually get along very well with everyone I meet. I can be very difficult to work with at times and I have no illusions about that. But I can also tell you that, from what I've seen this week, I think you and I do work well together. I'd like to continue that. You are intelligent and a quick learner, and those are important qualities to me in someone I work with. If I have behaved unprofessionally in any way this week, and you have felt uncomfortable with that, then I am sorry. I wanted to do the things we did this week because, quite frankly, I had never done them before myself, and I knew you would enjoy them, too. Document reviews can be awfully dull, as I'm sure you already know, and in this case I saw an opportunity to try to make it a little more enjoyable for the both of us."

Jess stopped speaking briefly and let her expression and her voice soften slightly. "And for the record, I never, ever once felt in any way obligated to do any of those things with you. I wanted to do them with you because I wanted to do them with you. End of story." Jess then reached across the table to where Robin's hand was resting and gently covered it with own, whispering intently to her, as if it were the most important thing she had ever said. "And if doing those things with you helped give you some small measure of comfort, and take your mind off of things that trouble you, even for a brief moment, then I am most certainly not sorry about that. You got that?"

Robin swallowed. "Got it. Thanks. Sorry…I just had to know." She cleared her throat and took a sip of water.

"That's okay." Jess nodded and gently let go of her hand.

After perusing her menu again for a few moments, Robin looked up and over to Jess with a grin now playing across her face. "Can we eat now?"

Jess chuckled. "You betcha, kiddo. So what are you going to have?"

"I think I'll have the blackened redfish. You?"

Shrimp Creole for me." Jess motioned the waiter over.

Robin closed her menu. "What is it with you and shrimp, anyway?"

"Wouldn't you like to know?" Jess wiggled her eyebrows suggestively.

And so it went. They ate their dinner in relaxed conversation and light banter, all seriousness put aside, to enjoy their last night in New Orleans and each other's company. The jazz band played merrily in dinner accompaniment until all serving had been completed, then the tables were moved away to reveal a wide open dance floor, and the band picked up again with more festive Dixieland Jazz ensembles.

"Want to go up on deck for a while or stay here and listen to the music?" Jess asked as she stood up and waited for Robin to do the same.

"Let's go up on deck, then come back down later on for some Irish Coffee." Robin slid on her light sweater.

"Sounds like a plan." Jess grinned. "Lead on, mademoiselle."

****

They made their way out the narrow passageway and up the stairs into the crisp night air, walking slowly along the deck and finally stopping at a railing toward the back section of the riverboat. Robin rested her hands on the top of the rail and took a deep cleansing breath, the strong breeze feeling almost cold against her body. She gazed out at the river, with its black waters moving in quiet grace, and the half moon casting a silvery glow upon the rolling waves. The large, paddled wheel at the stern of the boat churned softly in the background, slowly propelling the riverboat forward in all its quiet majesty.

"This is really beautiful." Robin sighed and marveled at the view from the upper deck. A dim light flickered in the distance up stream, and Robin struggled through the moonlit darkness to see what it was. "What's that?" She extended her arm and pointed up ahead. As she spoke, a tall presence moved up behind her, cutting the feel of the blowing wind at her back, and although not quite touching her, surrounding her with an overwhelming and delicious warmth.

"Where?" A low voice asked close to her ear, its timbre affecting her senses and sending a curious tingling sensation down her spine.

Robin swallowed, then spoke softly. "Over there, Jess, see?" She felt the same warmth which had enveloped her just moments ago, intensify as the body pressed forward lightly against her back.

Jess peered over Robin's shoulder in earnest and followed the aim of Robin's finger toward the object in question. "Don't know. Could be another boat on the river tonight. The Mississippi is a well-traveled trade route to the Midwest states, you know." Her breath gently caressed the petite ear as she spoke.

Robin nodded at the answer, but in reality did not hear a word that was said, her mind lost in the delicious sensations she felt from the presence behind her. Whether it was the wine she had with dinner or simply the serene beauty of the river itself, it did not matter, for Robin was momentarily lulled into a tranquil haze, unwilling to break free from the warm and cozy cocoon surrounding her.

After a few minutes passed, Robin suddenly put her foot on the bottom rung of the metal railing and hoisted herself up several feet, leaning her body half-way over the edge of the top rail to peer intently into the water below.

With that movement, two strong arms suddenly closed protectively around her waist from behind, hands clasped tightly around her stomach, pulling her swiftly backward from the railing.

"Hey!" Robin yelped in surprise.

"Hey, nothing. Get down from there." Jess's voice echoed in alarm as she lifted Robin completely off the railing and set her gently back down on the deck. "We wouldn't want you falling overboard, now would we?" She arched a dark eyebrow to make her point.

"I wasn't going to fall overboard, dummy. I just wanted to see the big paddle wheel turning, that's all."

"Yeah, yeah, right. I can see me now, standing in Harry's office, trying to explain how I lost the new associate somewhere in the middle of the Mississippi River. I don't think that would go over very well." She shook her head and gazed out at the river, then shrugged. "Besides, I'd kinda miss ya."

Robin glanced up at her. "You would? Miss me, I mean?"

"Sure," Jess chuckled and slightly cocked her head to one side. "Then who would I get to do my legal research?"

"Oh, so I get it." Robin spoke playfully. "You only need me around to do your grunt work for you, huh?"

"No, not entirely." Jess furrowed her brows. "I'm sure there are other reasons I'd miss ya."

"Yeah? Like what?" Robin bantered.

Your beautiful green eyes. Jess stepped closer and spoke in a low deep voice directly into Robin's ear. "Give me some time. If I think long and hard enough, I'm sure I can come up with something." Jess stepped back and winked.

The darkness of the night hid well the deep blush covering Robin's face.

For the next moment, Jess stared at the magnificent view over the water, tapping her fingers lightly on the metal railing. "It's getting a little cold out here. You want to go back inside and get warmed up a little?"

I'm already pretty warm right now, thank you very much. "Okay by me." Robin followed the junior partner toward the stairs.

"Oh, and Robin." Jess stopped briefly and pointed a playful finger at Robin. "Do not step foot on another railing. Got it?"

"Aye, aye, Captain. No feet on railings. Got it." Robin laughed and gave a mock salute as they made their way down below.

****

Festive Dixieland jazz and several Irish Coffees later, Jess and Robin disembarked the riverboat after it had pulled back into its moorings alongside the dock to unload its weary passengers. Jess and Robin headed back to the hotel where they had agreed to share one of their previous rooms. Robin had checked out of her own room earlier that day and moved her things across the hall into Jess's room for the night. Whether it was because of the full day or the effects of the Irish Coffee, they were both rather exhausted by the time they entered Jess's room.

"Go ahead and get changed first," Jess said. "I need to send a quick e-mail to one of our clients."

"Sure." Robin grabbed her oversized t-shirt and toothbrush and headed into the bathroom.

After Jess completed typing her e-mail, she hit the send button, and then powered off her laptop. She pulled a light flannel nightshirt out of the top dresser drawer and smiled to herself. *You enjoyed yourself tonight, didn't you, Jess. It's been such a long time...* She didn't have time to complete that thought as she heard the bathroom door open.

Robin finished brushing her teeth and stepped out of the bathroom letting Jess take her turn. She got directly into one side of the large king sized bed, and laid her head back upon the soft pillow, thinking about the evening they had just spent. *What a wonderful night.* She sighed. *It's funny, I've never really felt this comfortable with anyone before. Not even with David. It should feel strange, but it doesn't.* Her eyes closed as she snuggled down deep in the warm covers.

Jess returned to the room, and thinking Robin was already asleep, quietly got into her side of the large bed and clicked off the nearby light.

"Thanks for tonight, Jess," a small voice came from the opposite side of the bed.

"You're welcome. Goodnight, Robin."

"Goodnight." A long moment passed. "Um...Jess?"

"Yes."

"Remember what you said earlier about your being sorry if anything you did ever made me feel uncomfortable?"

Shit. Jess tensed and closed her eyes tightly. "Yes, I remember."

"Well, just for the record, I never, ever once felt in any way uncomfortable around you this week."

Jess slowly released the breath she was holding. *God, that was close.* "Thanks for saying that," she replied softly. "Goodnight, Robin."

"Goodnight, Jess." *Sleep well.*

****

Jess was the first to awake Saturday morning, feeling something warm and soft pressed up next to her. She looked down to see Robin curled up on her side, both hands drawn neatly under her chin, and her body resting lightly against Jess's. Robin's short hair was in disarray from sleep and her warm breath tickled Jess's arm as she breathed deeply in slumber. *She looks so cute when she's sleeping.* Jess thought to herself. *But how'd she get all the way over here?* Sometime during the night, Robin had somehow strayed halfway across the bed to lay more on Jess's side than her own. Jess watched Robin sleep for a few moments. Her soft blonde eyelashes curled adorably past her eyelids and her expression was one of quiet innocence. *You need to figure out what's going on here, Jess, and do it fast.* After another long moment, Jess reluctantly got herself up, trying not to disturb the sleeping form as she did so, and made her way quietly into the bathroom.

A short while later, Robin awoke, at first feeling a bit disoriented then realizing where she was. She took a moment to gather her bearings and then remembered the previous evening. *The riverboat.* She smiled to herself at the memory as she registered the sounds of the shower coming from other side of the bathroom door. Robin stretched her arms above her head and debated with herself whether to get up or go back to sleep. Before she could fully make up her mind on the matter, the bathroom door opened and Jess quickly stepped out into the room, her hair wet and her body wrapped only in a large towel.

Momentarily startled, Robin blinked her eyes in surprise, her mouth slightly open, as Jess padded across the carpet. *Hello.*

"Ah...sorry...I uh...didn't mean to...um...scare you. I thought you were still asleep." Jess turned quickly to pull some clothes from the dresser drawer and headed back toward the bathroom. "I'll only be another minute, if you'd like to get in there."

"Sure...um...yeah. That would be great. Take your time." Robin managed. As the bathroom door closed shut, she let her head fall back to the bed and threw a pillow over her face. *God...I can't believe I stared like that.* Trying to distract herself from her thoughts, she set the pillow back down and got out of bed, padding over to the closet to pick out something to wear for the day.

After they were both dressed and ready, they quickly ate breakfast and then took a stroll along the Riverwalk where they could enjoy the beauty of the river and get a little shopping in as well. It was a bright fall day, crisp with an autumn breeze, and perfect weather for enjoying the charm of the old city. The better part of the day was spent wandering around the less traveled areas of the French Quarter, window shopping for antiques, and admiring the ornate balconies of the Spanish occupation. Robin's favorite part was learning about the city's French and Spanish history and exploring the hidden courtyards, which echoed the themes of the American Civil War and the early and mid-19th Century Confederacy. Robin and Jess also spent some time down around Jackson Square and the St. Louis Cathedral, watching the sidewalk artists as they created and captured on canvas scenes of the old French Quarter and the mighty Mississippi.

At day's end, Jess and Robin caught their flight back to Orlando, exhausted but content. In reflection, it had been a wonderful day, a good week, and the beginnings of a friendship both were glad to have made. But it was also something more, something deeper, and even though both had felt its stirrings too strong to deny outright, neither had consciously acknowledged just exactly what it was. They had just met, after all. Spent a few days together on a case. That was it. Not a big deal. But somehow, it was. And neither one of them could shake the lingering feeling of a familiar euphoria that stayed with them long after they had left the city of New Orleans.

"You realize you've just spoiled me for any future document reviews, don't you?" Robin buckled her seatbelt and braced herself for the plane's take-off.

"You think so, huh? Well don't tell anyone. I have a reputation to uphold. Can't have people thinking that my document reviews are actually fun, can we?" Jess raised an eyebrow and stowed her laptop beneath the seat in front of her.

As the plane gained momentum and prepared to lift off the ground, Robin nervously clung onto the tops of the armrests, her knuckles almost turning white and her jaw tightly clenched.

"Hey, take it easy there." Jess reached over and grasped Robin's hand in her own. "Just hang onto me until we're up and leveled off, okay? I promise I won't let go." Jess smiled reassuringly. *I promise I won't let go.*

Chapter 2

Robin stepped off the elevator and walked to her office, her short blonde hair slightly damp from the drizzling rain. It was a miserable gray day, having rained all evening, and now the rain continued well into the morning, leaving the earth a wet and soggy mass. Traffic was tied up all over town, the drive in to work stop and go, causing Robin to run rather late this day. *I hate Mondays.*

After having been gone a week in New Orleans, she had spent all day Sunday catching up on her mail, grocery shopping, and performing other mundane chores in between trying to complete the unfinished unpacking she still had left over from moving.

She entered her office, set her briefcase down and powered up the computer. It was then that she noticed something sitting on her desk, right next the stack of deposition transcripts she had waiting to review. As she sat down in her chair, she reached out and picked up the object. *Café du Monde Coffee with Chicory.* A can of the wonderful coffee she had liked so much in New Orleans. She smiled to herself. *Jess.* Under the can was a scribbled note.

R –

Thought you might like to enjoy some of New Orleans in Orlando. There's also an order form in case you want to order some more later.

J –

Robin shook her head in quiet amazement. She opened up her e-mail program and typed in a short message.

Jess,

Got the coffee you left. Is there no end to the lengths you will go to bribe me into doing your grunt work for you? Chicory coffee works for me! Thank you.

Robin

She clicked the send button and looked up in time to see Paul Franklin standing in her doorway, his lanky build leaning casually against the door frame.

"So, I see you made it back from your first document review, all in one piece, I may add." He chuckled and stepped into the office, taking a seat. "Hopefully, Jessica didn't torture you too badly."

"Well, it wasn't as bad as I thought it'd be. I mean, we did get to see some of New Orleans while we were there, so that kind of made up for it." Robin had a distant look in her eyes for a brief moment.

"Well, I'm sure you did your best to get Jessica out for a little fun. She doesn't go in much for play. Pretty much all work." Paul leaned back in the chair and stretched out his legs. "I remember the first document review I had with Jessica. We went to Atlanta and proceeded to spend all day and all evening knee deep in financial records. I remember thinking that somebody should just shoot me and put me out of my misery." He laughed slightly.

"Ooooh. That sounds bad. I hope I don't have that in store for me later on." Robin relaxed in her chair and regarded Paul. He was a senior associate, rather tall, with slightly wavy graying brown hair that made him appear older than he was. "Did you need help with something today?"

"Yes, a couple of things, if you have time." He leaned forward slightly and looked at her gently with warm brown eyes. "I was hoping you could draft a couple of motions to dismiss for me. I'll be in a mediation the rest of the day and I really need to get them out. One of the paralegals can get you the forms." His gaze lingered, and he gave Robin a charming smile as handed her the files.

He's flirting. "Sure, Paul. I'll take care of it. Go on to your mediation."

Robin stood up as Paul left the office and turned to stare out the window at the gray morning light, the outline of the lake below barely visible through the haze of the rain. She shook her head. *I'm not going to get involved with anyone right now. I just can't do that yet. It's only been a few months.* It was a defiant thought, maybe in spite of herself, but she was adamant just the same. And although she didn't exactly know why, she came to realize that she didn't quite feel comfortable with that decision.

****

Jess sat in the high backed, largely uncomfortable, velvet covered chair in Harry Roberts' office, staring out the large windows and patiently waiting as he completed his phone conversation with the managing partner, Gordon McDaniel. Work had seemed to pile up while she way away, as it always does, and she knew she had some long nights ahead of her this week in order to catch up. Sometimes going out of town was just not worth it. Jess smiled to herself. *But this time it was worth it.*

Harry put down the receiver and looked over at Jess, appearing somewhat preoccupied. He frowned. “I haven’t seen our new associate today. Have you? You didn’t scare her away already, did you?”

“Oh, be serious, Harry. It’s a mess out there. She’s probably just running late.”

“Maybe. How did you two do in New Orleans? Any problems?” Harry took a sip of his now cold coffee, then pushed his intercom button. “Betty, could you bring me some more coffee, please.” He looked at Jess. “Want some also?” Harry was from the old school, having yet to realize that most legal secretaries don’t normally fetch coffee nowadays.

“No, thanks. Um...we got everything we needed from RSJ. I think Robin will work out well. She found some key documents for us and seems to able to grasp some of the relatively finer issues of the case. I’d like to put her on my trial team.” The secretary stepped quietly into the office and set a fresh cup of coffee down on Harry’s desk before retreating back to her work station.

“You want Robin on your trial team? So soon? You know we usually send in more experienced associates.” Harry took a sip of his now hot coffee and considered the request. His frown deepened as he mulled over the thought in contemplation. “Alright, this is what we’re going to do. You can put her on your trial team, for now, and we’ll see how it goes. If you feel she’s in over her head, I want you to tell me immediately and we’ll get Keith or Mark in there.” He looked at Jess directly, the silent warning evident. “There is no substitute for experience. We can’t compromise the client’s case for training purposes.”

Jess pursed her lips and gave it some thought, not for the first time mind you, and asked herself again just why it was she wanted Robin on her trial team. Sure, it was unusual for a first year associate to be placed on a trial team. But Jess was certain Robin could handle it. *Robin’s sharp. Her instincts are good. And I need someone who can work with me*. But in the back of her mind the question lingered. Was there some other reason? *Would I be compromising the client’s case?*

“Alright, Harry.” Jess nodded. “But if it comes down to it, I’d rather not work with Mark again after the that little near-malpractice screw-up the other week." She grimaced at the memory, then stood up and walked toward the door. "If I feel Robin can't handle it, I'll let you know."

And, with that little piece of business out of the way, Jess headed toward her own office. She stepped inside and plopped herself down in her burgundy leather chair, idly noting that most of the morning had been frittered away. She looked for a particular piece of correspondence that urgently demanded her attention, digging her way through the mass of papers strewn haphazardly across her desk, until finally coming across it. Neatness was never a strong suit.

Almost as an afterthought, Jess glanced at her computer, seeing and then reading a lone e-mail message from Robin. *She got the coffee.* Jess smiled gently to herself, then typed in her reply.

R,

Glad you liked the coffee. By the way, I didn't know you were immune to my bribing techniques.

J

She clicked the send button and promptly turned her attention to her overflowing in-box. A few moments later, a message came back.

I never said I was immune to your bribing techniques.

R

Jess arched an amused eyebrow. *Is that so? Well, Jess, it looks like you're going to make use of your bribing skills after all.* And somehow, she found that thought quite to her liking.

****

The evening descended rather quickly, the rain never letting up, and the work seeming to multiply during the day faster than rabbits. Most everyone had left the office by now, and Jess knew it would be a long night, as the dreariness of the day settled deep within her, and her disposition soured along with the weather.

Robin, on the other hand, had completed most of her urgent tasks and was headed toward the elevators, umbrella in hand, when she heard Jess's deep alto voice in subdued dictation coming from down the hallway. *She's working late. Bet she hasn't eaten.*

Robin made a decision. She quickly walked back into her own office, dialed the phone, and ordered some take-out for dinner. A half hour later, she had procured said take-out and made her way over to Jess's office, where she found Jess as she was before, dutifully dictating into her hand-held tape recorder.

"You still here?" Robin poked her head inside the office door.

Jess looked up and smiled, her mood suddenly and inexplicably brightened. "Yep. See what you get to look forward to?"

"Um...I figured you probably hadn't eaten, so I took a chance and ordered some dinner. I hope you like Chinese." Robin held up a bag in front of her, presumably containing the food in question. "Care to join me?"

A delighted grin. "I would love to. I was going to take a break soon anyway." Jess looked down at her paper-covered desk "Let me just see if I can clear off a space here somewhere. Sorry it's such a mess." Jess apologized and gave a wry smile. "So, what did you get?"

Robin sat down and set out the paper plates. "A couple of egg rolls, moo goo gai pan, and shrimp with lobster sauce." She looked up at Jess expectantly.

"Ooooh, shrimp with lobster sauce. That's one of my favorites." Jess eagerly opened one of the containers and started dishing out its contents.

Robin simply shook her head and grinned uncontrollably.

"What?" Jess took a bite.

"I think you just might have an incurable preoccupation with shrimp." Robin chuckled.

A raised eyebrow. "Sounds serious." Another bite. "What would you prescribe?" Jess studied her intently.

"Well, seeing as it's incurable, I'd definitely say it would require lots and lots of personal attention." Green eyes locked onto blue.

Personal attention? "I see." Blue eyes held the gaze. "Is my condition...hopeless?"

"Most definitely. We need to start the necessary treatments right away." Robin looked away, then cleared her throat. "And, if you can tear yourself free from work tomorrow night, we could start with a home cooked meal at my place." She smiled. "Can you make it? "I wanted to break in my new apartment. You'd be my first visitor."

"Ah, well, now how can I turn that down?" Jess smiled back and took another bite. "Should I bring anything?"

Just you. "No, just you." A beat. "And no, we're not having shrimp."

Jess let go a laugh. *Jess, you are so in over your head.*

****

The next day, the sun had returned and most of the dreary moods from the previous day had brightened accordingly. The day was unremarkable for the most part, save for the not so subtle attentions directed by one particular senior associate toward one particular new associate, which did not go unnoticed by one particular junior partner. As was the case, Paul seemed to spend an amusingly inordinate amount of time hanging about, and in the vicinity of, and generally near, Robin's office. The office gossip mill was in full force that day, and as was also the case, said gossip did not go unnoticed by that same particular junior partner.

As the day came to a close, Robin rushed home to prepare what was soon to be her first formal dinner in her new apartment. Jess was expected to come over at 7:30, and Robin began preparations for the meal in earnest, seeking to make this first dinner quite perfect.

Shortly after 7:30, Jess arrived, appearing a bit tired, but otherwise in a relatively good mood, considering it had been another full day, even if a little routine.

"Hi." Robin answered the door. "I see you found this place okay."

Jess stepped inside. "Yeah, no problem, though I had to take a detour to get here."

"How come?" Robin gestured for Jess to sit down on the fluffy sofa.

"Well, I stopped to pick up something. I know you said not to bring anything, but just consider this a housewarming gift. From me." Jess handed her a medium-sized box.

Robin's eyes lit up. "You didn't really have to do that."

"I know. Open it." Jess grinned.

Robin opened the box with a contagious enthusiasm, at last revealing a large, berry scented candle in a beautifully carved wooden centerpiece. "It's beautiful, Jess." Robin fingered the carvings. "Thank you."

"I thought maybe you could keep it on your dining room table for decoration, if you didn't already have something, and of course, if you like it." Jess smiled a bit shyly.

"I do like it. Very much." Robin glanced up, and then turned her attention toward the dining room. "Let me put it on the table and see how it looks." Robin stepped over to the table and placed the centerpiece carefully on the tablecloth, admiring the way the simple elegance of the candle added a certain beauty to the arrangement. "I like it." She turned to Jess. "Want to see the rest of the place?"

"Sure. Lead the way." Jess dutifully followed after the petite woman, exploring the small, yet cozy, one bedroom apartment, complete with vaulted ceilings and kitchen nook.

After the grand tour, Robin led them through the short hallway and back into living room. "So now you've seen my humble abode." Robin smiled modestly. "Not much, I know, but I don't need too much right now."

"I like it just fine." Jess looked around. "It's a bit larger than the apartment I had when I first came here. You've done a great job fixing it up, too."

"Thanks. It took me long enough." Robin grinned widely and then headed into the kitchen. "Dinner's ready. Go sit down and I'll get everything. I made Chicken Parmesan." She stuck her head back out the doorway. "Sorry, no shrimp."

"I think I'll live." Jess cracked a smile and took a seat at the table. "Smells great, by the way."

The dinner was quite delightful. They ate together and engaged in easy conversation and comfortable companionship, warmed by the soft glow of the candlelight which danced merrily off the berry scented candle sitting nobly in the center of the table. It was, of course, all rather pleasant, and carried with it a hint quiet familiarity, though neither Robin nor Jess could quite place the feeling.

"Can I ask you a question?" Robin pushed the food around on her plate for a moment.

"Sure."

"Um...what do you think of Paul?"

"Paul?" Jess looked a bit surprised. "Well, let's see, he has the makings of a great litigator and certainly will be up for partnership next year." Jess took a sip of her wine.

"Yeah. That's not quite exactly what I meant." Robin up shyly through blonde lashes. "Um...I mean, what do you think of him...as a person?"

"Oh." Jess mulled that thought around for a moment, not really knowing why she felt a sudden uneasiness settle over her. "He's a nice person, quite charming, although a bit arrogant sometimes, and certainly available. All in all, I'd say he's quite a good catch for someone, if they could catch him, and no one has yet. Why?"

Robin leaned over and whispered in all seriousness. "I think he's been flirting with me."

Jess dropped her fork to her plate, and proceeded to laugh uncontrollably until the beginnings of tears formed in her eyes.

"What?" Robin asked perplexed. "Why are you laughing?"

Jess calmed down enough to speak. "He's been flirting with you?"

"I think so."

"And you've just now figured this out?"

"Yes. So?" Robin raised both eyebrows.

"Robin, I hate to break this to you, but the whole office has known this for weeks." Jess failed miserably to suppress another laugh.

"And you knew? And you didn't tell me?" Robin gave Jess a playful slap.

"Hey, no hitting. I'm sorry, I thought you knew." Jess also failed miserably to sound sincerely apologetic.

"How was I supposed to know? We were gone a whole week." Robin shook her head. "I should be really mad at you for this."

Jess, after much difficulty, was finally able to compose herself. "Okay, I am duly chastised. I should have told you." She then gave Robin an amused look. "Well?"

"Well, what?"

"Well, are you interested?" Jess waggled her eyebrows. *Do you want really to know this, Jess?*

Robin chuckled softly. "Well, no. Not really. I um..." She quietly sobered somewhat as she watched the firelight flickering from the slowly melting candle top. "I don't think I can...you know...be involved with someone right now." This last part was said in almost a whisper.

Damn. Jess closed her eyes briefly in regret. *What's the matter with you, Jess?* "Robin, honey, I'm so sorry. That was very insensitive of me." She placed her hand over Robin's and ducked to look into green eyes. "Forgive me?"

Robin nodded, an almost sad smile crossing her features. "You shouldn't have to watch everything you say around me. I'm the one who should be sorry. This is something I have to deal with for myself."

"No, Robin." Jess gave her hand a gentle squeeze. "You don't have to deal with this alone. I'm here. Will you remember that?" Blue eyes pleaded in genuine sincerity.

Robin took a deep breath and offered a brave smile. "You are so sweet to care the way you do." She whispered. "I'm not sure I deserve that."

"You deserve that and more." Jess nodded and squeezed Robin's hand once again, then released it. "Now come on, let me help you get this stuff cleaned up, okay?"

They both got up from the table and cleared away the dinner dishes. While Jess was still in the kitchen, Robin stepped over to the quietly flickering candle, made a silent wish and then blew out the flame, watching as the tiny wisps of smoke trailed behind and then disappeared into the air. The wish she made was private, something which her heart had already acknowledged, but her mind, in all its meanderings, had been slow to recognize. Until now. Verbalizations failed her, but her wish, nevertheless, remained intact.

When the dinner dishes were finally finished, Robin went over to the freezer and pulled out her newly acquired can of official Café du Monde Coffee with Chicory. "Want some?" She looked over to Jess expectantly.

"What a treat. I get to share your coffee. I would absolutely love some." The dark-haired woman went into the living room as Robin set the coffee maker to its task.

If you want to watch TV, go ahead and turn it on." Robin called back from the kitchen. After a moment, she poked her head back out the kitchen doorway. "So how did you manage it anyway?"

"Manage what?" Jess put down the remote control and looked at Robin quizzically.

"The coffee. How did you manage to get it without my seeing you?" Robin brought out the hot beverages and set them down on the coffee table.

"There were *some* times when you weren't looking, you know."

Robin shook her head "That's hard to believe." She sat back next to Jess on the fluffy sofa. "I thought I had my eye on you the whole time."

A dark eyebrow shot up. "Did you, now?" Jess slowly set down her coffee cup and leaned back, staring intently into the green eyes just inches from her own. "And did you see anything...interesting?"

Robin took a sip. "Perhaps." She looked away for a moment, then turned her attention back to Jess. "But I didn't see you get that coffee."

Jess grinned and leaned forward slightly, tilting her head so her forehead rested neatly against Robin's. She gazed into eyes the color of the sea, and whispered very softly, her breath gently caressing Robin's face. "Then I guess, Robin, you aren't as observant as you think."

Oh God. Robin sat mesmerized for a brief moment, her eyes locked by a penetrating blue. Her heart rate had curiously sped up, and she was unable to move, the intensity of the gaze too much to resist, and the proximity of Jess too much for her senses to ignore. At last, shaking herself free from her captivity, she broke the gaze and relaxed back against the fluffy sofa, as Jess likewise did the same.

For the rest of the evening, they managed quite effectively to carry on in casual conversation, neither seeming to notice how quickly the minutes passed, until Jess looked at her watch and offered a silent frown. "I wish I could stay a little bit longer, but it's getting late. I still have some work to do tonight, and you should get some rest." *It's getting harder to leave her.*

"Thank you for coming over. And thank you for my lovely housewarming gift." Robin smiled. "I really do like it." They both stood up and Robin gave her a quick hug.

"It was my pleasure. And thank you for a wonderful dinner and truly wonderful company. I'll see you tomorrow." Jess opened the front door and stepped outside into the autumn's night air. "Goodnight."

"Goodnight, Jess. Drive safely," Robin called out as Jess turned and walked toward her car. She watched Jess drive off and then stepped inside and closed the door. She stood by the door for a moment, then walked into the dining room and over to the table where the wood-carved centerpiece stood holding its candle in quiet grace. She lifted the centerpiece almost reverently and studied the intricate carvings which adorned its base, tracing their delicate shapes lightly with her fingertips. She recalled the wish she'd made earlier that evening, as the candle had been finally extinguished, and she hoped now, above all hope, that her heart's wish might somehow come true. What she didn't know was that it already had.

****

Robin set the case file down and picked up the ringing phone. "Robin Wilson."

"Robin, it's Jess. Can you come down to my office. I need to go over some things with you."

"Sure, I'll be right there." With that, Robin started down the hallway, side-stepping an admiring Paul, and dodging the hushed voices and veiled stares of certain gossip propagators along the way. *Jeez, I wish he'd just go away.* She rapped lightly on Jess's door, and was quickly motioned inside.

"Good, you're here. Close the door." Jess peered at Robin over a mountain of paperwork. "I just wanted you to know I've asked Harry to assign you to my trial team. He's agreed."

"Okay." Robin appeared a bit unsure.

"Listen, I know you don't have any trial experience, but I also know from working with you that you would do an excellent job with some of the things we need done. I will not expect you to handle anything I feel you are not sufficiently prepared for. Keith is our back-up and can assist us as necessary. We've got a lot to do here to prepare witnesses and pull together our exhibits." Jess handed Robin a list of due dates. "I need you to make sure everything gets done by these deadlines."

Robin nodded. "I'll take care of it."

"Good. And Robin," Jess looked across the desk. "If at any time you feel you're having trouble with something, or need help, please come to me right away, okay?"

Robin smiled, a bit more confident now. "Okay."

With that out of the way, Jess stood up and stretched. She had been sitting in one position all afternoon and needed to take a little break. "Now for the fun stuff." She gave Robin a small wink and sat on the edge of her desk. "The firm gets tickets to the Broadway Series every year and most of the time I never use mine. I don't usually like going alone. But this time the tickets are for *Cats* which I'd really like to see. I've got an extra ticket." Jess fidgeted. "Would you like to go? It's Saturday night."

"I love *Cats* and I would definitely like to go." Robin gave a broad smile. "Where is it playing?"

"At the Performing Arts Center. The show starts at 8:00. I could come get you and we could drive down together, if you'd like."

Robin thought for a moment. "Well, maybe I should drive. I'm farther away from where we're going and it's easier for me to pick you up on the way than you coming all the way out to get me. You just have to give me directions." She grinned. "Easy directions."

Jess grinned back. "Okay, that'll work. I'll e-mail you the directions to my place. They're easy. Come pick me up at 7:00, okay?"

"You got it." Robin stood to leave. "Thanks for inviting me, Jess. I'll leave you to your paperwork now." A sly grin as she headed out the door. "Don't get lost in there."

"Yeah, yeah. Everyone's a comedian." Jess sat back down behind the mountain of paper on the desk, grinning broadly from ear to ear. *Jesus, Jess, get a grip, will you?. You'd think you were going on your first date or something.* She raised a dark eyebrow at the thought.

Indeed.

****

Robin pulled her blue Miata into Jess's driveway and honked the horn, the evening chill forcing her to keep the convertible's top up. A moment later, Jess came out of the house, set the alarm, and then made her way to Robin's car.

"Hey there." Jess got in the car and buckled her seatbelt.

"Hey." Robin pulled out of the driveway and made her way toward downtown. "I don't know my way around yet, so can you tell me how to get to the Performing Arts Center from here?"

"You're in luck. I am an expert back-seat driver." Jess grinned proudly. She turned around and looked over her shoulder. "Ooops, you don't have a back seat." A shrug. "Sorry, can't help you, then."

Robin giggled. "You are such a goofball. Just point me the way, will ya?"

They arrived at the Performing Arts Center with plenty of time to spare, in spite of one minor directional mishap, and took their seats for the show. All in all, it was a perfect evening, as they both enjoyed the performance immensely. Robin appeared captivated by the musical, and every once in a while during the show, she would tap Jess lightly on the arm and whisper a commentary or two about the production. At one particularly compelling part of the show, Robin let her fingers linger lightly on Jess's arm as the performance continued, though Jess would be hard pressed to tell anyone exactly what that one particularly compelling part was, having been too distracted at the time to notice.

At the show's conclusion, they headed back home, Robin needing directions again, in reverse order, on how to get back to Jess's house. As she pulled into the driveway and stopped the car, Robin quietly marveled at how much she had enjoyed the evening and just how much she had enjoyed being with Jess. It was a feeling unlike anything she had ever experienced, a feeling of complete and absolute contentment, as if this was exactly where she was supposed to be.

"Thanks for the show, Jess. It was really great." A wide grin. "And you give excellent directions. I only got lost once."

"You're welcome. And just for your information, it wasn't my directions that got you lost." Jess pointed a playful finger. "If you will recall, I specifically told you that it was a one-way street long before you turned down it, going the wrong way, I might add." She unbuckled her seatbelt.

"Well, if the direction giver would have given the direction taker a little more information in the first place, then maybe the direction taker would not have turned down the one-way street going the wrong way."

A bored look. "Are you finished?"

"Yes."

"Good." Jess reached for the car's door handle. "Hey, you haven't seen my place yet. Would you like to come in? I'll give you a tour." Jess raised both eyebrows expectantly.

"Sure." A chuckle. "That way I can see how you big-time

partners live." Robin turned off the ignition and followed Jess to the front door and waited as she turned off the alarm.

Once inside, Jess proceeded to show Robin every single room, nook and cranny of the large four bedroom house. It was, quite simply, an expansive ranch style house, very well appointed with modern furnishings and plush wall to wall carpeting, complete with a swimming pool out back.

"Well, there you have it. This is how us big-time partners live." Jess winked and spread her arms wide to each side.

"It's...um...wow...really nice...and big." Robin stood in awe. "There's so much space...just for you?"

"Well, yeah, just for me. Have a seat in the living room. Want something to drink? I have soda." Jess entered the kitchen.

Robin walked over and sat down on the plush, soft sofa. "Okay, soda's fine." She tried to take in the sheer vastness of the house and offered another chuckle. "You know, I think I'd get lost in here."

"You think so?" Jess brought out the beverages and set them down on the pine wood coffee table before taking a seat on the sofa next to Robin. She then leaned her head toward Robin, as if telling her a carefully guarded secret, and quipped. "There are no one-way streets in here, Robin, so I think you'd be okay."

Robin squinted her eyes. "You are such a brat." She playfully tugged at Jess's shirt sleeve. "I will definitely get you for that"

"Yeah, yeah. Promises, promises."

Robin looked around again, a gentle curiosity crossing her features. "If you don't mind my asking, why did you decide to get such a big place...I mean...just for yourself?"

Jess sat up a little straighter and tensed her jaw slightly. "It wasn't supposed to be just me. It's a long story. You don't want to hear it." She turned her head and focused her attention on the corner of the coffee table, making it clear that she did not want to continue further.

"I'm sorry. It's none of my business. That was rude of me."

"No, it's not that. It's just that it's not a pleasant memory."

"I'd listen, if you wanted to tell me. After all, you've listened to me." Robin tilted her head sympathetically. "But if you'd rather not, that's okay, too."

Do I really feel like dredging all this up? Jess sighed. "Alright." She took a deep breath, then paused briefly to collect her thoughts. "When I first started working for Roberts & McDaniel, I met James. He was a little on the wild side, but I fell head over heals for him and we got along very well. He was majoring in Engineering at the University here, and somehow he had lost his scholarship mid-way through completing his degree. I agreed to put him through the rest of his coursework." Jess glanced up slightly at Robin to gauge her reaction. "We made a lot of plans together. We were going to start our own company. I'd be the legal counsel...we'd take over the world, so to speak." Jess shook her head. "It all seems so stupid now. I was very young and very naïve. When James finally graduated, I thought we should start out right, so I bought this place, sort of as a celebration of his graduation. The place I had was really too small."

Jess fixed her eyes on an imaginary spot on the wall and her voice took on a more dispassionate tone. "The day after James graduated, I came home. He was gone, and all his things were gone. He left a note on the table saying thanks for everything, but that he needed to move on. He even cleaned out our bank account." Jess let go a disgusted laugh. "I was such an idiot to have trusted him. I was a meal ticket, that's all. He got what he wanted from me, and I mean that in every possible way, and then he just skipped out."

Jess looked down at her hands now, suddenly feeling sick at the memory of the betrayal, her voice nearly a whisper. "Now you know what a fool I was...am." Just then, two gentle arms surrounded her in a quiet embrace, holding her high above the drowning waters, and offering her soul safe harbor from the storm within. Jess closed her eyes and sank into the welcoming contact, savoring the feeling of gentle warmth and comfort such as she had never known before.

After a long moment, Robin released her hold and looked up firmly into cerulean eyes. "You are not a fool to me, Jess. Never. You are a wonderful person who I am proud to know. I'm sorry he hurt you." *I would never hurt you.* "You didn't deserve that."

"Thanks." Jess sat back against the sofa and then cleared her throat. "I told you it wasn't a pleasant story." She gave Robin a weak smile and continued. "After he left, I moved in here myself. I refused to let him take this home away from me , too."

Robin took Jess's hand and gave it a firm squeeze. "Thank you for telling me. And I do like your home." She offered a warm smile. "Very much."

They sat there for a few moments longer before Robin, already quite tired, stifled a small yawn. She leaned her head back against the sofa and briefly closed her eyes. "I'm sorry. It's getting late. I really should go home so you can get some rest, too."

Jess nodded and then stood up, leading Robin toward the door. Though she was afraid to admit it, the truth was, she really did not want Robin to leave. Their daily separations were becoming curiously quite difficult, and the sense of loss, at times, seemed increasingly present. *Don't go.* Jess hesitated. "Stay?" It was a simple request.

A blonde head swung up in surprise. "What?"

"Stay. I mean, it's late and tomorrow's Sunday and unless there's something you have planned...um...I could fix up the guest room for you." Jess glanced at Robin hopefully, and then paused slightly. "But if you can't stay...."

"Yes."

"Yes?

"Yes, I can stay." Robin smiled. "Don't go to the trouble of fixing up the guest room. I can sleep right here on this nice, cushy sofa." She pointed to the object. "It looks pretty comfortable to me."

"It's not."

"No?"

Jess shook her head. "Horrible. You'd be much better off sleeping in a bed. If you don't want me to fix up the guest room, the only other room with a bed is my room." Jess pointed to the room in question and arched an eyebrow. "We'd have to share."

"I really don't want you to go to any trouble." Green eyes fixed on blue. "So, I see no other alternative. We have to share." Robin gave her a wide grin. "We did share once before, as I recall. And I still think you're pretty trustworthy."

"Trustworthy is a such relative term." Jess winked and grinned back. "I've got a nightshirt you could use. It'll be a bit big, though."

"That's okay, I like wearing them a bit big."

They performed their nightly routines, Robin sans toothbrush, although mouthwash worked as a temporary substitute, and changed into their sleep clothes. Thanks to Jess, Robin donned an over-sized sleep shirt, and Jess pulled on her favorite Calvin Klein boxer shorts with matching shirt. Both were quite tired as Jess turned off the nearby light and they snuggled down deep into the cozy queen-sized waterbed.

"I've never slept on a waterbed before." Robin waited for the slight wave motion to settle down and then chuckled. "I won't get seasick, will I?" She looked over to Jess in the dark.

"No, I can personally guarantee that you will not get seasick."

"Good, because that would be quite unpleasant." Robin grinned and closed her eyes. She took a quiet moment to absorb the crisp, light scent around her, of wood and fresh pine, and another scent, which she found quite indescribable, but which she came to immediately recognize as belonging to Jess. She took a deep breath of air into her lungs, holding it for a brief moment and committing the now familiar scent to memory, forever imprinting it in her conscious mind.

"Jess?"

"Yes."

"Can I...um...?" Robin suddenly fell silent, unsure of how to say what she wanted to say. It was an unusual request, to say the least, and she wasn't at all quite sure of how it would be received. Finally, she gathered her courage and just simply asked. "Would it be alright with you if I...um...came over there?" She pointed over to Jess's side of the bed. *I don't know why, but I need to feel you next to me right now.*

Jess opened her eyes in minor surprise. *Is she asking what I think?* She quickly gave herself a mental warning. *Not wise*. "It would definitely be alright." She heard herself say it before she could stop herself. "Come on over here." Jess patted a spot next to her.

With that, Robin quietly slid across the bed and rested her head partially on Jess's shoulder. She wrapped one arm lightly around Jess's waist, and then let herself savor the feeling of the comforting warmth of the body next to hers. She closed her eyes and snuggled down contently, breathing in the wonderful scent that she had committed to memory just moments ago, her mind immediately knowing the undeniable truth. *I'm home.*

After Robin was comfortably settled, Jess, almost without conscious thought, silently lifted her free hand and placed it lightly on top of Robin's back, slowly moving her fingertips back and forth against the fabric of Robin's sleep shirt. *You like this too much, Jess.*

Robin let go a small sigh. "This is nice."

"Yes, it is." She idly traced a petite shoulder blade.

"Does it bother you?" Robin spoke in a hushed tone. "Being this close, I mean?"

"No." Jess drew tiny circles with her fingertips. "How about you?"

"No." Robin whispered. "I like being close to you."

"Me, too." It was all Jess could manage. "Goodnight, Robin."

"Goodnight, Jess. Sleep well."

****

Bright sunlight filtered through the Venetian blinds as the early morning sun made its way up the horizon. Robin awoke first, somewhat disoriented, and then suddenly remembered where she was, and more specifically, who it was she was partially lying upon. She blinked her eyes open more fully, then squinted again as her eyes slowly adjusted to the daylight.

She looked around, then found that her free hand was curiously placed on Jess's hip, and one leg was nudged haphazardly over Jess's thigh. Robin studied the body she was lying on, and with a quiet, yet ardent fascination, she slowly trailed her hand from its perch on Jess's hip, northward, over Calvin boxers, and underneath the bottom edge of a Calvin shirt, until it came to rest lightly on top of Jess's stomach. Jess's bare stomach. Jess's bare, warm stomach. Robin suddenly felt that same stomach quake with subdued laughter, and she guiltily turned her head up to meet the owner.

"Hi there." An amused blue eye regarded her. "What are you doing?"

Robin blushed. "Hi. I was just, um...getting comfortable."

"I see." A grin. "And are you um...comfortable now?"

"Yes, very."

"Good. We aim to please." *Shut up, Jess*. A moment passed. "Do you know what today is?"

"Sunday?"

"Yes, but what else?" Silence. "Let me give you a hint. Boo."

"Boo?"

"Yes, Boo."

A chuckle. "You are very weird." Robin snuggled down further. "I have absolutely no idea what today is, other than Sunday. What is it?"

"Do I have to tell you everything?" Jess lightly rapped her knuckles against the very top of Robin's head and then lowered her voice. "It's Halloween, silly." Another grin.

"Oooh, and I must look a sight, too." Robin made a face. "I am definitely not a morning person. I probably scared you half to death when you woke up and saw me." *And saw what I was doing*. She grimaced. "I probably look a mess right now."

Jess observed Robin's slightly mussed hair and eyes still drowsy with sleep. "Nah, I think you look cute." *You're so adorable.*

"Thanks. Can I go back to sleep now?" Robin pulled the covers up around her more tightly.

"Sure, but I'm getting up. I'll fix breakfast."

A green eye opened. "You cook?"

"Well, I guess you will just have to wait and see, now won't you." A playful eyebrow wiggled. She extracted herself from the almost dozing form, careful to remove certain body appendages lying on top of her which were not her own, and headed for the kitchen.

After some undefined period of time, Robin felt the gentle

rocking of the waterbed as it suddenly moved to accommodate a larger weight making its presence known beside her. She looked up to find sparkling blue eyes staring back at her. "Hi." A sleepy voice managed.

"Glad to see you're awake, sleepyhead." Jess grinned "I made breakfast. Want some?"

Robin slowly sat up. "Yes, I'm starving."

"What a surprise." A grin. "I thought we'd eat breakfast in here. It's Sunday, after all." Jess brought two trays of food over to the bed, set them down., and then sat herself on top of the bed covers next to Robin.

Robin's eyes lit up at the sight. "You made pancakes, and sausage, and, oooh, there're strawberries, too." Robin picked up a strawberry and plopped it into her mouth.

Jess nodded. "Yep. I, myself, personally like to eat strawberries when they're dunked in sugar. Here, try one." Jess took a strawberry, coated it with sugar, and held it out for Robin to take. Instead of just reaching out and taking it, Robin leaned over unexpectedly and took a bite of the sugar-covered strawberry directly from a very stunned Jess's hand, her soft lips lightly grazing Jess's fingers, and the sensation sending a wonderful and not too subtle tingle down Jess's spine. Jess couldn't have moved her hand away if she'd tried, so transfixed by the sight, and caught in a wave of sensory overload. She felt her breath catch at the delicious contact, while her mind suddenly and frantically cried out in alarm. *You're feeding her, Jess.* Jess pulled her hand away.

"That was good." Robin smacked her lips.

Oh God. It was all Jess could do to swallow. "Glad you liked it," her voice almost croaked. A moment's pause and then Jess cleared her throat. "So, what do you have planned for today?"

"Nothing special." Robin took a bite of her pancake. "The usual Sunday chores, grocery shopping, laundry, house cleaning stuff, you know. You probably have a housekeeping service do yours, huh?"

"What, you don't believe I'm domestically inclined?"

Robin chuckled. "I would hardly think so, although you can cook, so you get two points for that."

A raised eyebrow. "Really. Tell me more about this point system of yours. Do I get points for everything I do or just for certain things?"

"Only certain things, and you have to be really, really good at them."

"And who decides what those certain things are and if I'm really, really good at them or not?" Jess finished her last bite.

Robin pondered that question for a moment. "Since it's my point system, as you say, then I would be the one to decide what those things are and if you were really, really good at them."

"I see." Blue eyes locked onto green. "And when I get enough points, what do I get?"

Anything you want. Robin held the gaze and smiled just a bit. "I can't tell you specifically, but I can definitely guarantee it will be well worth your effort."

Oh boy.

****

They finished their breakfast amicably and got dressed, Robin needing to return home for a shower and a fresh change of clothes before beginning her Sunday chores. Jess sent Robin happily on her way and then proceeded into the kitchen to take care of the breakfast dishes. When all such chores were completed, Jess made herself a cup of coffee and sat down on the plush sofa in the living room. She'd had a silly grin on her face all morning, and her mind was making sure she took proper notice of that fact, her internal voice making itself known today with a persistence not even she could suppress.

Something's going on, Jess. And it's making you a bit nervous, isn't it?. You're a smart person, an intelligent lawyer at a top rated law firm. Surely you can figure it out. Maybe we should think about this.

She put her feet up on the coffee table and set down her coffee cup, then relaxed against the back of the sofa, and prepared herself for some quick self-analysis, with a little cross-examination thrown in.

First things first.

You like Robin.

'Yes, we've become good friends.' Her alternate internal voice mentally supplied.

Maybe it's more than simple friendship.

'Nope, just friends.' The alternate internal voice happily assured.

But friends don't normally do some of the things you've done.

'Such as?' The alternate internal voice cautiously asked.

Let's look at the evidence, shall we? You've slept in the same bed twice, very closely I might add. You buy gifts for her, you take her to Broadway musicals, you feed her with your hands, you can't wipe that silly grin off your face, and you're constantly flirting with her. Yep, that about covers it.

'I do not flirt with her.' The alternate internal voice was raised up a notch.

Oh, please. The windows fog up every time you two are in the same room together.

'I don't know what you're talking about.' The alternate internal voice was indignant.

Don't you? Let's take a look at some other things. Just answer the following questions. Do you like her?

'Yes, I already said that.' The alternate internal voice answered.

Do you want to be with her all the time?

The alternate internal voice became restless. *'Yes, so what?'*

Do you think she's cute?

'Yes. She's adorable. Next question.' The alternate internal voice was clearly agitated.

Do you have romantic feelings toward her?

'Hold it right there, buddy.' Her alternate internal voice was more than angry. *'That is way out of line. I do not have, nor have I ever had romantic feelings toward a woman.'*

But this isn't just any woman. This is Robin.

'So what?' The alternate internal voice was fuming. *'I am not interested in her that way. End of story. And even if I was, which I'm not, she most certainly is not interested in me that way.'*

Is that what you're really afraid of? That she wouldn't return your feelings? Or are you really just afraid to admit to yourself that you might have romantic feelings for her? Or both?

The alternate internal voice calmed down a bit. *'I...don't know. I have feelings for her, yes. Things I've never felt before. Things that make me crazy. I'm just not sure they're romantic. And I'm not sure I'd be even be comfortable with that. Even if I did have romantic feelings for her, and even if I was totally comfortable with that, I still don't think she would feel the same way about me.'*

So that's really what's going on then, isn't it? Even if you did have romantic feelings for her, which we're not clear you do, you're not sure you're totally comfortable with that idea.

'Correctamundo.' The alternate internal voice concluded.

And even if you were comfortable with your feelings, you're afraid Robin would not have those same feelings for you, and you would never, ever want to do anything to hurt Robin in any way. Is that it?

'Correctamundo again.' The alternate internal voice was now resigned.

So maybe you should just do your best to fight whatever feelings you might have until you're sure.

'Maybe I should do that.' The alternate internal voice answered, sounding quite glum.

Good. Feel better now?

'Just dandy.' The alternate internal voice responded a bit sarcastically. *'I'm so glad we had this little chat.'*

Chapter 3

Jess had seen better days. Of course, all the days Jess had seen lately had seen better days. Today was no exception. First, there was a screw-up in the filing of a court document, that particular screw-up being that it never got filed in the first place, deadlines notwithstanding. Then, there was the tedious chore of reviewing the clients' billings on each of her files from the previous month, writing off certain time entries and correcting billing errors. *You'd think educated law professionals could provide better billing descriptions than 'prepare documents.'* She rubbed her tired eyes and grimaced at the pile of yet to be reviewed client bills. *I hate the beginning of the month.*

So, by the time the day came to its close, Jess was in a mood. She got up from her desk and took a walk down the hallway, stopping briefly by Robin's office. Robin had a wonderful way of brightening up her frame of mind, even when Jess was in the most crankiest of moods. She looked inside Robin's office. *Not there.* She frowned unhappily, and after checking around the firm a little more and still not being able to locate Robin, Jess went to the one place she knew she'd definitely find the answer--Paul.

"Hi, Paul." Jess stepped into his office. "Have you seen Robin anywhere?"

Paul looked up from his computer. "I think she's already left for the day."

Damn. "Okay. Thanks."

Now a bit sullen and sulking just a little, Jess's mood soured even further as she returned to her office to complete the rest of her tedious billing review. By late evening, she had finally finished the task and headed home, very weary and very cranky. She pulled her silver Mercedes into the garage, went inside and set the alarm. Her body, stiff from sitting all day, was in definite need of a nice, hot, long bath. After running the steaming hot water for several moments, Jess stepped into the imported marble oval roman tub, turned on the Jacuzzi power jets, and simply relaxed into the delightful warmth. And it felt good. Very good. She let her mind wander aimlessly, the ache in her muscles slowly easing and the tension evaporating. *Now, if only Robin was...*She shook her head in silent warning. *Don't go there, Jess.* She mentally chastised herself for her momentary lapse and then relaxed herself against the back of the tub, her disposition still not improved but her muscles less sore. She closed her eyes as she let all the tension of the day evaporate and finally drift away.

What a shitty day.

****

"So, you're telling me they entered a default? Damn it" Jess was livid. "What the hell were you thinking?" Her arms flailed wide in animated gesture. "How could you let that deadline pass?"

Mark Stevens, the third year associate infamous for the near-malpractice meltdown a few weeks prior, shrank back in his chair, his eyes wide with more than a twinge of fear. Jess was in rare form today and he was not willing to risk speaking. Not if he wanted to save his tongue.

"I want you to do a motion to set aside the default. I will cover the hearing." Jess leaned over the desk and gave him a menacing glare. "Just find me one case, one simple case, to take into that hearing. That's all I ask." She abruptly turned and headed back to her office, wondering what the hell she had ever done to deserve such incompetence. Almost as an afterthought, she took a slight detour, through the lobby and past the reception area, over to Robin's office. Jess looked inside. *Not there. Damn.* Jess scowled and then spied Paul at the far end of the hallway, lingering casually about the coffee maker. She rapidly made her way toward him.

"Jessica, hi. We have hazelnut flavor this morning." Paul poured himself a cup.

"Yeah, yeah. Paul, I need to find Robin. Have you seen her?" Jess chose the regular coffee blend.

"Uh, I think she called in. Sick, I think. Anyway, she won't be here."

Jess's head snapped up. *Robin's sick?* "Uh, thanks, Paul."

"Hey, Jessica?" Paul leaned back against the wall and spoke in a quiet tone. "I wanted to ask you, since you know Robin somewhat, um..." He stammered. "Do you know if she's seeing someone right now?"

I definitely do not need this. "I don't think so, but this is a conversation that you should be having with her, not me. Okay?"

"Right. Thanks." Paul nodded, appearing to concentrate heavily on her words.

Jess turned quickly and started walking purposefully toward her office, seemingly deep in thought, only one thing taking precedence in her mind at this precise moment. Once inside her office, she closed the door and sat down, idly noting the time and wondering if it was too early to call. She made the decision anyway, and picked up the phone, dialing the number she had already committed to memory.

Amidst the quiet of the mid-morning, the noisy, insistent ringing of the phone woke Robin up from a restless slumber, her headache pounding hard and her throat unbelievably sore. What had started out as a minor cold, had quickly become worse, and she had mostly slept the past twenty hours away, unable to do even the simplest of things.

"Hello." Robin's voice was low and horse, laryngitis nearly settling in.

"Robin, it's Jess. Sorry. Did I wake you?"

"Yes, but it's alright." Robin suddenly felt soothed by the familiar sound on the other end of the line.

"I heard you were sick. How are you feeling?" Jess asked, sympathy touching the edges of her voice.

"I have the flu, I think. Feel bad. Can't talk real well. Really tired." Robin closed her eyes again and nearly fell back to sleep.

"Robin?" Silence. "Robin?" Jess's voice became tinged with slight alarm.

"I'm here. Just tired."

Jess became slightly more worried. "Listen, let me come by a little later on and check on you, okay? Will you let me stop by?"

"Don't go to any trouble, but if you want to come by, it would be okay. There's a spare house key in the top right drawer of my desk at work in an envelope. It's not labeled. You can use that to get in if I'm asleep." Several long, quiet breaths. "Can I go back to sleep now?" Robin's voice faded out.

Damn. This did not sound good. "Sure, you get some rest. I'll be over a little later on." Jess ended the call and stood up, pacing lightly. She ran her slender fingers through her dark hair and blew out a long breath. Jess went through the logic in her mind, trying to convince herself of all the facts. It was just the flu, after all. Not a big deal. A little uncomfortable, yes. Not an emergency situation. She finally, with a little effort, managed to calm herself down and decided to do something she had never done before. She decided to take off work a little early that afternoon and go check in on Robin.

****

Though mostly distracted for much of the remainder of the day, Jess completed several of her more urgent tasks before making her way out the door. She stopped at the grocery store for a few items and then proceeded directly to Robin's apartment, knocking lightly on the door and then letting herself in with the spare key. Setting the grocery items down, Jess immediately headed back toward the bedroom, intent on checking on her sick patient. Standing quietly in the doorway, Jess observed Robin, curled up and sleeping, the room darkened and quiet. She crossed the room and sat on the edge of the bed, concern etched on her face, and then brought her hand up and lightly brushed the strands of short blonde hair away from Robin's eyes.

Green eyes fluttered open, the voice barely a whisper. "Jess." Robin smiled weakly. "You're here."

"I'm here." Jess smiled, putting her hand up to Robin's forehead, and then frowned. "You have a fever. How are you feeling?"

"Yucky. I have a horrible headache, and a sore throat, and an achy back, and a stuffy nose." *But I'm better since you're here.* Robin furrowed her brows. "Shouldn't you be at work?"

"Don't you worry about me. Let's take care of you." Jess gently brushed another strand of hair from Robin's forehead. "How about if I get you something to drink and you can take some aspirin for the fever, and then we'll see if you're hungry, okay?"

Robin closed her eyes. "Okay."

Jess proceeded into the kitchen, opened the bottle of sports drink she had bought to take care of any dehydration, and poured some into a glass for Robin. She then heated up some chicken soup and brought everything back into the bedroom on a small tray, finding Robin asleep once again. Jess set the tray down, turned on the small lamp on the dresser, and sat down on the bed to gently wake Robin.

"Robin, honey, come on, wake up." Jess spoke quietly. "You need to take some aspirin now and try to eat a little something, okay?"

Robin groggily stirred and slowly opened her eyes. The dim light from the small lamp cast an almost celestial glow around the room, and in Robin's fever induced haze, the vision in front of her left her momentarily dazed. "Jess," she whispered in awe. "You're an angel."

Jess offered a perplexed smile. "No, Robin, most people would definitely not say that. Now try to sit up a little, okay?"

Robin complied and sat up, albeit with slight difficulty. "I need to get something to drink."

"You're in luck." Jess smiled. "I've got something right here. Take these aspirin, too." She handed them to Robin. "Now, let's see if you can eat." She took the hot chicken soup from tray, stirred it, and then blew on a spoonful to cool it before leaning over with it toward Robin. "Here, try some of this, okay?"

Robin took several spoonfuls of the soup, then leaned her head back against the pillows. "You take such good care of me." She gave Jess a contented smile and then closed her eyes. "You're even feeding me."

Jess gave her a very warm smile back. "Yes, I know."

****

Robin fell back to sleep very shortly after eating some of the chicken soup Jess had prepared. For a few moments, Jess sat on the edge of the bed, watching quietly as Robin slept. She reached up and tucked the covers gently up around the sleeping form, and briefly debated with herself as to whether she should go on home, finally deciding that there was really no contest on the matter. It was quite difficult to imagine herself at her own house while Robin was here, sick. So, Jess opted to stay, and pulled in an easy chair from the other room in order to sit and keep silent vigil.

Later, at some indiscernible hour of the night, Robin awoke feeling suddenly thirsty. She took a small sip of water from the glass on the nightstand, then looked around the room, the soft glow of the dim lamplight casting long shadows across the far wall. It was then that she noticed the sleeping form in the easy chair at the foot of the bed. It appeared that Jess had fallen asleep, her stocking feet propped up on the bed, and a thin blanket draped partially around her long frame. Robin smiled to herself. *Jess is here.*

Robin laid back down against the pillows, thinking that the sight of Jess sleeping by her bed was quite possibly the sweetest thing she had ever seen in her life and the sweetest memory she would ever take with her. She took a deep breath, and then, quite unexpectedly, she felt a sudden, overwhelming build-up of intense emotion wash over her, perhaps as a result of the fever, or the cold medicines she was taking, or the result of a myriad of other reasons her mind couldn't possibly process. But at that precise moment, in the quiet stillness of the night, Robin couldn't quite stem the tears that began to flow, as she gazed through the dim light at the partially shadowed form sleeping in the easy chair at the foot of the bed. *Jess is here.*

Her mind drifted back over recent events. Her law school graduation, the horrible fight with David and then his sudden death, the move to Florida, the new job...Robin's whole life had changed in just a few short months. Nothing was as it was supposed to be. David was her life before, and was to be her future, as well. Now, he was gone, and there was left behind the anguish of guilt and loss that still had yet to heal. And in the midst of enduring her silent pain, in the midst of her uncertainty of what the future held, someone had walked into her life as if truly sent by the angels above. *Jess is here.*

The connection she felt to Jess was real. That she knew. But the closeness, the indescribable, indefinable, undeniable feelings she had when in her presence seemed to penetrate deep to her very soul. It had crossed her mind, more than once, that she might be filling an emotional void left by David's death with Jess's friendship. But, in reality, what she felt for Jess was much more than simple friendship. It was something which was never present in her life before, not even with David. And it was intense. Very intense. And so, tonight, looking once again over to the sleeping form at the foot of the bed, the tears came, faster and harder, and they just simply wouldn't stop. *Jess is here.*

Jess awoke at that very moment, perhaps from hearing the muffled sobs or sensing some sudden, unyielding distress, and looked over to the bed to see Robin softly crying. Jess rushed from the chair to Robin's side in an instant, kneeling beside the bed, her gently soothing fingers wiping away the tears as they fell.

"Robin," she whispered tenderly. "What is it, honey?" Jess wiped away another tear. "What's wrong?"

And the tears came harder still. "Jess?"

"Yes."

"Jess?"

"I'm here."

Robin really didn't know where all the sudden insecurity had come from, only that it was there, and that it all came crashing down around her at once, in seemingly unstoppable measure. She looked up at Jess with pleading and tear-filled eyes and whispered softly. "Please, don't leave."

"No, honey." Jess shook her head and then climbed onto the bed next to Robin, swiftly gathering the sobbing form into her arms. She hung on tightly, rocking gently back and forth, all the while whispering quiet assurances. "I won't leave. I'm here, sweetheart. I'm here." *I will always be here.*

Jess held Robin in a that quiet embrace, until Robin's tears finally subsided and they both fell into a light sleep.

****

The dawn's early light filtered through the window blinds as Jess awoke. She carefully rose from the bed, trying not to disturb Robin as she slept, and then glanced back at the clock. She had just enough time to return home to shower and change for work. As Jess was gathering her things, trying to be as quiet as possible, green eyes opened and watched her silently.

"You're going to be late." Robin sat up slightly in the bed.

"No, I have enough time. Just take it easy for today, okay? Call me if there's anything you need. Will you do that?" Jess folded the extra blanket and placed it neatly on the easy chair.

Robin nodded. "Yes. Jess, um..." She didn't quite know how to put it. "Thanks for staying with me last night. I'm sorry about...well, sometimes the nights can be a bit hard for me." Robin fingered the edge of the blanket for a brief moment in slight embarrassment and then looked up to see compassionate blue eyes regarding her gently. "It meant a lot to me that you were here."

"No problem, kiddo." Jess smiled warmly. "Now, you make sure you drink your fluids today and I'll come back by to check on you later, alright?" She headed toward the doorway. "Call me if you need to for any reason."

Robin nodded. "See you later, then. Have a good day." She watched Jess leave and then fell again into a dreamless slumber, somehow feeling much better today than she had a right to expect, considering her condition, but knowing just the same the exact reason why.

****

When Jess arrived at Robin's apartment that evening, she was a little surprised, but rather pleased, to find Robin awake and sitting up in bed.

"You're up. How are you feeling, kiddo?" Jess stepped inside the room.

"Hi. Much better, thanks. I was just going to get something to eat. I think my appetite is coming back." Robin grinned and then stepped gingerly out of bed, going over to the closet and putting on her robe and Bugs Bunny slippers.

"That's good." Jess was trying hard to suppress a laugh.

"Is there something you find funny?" Robin started walking toward the door.

"No, nothing." Jess chuckled.

"You're laughing so something must be funny to you." Robin stood in the doorway.

"Well, if you insist on wearing those, I can't be held responsible for my lack of composure while I'm around you." Jess pointed to the bunny slippers and laughed out loud.

"You're insulting my slippers? I think I take that rather personally."

"No, no. I'd certainly never dream of insulting your choice of footwear." Jess shook her head, trying miserably to suppress another laugh. "Why don't you take you and your....slippers into the living room and I will fix us something to eat." Jess chuckled rather loudly now, giving up all hope of being able to maintain her composure for any length of time.

"Yeah, yeah. You just wait until you're sick and see if I don't laugh at you." Robin walked into the living room and turned on the TV.

A short time later, Jess had prepared a light meal for herself and Robin, complete with chicken soup. They ate casually in the living room as they watched TV, not speaking much, but not really needing to just the same.

"That was good, Jess. Thanks for making me something to eat." Robin set her bowl down and sat back against the sofa, propping her feet up on the coffee table. "You have excellent chicken soup making skills, among other things."

"Oh, do I, huh?" Jess put her own soup bowl down and sat back next to Robin. "And just what might those other things be?" She arched a dark eyebrow.

"Well, let's see. There's your bribing skills for one thing, and your direction giving skills for another...on second thought, let's not include that one for now, your breakfast making skills, and, well, I'm sure I haven't seen everything yet."

Jess turned and looked at Robin directly in the eye. "Oh I can assure you, Robin, you most definitely have not seen everything yet" Jess winked.

All Robin could do at that point was sit there, very still, and quite speechless. *Oh yes, I am definitely feeling better.*

****

That evening, after Jess had cleared away the supper dishes, she walked back into the living room carrying a pillow and a light blanket in her arms. "If you're going to stay up, I brought you a pillow and blanket. You can go ahead and lie down on the sofa." Jess placed the pillow behind Robin's head and spread the blanket out wide over her.

Robin situated herself and then frowned slightly. "There's nowhere for you to sit."

Jess promptly went to the opposite end of the sofa, lifted up Robin's feet and sat down, placing the feet in her lap. "There." She grinned. "I'm pretty comfy now." She looked at Robin's bunny slippers. "But I absolutely, positively cannot have these things here staring at me in the face. I'd die from laughing hysterically. I'm barely keeping it together as it is." Jess then proceeded to remove said slippers and place them on the floor, taking care to ensure that they were sufficiently and conspicuously out of sight.

"I think you secretly wish you had a pair of your own." Robin wiggled her toes.

Jess placed her hands on Robin's feet and began to lightly massage them. "If I ever have a pair of slippers like that, you must promise to have me committed."

"This is slipper abuse, you realize." Robin closed her eyes.

"Do tell. We certainly wouldn't want that, now would we?" Jess smiled sweetly.

Robin enjoyed the feeling of Jess's hands gently kneading the tiny muscles and tendons in her feet, the fingers massaging and spreading a tingling warmth as they trailed from heel to toe and back again. The touch was light, but firm, and seemed to know exactly where the pressure could be best applied to relax each muscle in detail. The massage continued on its tour, magic fingers rubbing lightly over her ankle, and then over the skin on top of her foot, and then onward again toward her toes, in feather-light caresses, alternating between long strokes and small circular motions. It was all having a wonderful effect on Robin, the delicious sensations both relaxing and exhilarating at the same time, and the delightful sensuality of the touch curiously noticeable, despite her still flu-bound condition.

"You're really good at this, you know." Robin chuckled contently. "I think we should add foot massaging to your list of skills."

"Okaaay." Jess slowly massaged a toe. "Do I get points under your point system, as well?"

"Absolutely. You definitely get points for your foot massaging techniques." Robin slowly opened her eyes.

“Good.” Blue eyes gazed down at green. “So tell me, how would you say I’m doing in the point department so far?”

Green eyes held the gaze. “Well, I would say you are definitely doing very well.”

Jess moved to another toe. “And how do you keep track of these points? Do you keep score?”

Robin looked away, then fixed her gaze back on Jess. “I can assure you that I am most definitely keeping score.”

I should never have had that little chat with myself. Jess rested her hands on top Robin’s feet. “All finished.”

“Thank you. That felt wonderful.’’ Robin closed her eyes again, the lids very heavy by now, and then let out a restrained yawn. “Boy, you did such a good job relaxing me, I’m about to fall asleep.”

Jess smiled. “You go ahead and get some rest.” She lightly grasped Robin’s hand and spoke to her with a quiet sincerity.” Will you be okay tonight? I can stay if you’d like?”

Robin squeezed Jess’s hand lightly. “Thank you for offering. I’m fine. Really. You should go home and get a proper night’s rest.”

A dark head nodded. “Okay. But if you need anything, I want you to promise me you’ll call me, no matter what time it is.” Jess stood and made her way for the door. “Deal?”

“Deal.” Robin grinned. “I promise. Goodnight, Jess.”

****

“Where are we going?” Robin sat in the passenger seat of Jess’s silver Mercedes as they drove down the main highway.

“Can’t tell ya.” Jess turned onto a side street.

“Why?”

“Just can’t.”

“First, you kidnap me, luring me away from my apartment on a Saturday afternoon, with vague promises of fun and a ride in your fancy car, and now you won’t even tell me where we’re going.”

“I did not kidnap you. As I recall, you came along quite willingly as soon as I mentioned lunch.”

Robin dropped her sunglasses from her eyes. “I came along willingly only because I couldn’t stand to see you pout.”

“I was not pouting. I was merely making my point that we needed to leave or it would be too late to eat.” Jess turned onto another back road.

"I think it was your plan all along to drive me out into the middle of nowhere." Robin chuckled. "I see absolutely no place around here to eat."

"Just wait." Jess drove down the winding road and then pulled the car alongside the bank of a splendid free flowing river. "We're here." She looked out over the sparkling river waters. "I just thought that since it was such a nice day, and you were feeling better, we could maybe come here and relax by the river for a while." She looked at Robin expectantly. "What do you think? I brought a picnic."

Robin's eyes lit up, first at the idea of a picnic, and next in a surprise mixed with a bit of awe as she took in the sights all around her. "Jess." She looked around again. "It's beautiful. I didn't know this place was here." She looked across the river to see a hawk gracefully swooping high above the tree tops, the soft rustling of the breeze in the branches and the quiet rush of the flowing river giving an aura of solitude to the surroundings. She turned to meet Jess's quiet gaze. "I would really love a picnic."

"Good. Let's get settled."

They retrieved the picnic items from the trunk of Jess' car and proceeded to spread them out along the riverside, taking care to choose a particularly flat area of ground and one with equal amounts shade and sun. The fall day was cool, but not cold, and the gentle breeze carried nature's wonderful scents on the freshness of the forest air.

"What is this place?" Robin asked as she spread out the blanket on the grass.

Jess knelt down with the cooler. "It's a small river which feeds into a larger river downstream. The river and park are run by the Parks Department. It's a little get-a-away I like to come to sometimes, mostly on weekends. It gets me away from the city for awhile to clear my head." Jess popped open two sodas and gave one to Robin. "Out here, the wilderness is all around you. You just have the forest and the birds and the river."

Robin grinned. "You amaze me sometimes."

"I do? How so?"

"Well, I never would have figured you for the type of person to seek out the outdoors like this." Robin sat down on the blanket and stared at the sunlight sparkling off the ripples on the river, the shimmering light almost blinding in its intensity.

"You thought I just went in for creature comforts?" Jess raised an eyebrow.

"Well, sort of." Robin furrowed her brows quizzically and then chuckled. "The more I find out about you, the more I find there is to know."

Jess looked down at the ground, suddenly shy, and spoke softly. "Do you like what you're finding out about me?" She glanced upward toward Robin through dark eyelashes, insecurity plainly visible in her azure eyes.

Green eyes met the gaze, offering the reassurance so plainly sought. "Yes. I definitely do." Robin glanced at the river and then continued. "The more I find out about you, the more I find out how much I really like you. Which, by the way, is very much."

With that, Jess broke into a bright smile, one which rivaled the sparkling lights off the flowing water. "Thank you." She turned her attention to the picnic basket. "So, are you ready to eat? Oooops, what a silly question."

Robin narrowed her eyes playfully at Jess, then peered with intense curiosity at the picnic basket. "What did you bring?"

"Well, let me see here." Jess looked inside. "Okay, we have shrimp salad, shrimp cocktail, shrimp roulade, and some jumbo shrimp for grilling on that barbecue over there." She pointed toward a barbecue grill a few feet away. When Jess finally looked up, Robin was sitting completely motionless with her mouth wide open, her eyes staring ahead in utter astonishment, and a completely bewildered look on her face. "What?" Jess asked quite innocently.

Robin shook her head in disbelief. "You've regressed! And you were doing so well, too."

"It just goes to show you that I will need much more intensive therapy on the matter." Jess arched an eyebrow in mock seriousness. "I think this will require further sessions, doctor."

"I think you're right." Robin played along and gave a light chuckle. "So tell me, what did you really bring?" She reached across the blanket for the picnic basket.

"Be patient." Jess playfully slapped her hand away, then noted Robin's pouting. "Okay, fine. If you must know, I brought fried chicken, potato salad, and coleslaw."

"That's better."

"And shrimp." Jess tilted her head and looked at Robin smugly.

"You are so hopeless."

"So you keep saying."

****

After they had finished eating, Jess and Robin sat together warming themselves in the autumn afternoon's gentle sunshine. Robin relaxed back against a nearby tree, most of its shade off to the opposite side.

Jess stretched her long frame out beside her and put her hands behind her head. "I am really sleepy now after having eaten. Lunch sometimes does that to me."

Robin patted her lap. "Come over here and lie down." She grinned. "I'll be your pillow."

Jess raised an eyebrow. "I wouldn't want to squish you."

"You won't squish me. It's perfectly safe."

It most definitely is not safe. Jess accepted the invitation, and then positioned herself on her back, her head lying across Robin's lap. She slowly closed her eyes, the sudden peace and contentment of the moment flowing over her like the gentle breeze rustling through the trees.

"Is that better?" A petite hand reached up and softly stroked Jess's forehead.

"Yes. It's very nice."

The petite hand went about tracing with interest the finely chiseled features of Jess's cheek bone, then down across her sculpted jaw, and around her firm chin, the touch light and delicate. The soft, gentle fingers slowly stroked their way through her ebony hair, and behind her ear, before finally coming to rest at the base of her neck. Robin then used the very tips of her fingers to slowly trace back and forth against the skin from just below her ear, downward to the pulse point in her neck, and then back up again, in a soothing caress.

Jess was lost all at once in the sensations, immobilized by the tingling touch. She felt every nerve ending become sensitized, each gentle stroke more charged than the one before, and every fiber of her being crying out for more. She turned into the soft touch, craved it even, as if her very life depended on it, as more than one shiver traveled down her spine. It was an utterly intense and delightful feeling. After a few quiet moments, Jess slowly opened her eyes and looked up into sea green. As if guided by some unseen force, their gazes were magnetically locked.

Robin spoke first, her voice very soft, her fingers tenderly brushing the strands of dark hair away from blue eyes. "Jess," she whispered and swallowed back a hidden emotion. "Remember when I was sick and you came and took care of me?"

Blue eyes still held the gaze. "Yes, I remember." Jess's voice was just above a whisper.

"I remember at one point during the night, I woke up and saw you, and for a moment, I thought you were an angel." Robin gave a small smile. "You told me that you didn't think anyone thought of you like that." A pause. "But that's not true." Another longer pause as Robin tried to keep her emotions under control. "You were an angel to me. Thank you for being my angel that night."

Jess continued to look into unwavering green eyes long after the words were spoken. Suddenly, a tiny tear made its way silently down Jess's cheek, the words having touched her heart so profoundly, unlike anything had before. Robin reached down and tenderly wiped away the tear with her thumb, and then placed a gentle kiss on Jess's forehead. Jess closed her eyes and let herself doze off for a while, sinking into the comforting cocoon of warmth as Robin held her gently in her lap.

Later, as the sun started making its descent from the sky, Jess reluctantly sat up and stretched. "That was a great nap. You make an excellent pillow." She winked. "We should really get packed up now. They'll be closing the park soon."

Robin nodded and stood up, putting on her sunglasses. "Thanks for bringing me to this place, Jess. It was a wonderful picnic." She gathering the picnic items and headed for the car.

"I'm glad you enjoyed it." Jess picked up the cooler and followed Robin. "What are your plans tomorrow? Oh, that's right. You have your Sunday chores." Jess got in the car and started the ignition.

"Well, I suppose I maybe could be persuaded, perhaps, to postpone those chores if you had something interesting in mind."

Jess grinned. "Want to go to the beach?" She waggled her eyebrows.

Robin pulled her sunglasses down off her nose, in a trademark showing of 'you must be crazy' and gave Jess a incredulous look. "It's November."

"True, but this is Florida. It's not freezing. We could go to the coast, drive around a little bit, play on the beach, and then catch the sunset." Jess pulled out onto the main highway. "Want to?" She looked over to Robin.

Robin furrowed her brows and pondered this idea for a moment. "Okay, on one condition." She offered a grin.

"What's that."

"You let me drive. You give the directions and I will drive." Robin gave Jess a serious look. "I think giving directions is one area you still need a little work on."

Jess gave Robin a serious look back. "Fine. You can drive, but you realize then, that people may not see us again until next Tuesday."

****

After leaving the park, Robin and Jess headed back to Jess's place and ordered a pizza for dinner. Once finished eating, Jess stretched herself out on the plush sofa, dangling her feet off to one side. Robin sat on the floor directly in front of the sofa. They watched a little TV for a while, the old re-runs still offering amusement even decades later, until Jess finally stretched her arms above her head and suppressed a tired yawn. "I should really be getting you home, seeing as I kidnapped you and all."

"Well, I was kind of thinking about that." Robin turned around on the floor so she was facing Jess. "I was thinking that maybe if I were to stay here tonight, then tomorrow morning we could stop off at my place so I could change, and then we could just go directly to the beach from there. That way, I wouldn't have to come all the way back over here in the morning to pick you up." She furrowed her brow in thought. "I think it would save some time."

Jess contemplated that idea. "You think so?" Blue eyes locked on green.

"Definitely." Robin assured. "I think it would be the best thing to do." Green eyes held the gaze.

Jess arched an eyebrow. "If you think it's best."

"It is."

Jess nodded in agreement and then looked at Robin out of the corner of her eye. "Guest room?"

Robin shook her head very slowly. "Waterbed."

"I see."

They once again performed their nightly chores, Robin donning the usual over-sized nightshirt, and Jess her favorite Calvin boxes and shirt. Jess reached into the medicine cabinet and pulled an object out just as Robin entered the bathroom.

"Here." Jess handed the item to her. "I picked this up for you."

Robin took the item, a full grin spreading widely across her face. "A toothbrush."

"Yeah, well, you never know when having one around here might come in handy." Jess winked.

With their nightly preparations completed, Jess and Robin snuggled down into the waterbed on their separate sides. Jess laid on her back, her eyes closed for a moment before she opened them again to stare at the darkened ceiling. She closed her eyes once more, and then another moment later, opened them yet again. She went through this exercise three more times until she finally turned her head to look over to Robin.

"Um...Robin?"

"Yes." Robin waited.

Jess spoke nonchalantly. "If you wanted to come over here, that would be okay."

Without a word, Robin slid over next to Jess, placed her head on Jess's shoulder, and wrapped an arm lightly around her waist. It wasn't long, as they lay snuggled together, before they both drifted off fast asleep.

****

Morning came quickly and Jess awoke first to find that it was still quite early, the first rays of sunlight barely edging their way past the horizon and in through the tiny cracks in the Venetian blinds. Jess took note of the quietly slumbering form next to her. Robin was curled up on her side facing away from Jess, with Jess spooned tightly up against her back. In the stillness and silence of the early morning, Jess let her mind take control once again, her unrelenting internal voice making itself heard with a renewed vigor.

It seems we might need to go back and review what we discussed before.

'Nope, I am well aware of all that.' The alternate internal voice responded.

Things might be getting a little out of hand.

'Nope, again. I have everything perfectly under control.' The alternate internal voice replied confidently.

Is that so? Then, what are you doing?

'What do you mean? I'm sleeping. What do you think?' The alternate internal voice became a bit testy.

You mean you're sleeping in the same bed with Robin, again.

'Yes, so what? Like I said, I have everything perfectly under control.' The alternate internal voice replied defensively.

I see. Where is your hand?

'What?'

Your hand. Where is it?

A moment to ascertain where said hand was located. *'Around Robin's waist.'*

And how did it get there?

'What do you mean?' The alternate internal voice was a bit perplexed.

How did your hand get around Robin's waist?

'I presume I must have put it there sometime during the night.' The alternate internal voice was now quite annoyed.*'*

And did you put your hand on the outside of the nightshirt she's wearing?

A moment to check once again. *'Nope, on the inside.'* An audible gulp. *'What's your point?'*

Your hand is around her waist, on the inside of the nightshirt. The nightshirt comes to her knees. Think about it.

A moment. *'Oh, Shit. Oh, Shit. Oh, Shit.'*

Calm down.

'Not possible.' The alternate internal voice was clearly panicked.

Sure it is. Now think. You don't see Robin running for the hills, do you?

'She's asleep. She doesn't know.'

You're presuming she's asleep and you're presuming she doesn't know. Try a little test.

'A test?' The alternate internal voice asked a little uneasily. *'Is that fair?'*

Sure it's fair. Do this. Try taking your hand away without waking her up.

A moment's contemplation. *'Alright, fine.'* As the hand in question began to remove itself from the waist in question, a petite hand swiftly reached out and grasped the moving hand and replaced it back to its original position.

There's your answer. She knows and she likes your hand exactly it where it is.

The alternate internal voice refused to believe it. *'It could be just a reflexive reaction.'*

Doubtful. So, now that we've cleared up that little matter, it seems you may have something else on your mind.

'Gee, you're full of insights this morning.' The alternate internal voice replied sarcastically.

You've noticed that Robin's been rather emotional lately.

'She was sick.'

But maybe it wasn't just being sick. Maybe her emotional state had to do with David.

'I'd rather not think about him.' The alternate internal voice tried to avoid the subject.

Why? Could it be because you think that Robin might be transferring her emotional needs from David to you?

'Perhaps.'

And that if she ever were to return any romantic feelings you might have, it would only be temporary, until she was sufficiently past the grief of losing David?

'Very good, Einstein.'

And if that were the case, she might ultimately decide she didn't really want to be involved in any relationship with you?

'Bingo. Give the guy a gold star.'

And then she might skip out on you?

The alternate internal voice became quiet. *'Yes.'*

Because she wouldn't need you anymore?

The alternate internal voice became quieter still *'Yes.'*

Just like James.

'Yes.' The alternate internal voice responded sadly. *'Just like James.'*

Maybe you should clear some of these things up with Robin before you start any type of relationship with her, if you do so.

'That would be a very good idea.'

****

They packed up their beach gear, complete with beach blankets, folding beach chairs, and sunscreen and headed off to the beach. The weather was very nice in the sun, not hot and not cold, but with a pleasant, fresh fall breeze just the same. They each wore jeans and a light long-sleeved shirt, bringing along a light sweatshirt in case it was needed later in the day.

"I thought the beach was in the other direction." Robin drove down the main highway in her blue Miata.

"Are you gonna let me give the directions? We're going to the Gulf, not the Atlantic. The Gulf of Mexico beaches face west. The sun sets in the west. Ergo, we want to go west." Jess put on her sunglasses and sat back in the passenger seat.

"Makes sense. What's the difference, other than the direction, between the Gulf beaches and the Atlantic beaches?" Robin was genuinely curious.

"The Gulf water is warmer and doesn't have as many waves. Some beaches can be quite nice. The Atlantic is rougher, with larger waves. Some beaches, like Daytona Beach, have hard sand that you can drive on, but other beaches have soft sand. The water is colder, too." Jess looked over to Robin. "We can go over to the Atlantic some other time, if you'd like."

"I would like that. I've never spent much time at the ocean before, since Michigan is rather far away from the nearest coast. We have the Great Lakes, which are nice, but they're not the ocean beaches." Robin furrowed her brows in thought. "Is the water too cold to swim in now, since it is November?"

"A little, yes, unless you really wanted to swim. But it's nice just to sit on the beach and enjoy the surf and the pelicans, or take a walk down the beach along the shore." After a moment, Jess glanced at the rearview mirror. "What's this?" She pointed to a miniature doll in the shape of a chimpanzee dangling from the bottom of the mirror.

"That's Al."

"Al?"

"Yes. He's my good luck charm." Robin chuckled "I got him when I first moved here, and ever since, I've had very good luck." Robin glanced over at Jess. *Like meeting you.*

They drove for a while longer and made their way over to the Gulf, finding a beach spot not too far from the main highway. It was also close enough to walk to an old fort which had been used centuries ago by the Spanish.

"Do you want to explore the fort first? It's open on Sundays." Jess got out of the car after retrieving some things from inside.

"Let's do that and then we'll have the rest of the afternoon to sit on the beach. I've never seen a fort before." Robin had a contagious exuberance that Jess couldn't help but catch. It was like seeing things through Robin's eyes for the very first time.

They took their time exploring the old fort which the Spanish had used to guard the coast when they occupied Florida almost two centuries ago. It was fascinating to Robin, seeing the old cannons and cannon balls, and the layout of the fort itself, a piece of history she could experience firsthand.

Next, Robin and Jess set up their beach gear out on the beach. They sat on the beach blanket for a while and enjoyed watching as the calm waves lapped gently at the shoreline, and the seagulls swooped above the water, their cries echoing through the mostly quiet and deserted beachfront.

Jess stretched out her long legs and rested back on her elbows, staring straight ahead at the relatively calm water. After a few more moments of seagull gazing, she glanced back over at Robin, seeing her curiously squirming around a little bit. Jess raised an eyebrow.

"Is there a problem?" She asked in a decidedly semi-bored tone.

"No. No problem." Robin squirmed around some more.

Jess furrowed her brows in slight amusement. "Are you sure?"

"Yes. I'm sure. No problem." Robin squirmed around yet some more.

Jess watched her again for a brief moment, baffled, then shook her head. "What is the matter?"

"Nothing. I just um...well, I think some sand got down in my pants." Robin squirmed yet again.

At this, Jess was simply unable to contain the laughter that followed, the tears streaming down her face. It was all just too priceless. She tried after a moment, though in vain, to regain some semblance of composure. "Robin, all you have to do is stand up and shake the sand out." Jess laughed uncontrollably again. *God, she is so damn cute.*

Robin lowered her sunglasses and squinted her eyes at Jess. "Fine, Miss Beach Expert." She pointed a playful finger. "You go right ahead and laugh about it all you want, but I promise I will get you back when you least expect it." Robin stood up and shook the sand out of her jeans.

"Yeah, yeah. I've heard it all before." Jess was now finally able to calm herself down. She turned her attention for a moment back to the seagulls congregating on the shoreline, and then she just couldn't resist any longer.

"You know, Robin, I seem to be feeling quite lucky right about now. After all, it seems no sand got down in my pants." Jess crossed her legs out proudly in front of her and sat back with a self-satisfied grin on her face. "I'd say your good luck charm is working out rather well."

Robin immediately sat down next to Jess and turned toward her, narrowing her eyes, and annunciating her words very slowly. "What exactly do you mean?"

Jess grinned mischievously. "Well, I can't let you have a monopoly on all the luck, now can I?" She reached into her jeans pocket and pulled out Al, dangling him in front of Robin's face.

Robin's mouth flew open wide. "You are in so much trouble. You give him back." Robin reached for Al. "I can't believe you took him."

"I'm just borrowing him. I'll give him back later." Jess placed Al in her front jeans pocket.

With lightening speed, Robin reached over and grabbed Jess's arm, moving it out of the way and reached her other hand down into Jess's jeans pocket, searching around quite thoroughly for Al.

An amused blue eye regarded her antics for a moment. "Are you...having fun?" A grin.

Suddenly aware of what she was doing, Robin stilled her still searching hand and blushed profusely. "Um...well, if you mean, did I find what I was searching for, then yes." She pulled her hand from Jess's pocket and dangled Al in front of her, and then sat back on the other side of the blanket.

Jess looked over intently at green eyes. "I'm very glad you found what you were searching for, Robin, but that is certainly not what I meant." Jess winked and then turned her attention to a passing seagull, almost. but not quite, missing the even brighter blush that now fully covered Robin's face.

After all their fun and games were over, Robin and Jess spent a leisurely day on the beach, enjoying the atmosphere of the waves and the sand, and the scent of the salt air permeating the seashore. Finally, the sun began its descent from the sky, and Jess and Robin donned their sweatshirts to ward off the early evening chill.

"Care to take a walk with me?" Jess stood up.

"Sure, I would love to." Robin stood and then went down to the water's edge to walk with Jess beside the shoreline. "My mom called the other day." Robin frowned slightly. "She wants me to come home for Thanksgiving."

"Are you going to go?" Jess continued to walk, staring straight ahead at the horizon.

"Yes. I am. But I wish I weren't. I'd rather not go back there, you know, so soon after....everything." Robin stared down at the sand in front of her. "There're just too many memories there that I can't deal with yet."

Jess nodded in a quiet understanding. "Have you seen anyone to help you work through some of the...you know...grief and pain you're feeling? I mean someone professionally?"

"No," Robin replied softly. "I think that most of the time, I deal with it okay. But I admit that sometimes, it is very hard for me."

"It might help to talk with someone, you know, if it's hard for you emotionally to work through this on your own. I imagine it can be hard to start your life over again after something like that." Jess spoke in a quiet empathy. "It must be very difficult for you at times."

"It is, but I know that I have to deal with it. I have to move forward. Nothing can change the past." Robin stopped and then grasped Jess's hand gently. "You have helped me more than you know, Jess. Because of you, I now know that it's possible for me to move forward, that I do have a future." She swallowed back an unseen emotion. "Thank you for that."

"You're welcome." Jess spoke sincerely and offered a reassuring smile. They slowly resumed walking, hands still linked. "I want you to know that I am here for you, and I will always be here for you. But if you need to, we can find someone professionally for you to talk to about things, to help you through some of the harder times. You just let me know if you want to do that, okay?"

"Okay." Robin gave Jess a small smile and shook her head in slight amazement. "Sometimes, I don't know what I did to deserve you."

Jess rolled her eyes in self-deprecation and gave Robin a crooked grin. "You're just lucky, I guess."

Lucky. Robin nodded quietly and then stopped and reached into her pocket, pulling out Al. She looked at the tiny figure in the palm of her hand, fingering it lightly, and then held it up tightly to her heart, whispering a silent thank you to whatever force in the heavens or on the earth was responsible for that one good fortune. Some might call it luck, others fate, and still others destiny. But whatever it was called, it was looking back at her with incredibly deep blue eyes.

Robin gazed out at the small waves lapping at the sand, as a pelican landed on nearby pier. She put Al back in her pocket and turned toward Jess who was watching the same pelican as well. "Hey, Jess, do you think the water's cold?"

"Probably a little." Jess raised her eyebrows playfully and then stood behind Robin with a teasing grin on her face. "But I suppose you could find out first hand. I'd be happy to assist you in that matter."

"Oh, no. No, you don't." Robin took off running down the beach with Jess chasing closely behind her. A moment later, Jess caught up with Robin, clasping her arms tightly around her from behind while Robin, giggling lightly, playfully struggled to get free.

Jess spoke softly into Robin's ear, her warm breath caressing the very back of Robin's neck, sending small delicious shivers down Robin's spine. "You can run, Robin, but I promise you, I will always, always catch you. Remember that."

I think I'm counting on that. Robin stood in the delightful embrace for a moment longer and then spoke softly, green eyes locking firmly onto blue. "I'll hold you to that."

Jess smiled. "The sun's setting. Let's watch." Jess had not moved from her position behind Robin, her arms still wrapped snugly around Robin's waist, and her chin now resting on Robin's shoulder.

They stood in silent wonder and watched the sunset together, the oranges, purples, pinks, yellows and mauves merging in a timeless array. Robin had never seen a more beautiful sight, or felt a more contented or peaceful moment, as when this warm, and yes, loving embrace, completely engulfed her, setting her heart free from its guilt and pain, and carrying her soul safely to the nearest shore.

****

Jess and Robin arrived back in town a little later that evening and ended up at Jess's house, having eaten dinner at a small seafood restaurant they encountered along the way back from the coast. The restaurant, of course, was minus one shrimp special upon their leaving. Upon arrival at the ranch style house, or "The Ranch" as Robin referred to it, Jess offered Robin the use of the guest bathroom in order to shower and change clothes, and of course, remove any lingering sand from any and all unwanted places. Robin had the foresight to bring a change of clothes, and if truth be known, an extra change of clothes had become a permanent resident of her car in case of any unplanned sleepovers. Jess, likewise, showered in the master bathroom and donned a clean pair of jeans and a light-weight cotton pullover shirt.

Upon changing into her twill pants and polo shirt, Robin stepped out into the living room in time to see Jess start a fire in the fireplace. Though not a particularly cool day, a fire was always a nice addition in the winter months, and the glass doors in front of the fireplace served to keep the extra unneeded heat from entering the room, if necessary. The stereo was playing softly in the background, tuned to the local soft rock radio station.

"Wow, a fire. I didn't think people in Florida needed fireplaces." Robin sat down on the plush sofa opposite the fireplace.

"We don't. But it's nice and it's one of the things I like most about this house." Jess sat her long frame down on the sofa next to Robin, the soft, orange glow of the fire the only source of light in the room. "I sometimes like to relax in front of a cozy fire. It makes it seem more like winter's coming."

Robin leaned her head against the back of the sofa and sighed. "Yeah, it is nice." A moment passed. "It was a wonderful weekend, Jess. After being sick, it was really nice to get out again and enjoy the day. Thanks for spending it with me."

"You're welcome. And I'm glad you're better now, so you could come out and play." Jess grinned widely and then relaxed back against the plush cushions, putting her feet lazily on the coffee table.

They sat silently curled up together on the plush sofa, side by side, arms and legs barely touching, and listening contentedly to the soft music from the stereo. They watched the play of the flames dancing from the fireplace, the shadows promenading merrily across the far wall of the darkened room. Just then, as the dim light of the fire flickered hypnotically, and its luminance cast an ethereal quality all around them, a soft melody filled the room, a familiar tune which both Robin and Jess immediately recognized, the words themselves penetrating into their very thoughts. And so, as the music played softly in the background and the sound of the words filled the room, it all began.

I can't fight this feeling any longer
And yet I'm still afraid to let it flow
What started out as friendship, has grown stronger
I only wish I had the strength to let it show

Green eyes turned and looked questioningly up to blue.

I tell myself that I can't hold out forever
I said there is no reason for my fear
'Cause I feel so secure when we're together
You give my life direction
You make everything so clear

Blue eyes locked onto green.

And even as I wander
I'm keeping you in sight
You're a candle in the window
On a cold, dark winter's night
And I'm getting closer than I ever thought I might

Robin turned and shifted closer to Jess.

And I can't fight this feeling anymore
I've forgotten what I started fighting for
It's time to bring this ship into the shore
And throw away the oars, forever

And studied her beautiful face with silent and intent curiosity.

Undeniable

Cause I can't fight this feeling anymore
I've forgotten what I started fighting for
And if I have to crawl upon the floor
Come crushing through your door
Baby, I can't fight this feeling anymore

Azure eyes stared back intensely, heart racing and breathing becoming shallow.

My life has been such a whirlwind since I saw you
I've been running round in circles in my mind
And it always seems that I'm following you, girl
Cause you take me to the places that alone I'd never find

And Robin slowly brought her palm up to Jess's face and lightly caressed her cheek.

And even as I wander
I'm keeping you in sight
You're a candle in the window
on a cold, dark winter's night
And I'm getting closer than I ever thought I might

And tenderly traced a petite finger across the curve of Jess's jaw.

And I can't fight this feeling anymore
I've forgotten what I started fighting for
It's time to bring this ship into the shore
And throw away the oars, forever

And Jess felt a sudden dizziness at the gentle, almost reverent touch.

Cause I can't fight this feeling anymore
I've forgotten what I started fighting for
And if I have to crawl upon the floor
Come crushing through your door
Baby, I can't fight this feeling anymore.

And then Robin slowly leaned in very close to Jess, their breaths mingling together for what seemed like an eternity, their eyes locked in an unyielding gaze, until, at last, Robin's lips finally brushed against

Jess's in the softest of tender kisses. And with that connection, time, in all its eternal wonder, seemed to stand still, and Robin somehow forgot to breathe for a brief moment, the intensity shaking the very foundations of her entire being, refusing to let go. She pulled back slightly, her hand still resting lightly on Jess's cheek, and searched the clear blue eyes briefly, before leaning in again, and placing another soft, delicate kiss on Jess's lips. Robin closed her eyes, barely able to breathe, her voice almost shaky. "Jess."

Immediately, Jess pulled her into her arms and gently held her close, kissing her intensely with a final release of tender emotion too long denied, too long contained, too long suppressed. She felt Robin's arms go around her shoulders, Robin's palms laying flat on her back, wanting to maintain the contact and prolonging the connection. And all at once, in that fleeting instant, in that one immeasurable second of time, Jess knew, beyond any doubt, that what had once been denied, was now incomprehensibly undeniable. Her head was spinning with a concentrated mixture of emotion too intense for her mind to perceive, the realization finally dawning across the span of timeless ages, as if her soul was desperately reaching out for its missing half, calling it home once again. *It's you.*

Jess gently broke the kiss, closing her eyes and resting her forehead lightly against Robin's, trying with all her might to catch her breath and still her racing heart once again. Her arms still held Robin in a tender embrace, as Robin slowly moved her hands from Jess's shoulders up to softly caress her face. Jess almost melted under the tender touch, and then softly gazed into the green eyes so close to her own, and whispered, almost desperately. "I can't fight this any more." She took a breath and looked up, trying to steady her emotions. "What I feel, what I am feeling, Robin, I can't fight it."

Robin closed her eyes tightly, her forehead still resting against Jess's, and without moving, tenderly placed a delicate kiss on her cheek. "I know, Jess." Robin swallowed "Neither can I." Robin spoke in an unsteady voice, then dropped her head, resting it on Jess's collarbone and wrapped her arms tightly around the strong shoulders once again. She hung on, seemingly for dear life, as she let the emotions ease their way over her in silent waves.

Jess put her cheek on top of the blonde head and held Robin closely, unable to keep the intensity of the moment from reaching up and claiming her, as well. She heard Robin gently sniffle back the tears, and felt her own eyes well up as she clutched Robin to her, holding on with all her might. She moved her hand back and forth slowly against Robin's back in a soothing motion, her own silent tear falling now.

"It's okay, sweetheart. It's okay." Another tear made its way from her eye. "I've got you, honey. I've got you. We're going to be okay."

After several long moments, now more composed, they pulled apart and sat back against the cushions on the sofa.

Robin reached for Jess's hand and held it tightly, linking their fingers together. "Are you okay?"

Jess turned her head to look at Robin, smiling gently. "I'm good. You?"

"Good, too." Robin gently brushed her thumb back and forth against the palm of Jess's hand in a soothing rhythm for several moments. "We should talk about this."

Jess nodded. "Yeah, but um...would it be alright if we do that another time?"

Robin nodded, knowing they both needed time to process what had just happened before putting voice to their thoughts. They both sat together in quiet solace for a very long while, curiously unable to break themselves completely free of the connection which had formed between, as they watched the fire's dying embers slowly burn down.

Robin softly spoke again. "It's getting late. I should go. Tomorrow's a school day." She smiled. "I mean work day."

Jess gave her a warm smile back. "Okay." She stood. "I'll see you tomorrow, then."

Robin followed her to the front door, gathered her things and stared silently for a moment, before reaching up and giving Jess a lingering hug. Jess wrapped her in her arms, and kissed the very top of her head before gently releasing her.

"Goodnight, Jess." Robin stepped out into the surprisingly chilly air.

"Goodnight. Drive safely, okay?" Jess watched as Robin got into her car and pulled out of the driveway and out of her sight. *Jess, I hope you know what you've just done.*

Chapter 4

It had gotten unexpectedly cold during the previous night. As Robin made her way inside the downtown office building, the slightly burnt smell of heated air lightly hit her, signaling the first day the building's heat generators had been turned on this fall. She made her way up the elevators to her office, closed the door, and powered up her computer. Her mind, of course, was elsewhere, and the distraction persisted as she absentmindedly gazed out the window toward the lake below. *I need to see Jess.* Just then, she heard a light knock at her door.

"Come in." Robin sat at her desk, half expecting and more than a little hoping to see Jess walk in.

It was Paul. He opened the door and stepped inside her office. "Hi. I see you've fully recovered. The flu, wasn't it?" He awkwardly leaned against the interior of the door frame.

Robin sighed. "Yes, but I'm all better now." She smiled politely, then picked up her pen to begin to write. "Did you need something?"

"No, nothing, really. Just wanted to see if you were back." He fell silent for a moment. "Listen, Robin, I was wondering, if you don't have any other plans, if you'd like to go to the basketball game with me on Friday night. I have tickets." He looked at her hopefully.

Robin sighed again. *Could this get any worse?* "Paul, thanks, but I can't make it. Thank you for asking, though."

Paul looked at his feet for a moment. "Sure, maybe some other time." He smiled slightly. "Glad you're back." Another brief smile, and then he left Robin's office, closing the door again.

Robin mentally noted that she needed to have a nice, little chat with Paul, and then began to make her way in earnest through the pile of work that had built up during her absence. After hours of pouring through potential trial exhibits and preparing pre-trial affidavits, Robin glanced briefly at her watch to find that it was nearly lunch time. She had not seen Jess all morning, and Jess had not called or e-mailed either. Robin sat for a moment, idly wondering if Jess might be free for lunch, and then decided to make her way over to Jess's office to find out firsthand. As Robin turned the corner and walked down the hall toward Jess's office, she saw that the door was closed, which usually meant that Jess did not want to be disturbed. As Robin approached, she hesitated for a slight moment, then knocked lightly.

"Come in." Jess's muffled voice came through the thick wood door.

Robin opened the door slowly and peeked inside. "Hi." She smiled, slightly unsure. "Are you busy?"

Jess glanced up from her desk, an unreadable expression on her face, and motioned Robin inside the office. "A little. Go ahead and close the door."

Robin did so and took a seat opposite Jess, deciding it was best to just get straight to the point. "Um...I was wondering if you'd like to go grab some lunch. Are you free?" She looked at Jess expectantly.

"No." Jess shook her head. "Thanks, but I'm really busy and I think I should just work straight through." She relaxed a little and let go a small smile. "I played hooky this weekend."

"I know." Robin returned the same smile. It was true, they had played all weekend, but Robin desperately needed to talk to Jess, and she just couldn't let the day pass without attempting her best to do so. "Can you come over tonight? I can fix something for dinner and then maybe we can talk a little bit." Robin was insistent, a bit of desperation coloring her voice.

There was a long silence. Longer than it should have been, and Robin was growing nervous. Jess's unreadable expression had not changed, and it was impossible to discern what was behind those extraordinary blue eyes. The silence lingered, and after another long moment, Jess finally spoke. "Tonight's bad for me, Robin. I really have a lot of work to do, and I really need to catch up on some of this stuff this evening."

Something's wrong. "Okay." Robin tried not to let her disappointment show and took a long breath. "Then, how about tomorrow night?"

Jess focused her attention out the large window and stared at the downtown skyline, her jumbled thoughts racing through her mind. She was trying, though a bit unsuccessfully, not to deal with the events of this past weekend. A part of her wanted to fall head first into the sea green comfort Robin provided, and another part was just plain afraid to take the risk. It was as simple as that. But they did need to talk, and it really wasn't something that could be avoided. Jess closed her eyes. She was considering perhaps waiting a few days, and then dealing with things when she'd had more time to think, but the question in Robin's voice seemed to hold more urgency. Jess shook her head and mentally berated herself. *Don't do this to her, Jess. She doesn't deserve this from you. Deal with it now.*

"Jess?" Robin broke through Jess's thoughts and looked over to see the apprehension on her face. It was then that Robin sensed what seemed to have been troubling Jess all along. *She's afraid.* Robin mentally noted to herself. *I am, too.* She cautiously asked again. "Is tomorrow evening, okay?"

Jess silently made up her mind and then slowly nodded, clear blue eyes now suddenly quite readable. "Yes."

Robin let out a relieved breath. "Great. Come over about 7:00, okay?" She stood up to leave, but suddenly and without thinking twice, she instead stepped around Jess's desk and knelt by her side, resting her hands lightly upon the arm of Jess's desk chair. Robin looked up and spoke softly, her voice quietly compassionate. "Whatever happens, Jess, we're in this together, okay?"

Jess gave her a warm smile and nodded slightly. "I'm counting on that, kiddo." The smile tuned into a full grin. "Now go get some lunch before you starve to death."

Robin stood up and grinned back. "You are so mean to me."

"Just stating the facts, kiddo." Jess turned and pulled out an envelope from her desk drawer. "Here. I forgot to return this to you from last week." She handed it to Robin.

Robin took the small, white envelope, the one with the spare apartment key in it, and stood silently in place for a moment. She then handed it right back to Jess. "Keep it."

"Keep it?"

"Yes, keep it. You never know when it might come in handy sometimes." Robin headed toward the door and grinned. "Especially if you play hooky again."

****

At 7:00 sharp Tuesday evening, Jess arrived at Robin's place, a little tired but more than a little anxious. Talking was never easy for her, and this night would be no exception, though she had decided that, if they were going to talk, everything should be dealt with head on. She pulled up to Robin's apartment building, sat for a few moments in her car, and then, taking a steadying breath, headed for Robin's door.

"Hey." Robin answered the door. "I'm glad you're here. Boy, it's getting cold out. Come on in."

Jess stepped inside and took off her light jacket. "Thanks. It smells good in here. What did you make?"

"Spaghetti. I thought it would be simple." Robin led Jess to the sofa and sat down. "You know, I thought you said it never got cold in Florida. I think you might have some explaining to do." She wagged a playful finger at Jess.

"What I said was, it hardly ever gets cold in Florida and that I wished it was cold more often." Jess sat down. "I never said that it never got cold in Florida. And for you information, it's not cold out. It's a little cool, that's all."

"Cool, yeah, right. Well I guess I'll have to drag out some of my sweaters to wear after all." Robin chuckled.

Jess shook her head. "The problem is, tomorrow it'll be warm again. The cool air only sticks around for a day or two before it warms back up." *I can't believe we're talking about the weather.*

"Right." Robin frowned. "Dinner's ready. Let's eat." She furrowed her brows. "You do like spaghetti, don't you?"

Jess gave her a bright smile "It's one of my absolute favorites, next to shrimp, of course." She laughed and followed Robin into the dining room, idly noting the carved centerpiece still displayed prominently in the center of the table. "You seem to always do all the cooking. You'll have to let me cook dinner next time. Deal?"

Robin grinned widely. "Okay, deal."

Dinner was quite informal and relaxed, the conversation light and comfortable. No matter whatever else, Jess and Robin seemed to fall into the content and familiar pattern of easy and gentle banter, both of them happy simply to enjoy each other's company. When dinner was finished and the dishes washed, they retired into the living room to talk.

"Come sit down." Robin patted the sofa and gestured for Jess to sit. "Thanks for coming over tonight." She watched in silence as Jess came over and sat down on the sofa next to her. "Um...Jess..." Robin bit her bottom lip lightly, trying to decide how to best start. "I want you to know something, first." Robin took a deep breath and steadied her voice. "If you'd like to keep things the way they were, you know, before, then I want you to know that we can still do that."

Jess was quiet for a very long moment, appearing to contemplate that statement at length and in great detail. She swallowed and softly whispered. "Is that what you want?"

Robin sat motionless. *How do I answer my own question?* There were so many things she felt, and none of them was easy to explain. She mostly felt fear and then a bit of guilt, as if by charging forward into uncharted waters with Jess, she was also perhaps betraying David's memory. But the question was, did she want things to go back to the way they were before? *No, definitely not.* "No," Robin finally whispered back. "I don't want that. But I'm not the only one here, and I would respect whatever you wanted to do."

Jess nodded and looked directly into sea green eyes. "I don't want things to go back to the way they were before, either." She reached down and took Robin's hand gently in her own. "I've thought of little else these past couple of days. I'm a little nervous about this, as you probably can see, but I do know that I want to be close to you."

"Jess, I want that too." Robin looked over at the far wall, not really seeing anything in particular. "I have to be honest with you about something." Her voice became shaky. "I've never felt this way before, not even with David. I'm a little bit afraid of these feelings. I've never um…." She paused trying to collect her thoughts and then whispered, slightly embarrassed. "I've never kissed a woman before." Her voice trailed off.

Jess closed her eyes and nodded. "I know what you mean. Neither have I." She opened her eyes again and stared intently at Robin. "I've never wanted to do that...before now. Before you." Jess fidgeted a little. "If we were to go forward, would you be okay with it?" She gave Robin a crooked smile. "The kissing part, I mean."

Robin smiled back a bit shyly and nodded. "Yes, I would definitely be okay with it."

Jess sat a little closer. "So how was it?" Her voice was a bit unsure.

"How was what?" Robin stared into blue eyes.

"The kissing part." Jess whispered. "Was it okay?"

Robin swallowed and moved closer to Jess. "Yes." She took a breath. "It was very okay."

"Would you want to maybe...try it again?" Jess's warm breath caressed Robin's face.

"Yes." It was all Robin could say before Jess's lips lightly brushed hers and then made firm contact, the softness exquisite and the sensation indescribable.

It was a chaste kiss by all standards, but Jess was spellbound just the same. Robin's lips were so soft, and the electrified jolt was enough to make her dizzy. She brought her hand up and placed it behind Robin's neck, pulling her in closer, while Robin lifted her own hand

and caressed Jess's cheek with her fingertips. The kiss turned into several more kisses, each more confident than the previous one, but yet, the kisses were also slow and gentle, and lingered over the span of several moments. Both Robin and Jess were all at once very lost in the new sensations, and more than a little overwhelmed by the intensity. Finally, they broke gently apart and leaned back against the cushions, both trying to calm the speed of their racing hearts.

"That was...um...wow." Robin shook her head in wonder. "I can't describe it."

Jess smiled. "Amazing."

"Yes." Robin smiled back. "Amazing."

Jess grew serious. "There's something I need to ask you, Robin, but I don't want to upset you."

Robin sat very still. "Okay."

Jess's voice was slightly above a whisper. "You mentioned David. I know his loss is hard for you, and the pain you feel must be very great." She glanced away for a moment then turned her attention back to Robin. "I just don't want you to do anything that you wouldn't be comfortable doing in light of that." She paused. "You once said that it was too soon for you to be involved with someone. What I mean is, are you sure you're okay with this...with us, and our going forward?"

What is it you're really asking? Robin looked at Jess, trying desperately to understand. "Are you asking if I would feel like I was betraying David by feeling the way I do about you?"

"Something like that." Jess turned her gaze downward toward the floor, unable to look at Robin directly, and almost afraid to hear the answer.

"Jess, will you look at me, please." Robin brought her hand to Jess's chin and gently lifted it up. "I will be honest with you." Robin spoke softly. "Sometimes I feel that I would be betraying his memory, yes. That doesn't mean that it's right for me to feel that way, or that I will always feel that way. I know in my mind that I have to move on with my life. My heart sometimes just has to catch up. I can't promise that I won't fall backward sometimes, but I'd like to count on you to be there for me if I do." Robin looked intently into apprehensive blue eyes, piercing the veil that shielded them. "I want you to know that the things I feel for you, Jess...I've never felt them before, with David or with anyone else. Just you."

Jess nodded, not taking her gaze away, and then continued. "If you couldn't do it, I mean, if you realized you didn't want to go forward after all, that this might not be right for you, you would tell me, right? You wouldn't just..." Her voice faded, unable to put words to the thought.

Leave.

Robin closed her eyes briefly. *I see it now. She's afraid I'll change my mind and then leave her. Damn you, James. I can't believe you did this to her.* Robin wrapped her arms gently around Jess's shoulders and held her close. "I promise you, Jess, I promise you, I'd tell you if there was any doubt." She then pulled back slightly from the embrace, green eyes staring resolutely into blue, and spoke very clearly. "There is absolutely no doubt, Jess. None." She offered a slight smile. "Scared, yes. Doubt, no."

"Thank you." Jess nodded and then was quiet for a long moment. "You, know, Robin, I'm really glad we talked about this tonight. I'm sorry if it seemed as though I was trying to avoid it." She gave Robin a crooked grin. "Alright, I was definitely trying to avoid it. But thanks for insisting. Sometimes, you just have to kick me." She laughed softly.

"I'll have to kick you, huh? I'll definitely have to remember that." Robin chuckled and fingered the fabric on the sofa cushion. "Um, Jess?"

"Yes."

Robin looked up a bit shyly. "Do you want to cuddle for a while?"

Jess gave her a warm smile. "Definitely. Come here." She stretched herself out on the fluffy sofa. "I want you to know that cuddling is my specialty."

Robin cuddled up facing Jess on the inside portion of the fluffy sofa. "I agree. You're an excellent cuddler." She chuckled. "We'll have to consider adding this to your list of skills."

Jess nuzzled Robin's ear. "Yes. And don't forget to give me points, too. I need lots and lots of points."

"Why is it you need lots and lots of points?" Robin gently kissed Jess's temple.

"So I get my prize." Jess ran her fingertips slowly through Robin's soft blonde hair.

"I see. Do you know what you want your prize to be?"

Jess gave Robin a devilish grin. "Oh, yes. After all, you did tell me it would definitely be worth my effort." She winked.

"So I did." Robin chuckled and then laid her head on Jess's shoulder, releasing a contented sigh. "I like it when you hold me like this. I feel safe with you."

Jess smiled. "Me, too."

Robin closed her eyes. *You are safe with me, Jess. I won't leave you.*

****

Jess stared intently at her computer screen, planning the trial calendar. She looked up from her work in time to see Keith enter her office. He seemed particularly quite anxious today.

"Keith, what can I do for you?" Jess sat back in her leather chair.

Keith Miller, a fourth year associate, had been assisting with trial preparations in Robin's absence and took up some of her workload while she was out sick. "I wanted to go over the deposition status with you, if you have some time."

Jess nodded. "Alright. Robin's back now so she can pick back up with the trial preparation matters. What is it?"

"Well, I had a question and I wanted to run it by you." Keith seemed nervous. "I noticed in reviewing the deposition transcripts that apparently we haven't deposed Anne Carver. I know she's a key witness for the opposing side and I didn't know why we decided not to depose her."

Jess frowned. "What do you mean, we haven't deposed her? I thought you and Michelle were deposing all the witnesses?"

"She wasn't scheduled. I didn't know about it until now." He looked at the floor. "The discovery deadline has passed, so we can't even try to schedule her for a deposition at this late date even if we wanted to."

Jess looked grim and tried to control her growing anger. "You know very well we can't go into trial without knowing what that witness will say. How can I cross-examine her when I don't know what the hell I'm supposed to ask her?" Jess's raised voice was heard well down the hallway. "Why wasn't she scheduled?"

"I don't know. Maybe you should check with Robin and see why Anne Carver didn't make it on the deposition schedule." Keith stood to leave. "Let me know if you need me to do anything with this." He left Jess's office, practically on the run, feeling fortunate to have escaped in one piece.

Damn it. Jess swiveled her chair and stared out the floor to ceiling windows at the downtown skyline. *Why didn't Robin schedule that deposition?* Something just didn't feel right. Robin wouldn't let this slip. It wouldn't be like her to forget the discovery deadline. Jess closed her eyes. Ordinarily, she would have been fuming, and she knew it. Didn't she just get all over Mark's case for missing a deadline? Suddenly, Harry's words came back at her. *'We can't compromise the client's case for training purposes.' Damn.* Jess dialed the phone to

Robin's office. "Robin, it's Jess." Her voice was neutral. "Can you come see me? I need to talk to you about the trial." She hung up the phone, and after what seemed like an eternity, Robin poked her head inside the office door.

"Hi. What did you need?" Robin closed the door and sat in a chair opposite the large, cherry wood desk.

Jess spoke in an even, businesslike tone. "Keith was in here a few moments ago. He was covering some of your work while you were out." She paused. "He tells me that we didn't depose Anne Carver and she wasn't on our deposition schedule." Jess looked intently at Robin. "Was there a reason?"

Robin flinched. "I spoke to opposing counsel and scheduled all the other depositions. When we came to schedule Anne Carver, he told me that they would not be calling her as a witness at trial, so it was not necessary to depose her. She was not going to testify."

"I see." Jess rubbed her fingers against her eyebrows and closed her eyes. She opened the case file and pulled out a document. "Here. Take a look at their witness list." She handed the document to Robin.

"I don't understand." Robin read the document. "He said she was not testifying."

Jess frowned. "Well, she is, and now we don't know what she's going to say." Jess sat back in her chair and was silent for a long moment. A seasoned associate would have recognized what was happening. Harry's words came back at her again. *'There is no substitute for experience.'* Jess spoke her next words carefully, making an effort to remain calm. "Robin, this is a very old trick which, quite frankly, most ethical lawyers don't use. They tell you that they don't intend to call a witness at trial so you won't depose the witness ahead of time. Then, once the discovery deadline has passed, they suddenly decide that they indeed intend to call the witness after all, and they amend their pre-trial witness list to include the new witness. That way, you won't know ahead of time exactly what the witness will say on the stand." Jess shook her head. "I've seen it done before, although the Court doesn't often let them get away with it." Jess softened her voice somewhat. "I should have warned you about our opposing counsel. He tends to be less than ethical."

"Oh." Robin grimaced. "Is there anything we can do?"

Jess thought about this, and stared out the window for a long moment. *Think, Jess.* Then, it suddenly hit her like a ton of bricks. It was so glaringly obvious, it practically called out her name. Jess looked over to Robin. "I just thought of something." Jess paced around the room "This tactic is a desperate measure and is rarely ever used. There is some particular reason opposing counsel did not want us to depose this witness ahead of time. Something probably big. Otherwise, he wouldn't have resorted to such an underhanded tactic in the first place." Jess tapped her fingers against the side of her chin in thought. "We just have to figure out what that particular reason is."

Robin looked at Jess apologetically. "I'm sorry I didn't catch what he was doing."

Jess nodded. "Not your fault. Besides, you'll learn as you handle more and more cases. It was my mistake in not alerting you to the type of person our opposing counsel is."

"He's a weasel?" Robin tried to lighten the situation somewhat.

Jess nodded again. "He is definitely a weasel, and we're going to bag this weasel before he knows what hit him." Jess gave Robin an almost feral grin. "This is what we'll do. I want you to go back through each and every document that has Anne Carver's name on it. Have one of the paralegals run a background check and an asset check on her. Then pull it all together and see what shakes out. There's something there, I just know it, and we're going to find out what it is. It might require some late nights, though." Jess raised her eyebrows expectantly. "Sound like a plan?"

"You got it, boss." Robin grinned. "I'll get right on it."

"Good." Jess's expression suddenly turned very serious. "Now, I have one very important question for you, Robin, and I need you to give me an honest answer."

Robin nodded slowly and swallowed, a bit unsure and more than a little apprehensive. "Okay."

With a still serious expression, Jess asked, "What are you doing Friday evening?" She arched a dark eyebrow.

Robin opened her mouth, but nothing came out. She then arched an eyebrow of her own and responded in an equally serious manner. "Working."

Jess shook her head. "Nope, wrong answer." She pulled something from her top desk drawer. "You're going to the basketball game with me. See, I have these tickets." She flashed said tickets at Robin. "These tickets always used go to waste because I didn't often go. Now, you can go with me." She grinned expectantly.

Robin looked at Jess and teased. "But what if I don't like basketball?"

"Then, you would be weird. Everyone likes basketball. But if you don't want to go...." Jess didn't get a chance to finish the sentence.

"I never said I didn't want to go. I just asked what happens if I don't like it. Actually, I don't know much about basketball. Football, yes. Basketball, no." Robin glanced at Jess. "So, what would happen if I go, and then I don't like it?"

"Well, then, I guess I'll just have to make it up to you some other way." Jess winked.

"Such as?"

"Such as you get to pick the next place we go. Deal?"

"You've got yourself a deal, boss." Robin got up and headed for the door. "As long as I get to be in charge."

"Alright, fine. You're in charge. Now get back to work. You need to be perfectly work-free by Friday night." Jess returned to her trial preparations as soon as Robin left her office. *You're getting too soft, Jess. There was a time not so long ago when you would have chewed someone up and spit them out for less than what happened.* She sighed to herself. *I guess we know who's really in charge here, don't we?*

Robin arrived back at her office and checked her e-mail, opening a mail message from the office administrator. *November Birthdays.* And there, in bold print amongst the other November dates, was the date that most caught Robin's eye. *Jess's birthday.* She smiled to herself. *Next week.* Robin sat back and considered for a moment just what it was she was going to do to celebrate that particular event.

****

"What row are our seats?" Robin stepped over to the sports arena's aisle stairway.

"Well, do you see those seats way up there?" Jess pointed her index finger toward the balcony seating.

"You're kidding. We're way, way, way up there?" Robin squinted to see the uppermost level.

Jess grinned. "No, I never said that. I just asked you if you saw them. We are way, way, way down there." Jess now pointed toward the lowest level seating. "Much better than those up there, huh?"

Robin gave Jess a playful swat. "You think you're so funny. You just like to torment me." Robin made her way down the aisle to the lower level.

Jess followed after her. "Yes, I think I'm funny, and yes, you're fun to torment." She stopped near a row of seats. "This is us. The law firm gets great seats, huh?"

"I'll say. This is a great view of the basketball court from here. You partners get all the perks." Robin took her seat. "You'll have to explain the basketball rules to me so I understand what's going on."

Jess sat down in the seat next to Robin. "Fine, but I have to warn you, it's a fast game and you're not going to learn everything all at once."

"Okay." Robin turned to look at the rows of seats behind her. "Oh no."

"What is it?" Jess looked around.

"Hide me." Robin sunk down into her seat and ducked her head behind Jess's shoulder.

"What?"

"It's Paul." Robin pointed two rows back. "Don't let him see me."

Jess followed the direction of Robin's finger. "So what if he's here. He's probably using firm tickets, too. Why does it matter if he sees you?" A pause. "Oooops, sorry, too late. He saw you."

"Great. Just great." Robin shook her head. "He asked me to come to the game with him and I told him I couldn't go. He's probably thinking horrible things about me right now." She hid her eyes behind her hand.

"So, you changed your mind. It happens. Big deal." Jess smirked. "If you feel so bad about it, why don't you just tell him you're not interested." Then, Jess quickly realized how what she had said sounded, and rushed to clarify. "I'm sorry. That was awfully presumptuous of me. I didn't mean to assume that you wouldn't be interested if you wanted to, you know, see him sometimes." *A little insecure aren't you, Jess.*

A little jealous, huh, Jess? "I'm not interested, and you know it. There's only one person I'm interested in at the moment, and it isn't Paul." Robin looked directly at Jess. "And if you don't know that by now, then we have a serious problem."

Jess stared at the far-end basket. "Oh." It was all she could say. After a few minutes, the announcer came across the speakers to announce the beginning of play, the deep voice booming throughout the arena. "Look, the game's starting now."

Robin tugged on Jess's shirt sleeve. "You won't forget to explain everything to me, will you?"

"Not likely, especially if you keep tugging on me like that." Jess grinned.

They watched the entire game, and the home team won in the end, with Jess dutifully and very thoroughly explaining all the key calls and rulings by the officials. Robin enjoyed the game fever, but still wasn't quite sure exactly how it all made sense. She did understand that when your team made a basket, it was good. After the game was over, Jess and Robin made their way back to Jess's car, since Jess had insisted that she should drive, primarily due to Robin's difficulty in navigating downtown one-way streets. They made their way out of the downtown area and headed back to what was now affectionately known as The Ranch.

"So, what did you think?" Jess opened the garage door via remote control and pulled her silver Mercedes inside.

"I think it was fun, but you'll have to explain it to me some more so I completely understand the game." Robin got out of the car and followed Jess inside the house. "Then, I think I might enjoy it better."

Jess went into the living room and sat down on the plush sofa, swinging her feet up onto the coffee table. "Well, it sure looked like you seemed to be enjoying the game fine to me." She raised both eyebrows in humor.

"And what's that supposed to mean?"

"Nothing. Nothing. Only that you practically had everyone in the whole arena staring at you whenever you did that little dance thingy of yours every time our team made a basket." Jess laughed at the memory.

"I was just cheering."

"Oh, is that what it's called? Your cheer was complete with little arm pumping motions, and little twirls around in circles, and a little hip wagging thing going on. It was quite cute." Jess laughed harder. *I liked the hip wagging thing the best.*

"Like you weren't out there, Miss Basketball Expert, with that 'Number One' finger foam hand thing, waving it around in everyone's face every time our team scored." Robin wagged her finger playfully at Jess. "You almost knocked me over with it several times. I can't believe I was still standing by the time the game was over."

"You were too busy dancing around in between the aisles for me to knock you over. Besides, you nearly scared the poor guy in the fourth row half to death when you let go that yell half way through the third quarter. I thought he was going to have a heart attack."

"I can't help it. I'm a very enthusiastic fan." Robin grinned widely. "When I'm quite enthusiastic about something, I tend to be extremely loud." Robin laughed hard, then froze for a moment, realizing an alternative, yet quite unintended, meaning to what she had just said. She blushed profusely, and then turned to look at Jess, hoping Jess hadn't picked up on her little faux pas. No luck.

Jess sat there, staring over at Robin, eyebrow raised, trying very hard to suppress a mischievous grin. "Is that so? You're extremely loud, huh?" Jess winked and stifled a laugh. "I certainly can't wait to see that." She whispered quite seductively. "So, tell me, Robin, what else besides basketball might you be quite...enthusiastic about?"

"Oh, God." Robin let go a loud and embarrassed sigh and then fell backwards on the sofa, hiding her face behind a large throw pillow. "I didn't mean it that way." Came the muffled voice. A green eye peeked out from behind the corner of the pillow. "And you knew that."

Jess was on the floor laughing herself silly. Robin was so much fun to tease, and Jess, it seemed, just couldn't resist. After a few long and giggle filled moments, Jess finally calmed herself down enough to wipe her eyes and sit up. "Boy, that was fun." She lifted herself back up on the sofa and took the pillow from Robin's face. "So how about you staying over tonight?" It was a lighthearted question.

Robin sobered quickly and snapped her head up, hesitation plainly written on her face. "Um, Jess...I um…." She stammered.

"What?" Jess looked genuinely perplexed.

Robin turned away, unable to look at Jess directly in the eyes. "I um...I'm just not ready to...you know." She took a deep breath and whispered. "I'm sorry."

Jess stared at Robin for a long moment, her mouth slightly open, trying to figure out what it was Robin was saying. Then, it suddenly hit her, and Jess's eyes grew wide in silent understanding. *Oh, no.* In light of their previous, albeit joking, conversation, it wasn't surprising that Robin thought Jess was asking something other than what she was really asking. Jess leaned back against the cushions and turned to Robin, speaking very softly. "Robin, honey, look at me, okay?"

Robin slowly turned her head toward Jess and nodded. "Okay."

"I didn't mean that the way it sounded." Jess paused briefly. "I know you're not ready. I don't think either one of us is ready for more right now. It's okay. We're going to go very slow here. If one of us isn't comfortable with anything, we just have to say something and we won't do it." Jess smiled gently. "Is that alright?"

"Yes." Robin gave a shy nod. A long silence passed and then Robin sighed heavily. "Jess, I um...guess I really should tell you that I um...I haven't, you know...other than with David, and it was only very recently. We were going to be engaged and we...." Robin's voice became a little shaky and then trailed off.

"Shhhh, honey. It's alright. I understand." Jess whispered and gently grasped Robin's hand. "For me, it was just James and a few others along the way. No women." She gave Robin a crooked grin. "All I really want right now, Robin, more than anything else, is to hold you tonight. Would that be okay?"

Robin nodded and gave Jess a small smile. "Yes. I would really like that."

"Good. Now let's get ready. The waterbed is waiting for us." Jess leaned in and placed a quick, chaste kiss on Robin's lips. "And your personal nightshirt and personal toothbrush are beckoning you." She smiled warmly.

After they had performed their nightly routines, Robin and Jess snuggled down deep in the slightly heated waterbed and cuddled together. Robin laid her head on Jess's shoulder, putting her arm snuggly around Jess's waist. Jess reached up and put her hand on Robin's back and began gently rubbing back and forth over the cloth of the nightshirt with her long fingers, the simple touch calming and reassuring.

"Robin?" Jess trailed a finger up to the back of Robin's neck.

"Yes."

"I want you to know something." Jess brushed a strand of hair behind a petite, delicate ear. "If I never do more than hold you like this, that would be enough for me."

Robin smiled in the darkness. "Thank you for saying that." A moment. "But, of course, we wouldn't have to limit ourselves to that, right?"

Jess swallowed. "Uh, right." *Oh boy.*

"Good."

"Yeah, good." Another moment. "Goodnight."

Robin reached for Jess's hand and intertwined their fingers, bringing their joined hands up and placing them beneath her chin. "Goodnight, Jess."

****

As morning arrived, Robin woke to the smell of coffee brewing and bacon cooking. She got up from the waterbed and padded her way into the kitchen. Jess was standing over the stove, spatula in hand, cooking bacon and scrambled eggs.

"Hi. Whatcha making?" Robin peered around Jess's shoulder.

"Hi, sleepyhead. Glad you could finally join the world of the living." Jess flipped the bacon. "I'm making bacon and eggs. Hope you like it, because there isn't anything else around here to eat. I haven't had much time to shop." She looked at Robin accusingly. "Wonder why?"

"Hey, don't blame me for your failure to attend to your grocery shopping duties. If you wouldn't work so late most nights, and then play hooky all weekend, you might have time to stock up on your food-related items." Robin sat at the kitchen table and poured two cups of coffee.

"My point exactly. I was playing hooky all weekend with you." Jess pointed the spatula at Robin accusingly and then finished scrambling the eggs.

"Sorry, Jess. You cannot use that as an excuse for your grocery shopping neglect."

"Well, then, maybe I should get a grocery service to deliver my groceries." Jess grinned mischievously. "That way I can have food in the house and still reserve all my free time for playing hooky." She waggled her eyebrows at Robin and turned off the stove. She then filled two plates with bacon and eggs, retrieved the toast, and sat down at the kitchen table. "That reminds me, I have something for you." Jess got up again and removed something from a nearby counter, handing it to Robin. "This is for when you want to play hooky, too."

Robin took the item. "A key?"

"Yes, it's a key to this house. I mean, it's only fair. You gave me yours, so I'm giving you mine. That way we can each play hooky whenever we want." Jess grinned happily and sat down, taking a bite of her toast. "I'll write down the alarm code for you, too."

"Thanks. A key to The Ranch." Robin smiled. "I know it'll come in handy, because there's a minimum weekend hooky requirement now, you know?" She took a sip of her coffee.

A dark eyebrow shot up. "Is that so? And what would that requirement be?"

"At least one day and one night per weekend, minimum. That's just the minimum. The recommended weekend allowance is far higher. For maximum hooky results, the entire weekend is optimal." Robin munched on a piece of bacon.

"Sorry, kiddo. Got to work tomorrow." Jess took another bite. "And don't forget, you've got to do your Sunday chores, which you neglected last week."

Robin pouted. "You're no fun. Can you at least play today?"

"What did you have in mind?"

"The mall."

"The mall?" Jess poured herself a second cup of coffee. "And we would go there, why?"

Robin chuckled. "To shop."

"To shop for what?"

"We won't know until we get there. That's half the fun. You go there without knowing what you'll find, and when you find something you weren't expecting, it's fun." Robin was quite proud of herself for explaining it so well.

Jess furrowed her brows. "I usually go to the store knowing what I want. I go in, I get it and then I get out. End of story." Jess nodded to herself. "Seems very practical to me."

Robin shook her head. "No, silly. The idea of shopping isn't to be practical, it's to go and have...."

"Fun." Jess interrupted.

"Exactly." Robin chuckled. "I knew you'd see the logic."

Someone save me.

****

"Jess, what do you think of these shoes?" Robin stood at the floor mirror of the fourth shoe store they'd been to that day. "I like the heels."

"If you like them, then get them." Jess sat in the chair and played with the foot measurer.

"Okay, I will." Robin went up to the cashier. "So, what store do you want to go to next?"

"I have a better idea." Jess grinned enthusiastically. "Let's go ride the train." She jumped up from the chair and waited for Robin to finish paying for the shoes.

"The train?" Robin looked at Jess with the trademark 'you can't be serious' look and followed Jess out of the shoe store and into the crowded mall.

"Yeah. It'll be..." Jess looked at Robin and smirked. "Fun."

"The train is for kids. It doesn't go anywhere, just around and around part of the food court."

"Doesn't matter. I like to ride it." Jess spoke to Robin matter-of-factly. "You don't have to come along with me, if you don't want to. But you'll be missing out."

Robin let out an exasperated sigh. "Oh, alright. Fine. Let's go ride the train. You're such a big kid, anyway."

They went and rode the train, three times mind you, until Robin finally had to put a halt to their train-riding activities, primarily due to the smell of food wafting throughout the food court. Jess and Robin decided to get a bite to eat before proceeding on their way to do some more shopping. Robin, of course, had an ulterior motive for wanting to get Jess to the mall in the first place. There was this little matter of someone's birthday coming up in a few days, and Robin thought she could get an idea of what that certain someone may want in particular as a birthday gift. Jess, of course, was not cooperating, until they finally came upon a specialty shop of hard to find and imported items.

"Ooooh, look at this." Jess went down an aisle and stopped in front of some carved onyx figures.

"What are those? Robin peered at the items in question.

"They're onyx chess figures. This is a carved onyx chess set. See, the quality is impeccable and the carving is very intricate." Jess picked up a chess piece and fingered the smooth, slick texture. "A set like this is very rare outside of Mexico and quite expensive."

Robin took a chess piece in her hand as well. "Do you play, Jess?"

"No, not really. My father used to. But that was a very long time ago, before he left." Jess set the figure down. "I always thought it would be nice to have a set and display it."

"Why didn't you ever get one, then?" The wheels began to turn in Robin's mind.

"No point to it. I don't play, so there's really no reason to have one. I just always thought the way they looked was neat." Jess shrugged and then turned to make her way back out into the mall again. "So, is there anywhere else you wanted to go today?"

"No, I think I'm finished. We can leave now." Robin glanced over toward Jess and smirked. "Unless, of course, you wanted to ride the train again."

"You're just jealous because I got to sit up front and ring the bell, which I consider my personal bell on all train rides." Jess poked Robin lightly on the arm.

"Yes, that's right, Jess." Robin humored her. "I'm jealous because you got to ring the bell. Which, of course, you rang extremely loudly, I might add."

Jess leaned in and whispered closely into Robin's ear. "I'm an enthusiastic train rider, Robin. When I'm quite enthusiastic about something, I tend to be extremely loud." She paused for effect. "And by the way, I'll let you ring my personal bell any time." Jess stood back and winked.

Robin nearly choked and then blushed tremendously. *I hate it when she does that. And I walked right into it this time.* "You are really a brat." She gave Jess a light slap on the arm and proceeded on to the car.

"Hey, don't hit." Jess yelled ahead to Robin in amusement. After a moment, they arrived at the car, with Jess still trying mighty hard not to venture a laugh, but failing in spite of the effort. She turned off the car alarm and unlocked the doors. "So, did you have fun shopping today?" Jess glanced over the car's roof to Robin.

Robin put her packages inside the car. "Yeah, it was a lot of fun."

"After all, the whole point of going shopping is to have fun, right? See, I learned that from you." Jess grinned proudly.

"Very good, Jess." Robin chuckled and then gave Jess a very sweet smile. "And the train ride was fun, too. Next time, though, it's my turn to ring the bell."

Jess, you are in so much trouble.

****

Robin and Jess returned to The Ranch and fixed a small dinner before deciding to go into the living room and relax. Though the weather, true to Jess's prediction, had turned a bit warmer by week's end, it was still not too warm for a fire in the fireplace.

"Would you like a fire tonight or do you want to just watch TV?" Jess entered the living room with Robin in tow.

"I think a fire would be nice. I really miss not being able to have a fire at my place. Not many apartments in Orlando come with fireplaces." Robin sat on the tile floor next to the hearth. "Do you have enough wood?"

"Yep, I have more in the garage. I use oak because it burns longer, even though the fire's not quite as hot as when you use pine." Jess lit the firelog and carefully placed several pieces of wood on top of it.

Robin sat on the floor, knees pulled up to her chin, and her arms wrapped securely around them. She stared at the fire and became mesmerized by the flames, as they started small and low in the fireplace and then grew to engulf the entire firelog, slowly catching the larger pieces of wood on fire in succession. The fire began to hiss and crackle. Save for the sound of the fire, there was complete silence, as Robin's mind drifted in quiet thought for a very long while. Jess slid down onto the floor behind her, and wrapped her long arms completely around Robin's shoulders, speaking in a low and gentle tone in a small ear.

"If you want to talk about it, I'm here." Jess's voice had a calming effect.

"How did you know?" Robin whispered.

"I just know." Jess rested her chin on Robin's shoulder and waited for a moment. "Come on. Let's go over to the sofa. It's more comfortable than this hard floor." Jess pulled Robin up and led her over to the plush sofa. She turned off the table lamp and stretched herself out on the cushions, opening her arms wide. "Come here."

Robin complied and curled up snuggly in Jess's arms, head resting gently against a broad shoulder. After a long moment more, Robin finally spoke. "Sometimes, I feel this overwhelming sense of guilt, and it comes over me when I least expect it. I feel very happy one moment, and then it sneaks up on me. I think sometimes that I don't deserve to be as happy as I am right now after...everything that's happened."

Jess kissed the top of Robin's head. "You deserve to be happy, sweetheart. Don't ever think you don't. Your being sad will not change anything." She stroked Robin's soft blonde hair and then asked something that had been on her mind all week long. "Robin, are you really happy?" It was said quite unsure and with more than a bit of nervousness.

Robin turned her head and looked up at Jess and then brought her hand up to caress Jess's cheek, her fingers gliding over the smooth, angular features. "I have never been more happy in my life than I am right now. Part of that is what scares me so much. It seems like I have no right to be happy considering everything." She laid her head back down on Jess's chest. "I don't deserve you."

Jess sighed. "Robin, you've said that now several times. Believe me when I tell you that I'm no great prize, but you have to believe that you deserve every happiness that comes your way." Jess smiled gently and kissed Robin's nose. "Even if it's me, for whatever that's worth." She rolled her eyes in self-deprecation. In spite of Jess's playful tone, she was actually beginning to get slightly worried about Robin's state of mind and her inability to accept the good things in her life.

Robin quickly slid up Jess's body to look directly into blue eyes, resting her weight on one elbow. She lightly traced Jess's soft lips with her index finger and then leaned in and placed a small kiss on those soft lips, savoring the feel of the tender connection. Robin pulled back slightly, green eyes staring intently into deep blue, and whispered very softly, her warm breath gently caressing Jess's face. "You are what makes me happy, Jess. And it's worth more than you know."

Jess reached up with her free hand and pulled Robin down to her, placing a tender kiss on her lips. Robin returned the kiss with equal tenderness, as the one kiss ultimately turned into more. Their kisses became long and slow, but not deep, as their hands gently caressed each other's faces, feeling the smooth skin beneath their fingertips, and then lightly stroked each other's silky soft hair. They kissed slowly and leisurely for several moments more, the firelight flickering in random patterns off the walls, and the slight crackle from the wood the only sound in the room. After an undetermined period of time, they broke away, and Robin slid down to resume her previous position across Jess's chest, closing her eyes contently.

"How is it that just by being with you, I feel so many things, so many emotions, that I can't even explain them to myself?" Robin brushed her fingers lightly back and forth over the fine hairs on Jess's arm.

"I'll be honest with you, Robin." Jess spoke in a hushed tone. "I've never felt this way before either and I'm not quite sure what to think about it." She lightly stroked Robin's cheek. "It feels wonderful, though." Jess thought about that fact for a moment. It did feel wonderful, and right, like this was the most natural thing in the world and the way it was always supposed to be, a connection that defied explanation and was as ageless as the universe.

Robin slowly opened her eyes and stared blankly at the orange glow of the fire. "I admit that I was nervous at first about being close to you. Being this close to a woman was something I had never considered before, and I wasn't at all sure I wanted to become involved in a relationship like this.

"Does that...bother you now?" Jess held her breath for a moment. She had very recently had these same thoughts and had come to the decision that she did indeed want Robin in her life. But what if Robin decided differently in the end? Jess's heartbeat sped up a little, waiting for Robin to give her the answer she was most afraid to hear.

"Hey." Robin could hear Jess's heart rate increase beneath her ear. She lifted her hand and put her palm directly over Jess's heart, feeling the strong, insistent beat, willing it to calm. "Jess, it's okay." She looked up and smiled tenderly. "It doesn't bother me, now. I've thought about this, and I believe that it's what's on the inside of a person that counts, not what's on the outside." She paused. "Although your outside is very nice." Robin chuckled lightly. "You're very beautiful, both inside and out. I mean that."

Jess gave her a very warm smile. "Thanks. You're very beautiful on the inside yourself, and your outside is very cute." Jess touched her finger to Robin's nose.

With sudden emotion, Robin reached up and grasped Jess's hand and brought it to her lips, kissing the knuckles gently. After a moment more, Robin spoke again. "It's the person's soul that matters, Jess, not the packaging. I believe that." She kissed the knuckles lightly again. "And I believe our souls are somehow connected, because I wouldn't feel this strongly about you if that weren't true."

"I think you're right," Jess whispered, also appearing to be caught in the tide of the existing emotion, unable now to speak any further.

They cuddled together for a long while, and when the last of the fire had nearly burnt out, Jess sat up and stifled a small yawn. "I have to go into the office tomorrow, you know. If you like, you can stay, or if you prefer to go home, that would be okay, too." Her eyes betrayed what she said. She most definitely did not want Robin to leave. The separations had become extremely difficult, almost painful, but she didn't want to pressure Robin into spending every moment with her either.

"I want to stay." Robin decided.

"But I have to leave early if I intend to get everything done tomorrow that I want to do."

"I want to stay." Robin confirmed.

"But I'll be gone when you wake up."

"I want to stay." Robin reaffirmed.

"If you'd rather go home, I would understand." It seemed now that they were really talking about something quite different than simply whether Robin should stay over that night. They were in reality speaking about a level of commitment to each other and to a relationship that they were both a bit afraid of, but which both of them wanted desperately to pursue."

Robin went over and gently laid her hand on Jess's arm. "I know, and I want to stay."

Jess smiled. "Okay." They walked toward the master bedroom. "Tomorrow morning you can stick around here as long as you want and then just use the key I gave you to lock up and set the alarm when you leave, okay?"

"Okay. Maybe I can meet you at the office later tomorrow and we can get some dinner together." Robin stopped inside the doorway. "I haven't met my recommended hooky quotient yet this weekend." She grinned.

"You're on." Jess grinned back. "Did I tell you that I'm really good at playing hooky. I think I should get a lot of points for my hooky playing skills."

"I'll take that under advisement. But remember, I am the one that makes the ultimate decision. I think it depends on what you do with your hooky playing time that determines what points you get." Robin winked. "So make it good." She gave Jess a quick pat on the arm and then turned to get ready for bed.

Yeah, so make it good, Jess.

****

Sunday found Jess dutifully working in her office, files and paperwork strewn about her desk and floor area, and much work yet to be accomplished. Her mind had wandered aimlessly on more than one occasion, causing her not to complete as much work as she had originally intended. As she sat at her desk, she idly swiveled her leather chair around toward the large pane windows and simply stared unseeingly out at the clear blue sky. A bird flew perilously close to the window, but Jess curiously appeared not to notice, as her internal thoughts overcame her mind once again.

Well, it seems you've been quite busy lately, and we're not talking about work.

'Don't you ever go away?' The alternate internal voice was quite annoyed.

You've plunged head first into this thing with Robin. Are you sure you can handle it?

'Yep. I'm handling it just fine, thank you.' The alternate internal voice answered confidently.

Perhaps, but there's more going on here than you think.

The alternate internal voice was dismayed. *'What's that supposed to mean?'*

It's not hard to figure out. In fact, it's quite obvious. You're hooked.

'Don't be ridiculous. I beg to differ with you, Sherlock. I like Robin. That is all.'

Are you sure it's not more than 'like'?

'Yep, just like.' The alternate internal voice responded surely.

Is that so? Lets review all of the evidence and let the jury decide. You've kissed her very affectionately, for one thing. You can't stand to be separated from her, you, for all intents and purposes, have entered into a serious relationship with her, you've lost all objectivity when it comes to her, and you've been entirely too distracted lately. Does that sound like it's just 'like' to you?

'Yes' The alternate internal voice replied defensively.

Think again.

'Okay, I like her...a lot. Happy now?' The alternate internal voice was not amused.

Wrong answer, again. Let's ask the question a little bit differently. Can you think of your life without Robin in it?

'Nope, I like my life right now with her in it.' The alternate internal voice responded happily.

I see. And what about next month, or next year? Can you think of your life without Robin then?

'Nope, again. She's right there.'

Now, how about ten years or twenty years, or even fifty years, from now? Is Robin in your life then, as well?

Silence.

Your answer, please.

More silence.

Your Honor, instruct the witness to answer.

The alternate internal voice was reflective. *'We've never talked about a long term relationship or commitment.'*

But that wasn't the question. Can you imagine your life at anytime in the future without Robin?

Silence again for another moment. *'No.'* The alternate internal voice was barely a whisper. *'No, I cannot.'*

So, now you've seen all the evidence. What does it tell you?

The alternate internal voice stalled for time. *'I don't know.'*

Yes you do. The jury's in. What's the verdict?

'The verdict is that I more than like her a lot.' The alternate internal voice evaded.

Be more specific, please.

The alternate internal voice finally gave in and finally gave voice to the ultimate realization. *'I love Robin very much and I want to spend the rest of my life with her.'*

There, that wasn't so hard, now was it?

'Speak for yourself, buddy.' The alternate internal voice became a bit defensive once again.

Okay, so now that you've determined that you love her and you want to spend the rest of your life with her, what are you going to do about it?

The alternate internal voice pondered that question intently. *'It seems, Holmes, that I have absolutely no idea.'*

Chapter 5

The early morning sunlight drifted lazily across the room through the small slits in the Venetian blinds, casting long, golden slivers of bright light against the far wall. The alarm suddenly sounded, loudly sending its shrill noise throughout the spacious room, then being abruptly silenced by a long, slender hand. Jess opened her blue eyes slowly, adjusting cautiously to the bright sunlight, before finally rolling over on her back to gaze up at the eggshell white popcorn ceiling. *Monday.* Her mind took a little more time to shake away the fog of sleep before she stretched her arms over her head and let herself lie in bed a few extra moments, contemplating the most recent events.

Her life was totally out of control. No more fun and games, no more taking things as they came along. Everything had turned upside down, spiraling forward at a break-neck pace. Robin had come into her life and set it into turmoil and confusion. Everything she had previously known or believed was now inexplicably irrelevant. A mental sigh. *Time to slow this baby down.* "Love" was simply not in her vocabulary anymore, and this relationship, or whatever it was called, had proceeded too far, too soon. The near-constant distraction was keeping Jess from focusing on her office work, something which had never happened before. Not to mention the fact that Jess had simply lost all objectivity when it came to Robin. Another mental sigh. *So, what to do.* Jess pondered the thought, carefully surveying her options. She could have a long talk with Robin. Tell her things were getting too serious. It's not that they were getting too physically serious...yet. But rather, it was the fact that they were getting too emotionally serious that concerned her. Robin, after all, was on the emotional rebound after David. She might not realize what she was really getting into. And Jess was certainly not emotionally prepared for all this intensity, let alone what entering into this type of relationship would really mean. There was just no way that this could work out. *Option One: Pull back. End it now.* Jess shook her head in annoyance at the thought, as a knot formed in her stomach and then tightened. *Nope, too drastic.*

She rolled out of the waterbed and padded over to the bathroom, turning on the shower. She adjusted the water to the right, hot temperature, and then opened the clear glass shower door and stepped inside the large tiled enclosure. As the steam cleared her senses and the hot water tingled her skin, she allowed her mind to continue its thought process. *What to do.* She could tell Robin they just needed to take a little break from each other. If the feelings were really genuine, they would still be there later on, wouldn't they? *Option Two: A break.* Jess snorted to herself in dissatisfaction with that thought, as well, as the knot in her stomach involuntarily tightened once again. *That would not go over well.*

Jess rinsed the soap off her skin and next lathered up her long, dark hair, the herbal shampoo's scent invading her nostrils. *What to do.* They could keep things friendly. Weekend sleepovers are okay. Some weekend play time together is okay. A little light cuddling is okay. Kissing would definitely *not* be okay. She frowned. *Well, maybe just a little bit of kissing would be okay.* Basically, keep things where they are now, but go no further. That way, everyone would be happy. It would allow each of them enough time to decide if this is what they really wanted, and it would allow them enough time to become comfortable with their new relationship without it getting too intense, too soon. *Option Three: Status quo.* Jess nodded her head to herself at the thought, as the knot in her stomach loosened just a bit. *It's a good solution.*

She rinsed out her hair and turned off the water, grabbing a huge over-sized bath towel from the towel rack. She stepped out of the shower and dried herself off, wrapping the towel around her head and putting on a soft, plush terrycloth bathrobe. *What to do.* Jess stood in front of the steam-fogged bathroom mirror and wiped a neat space in the center, staring intently at her own reflection, and mentally clicking through the options again. After a moment's contemplation, she finally decided. *I pick Door Number Three: Status quo.* A talk with Robin was in order. Invite her over to dinner and discuss things like mature adults. It was true, sometimes the intensity of the feelings and the emotions of the moment tended to cloud the mind, and in those instances, it was just not possible to think rationally about the appropriate course of action. So, keep the lights on, no fire in the fireplace and definitely no cuddling. Just sit down and talk it through. They'd keep things light.

No talk of any deep intense relationship thing, no talk of love and ever after commitment thing, just the status quo liking each other thing. *The perfect solution.* Jess gave herself a satisfied grin in the mirror. *The perfect solution.*

Right.

****

An unexpected fall chill filled the air as Jess made her way from her car, the leaves swirling about the grounds as gusts of blustery wind blew past her. *What's this? It's actually cold in November.* She made her way into work, being sure to stop into the little coffee shop just inside the building's lobby to pick up a cup of cappuccino. She stepped onto the elevator, pressed the button to the 16th floor, and watched as the doors began to close. Just at the last moment, Harry snuck inside.

"Cold day isn't?" He took his hands from his coat pockets.

Jess smirked. "Unbelievable."

The elevator rose, approaching the desired floor. "Listen, Jess, do you have a minute? I wanted to speak with you about something?"

The elevator stopped and both Harry and Jess stepped out into the firm's reception area. "Sure, come on down to my office."

They walked down the hallway and entered Jess's office, Harry promptly removing his coat and settling himself down in the nearest chair. *Coffee would be good right now.* He mentally debated whether to call Betty to bring him a cup of the brew, but then decided to wait until he was finished with Jess.

Jess closed the door and set her cappuccino on the cherry wood desk. "What was it you wanted to talk about?" She sat down in her burgundy leather chair and leaned back in a casual manner, flipping on her computer.

"How's everything going with the trial preparations?" Harry looked a bit uncomfortable.

"Fine." No further comment was forthcoming.

Harry cleared his throat. "The reason I ask is that I heard from Keith that there was a little snafu regarding the depositions."

Jess rolled her eyes in annoyance. "Harry, everything's fine. Our weasel of an opposing counsel tried to pull a fast one on us, but it's actually going to backfire on him and it will end up being to our benefit, instead." She looked at Harry a bit cockily and then shook her head. "He at first led us to believe that he would not call a witness at trial, and then later tried to add the witness back onto the pre-trial witness list after discovery cut-off, so we wouldn't be able to depose the witness ahead of time. If he was so desperate not to have us depose the witness, there must be something he doesn't want us to know, and we're gonna find out what it is."

Harry folded his hands in front of him. "I see. But it was Keith that called it to your attention, correct?"

"Alright, Harry." Jess's tone took on a decided edge. "What's your point?"

"An experienced associate recognized there was a problem and brought it to your attention. You told me you that if you thought this trial might be a little too much for Robin, you would consider our reassigning Keith to your trial team." Harry looked at her frankly. "What's it going to be?"

Jess's eyes narrowed slightly. "Are you pulling Robin off the case?"

"I just want to make sure that we're covering all the bases here. If you want Robin to stay, then fine. But you've got to take a more active role in the trial preparation and coordination of the pre-trial activity. I know you like to delegate, but either we have some experienced people in there or you pick up the supervision directly."

Jess was silent for a long while and turned her head to stare at the Florida Statute books lining her bookcase. "It's under control." *Nothing is under control.*

Harry softened his features somewhat. "Look, this is not a criticism of Robin. We're very pleased with her. She's done a wonderful job for us for the time she's been here. But, a first year associate coming in fresh from law school needs guidance, and with time, will eventually learn a great deal. Robin has great potential and will be one hell of a litigator. She'll probably be wiping the floor with both you and me in a year or two. I just don't want her to be in a position that she's not prepared for, that's all. It's your case, Jess. You make the call. I'll respect your decision and I won't interfere."

Jess's eyes tracked back from the bookcase to Harry, as she paused in thought for a long moment. "Robin stays. I'll not take her off the case now. She and I work well together, and she does one hell of a job. I will take more of a supervisory roll with her, give her more guidance, and utilize Keith more."

"Okay." Harry stood up to leave and gave a small, but reassuring, smile. "You guys go get that weasel, then." He grabbed his coat and headed out the door. *Now, where's Betty so I can get my coffee.*

Jess took a deep breath and sat back in her leather chair. *Shit, shit, shit. Damn.* She knew her instincts were right on this one. Robin is the right person for this case. It was a gut feeling on Jess's part. She leaned back in her chair and thought about that. Or was it simply that she was just incapable of being objective here? *No.* Or maybe she was putting way too much pressure on Robin? *No.* She sighed and then decided it was better to ask Robin, anyway. The last thing she really wanted was for Robin to feel uneasy or afraid to talk with her about this or any problems she might be having. *Fine, let's go talk to her.*

Jess finished her cappuccino and then sauntered her way through the lobby and past the reception desk, until she reached Robin's office. She peeked inside and knocked lightly on the door frame. "Hi. Can I come in?"

Robin looked up from the pile of documents she was reviewing and smiled. "Sure, come on in."

Jess closed the door and took a seat opposite Robin's desk, idly gazing out the window at the lake below. "I had a talk with Harry. He says everyone is pleased with your work here." She started out the conversation carefully. "I may not be the best person to judge this, but I want to make sure I'm not putting an unreasonable expectation on you with this trial."

Robin put down her pen and folded her hands on her desk. "I see. Does Harry think there's a problem?"

Shit. "No. He and I want to make sure you're comfortable working on the case. You and I work so well together that I sometimes forget that you've only been at this a few months. I think I've neglected my role in providing you with the necessary direction so that you develop all the skills you need as an attorney. If that's the case, then it's my fault, and I want to apologize to you if I've put too much pressure on you." Now that Jess was finished with her little monologue, she looked up across the desk at Robin and smiled apologetically. "So, if there's anything you need help with or need guidance on, I want you to come to me. No hesitation."

Robin sat slightly stunned. It had never occurred to her that Jess might be putting undo pressure on her. "This has to do with the deposition incident, doesn't it?" Robin bit her bottom lip lightly at the memory. "You were right to call me on it."

"No, Robin. That was entirely my fault. But it's not fatal, and it could end up helping us in the end, especially if we find something to use out of all this at trial." Jess reached forward and tapped her long, slender fingers on the front of the desktop. "I'm more concerned with giving you the proper direction, which you have every right to expect from me. And I'm committed to spending more of my time giving you all the necessary guidance you need."

Robin sat patiently and listened to what Jess had to say. It was true, she was eager to do her best for Jess, not just because of their professional relationship, but because of their personal relationship, as well. She certainly didn't want to disappoint Jess under any circumstances. "Thanks." Robin accepted the offer. "I want you to know how much I enjoy working with you and learning from you, and I will take all the guidance you can give me." Robin smiled. "I happen to think you have a brilliant mind, you know."

Jess cocked her head to one side. "Is that so?"

"Absolutely. You have many fine attributes." Green eyes stared directly into blue. "And I don't think we should discuss all of them right now."

Jess blushed in spite of herself and cleared her throat. "I have an idea, then. As I recall, it's my turn to cook dinner, correct?" She didn't wait for Robin to answer. "So, come over to my place tonight for dinner at, let's say, 7:30. I'll even leave work at a normal hour. Then you can tell me more about my so-called fine attributes." She winked. *Jess, you're supposed to have that little chat with her tonight, not flirt with her some more.*

Robin nodded. "You're on. Dinner at the big house. I can't wait. I know you can cook breakfast. You'll need to pass the dinner test, too. I can foresee that there should be only one requirement."

"What's that?" Jess responded dryly.

Robin raised a blonde eyebrow. "No...."

"Shrimp." Jess interrupted. *We finish each other sentences.* "Sorry. Can't promise that, kiddo. You'll just have to take what you get when you're with me."

I'll take the whole package. "Don't I know it." Robin laughed. "That's the best part."

Enough flirting. Jess just couldn't help herself. There was something that was just so entirely infectious about Robin that made Jess grin from ear to ear quite involuntarily. Jess looked like an adorable love-sick puppy, and as much as her mind kept telling her to slow things down, her heart was not listening to a word of it, and was racing full steam ahead, totally out of control. "Are you free for lunch?" Jess heard herself ask. *What, dinner's not enough? You have to spend lunch with her, too?*

"I'm always free when it concerns lunch." Robin laughed at the joke at her own expense.

"Hey, you're stealing all my good lines. What will I have to tease you with?" Jess bantered.

"I guess that will make it more of a challenge for you, then. Maybe you'll need to improve your teasing skills." Robin's statement had a hint of a dare in her voice.

If we play this game, I will win. "I will definitely consider it." Jess focused her attention to the pile of documents on Robin's desk. "Are you having any luck with finding anything we can use?"

"Not so far, but I think you're right. There's something here and I'm going to find it. Give me a few days and I'll let you know. We've also ordered an asset check, a background check, a criminal check, and a bank account search. Something should turn up." Robin was quite pleased with the progress she was making.

Jess stood up and walked to the door. "It sounds like you have everything under control." Her gaze softened as it settled on warm green eyes. "I knew you would."

"Thanks, Jess. Your confidence in me means a lot."

Jess gave her a gentle smile. "Okay, kiddo. See you tonight. 7:30. And don't be late." Jess warned playfully. "I wouldn't want to have to eat all that shrimp by myself." She grinned smugly and then left the office.

Robin just smiled and shook her head. *I will definitely take the whole package.*

****

Robin arrived at The Ranch that evening, shivering intensely from the cold, not cool, weather that had befallen Central Florida, and knocked on the front door. Within a moment, Jess greeted her and ushered her inside.

"It's cold out there, Jess." Robin took off her jacket and set it on the coat rack in the foyer just inside the door. "I think you have some serious explaining to do."

"Hey, don't look at me. I don't make the weather, you know. And as I've told you before, just wait a day or two and it'll be back up in the 70's." Jess led them both into the living room. "It'll be a few more minutes until dinner's ready. Would you like some wine? I have both white and red wine."

Robin sat down on the plush sofa. "If you have a light red wine, maybe a pinot noir, that would be great." She noticed as Jess nodded in acknowledgement and left the room to fetch the requested wine. Robin called back to her. "Hey, what did you make for dinner? It smells really good."

Barely a moment later, Jess stepped back into the living room holding two full glasses of light red wine. "Your pinot noir, mademoiselle." She handed Robin a glass of wine and sat next to her on the sofa. "I made pork chops with a bing cherry glaze. It's always been one of my favorites. My mother made it for us during the winter months when I was growing up. I never make it for myself, though. It's hard to cook for one person most of the time." She smiled at Robin. "That's why I'm so glad you came over tonight. I get to have my one of my favorite dinners." The smile turned into a full grin.

Robin furrowed her brows. "I see. So, the only reason you invited me over tonight was so you could have one of your favorite dinners?" She took a sip of her wine. "I'm not sure whether I should feel offended by that."

"I think you should feel very fortunate that you get to enjoy such a fantastic meal," Jess replied with a perfectly straight face.

"So, are you saying that my being here, specifically, is not the driving force behind your meal enjoyment, but rather your cooking is?" Robin looked playfully into blue eyes.

"It's not every day that you would have such a wonderful opportunity as this, Robin. I am an excellent cook." Jess nodded in mock seriousness.

Robin set her wine glass down on the pine wood coffee table and looked intently at Jess. "You seem pretty sure of yourself."

"Yep."

"Well, then let me put it to you this way. If your dinner turns out to be as good as you say, then maybe some type of reward might be in order." Robin leaned closer to Jess. "But since your sole reason for wanting me to come here tonight is so that you can have one of your favorite meals, it seems that any reward there might be, would surely be insignificant."

Jess swallowed. "May I amend my statement to say that there are two reasons why I invited you over tonight. The first is so I could cook one of my favorite meals, and the second is because I absolutely and truly enjoy your company. The reasons are not necessarily in that particular order." She gave Robin a sweet smile.

Robin patted Jess on the knee. "I'm glad you understood my point so well." She sat back against the cushions and then broke out into giggles.

"What's so funny?"

"Nothing. I was just thinking about how much fun we have together." Robin giggled some more. "You can be such a nut sometimes."

"I think I resemble that remark." Jess laughed lightly along with Robin at her own silliness. After a moment, Jess suddenly stopped laughing and got very quiet, appearing to listen intently to something. "Did you hear that?"

"What?" Robin stopped and listened.

"Shhh." Jess held up her hand and cocked her head to one side and listened for another moment. "There it is again."

Robin strained to hear and whispered. "I don't hear anything."

Jess, still with head cocked, leaned over toward Robin. "It's seems to be coming from...." Jess held her ear intently near Robin for a moment, trying to hear the sound again. She then turned her head slightly to look Robin directly in the eye, speaking in a bored tone. "You're hungry, aren't you?" She tilted her head and pointed to Robin's stomach knowingly.

Robin's mouth flew open in mild surprise for a brief moment. She then narrowed her eyes and gave Jess a light poke on the arm. "You are so mean to me. Just for that, I might have to rethink my reward idea."

"Hey." Jess pouted playfully. "I was just having a little fun."

Robin couldn't help but laugh at the sight of Jess sitting there with her bottom lip sticking out. "Alright, Jess. You can have your fun. But just remember, the real fun happens when I," she pointed at herself in emphasis, "tease you."

Jess looked at Robin out of the corner of her eye. *Well, she certainly can tease.* "Hey, kiddo, dinner's about ready. Take a seat in the dining room and I'll bring everything out." Robin stood and followed Jess into the other room to begin their meal.

****

They ate their meal in complete enjoyment, with Robin making little "yum" sounds quite often throughout. When they were both too full to eat another bite, they got up from the table and set about cleaning up the dinner dishes. Once all that was completed, Jess and Robin headed back into the living room to enjoy some after-dinner coffee.

"Hey, Jess, can you start a fire?" Robin looked over to the fireplace expectantly.

"Sure." Jess got up from the plush sofa and began the task of setting up the firelog and wood. *You're not supposed to have a fire, Jess, remember?* Ignoring her inner voice, Jess lit the firelog and sat back down on the sofa next to Robin, leaving the glass doors to the fireplace open to spread the attendant heat throughout the room. "It's a good night for a fire since it's kinda cool out there."

"It's cold, Jess, not cool. Admit you erred a little bit as it relates to your weather forecasting skills." Robin moved in a little closer to Jess.

Jess shook her head. "I will do no such thing. I remain accurate. In two days, it will be warm again. Just you wait and see." She grinned smugly and then turned her attention back to the fire.

"I'm skeptical, but I'll give you the benefit of the doubt...this time." Robin kicked her feet up on the coffee table and patted her stomach lightly. "I'm stuffed. That dinner was very good, Jess."

"Told ya." Jess grinned smugly. "And I believe you mentioned something about a little reward if I was right?" She raised both eyebrows at Robin.

Robin turned to face Jess. "Yes, I believe I do recall something like that." She let her gaze travel to the edge of the sofa for a moment in thought and then looked back up into blue eyes. "But that particular reward is best saved for another time." She patted Jess indulgently on the stomach and resumed her watch of the now brightly glowing fire.

"Oh." Jess thought it best not to pursue that particular line of thinking just then. They finished their coffee, and after a few moments of quietly studying the flickering flames, Jess glanced over to Robin and spoke softly. "Can I talk to you about something?"

Robin looked back at her. "Sure, what's on your mind?"

Jess shifted her position on the sofa so that she was turned mostly toward Robin. She reached out with slightly shaking fingers and stroked Robin's hand, very lightly brushing her thumb slowly back and forth across the fair skin. "I think I need to tell you this." She paused. "Recently, I've felt so out of control, like things are happening too fast for me to catch up with them. I think maybe things are happening too fast here...for both of us." She took a deep, steadying breath, willing her trembling fingers to calm. "I was thinking that maybe we should keep things a little less serious until we both have time to adjust to everything that's been happening between us." Jess shifted her gaze from Robin, finally allowing it to settle across the room on the edge of the fireplace mantel.

Robin remained silent for a long moment, trying to process everything Jess was saying, and not saying. *She wants to slow down. We haven't gotten too physically serious. Maybe it's all the emotion. Has it been too emotionally intense?* Robin turned to completely face Jess, and took her trembling fingers into her smaller hands. "You're not comfortable with where we are right now, Jess?"

"I'm not sure I'm comfortable with how quickly it seems things are moving. At least they seem like they're moving quickly to me. I'm wondering if maybe we can both take a breath here and get used to things for a while." Jess rested the side of her head against the back cushion of the sofa. "What do you think?"

Robin mirrored Jess's position. *Maybe she's right. I need to more fully let go of the past before I can totally move on with the future.* Robin spoke her next words with a gentle understanding. "I think we should be completely comfortable with each other, Jess, and what we do together. Maybe we do need to take a breath and spend some time adjusting before moving ahead." She gently squeezed Jess's fingers with both hands. "Tell me the things that you would be comfortable doing."

"Well, what we've been doing is okay." Jess ventured a small smile.

"So...would our spending time together one or two evenings during the week be okay?" Robin asked unsure.

"Yes."

"Okay." Robin spoke more confidently. "Would spending hooky time together on the weekends be okay?" She gave a small grin.

"Yes, that would be okay." Jess nodded.

Robin picked lightly at the fabric on Jess's shirt sleeve, and spoke more cautiously. "Would weekend sleepovers be okay?"

Jess looked directly into sea green eyes. "Yes."

Robin hesitated for a slight moment before continuing. "And would cuddling by the fire be okay?"

"Yes, I think so."

Robin moved in closer to Jess. "It's okay?"

"It's okay, yes." Jess's breathing quickened at Robin's proximity.

Robin reached up and tenderly brushed the dark bangs from Jess's eyes and whispered. "Would kissing you sometimes be okay, too?" She let her hand trail down to Jess's cheek and rested it there as she awaited the answer.

Jess leaned in to the touch, unable to resist it, her eyelids fluttering at the contact and her voice barely registering sound as she spoke. "Yes."

"Okay." Robin placed a small, light kiss and Jess's lips and then reached over to the end table to switch off the lamp, casting the room into darkened shadows, the bright orange glow emanating directly from the flickering fire the only visible light. Robin laid herself back, resting her head against a soft throw pillow, and then stretched her petite form out along the length of the sofa. "Come here next to me."

Jess slid down and curled up alongside Robin with her back against the cushions of the sofa. She rested her head lightly on Robin's shoulder and placed her hand across Robin's waist, breathing out a heavy sigh. She watched the flames merrily dance and listened to the wood lightly crackle as it burned, as the warmth of the fire spread outwardly across the room. It felt so good to be held like this, in a complete and total embrace. Robin stroked her fingers through the long, dark hair, the comforting touch seeming to make all the anxiety disappear and soothing away any lingering tension. Jess could smell the light, clean scent that belonged to Robin, something which reminded her of springtime with a hint of fresh rain. And in that one moment of startling clarity, Jess finally came to realize that she could no longer attempt to deny the intensity of her feelings. All the apprehension suddenly vanished, and in its place settled a peace and serenity the likes of which she had never experienced before.

Robin stroked the dark head, resolving to give them both whatever time necessary to feel completely comfortable with their new relationship and the physical and emotional closeness they were experiencing. She knew there was a risk of letting too much of her inner self be seen too soon. Not even David had seen everything there was to see about her. No one had completely seen her inner thoughts, and fears, and wants, and dreams. If she and Jess were going to be comfortable sharing their complete selves with each other, if that's what ended up happening, then they were going to have to take time to feel comfortable at every step of the way, before they proceeded on ahead to whatever lie next.

They were both silent for a very long while before Robin spoke. "Are you okay? You've been quiet for a really long time." Robin continued to lightly brush her fingers through Jess's hair.

"Yeah. I'm fine. I almost fell asleep, though. You make a good pillow." She turned her head to look up at Robin and smiled fondly. "Again."

"I'm glad you find me so comfortable." Robin chuckled. "Hey, listen. What are you doing Thursday evening?"

Jess shifted to one elbow and rested her head in her hand while looking directly into mischievous green eyes. "Why?" She drawled.

"Because there's a certain person, who shall remain nameless, whose birthday it is Thursday, and I'm having a birthday party at my place for this person." The twinkle in Robin's eyes grew.

"I see. And who all will be at this party of yours?" Blue eyes studied Robin intently.

"Well, there's the host, which is me, and then, of course, there's the guest of honor."

"Anybody else?"

"Nope. I wouldn't want it to be too crowded." Robin gave a hint of a grin. "And did I mention that I am making the guest of honor's favorite shellfish for dinner?"

"Is that so?" Jess grinned affectionately. "Well then I think the guest of honor would be delighted to attend your party." Jess narrowed her eyes in a playful warning. "As long as you don't, of course, make the guest of honor do anything silly or embarrassing."

"I would never, ever do that." Robin winked and then moved her head over closer to Jess, whispering in a conspiratorial tone. "Besides, the guest of honor is rather prim and proper and would probably faint if I ever tried something like that."

Jess broke into a wide grin, and with a lightening speed, gathered Robin in her arms and hugged her fiercely, whispering into her ear. "Prim and proper? I'll show you prim and proper." With that, Jess ducked her head and placed several long and slow kisses on Robin's lips, lingering just a little to nibble on a petite chin, all the while hugging Robin closely to her body like a second skin. Completing her little demonstration, Jess pulled back slightly and gazed into sea green eyes. "Still think the guest of honor is rather prim and proper?"

Robin was still a bit dazed from the kisses. "Um...I think I'm going to have to rethink my assessment."

"You do that, or the guest of honor might just have to continue with demonstrations until you come to the appropriate conclusion." Jess winked and then sat up against the back of the sofa.

"I think more demonstrations might be in order, but I'll wait until Thursday night to inform the guest of honor of my final decision." Robin sat up as well and then looked at her watch. "Ooooh, it's getting late. Tomorrow's a school day. I really should go." She got up from the sofa, located her jacket from the coat rack, and pulled it on. "The party starts at 7:00 on Thursday night. Make sure the guest of honor is not late."

"I can assure you, the guest of honor will be right on time." Jess walked Robin to the door. "Thanks for understanding what I said earlier."

"There's nothing to understand. I feel exactly the same way." Robin leaned in and gave Jess a quick hug. "See you tomorrow."

"See you tomorrow, Robin. Drive safely." Jess watched her leave and then quickly shut the door to prevent the cold air from making its way too far inside.

I love parties.

****

It was late morning when Robin looked up from her exhibits, checked her watch and decided to refresh her cold cup of coffee. She stepped out of her office and around a group of huddled, whispering heads on her way to the galley. Selecting the freshly brewed flavor of the day, Irish Crème, she filled her cup and made her way back to her office. Just as she turned to go in through the doorway, Robin saw Paul over by the printer. A twinge of guilt made its presence known, and Robin decided that now was as good of a time as any to have that little chat with him.

"Hey, Paul." Robin called down to him. "Do you have a minute?"

Paul turned his head and nodded, pulling something off the printer. "Yeah."

"I wanted to talk with you about something." Robin waited as Paul approached her. "Could we talk in my office?"

Paul casually stepped inside and sat down in the chair opposite the desk. "Okay, shoot."

"Let me close the door." Robin swung the door shut and took a seat behind her desk, idly picking up her pen and twirling it nervously around in her fingers. "I wanted to explain to you about the basketball game." She looked at him a bit awkwardly.

"Really, Robin, there is nothing for you to explain." Paul didn't seem phased in the least.

He's not making this easy. "No, I think I need to explain something to you. When you asked me to go to the game with you, I really had no intentions of going. Later, Jess had extra tickets, and since we didn't have to work, I decided to go after all." *Technically, that was true.*

Paul nodded. "Hey, no big deal. Don't sweat it. I understand plans change." He then leaned forward, resting his forearms on the front of the desk, and gave Robin a truly charming smile. "Would you be interested in having dinner with me Friday night?"

A mental groan. *How did I manage to make this worse?* Robin twirled the pen faster in her fingers. "Um...that's the other thing I wanted to talk with you about." She blew out a breath, trying to order her thoughts. "I like you, Paul, but I'd rather keep things on a professional level. It's just that a lot of things have happened to me recently, and I'm not in a position to see anyone else outside of work." *That made no sense even to me.*

Paul sat back in his chair and folded his hands in front of him. "If you're saying you're already seeing someone, I understand and I won't mention anything again."

Robin twirled the pen dangerously out of control, and she debated with herself for only a split second before responding, a bit more forcefully than even she had intended "No." The minute she said it, a guilty look came across her face and she felt slight regret at the lie, as the pen now nearly flew out of her hand. "Um...it has to do with some other issues which I can't really get into. But, thank you for asking me out. That was very nice of you, and if things were different, I would definitely be interested." Robin smiled toward him now with genuine sincerity.

"Okay. But if things change, you'll let me know, won't you?" Paul winked cheerfully, trying to hide his disappointment.

"You bet. Thanks for understanding, Paul. Now, tell me what you need for the deposition next week so I'll have time to do the depo prep." For the next several minutes, Robin dutifully took down the key issues that Paul provided regarding the case, so that she was better able to pull together the relevant documentation for the deposition. When they were finished, Paul exited her office, leaving Robin with a vague sense of unease stemming from their prior conversation.

She sat back in her desk chair and stared unseeingly out the large glass window, the gleaming waters of the lake below going unnoticed. *I lied.* She tried to understand why that felt so bad. It couldn't have been avoided. How could she tell him the truth when she didn't understand it herself? It occurred to her that perhaps her discomfort with the situation was what Jess was referring to the previous evening. They both needed time to adjust. There were ramifications to their relationship, and they both needed to decide what to do and say, if anything at all.

As Robin gazed into the cloudless blue sky, she idly, and for no particular reason, had the thought that the sky somehow reminded her of Jess's amazingly beautiful blue eyes. She shook her head and mused to herself. *I am so hopelessly taken with her.* And that particular thought brought her to a whole new series of thoughts. How could she be totally consumed with this ever-present desire to be with Jess, and to be with her very affectionately? It was so soon, after all. Did her feelings for David just disappear overnight? Or were they never that strong to begin with? One thing was for certain. Any feelings she had for David paled in comparison to what she felt just being in the same room with Jess. It was a magnetic pull so strong that she couldn't deny the intensity of her feelings, even if she wanted to. *Jess.* What was it about Jess that made Robin's skin tingle at the merest touch? What was it that made Robin crave the slightest physical contact, or seek the comfort of Jess's protective embrace? There was the thrill of Jess's presence, and the complete and total sense of being right where she belonged. *Home.* And what was it that made Robin desperately want something even more intimate, even though she was terrified at the mere thought, just the same?

A flash of sunlight off the metal of a passing airplane caught Robin's eye, and all at once, as if the flash itself were the catalyst, Robin now knew, not only in her heart but also in her mind, that which seemed to have eluded her all along. Her reasoning progressed in logical sequence until she finally came upon the sought-after conclusion. If she had loved David and was willing to spend her life with him, and the feelings that she had for him did not come close to those she felt for Jess, then what she felt for Jess must far exceed that which she felt for David. But whether it was the hidden guilt and grief over David, or the fear of the unknown, or some as yet unanalyzed reason, something inexplicably still prevented Robin from putting a name to her feelings. The feelings themselves were realized, but the words were still left unspoken.

I need more coffee.

****

"Where are we going?" Jess sat in Robin's blue Miata as they headed down the main highway during the early evening hours.

"Can't tell ya." Robin concentrated on the road, not looking over at Jess.

"Why?"

"Just can't."

"First, you kidnap me, and now you won't tell me where we're going." Jess narrowed her eyes. "Not fair."

Robin turned her head and smiled at Jess sweetly. "Paybacks are a bitch, aren't they?"

"Now, it's definitely your turn to be in trouble." A pause. "Come on, just give me one little hint." Jess begged.

Robin shook her head playfully. "Nope. You can beg all you want, but it won't get you anywhere."

"I have a snappy remark to that, but it wouldn't be polite to make you blush." Jess gave Robin a look and then focused her attention on the rearview mirror, reaching up for Al.

Robin quickly swatted her hand away. "Don't you even think about touching him. The last time, as I remember, you took him and I had to go looking all over for him."

"I just borrowed him. And nope, you didn't go looking all over for him. You only looked in one particular location, as I recall." Jess now had a mischievous twinkle in her eye. "And I think you enjoyed that quite thoroughly."

Robin turned several shades of red, shielding her face from Jess's view, but not offering a single word in her own defense.

Jess was now laughing quite uncontrollably. "And here I was trying so hard not to make you blush."

Robin shook her head in exasperation. "Why is it that every time I think I've got you, you turn it around on me?"

Jess leaned in closer to Robin. "Don't you worry, Robin, you've got me, alright. She smiled affectionately.

"You can be very sweet, but I see through your little scheme, and I'm still not telling you where we're going." Robin headed toward the mall.

Jess pouted playfully. "Well, you can't blame a girl for trying." Noticing where they were headed, she cocked her head. "Don't tell me we're going to the mall again? Didn't you have enough 'fun' the other day?"

"We're not going to the mall, Jess, so be quiet."

"Can I ride the train again?"

"We're not going to the mall."

"I'll let you sit up front."

"We're not going to the mall."

"And you can ring the bell."

"Jess, we're not going to the mall." Robin enunciated the words very clearly. "Don't make me repeat it again." She chuckled, thinking the whole conversation was rather cute.

"But…." Jess started to speak once more, however Robin effectively stopped her by pointing a stern finger toward Jess's face in a silent warning.

"Be patient, Jess."

"Fine." Jess pouted some more.

Finally, a few moments later, Robin pulled the Miata into the local ice cream parlor, 102 flavors of ice cream, to be exact. "Okay we're here." She looked at Jess expectantly.

"Ooooh, ice cream." Jess slid out of the car, delighted. "How did you know I have a weakness for ice cream?"

Robin followed her inside the parlor. "Well, I didn't know that, but my weakness is ice cream, too." She grinned impishly "So, if you didn't like it, you were just going to have to stay here anyhow and watch me eat it."

They each got a cone with a double scoop of ice cream, Jess got mint chocolate chip, and Robin got chocolate peanut butter swirl. They, of course, had to taste each other's flavors several times, effectively sharing their cones the entire way until finished.

"That was delicious." Jess licked her lips. "I can't believe there are 103 flavors. I think we have to come back 103 times to taste them all."

"There're 102 flavors, Jess, and if you want to come back 102 times, I think that can be arranged." Robin chuckled, really enjoying the light banter between them. *She is so much fun to be with.* "Are you ready to go, now?"

"Yep." Jess got into the car. "Can we come back tomorrow night?"

"Nope. You have a very important dinner engagement, if I remember correctly." Robin started the car. "There's a party at my place and you're in charge of making sure the guest of honor arrives on time."

"Oh, yes. I have it on good authority that the guest of honor is quite looking forward to it." Jess stared out the window nonchalantly.

"Good. And make sure the guest of honor knows there's also going to be a surprise." Robin headed the car in the direction of The Ranch.

"Really? A surprise?"

"Yep. It's a birthday party after all." Robin grinned.

"I think we should skip the birthday part and get right to the surprise part. Tell me what it is." Jess was begging again.

"Nope. The guest of honor will just have to wait." Robin finally pulled into Jess's driveway. "Okay, here you are. Thanks for coming out to play tonight."

"I enjoyed it. Now I can get back to the work I brought home." Jess frowned a little at the thought, and sat in the car for a moment longer, not really wanting to leave. "Um...Robin, I think you have a bit of ice cream on the corner of your mouth." Jess shifted in her seat.

"I do?"

"Yes."

"Where?" *It's too dark for her to see anything.*

"There." Jess pointed.

"Exactly where?"

Jess leaned in toward Robin. "Right here." She brushed her finger against Robin's soft lips and then leaned in closer.

Robin melted at the touch and whispered. "Could you um...maybe remove it for me?"

"Yes." Jess whispered back and bent her head and kissed Robin's lips sensuously, making sure to thoroughly remove all imaginary traces of ice cream. After she was certain she didn't miss any spots, Jess broke away and sat back. "You taste good, very sweet."

Robin tried to regain her senses. "It's the ice cream."

"Not entirely." Jess cleared her throat. "Um...I think I had better go on inside. If I stay out here, there might be some more ice cream that needs removing, and then I'll never get any of my work done."

"And that would be bad?"

Jess grinned. "That, Robin, would definitely be very bad." She winked.

"Okay." Robin swallowed and then took a breath. "Goodnight, Jess. Don't forget dinner tomorrow."

Jess opened the car door. "I will make sure the guest of honor gets there precisely at 8:00." She spoke with a twinkle in her eye.

"Jess," Robin drawled, "It's at 7:00."

"Ooops, you're right." Jess got out of the car and leaned in the open window. "Okay, then, I'll make sure the guest of honor is there precisely at 7:00." She made her way up to the front porch.

"That's very good, Jess. Goodnight." Robin chuckled and started to pull the car away. "You are so hopeless."

"Goodnight." A pause. "And I heard that." Jess yelled back to Robin from the front porch as the blue Miata pulled away.

Jess, you are most definitely hopeless about her.

****

Early Thursday evening, Robin put the finishing touches on the special dinner she was preparing and chilled the light Chardonnay wine. She went over to the dining room table and gently lit the candle in the centerpiece, careful to arrange it so that the center of the table was clear for the placement of the dinner dishes. Satisfied that everything was in order, she went back into the kitchen to check the progress of her special meal. After a moment, she heard a light knock on the door, and went to answer it.

"Hi. Happy Birthday." Robin greeted Jess and motioned her into the living room. "Now the party can begin because the guest of honor has arrived, and on time, I may add."

"Hi. Thanks. Of course, I'm on time. Was there ever any doubt?" Jess asked innocently and made her way over to the sofa. "I can't believe you're cooking for me again. That must make it one million to only one for me."

"Perhaps, but this is a special occasion and it's not included in the dinner-making tally." Robin smiled warmly. "Would you like a glass of wine?"

"Alright." Jess relaxed on the fluffy sofa. while Robin left the room.

After a moment, Robin returned with two chilled glasses of Chardonnay. "Here you are." She handed a glass of wine to Jess sat herself down on the sofa. "So how has your birthday been so far?"

"Fine, I suppose. My mother called earlier today and my brother sent me a birthday card. I'm always amazed that he remembers things like this. Most guys don't." Jess took a sip of her wine. "By the way, that's a nice sweater you have on."

Robin looked down at her lightweight, short-sleeved, burgundy colored, velour sweater. "Thanks. I like the way it feels. It's so comfortable."

"It seems to be." Jess glanced over toward the window. " So, I think I was right."

Robin was puzzled. "Right about what?"

"You know."

Robin shook her head. "No, I don't."

Jess put her wine glass down on the coffee table and spoke as if it were common knowledge. "Monday, it was cold. Today's Thursday, and it was 70 degrees. Think about it. I think my weather forecasting skills are right on the mark." Jess gave her a smug grin. "You can now go ahead and admit that I was right."

Robin looked at Jess for a long moment. "I believe that's still open for interpretation, Miss Weather Expert, because it rained a little bit today, it's cool tonight, and another cold front is on the way. It'll be cold again tomorrow."

"It'll be cool tomorrow, and it doesn't matter because I correctly stated that it would warm up in a couple of days, and it did. Therefore, I was right." Jess touched her finger lightly to the tip of her tongue and made an imaginary chalk mark in the air in front of her."

Robin chuckled. “Because it’s your birthday, I’m not going to disagree with you...this time.” She rolled her eyes playfully and mumbled. “You were right.”

“I didn’t hear you.”

Robin blew out a breath and spoke louder. “You were right.”

Jess leaned an ear in closer to Robin. “I still didn’t quite hear you.”

Robin reached out with her hand and slowly turned Jess’s face so she was looking directly into blue eyes. She then leaned in very close, whispering softly. “You were right.” Robin’s warm breath caressed Jess’s face, and she leaned in further and punctuated that statement, placing a tender kiss on Jess’s lips.

Jess let the kiss linger for a moment, then sat back and grinned. “I definitely heard that.”

“Good. Now, dinner’s ready, so come on into the dining room. I hope you like what I made. It’s a recipe I actually got off the internet for Shrimp Dijon.” Robin went into the kitchen and returned with the entrée and side dishes.

“You are a very good cook and I know I’m gonna love it.” Jess heartily dug in, and all through dinner, she barely came up for air.

All in all, it was a wonderful dinner, to say the least, and after the table was cleared, Robin ushered Jess back into the living room while she prepared the dessert. Once everything in the dining room was set, Robin returned to the living room carrying a package wrapped in colorful wrapping paper and a decorative bow.

“I have a birthday present for you.” Robin sat on the carpeted floor in front of the fluffy sofa where Jess was sitting, and handed her the package.

“You got a gift? For me? That was very sweet of you, Robin.”

“Open it.” Robin couldn’t help the grin that spread across her face or the look of sheer excitement as she waited in anticipation for Jess to open her gift.

“It sure is heavy.” Jess meticulously and methodically unwrapped the present, first unwrapping each side of the box, then the bottom, and finally pulling the remainder of the wrapping paper away, revealing a plain looking brown rectangular box.

Robin was watching impatiently, the slow and deliberate unwrapping of the gift seeming to be pure torture for her. “Will you go ahead and open it, already?”

Jess smiled and opened the box, pulling out its contents. She sat there, silently stunned, as she pulled out, one by one, individually wrapped carved onyx chess pieces and next, the square solid onyx checkered game board. With slightly shaking fingers, she reverently unwrapped several of the chess pieces, taking one in her hand completely, and fingering the smooth, polished surface while intently studying the intricate carvings. During the whole process, Jess never said a word.

Robin broke the silence, speaking quietly. "Do you like it?"

Jess looked up, still clutching the onyx game piece. "It's one of the most wonderful gifts I've ever received." She took a breath. "I haven't told you this before, but my father used to play, and one of my few happy memories of him is when he would take me with him into his study, and show me how to move the pieces on the board in the proper way. I didn't quite understand it all, but I enjoyed that time he spent with me." She looked again at the game piece she was holding. "I'll never forget it."

"I'm glad you like it," Robin said simply.

"You must have spent way too much on this. I know how much these things cost, and one such as this is quite expensive. This is actually exquisite." Jess marveled at the quality of the carvings, her eyes sparkling.

Robin gave her a very warm and sincere smile. "I'd spend my last dime on you, Jess, if it meant I'd get to see, even for one moment, the look in your eyes right now. Happy Birthday." She reached up and grasped Jess's hand, which still had not let go of the onyx chess piece. "Now, come on." Robin tugged. "Dessert is waiting."

Jess set the game piece down and stood up. "It is chocolate?" She raised both eyebrows questioningly. "Because I love chocolate."

"I don't think I knew that, but yes, it's most definitely chocolate."

They walked into the dining room, and on the table sat a chocolate fudge cake with vanilla icing. Two places were set, each bearing a birthday party hat and a color coordinated napkin, with similarly colored balloons strung up from the mini-chandelier.

"Let me light the candles." Robin lit the six candles on the cake. "Put on your hat so I can sing." She grinned and put on her own hat as Jess, with a silly roll of her eyes, did the same. "Okay, now let me sing." Robin sang the entire verse of the birthday song, laughing most of the way through it. When she was finished, she glanced over at Jess. "What?"

Jess was suppressing grin. "Nothing."

"What? Tell me."

Jess silently raised an eyebrow. "Don't quit your day job."

Robin squinted her eyes and wagged a playful finger. "You are an unbelievable brat. Now, blow out your candles."

Jess did so, noticing for the first time the six candles. "Why six candles?"

"Well, there's three on the top and three on the bottom. That's how old you are, right? Thirty-three?"

"Yep. I didn't tell you that, though. How did you know?" Jess furrowed her brows, giving Robin her best menacing glare.

"I have my sources." Robin winked.

"Hmm. I just bet you do. I think I smell a spy somewhere." Jess cut two pieces of cake for herself and Robin. "So, now, let me see if I have this candle thing right. When it's your birthday, I would put two candles on the top and six candles on the bottom, correct?"

"Right," Robin stated matter-of-factly. "See how the system works? It all makes perfect sense."

Of course.

****

Jess and Robin lay stretched out on the carpeted floor in front of the coffee table in the living room, quite full from a delicious dinner. The soft glow of the single lamplight filtered its way in a dim manner throughout the room.

"I am so stuffed. That cake really did it for me. I'm gonna put on too much weight now and I won't fit into my jeans anymore." Robin patted her stomach.

Jess turned to look at her. "I can't believe you're going to gain weight just from one piece of cake. Ooops, I forgot, you had seconds, and then you finished the last bite of mine." Jess grinned.

"Yep." Robin stretched her arms above her head "And I also nibbled a little while I was making it. Trust me, I'm already gaining the extra weight as we speak."

"Let me check." Jess propped herself up on one elbow and lifted the edge of Robin's sweater just a bit to check the room at the waistline of said jeans. "You seem to have plenty of room here." Jess examined the area in question and then laid her hand flatly against the soft skin of Robin's stomach. "I think there's still space for a least one more piece of cake in there." Jess scooted in a little closer, and began to brush her fingers back and forth lightly against the silky smooth surface of Robin's stomach. A chain bracelet Jess had on her wrist moved in unison with her fingers, as they grazed the velvet softness of the fair skin, sending goose bumps trailing in their wake.

Robin's mind couldn't process the array of sensations all at once, and she heard herself gasp at the contact. Jess was now only a few inches away from her, and their eyes met and locked, green holding blue, as the gentle touch continued.

"I love the way you do that." Robin whispered.

Jess smiled, the cerulean gaze searching and then penetrating sea green to a new level of awareness.

"I love how you care about me, Jess. And I love all the things you do for me." Robin smiled tenderly, spellbound. "I love your eyes and your smile. I love everything about you." She brought her hand up to rest gently against Jess's cheek. "I love..." She searched azure eyes and whispered fervently. "You."

Jess closed her eyes at the contact, and then upon hearing the last words, dropped her forehead to rest against Robin's shoulder, her breathing quick and shallow.

Not a word was spoken for what seemed like an eternity, until Robin finally reached up and placed her hands on either side of Jess's dark head, swallowing hard before speaking. "Jess, I'm so sorry if that made you feel uncomfortable. I know we agreed to stop and take a breath here, so we could get used to things." Robin stared up at the ceiling to collect herself. "I shouldn't have said that out loud."

Jess lifted her head, a lone tear making its way down her cheek, as she inched her way up so that her face was even with Robin's and not more than a hair's breath away. She stared into green eyes for a long, quiet moment, and tenderly caressed a fair cheek, whispering softy. "You love me?"

Robin nodded solemnly.

Jess brushed the blonde bangs away from Robin's forehead, having difficulty breathing, and trembling slightly. "I have loved you forever, Robin. I just didn't realize it until now." She leaned in, and with a tenderness neither previously thought possible, kissed Robin's soft lips.

Robin was overcome with emotion, and she felt hot tears make their way from her eyes, immediately to be kissed away, as Jess lovingly memorized every inch of Robin's lovely face. Robin did the same with Jess, tasting the saltiness of the errant tear that had previously strayed. They both took a moment to steady their emotions somewhat, then Jess shifted herself onto her back, laying flat against the carpet. Robin curled up next to her, resting her head in the crook of Jess's neck.

"I love you, Jess, with all my heart." Robin took a deep breath. "It feels good to finally say that."

Jess kissed the top of the blonde head. "And I love you, Robin, very much. I don't know why I was so afraid to acknowledge that. I think it scared me to think that I was so completely out of control. I tried to deny the feelings, and then when I couldn't deny them any longer, I tried to slow them down." She kissed the blonde head again and hugged the smaller woman closer to her. "But you took over my heart, and you wouldn't let go. It was like you were a part of me, and I ached when you weren't there."

Robin placed her hand at the base of Jess's neck and felt the strong pulse, and then kissed the exact spot. "We're a part of each other, Jess. I believe that." She then shook her head slightly and gave Jess a small, crooked grin. "So much for taking time to adjust, huh?"

Jess let the corner of her mouth turn up in a half grin, as well, and quipped. "Sometimes, my plans don't work."

They both chuckled and laid there quietly together for a while, each trying to process what had happened between them. A few moments later, Robin decided to bring up a topic which she knew they needed to discuss. She shifted her position and lifted herself up on one elbow. "I spoke with Paul the other day."

"What did you tell him?" Jess stroked her fingers through Robin's short blonde hair.

"I told him that because of some things that had happened to me recently, I wasn't in a position to see him."

"What was his reaction?" Jess traced a petite earlobe with her finger.

Robin stared intently at the far corner of the room, as if it held some particular fascination. "He asked me if I was seeing someone."

Jess's hand stilled and her eyes widened. "How did you answer that?"

Robin grimaced, and then closed her eyes briefly. "I lied." She picked at imaginary lint on Jess's shirt. "I didn't know what to tell him. We hadn't talked about what to say to people." She whispered. "I didn't want him to know."

"Do you want anyone to know?"

Robin looked away again, slightly embarrassed. "No."

"I see." Jess sat up. "Let's go sit up on the sofa where it's more comfortable." They got up from the carpeted floor and sat together on the fluffy sofa, cuddled up next to each other, as Jess continued. "We need to talk about this."

"I know."

"Do you want to keep it a secret?" Jess didn't know, herself, the answer to her own question.

"Yes, I think I do. This is just so new to me. I don't feel comfortable yet telling anyone about us." Robin stared across the room. "There are a lot of ramifications that I'm not ready to deal with." She then looked fondly at Jess and hastened to add. "I'm not ashamed of you."

Jess nodded. "I know. I have to tell you that I can't see me telling anyone either." She chuckled softly. "I could hardly even admit it to myself, much less anyone else." She turned her head and tilted Robin's chin up, looking her squarely in the eye. "And I will never, ever be ashamed of you. You are the most wonderful thing that has ever happened to me. I just think that what we have is private, and should remain between us, and no one else."

"Do you think someone could find out?" Robin's voice sounded quite apprehensive.

"Honey, if someone finds out, there's nothing we can do about it. Unless and until that happens, this can just be a private matter between you and me. I think it should be private, anyway. It's nobody else's business." Jess brought her lips to Robin's and gave her a gentle kiss. "Nobody else could understand the way I feel about you."

Robin hugged Jess tightly, burying her face in Jess's shoulder. "I wish you didn't have to leave tonight. But I know tomorrow's a work day. I just feel so close to you right now that I don't want to be separated from you. Does that make sense?"

Jess smiled at the sentiment. "That makes perfect sense, and I feel the same way. When I'm apart from you, I ache inside."

Robin sat upright. "Then stay. I mean, I'm sure I could find something for you to sleep in, and then we could sleep together tonight."

"What?" Jess's tone was more than a little shocked.

Robin had a quizzical expression on her face, and then suddenly realized what she said. "Oh, no. No, no, no, no. I didn't mean...I meant..." Robin stammered. "We would just go to sleep...together...rather than apart. I mean…." Robin was trembling at this point.

"Shhhh, honey, it's okay" Jess pulled Robin into a tight embrace. "I know what you mean. We're both a little emotional right now. As much as we feel for each other emotionally, neither one of us is ready for anything more physically at the moment. Am I right?"

"Yes." Robin nodded slowly and then became pensive. "You know, it's funny. I always thought the physical side came first, even if you didn't act on it right away, and then you grew into the emotional side. But with us, it's everything all at once, and I feel it's more than just physical or emotional. There's also an almost spiritual side. It's the whole package." She gave Jess a small, shy smile. "Does that make sense?"

"Yes, I would say so, but I have one small caveat." Jess offered a wry smile.

"What would that be?"

"Sometimes, the physical side gets very strong." Jess grinned adoringly. "Because you absolutely take my breath away."

I'd faint if I were standing up. Robin blushed. "I stand corrected. You have the same effect on me." She got up from the sofa and tugged at Jess's arm. "Come on. Let's find you something to sleep in."

They headed for the bedroom and Robin found a slightly large t-shirt for Jess to wear, while Robin changed into her nightshirt. After they had turned out the lights and were safely snuggled in the bed, Robin turned to Jess and grasped her hand, linking their fingers together. "Happy Birthday, Jess. I hope you had a good day."

"Yep. It was the best birthday I've ever had." Jess turned on her side and looked tenderly at Robin through the darkness. "It was very special. Thank you."

Robin smiled and then positioned herself back against Jess so that they were spooned tightly together, as Jess wrapped a long arm around Robin's waist. After barely a moment, Robin lifted Jess's arm and took the larger hand in her own, gently guiding Jess's hand from the outside to the inside of the nightshirt and around her bare stomach. "I like your hand there."

Oh, God. I'd say that physical side is really strong right about now.

"Goodnight, Jess. I love you."

"I love you, too, sweetheart. Goodnight." Jess tightened her hold on Robin's waist, feeling the soft skin of Robin's stomach against her hand. *Let me amend my previous statement. I'd say that physical side is really, really strong right about now.*

Chapter 6

Jess had worked the entire weekend. With trial looming just around the corner and much preparation left to do, not to mention her new more supervisory role on the case, Jess unfortunately had little time to play all weekend. Hooky time, as Robin called it, had to take a rain check this time. It was Monday again, and the work just never seemed to end.

Jess arrived to work very early that morning, grabbed a cup of cappuccino from the lobby coffee shop, and made her way up the elevator to her office. The law firm's office suite at this hour of the morning was nearly empty, and Jess found herself wandering through the darkened reception area a little preoccupied. She strode down the long hallway to her own office, opened the door, and turned on the light. The morning sun had just started to peek its way above the horizon, the first warm rays blanketing the city below in golden hues. She approached the large, floor-to-ceiling glass window and gazed momentarily at the rising sun, idly noting the slight haze which had settled over the skyline. Not lingering too long at the window, she set her briefcase and her cappuccino down and quickly started up the computer. As she sat in her burgundy leather chair waiting for her computer to come to life, she glanced across the top of her desk, intending to survey the ever-increasing contents of her in-box, most of which she never even put a dent in over the weekend. At that particular moment, an object, neatly nestled on the inside corner of her desk, suddenly caught her eye. Leaning in for a closer inspection, Jess reached out her hand and pulled the object toward her, picking it up and studying it intently. *What's this?*

It seems that a slender glass vase with a single, perfect red rose had been deposited on her desk. This miraculous floral depository had somehow occurred at some point after Jess had left the office the previous evening and prior to her arrival this morning. She looked down at her desk again to see that a small, simple card had also been placed beneath the small vase. She reached out and picked up the card, turning it over, and reading the three simple words on the card to herself. And then she read them again.

'I missed you.'

That was all the card said. It was not signed, and yet there was no question in her mind who it was from. Jess stared at the card for a long while, then over to the red rose, and then back again at the card, wondering just when, exactly, it could have been placed on her desk. There was only one possible explanation. *She's here.* Jess hastily set both the card and the rose down, got up from her chair, and dashed out the door of her office, not slowing down as she crossed the lobby and the darkened reception area. She rounded the corner and headed down the hallway, finally reaching her destination. Stepping rapidly inside the occupied office, Jess quickly closed the door and stepped around the desk, kneeling down just next to the desk chair, and staring into warm green eyes.

"Hi." Robin smiled.

Jess smiled but was otherwise was silent.

"Jess?"

More silence.

It seems Jess had been mentally evaluating whether she should just give in and do what it was she really wanted to do, even though she and Robin were unquestionably in a business setting. Coming to the conclusion that there was probably no one else in the office at this hour, and that Robin's office door was now sufficiently closed, Jess finally chose to do exactly what she had wanted to do from the first moment she had seen that perfect red rose on her desk. She carefully leaned in toward Robin and placed a tender kiss on her lips. She then wrapped her long arms around Robin in a complete and warm embrace, whispering softly into her ear. "Hi. I missed you, too."

Robin hugged her tightly, and then pulled back and smiled. "My, you're here early."

"I could say the same about you." Jess gave her a tender smile in return. "And you've been very busy, I see."

Robin chuckled "Yeah, well, you see, I have this particular boss, who's a real slave-driver, and has loaded me down with preparing massive trial exhibits." She grinned widely.

"I see." Jess stood up and stepped over to sit in the chair across from Robin's desk. "And so, was the rose just a ploy to butter up said slave-driver boss?"

Robin furrowed her brows in thought for a moment. "Did it work?"

"Yes."

"Then, absolutely. It was definitely a ploy to butter up the slave-driver boss." Robin chuckled. "And there's more where that came from."

Jess arched a dark eyebrow. "Is that so? Well, then, I think your slave-driver boss might be in dire need of more of your buttering up techniques real soon."

Robin shook her head playfully. "Nope. Not so fast. I have to have proof that my so-called buttering up techniques are actually working first, before I proceed further."

Jess pondered that thought for a moment. "Well, Robin, I think I demonstrated quite well when I first came in here this morning how effective your buttering up techniques are." Jess pursed her lips in concentration. "You don't agree?"

"Well, let's just say it was a good start." Robin nodded seriously. "But I will definitely need more convincing on the matter."

"Okaaay." Jess tapped her fingers on the front of the desk pensively. "It seems that your slave-driver boss is free for dinner tonight. If you happen to be free as well, then perhaps said slave-driver boss could take you someplace nice to eat. Would that help to convince you that your buttering up techniques are working?"

Robin got up from her chair and stepped around her desk, leaning lightly against the front edge facing Jess. "That might help."

"But you would still need more convincing?" Jess queried.

"Yes."

"Such as?"

Robin leaned in close to Jess and whispered into her ear. "That particular part of the convincing would come after dinner." She winked.

Jess sat there staring at Robin for a long moment, not speaking and her mouth slightly open.

Gotcha. Robin started laughing very hard and pumped her arms jubilantly. "Yesss. I got you. I finally, finally got you."

"It's not that funny, Robin." Jess tried to dismiss the matter.

"Oh, yes it is. You're just mad because I finally got you." Robin pointed a playful finger accusingly at Jess. "When you get me, you laugh about it for days. When I get you, it's supposedly no big deal."

She smirked. "I don't think so."

"Listen, you did not get me. I knew all along what you were going to say. I was just playing along." Jess stood up.

"You just can't admit it, can you?" Robin stepped closer.

Jess leaned down to look directly into green eyes. "There's nothing to admit."

Robin shook her head. "I can't believe you." She then whispered softly. "You are so hopeless."

"So you keep saying." Jess whispered back and then leaned in and gave Robin a tender kiss, which turned into several more kisses and then into several more after that.

"Um...." Robin stepped back. "We shouldn't be doing this here."

Jess took a deep breath. "Right." *But I can't help myself.* "Okay. I've got to get to work, and so do you. So, tonight, dinner, my treat. Got it?"

"Got it." Robin grinned.

"Good." Jess approached the door. "And Robin?"

"Yes?"

"As it relates to the sufficiency of your buttering up techniques, I plan on doing quite a bit of convincing on that matter later on this evening after dinner." Jess winked. "Just thought you should know that." Then, without so much as another word, she strode out the door leaving Robin a bit speechless.

Oh boy. She is good.

****

The candle flickered in its glass holder on the tablecloth in the intimate little French restaurant as Jess and Robin sat quietly at a small table in the corner. As promised, Jess had taken Robin out to dinner in this exclusive little restaurant, one in which she was sure Robin had not been to or even heard of in her short time in the city. Dinner had been an enjoyable but subdued affair, the food delicious and the conversation light. Still, the undercurrent of something else seemed to be present, something absent from all their dinners at home together, something which imposed a sort of self-awareness of their particular situation. Being out in public. It seemed to arbitrarily place boundaries on their normal interactions with each other, each having to take extraordinary care not to appear overtly affectionate. And the fact of the matter was, it all was done entirely without conscious thought or effort, just a natural and instinctive distancing that took place due to the intimate nature of the setting.

"You seem quiet tonight." Jess sipped her after-dinner café au lait.

"Just a little tired, I think. It's been a long day." Robin looked across the table at Jess and smiled. "Especially since I got to the office so early this morning. You know, I'm definitely not a morning person." The smile turned into a full grin.

"Is that so? I hadn't noticed." Jess responded dryly.

"Just as long as you don't get used to it. I just went in early today to get caught up on some things before the long holiday, but it's not going to be a regular occurrence." Robin finished her chocolate mousse dessert.

A dark eyebrow shot up playfully. "So, no more roses, then?"

"I didn't say that," Robin winked.

"Good, because I'd still be susceptible to any and all buttering up techniques." Jess motioned the waiter over to request the check. "You can feel free to butter away, if you'd like."

"I'll keep that in mind." Robin chuckled and then looked over to Jess as the soft candlelight highlighted her striking features. Robin almost, for a split second, reached across the table to lightly grasp Jess's hand, but before the thought even became conscious, Robin looked away, finding other things in the restaurant of seemingly great interest. Had Robin acted on the impulse, the irony of the situation was that the waiter would have chosen that exact moment to return with the check. The waiter did, in fact, return with the check and Jess paid for the meals, leaving a hefty tip in the process.

"Let's go." Jess stood up and headed toward the door with Robin following closely.

As they reached the main entrance and lobby area, a familiar voice called to them from the restaurant bar. "Hey, Jess, Robin." They both turned around instinctively at the same time to see Harry and his wife Barbara seated at a small table in the bar area. Harry stood up and motioned them both over to their table.

Jess waved and acknowledged him, and then spoke to Robin, somewhat apologetically. "Let's just go over and say hello, and then we'll leave, okay?"

"Sure." Robin nodded a bit unenthusiastically and followed Jess over to where Harry and Barbara Roberts were seated.

"Well, if it isn't the best team of litigators our firm's seen in a long time." Harry grinned. "Fancy seeing you guys here. What's the occasion?" He was merely making conversation.

"Hello, Harry. Nothing special. Robin and I just left the office a little while ago and thought we'd check this place out for a nice meal." Jess tried not to be too specific with her answer.

"Good, good. You remember my wife, Barbara?"

Jess smiled politely. "Yes, we've met a couple of times at some of the firm functions. It's nice to see you again, Barbara. And this is Robin Wilson, one of our new associates."

Robin gave Barbara Roberts a courteous nod. "It's nice to meet you, Mrs. Roberts."

"It's a pleasure to meet you, too, Robin, and it's good seeing you again, Jessica." Barbara Roberts' manners were impeccable.

"Care to join us for a drink?" Harry motioned for Jess and Robin to have a seat.

Jess cast a slight glance toward Robin and then declined his offer gracefully. "Thanks, Harry, but we were just heading out. It's been a long day for the both of us. Another time?"

"Sure. How was the meal?" Harry politely inquired.

"Very nice, thanks." Jess turned to leave, lightly guiding Robin ahead of her. "Have a nice dinner. Goodnight." Jess and Robin exited the restaurant bar.

If Barbara Roberts considered her observations upon her brief encounter with the two women, she never mentioned a word of it to her husband.

****

Jess pulled her silver Mercedes up to the front of Robin's apartment building to drop her off after their dinner together. "Thanks for joining me tonight."

"Will you come up?" Robin asked a bit shyly.

Jess idled the car. "Not if you're too tired."

"I'm not." Robin lightly touched Jess's arm. "Come up for a little while." She almost pleaded.

"Alright." Jess turned off the ignition and got out of the car, following Robin up to her apartment.

Once inside, Robin turned on the lights and sat down on the fluffy sofa, kicking off her shoes in the process. "It feels good to finally relax." She put her feet up on the coffee table and sank back into the cushions.

"You do seem a bit tense." Jess joined her on the sofa.

Robin nodded. "I think I'm just a little nervous about Harry seeing us at the restaurant."

"Why?"

"I don't know." Robin became pensive. "It might seem unusual for us to be there."

"Trust me, Harry thought nothing about it." Jess removed her shoes and placed her feet up on the coffee table, as well.

"I hope so." Robin let out a faint sigh.

Jess turned to look at Robin with a bit of concern. "There's something else, isn't there?"

"You know me so well." Robin gave a small, almost sad smile and shifted her position toward Jess. "I'm leaving on Wednesday morning to go to Detroit for Thanksgiving." She looked down at the fabric on the sofa and traced a small pattern with her finger. "I don't want to go back there."

Jess didn't know what to say. "How long will you be gone?"

"I'll be back Saturday evening." Robin leaned her head on Jess's shoulder and spoke in a distant voice. "Will you tell me that everything's going to be okay?"

Jess wrapped a long arm around Robin's shoulders and hugged her to herself tightly. "As long, as I'm around, kiddo, I promise you, it will be okay." She smiled warmly and gave Robin a light kiss on the lips. "I promise."

And at that precise moment, wrapped in Jess's protective embrace, Robin had the distinct feeling that everything would indeed be alright. All of the pain, the sorrow, and the guilt that had been gnawing at her so strongly for the past several days, seemed to ease somewhat as she sat cozily on the sofa curled up next to Jess. *It's amazing how I always feel better when she's here.* "What are you going to do for the holiday?"

"Going to my mom's in Tampa. My brother and his wife and kids will be there. It's always a lot of fun when we get together." Jess smiled at the memories.

"I'm glad you have some place to go. I was worried that you might be here by yourself." Robin crossed one ankle over one of Jess's and leaned into the embrace further.

"Nope, I'm good." Jess sat silent for a moment, fingering the collar of Robin's silk blouse, then spoke again. "I hope things go okay for you in Michigan." She really didn't know what, specifically, Robin was worried about, but she had a general idea. "Will you need a ride to the airport?"

Robin shook her head. "No, I'm driving myself there. Besides, you'll be at work." She laid her head back against the cushions and stared into concerned blue eyes. "I'll manage just fine, and I do know how to get to the airport. You don't need to worry about me."

I always worry about you. "If you say so." Jess offered a small smile. "But call anyway, if you change your mind."

"Thanks, I will." A moment's pause. "Thanks for dinner tonight, Jess. It was a lovely restaurant." Robin smiled warmly. "Of course, the company wasn't so bad, either."

"Good, because there's plenty more where that came from." Jess touched her finger to Robin's nose and attempted to lighten the mood. "And as I recall, I believe my task for this evening was to convince you that your ploy to butter up the so-called slave-driver boss was working. So, are you convinced yet?"

Robin turned fully so that she was leaning entirely against Jess's body, bracing herself with her forearm resting on the back cushion. She traced a delicate finger over a strong jaw and whispered. "Perhaps more buttering up is in order." With that, Robin, pressed her lips to Jess's, tenderly at first, and then slightly more forcefully.

Jess returned the kiss in kind, reveling in the feel of the weight of Robin's body on her own, and the indescribable sense of some indefinable inner connection that passed between them at the contact. The kiss turned into a series of kisses, very long and very slow and deliberate, but as always before, they were not deep. After several moments, Jess pulled away slightly and grinned. "Buttering up is good."

"I'm glad you think so." Robin punctuated that statement with another light kiss. "Have I told that you do that really well?"

"Do what?"

Robin gently brushed her fingers lightly across Jess's lips. "Kiss. I think you definitely get points for your efforts in that department."

"Is that so?" Smiling blue eyes stared into green. "And how is my point progress coming along?"

Robin grinned. "You're winning."

"I am?" Jess stroked Robin's short blonde hair

"Yes."

"And just so I'm perfectly clear on the matter, what exactly do I win?"

Robin tilted her head slightly. "You keep trying to get me to tell you what your prize is. Like I told you before, I can't tell you specifically, but it will definitely be worth your effort."

"So you say. Can't you at least give me a little hint?" Jess reached up and placed a light kiss on Robin's forehead, and then her cheek.

Robin stared thoughtfully at the wall behind Jess's head, pretending to ponder the question seriously, then looked directly into blue eyes. "Nope."

"Well, then, you might just have to provide me with a little more incentive, lest I lose interest."

Robin bent her head and nibbled on a convenient earlobe and then whispered softly. "Jess, I can personally guarantee that you will definitely not lose interest."

Oh boy. Jess swallowed audibly and cleared her throat. "I see. Um...well, it's getting pretty late, you know."

"I know." Robin shifted her weight off Jess to sit directly on the sofa. "I should let you go home."

"Yeah. Do me a favor, though?" Jess sat upright and put on her shoes. "Promise me you'll call me at any time this weekend if you need to. If I'm not here, I'm in Tampa. I'll give you the phone number to my mother's house."

Robin stood up and walked Jess over to the door. "Okay, I promise." She placed her hand on the brass doorknob but did not open the door. "I'll miss you."

Jess stepped forward and wrapped Robin in a tight embrace. "I'll miss you, too, kiddo. I'll see you tomorrow at work, right?"

"I'll be there." Robin reached up and gave Jess a lingering kiss, and then watched as Jess stepped outside the door and made her way down the stairs. "Goodnight, Jess. Drive safely." Robin stood in the doorway as Jess got into her car and pulled out of sight, the red tail lights finally disappearing around the bend. Robin walked back inside, her thoughts many miles away, as she mentally began the process of determining what to pack for her trip. *This week cannot be over soon enough.*

****

Robin stepped off the jet way and into the Detroit airport, the chilly air hitting her squarely before a blast of heated air came her way from the airport's gate area. She glanced around and finally spotted her mother and father off to one side waiting patiently for the passengers to disembark the plane. Robin strode over to them.

"Hi, Robin, honey, how was your flight?" Colette Wilson hugged her daughter. "Did they feed you?"

"Hi, Mom. The flight was fine and I did get lunch earlier." Robin turned to her father. "Hi, Dad."

"Hi, honey." Thomas Wilson gave her a hug. "Let me take your bag."

"Let's get you home and I'll fill you in on all the plans for Thanksgiving. I'm so glad you decided to come home." Colette Thomas rattled on about everything and nothing in particular as they made their way through the airport terminal and on to the car.

When they arrived at the Wilson home, Robin took her things upstairs into her old room and unpacked. The room was just as she had left it. The desk where she used to study, the old stereo, the old high school yearbooks, and all of her childhood things lay still as they had so many years before. Nothing was out of place and everything was the same. It was as if it was all from another lifetime ago. But the reality was, it wasn't. Robin went over to the dresser, and opened one of the top drawers. Inside was everything she most wanted to forget. Letters, mementos, a class ring, a varsity letter, and pictures. Lots of pictures. She shut the drawer abruptly and proceeded to unpack and put her clothes away, hanging most of her things in the closet. Once finished, she sat on the bed and pulled a piece of paper out of her wallet. It contained one very important phone number. She stared at the number for several moments in silent debate. *I want to call.* But she resisted the urge.

Thanksgiving would be stressful enough, the family gatherings always taxing. But she knew there was one particular thing she had to do while she was in Detroit. The one thing that would probably be the most difficult thing she would ever have to do. Robin got up from the bed and walked back over to the dresser, opening the top drawer once again. She lifted out a black velvet box and opened it, revealing a gold and diamond ring. Lifting the ring out of the case, she slowly fingered the beveled cut surface of the diamond. *We picked this out together.* She had never worn it. It had arrived a week after the accident. Their parents had planned the engagement party for the following week, which, of course, never took place. Robin sighed and reached inside the drawer once again, pulling out a photograph. *David.* He was handsome and tall with sandy blonde hair, hazel eyes, and a wide smile on his face as he stood with his black Labrador Retriever, Buddy. Robin looked at the picture for a moment and then lifted out another photograph from the drawer. It was one of herself and David together by the lake. She looked so happy then. She wondered if she ever was really as happy as she looked in the picture. Sighing heavily, Robin quickly replaced all the items in the drawer, and went back over to the bed to lie down, curling up on the edge. Her eyes tracked to the piece of paper with the phone number lying on the nightstand. *I want to call.* But she resisted the urge again.

As she lay on the bed, tightly curled up, waves of sorrow and guilt made their way mercilessly over her. If only she hadn't been so selfish. If only she had tried to work things out instead of getting upset. If only she hadn't said those horrible things to him. If only. Things would have been different. He never would have left so angry and he would still be alive. She felt her eyes well up. Tomorrow she would go. She hadn't gone before. The service had left her too emotionally upset. The hearse took him away and she never said goodbye. And she never went back to visit him. Ever. So, tomorrow she vowed to herself that she would finally go. Finally. To tell him goodbye and to say that she was sorry. Maybe it was closure she needed, or maybe the feelings would never go away. She wondered if she would she ever be able to put everything in the past and move forward. A single tear now tracked its way down her cheek and she looked over again at the piece of paper with the phone number written on it. *I want to call.* But she resisted the urge yet another time and instead, clutched the piece paper in her hand, finally falling into an uneasy rest.

****

"Robin, honey, tell me about how you're doing all the way down there in Florida." Colette Wilson poured herself another cup of tea. "Your father and I have been so worried about you down there all alone."

Robin sighed. *I'm not alone.* "I'm fine, mom. My job is great. I'm working on a trial which will take place in a couple of weeks, and I really enjoy it."

Colette nodded. "Yes, I'm sure you do. But we were thinking that maybe you should come back here. You could get a job at a local law firm here in town. Your father has many connections."

Robin finished her breakfast. "Mom, I like it in Florida and I want to stay."

"But your family is here, dear. And don't you miss all your friends?"

"I have friends in Florida." Robin really did not want to continue this conversation.

"Well, we're worried about you. It's a big adjustment for you to be so far away. Your friends in Florida don't understand everything that's happened." Colette began the preparation of the turkey.

"Mom, please. I'm staying in Florida. I'm doing fine and I've talked about everything with a friend there. My friend understands." Robin finished her coffee.

"Well, let's not worry about it now. We'll discuss it some more when you're here at Christmas time."

Christmas? "Mom, I want to stay in Florida for Christmas." Robin stated it a bit defiantly, and mentally braced herself for the expected reaction.

"What?" Colette looked up from her turkey preparation in surprise. "I thought you'd want to spend the holidays with your family."

The guilt trip starts. "Mom, I'm here now. There is no reason for me to come back in another month. I want to spend Christmas in Florida this year." Robin got up from the breakfast table and started to head out of the kitchen.

Colette called back to her. "Well, if you insist on staying down there at Christmas time, then perhaps your father and I will come visit you."

Robin stopped dead in her tracks and slowly turned around. "You would come to Florida?"

"Yes, of course. We'd like to see where you live and you can show us where you work. We'll have a nice time." Colette finished stuffing the bird.

Robin now turned fully to face her mother. "You and dad always go to Aunt Martha's for Christmas."

"Yes, but this year, we can do something different. Your Aunt Martha will understand. We'll see her another time." Colette considered the discussion closed and placed the bird in the oven.

Robin allowed a brief scowl to cross her features. *Great. This is not exactly what I had in mind for Christmas.*

Setting the oven timer, Colette glanced at the wall clock. "Now, remember, we're eating at 3:00 today, so if you have any plans, please be back before then."

Robin took in a deep breath. "Actually, I was wondering if I could borrow the car. There's someplace I wanted to go today."

"Of course, dear. Take the sedan." Colette next began to prepare the candied sweet potatoes, mumbling quietly to herself. "I thought for sure I had cinnamon."

Her disposition a bit sullen, Robin quickly made her way up the stairs to her room and threw herself onto the bed, mentally preparing herself for the day's events. She groaned to herself. *I am so not in the mood for this.* She was tempted just to put everything off and go back to sleep, but avoidance, of both her family and the other matter she vowed to take care of, was simply not the answer.

****

It was a short time later that Robin found herself driving down the winding road, around the spreading oak trees and the small serene lake, back into a recently opened grassy area. The markers were placed flatly on the ground, surrounded by the perfectly manicured green lawns. *How do they keep it so green in the wintertime?* She knew where to find him, having gotten the directions many times before, but in the end, she never had been able to bring herself to go. One particular time, she had actually found herself at the entranceway to the cemetery, staring down the winding driveway, willing herself the courage to go inside. But as was always the case, she had felt an overwhelming sickness come over her at the thought of seeing where he lay, and couldn't bring herself to drive through the gate, instead turning the car around without even so much as stepping outside. But here she was today. Thanksgiving day. She thought about that. What was there to be thankful for? She suddenly had a thought, something which she felt betrayed him and his memory, and so she quickly shoved that particular thought back into the recesses of her mind, and set herself to the matter at hand.

Robin parked the car and walked over to the designated marker, kneeling down on the green grass a little off to the side. As she gently fingered the brass nameplate, a few small tears escaped her eyes, and she had to fight with herself not to just get up and run away. Again. She quietly composed in her mind what she wanted to say to him, hoping that the act of saying what she needed to say would somehow bring her some measure of peace. And so, having gathered her thoughts together, she began.

"Hi, David." She whispered softly and then paused. "I'm sorry it's taken me this long to come visit you. I wanted to come and tell you about a few things. I've been trying to start my life over. It hasn't been easy, but I've got a great job now at a law firm in Florida. Florida is warm and sunny most of the time. No snow. You would like it." She smiled. "I also wanted to tell you how sorry I am for the things I said to you that night. I didn't mean any of them." The teardrops fell faster, and she looked up at the clouding sky trying to place her emotions under control. Robin fingered the brass nameplate again, and then reached into her purse and pulled something from it. "I have something to return to you. I'll send it to your folks, but I thought I would tell you, first." She held the small velvet box in her palm and opened the lid. "I remember when we picked this out. You wanted to have this one specially made for me." Robin ran her thumb over the oval diamond setting. "It's beautiful, and I will always remember it." She stopped for a short moment, then continued. "But, David, I can't keep it." She set the box down on the grass by the marker.

"I met somebody in Florida who's helped me to adjust." Robin absently looked down at her restless fingers. "Her name is Jess, and she's been wonderful to me. We get along so well. She works at the law firm I'm with now." Robin paused again. "I love her, David. Does that seem strange to you? Sometimes it seems strange to me, but it doesn't change the fact that I do. She makes me happy. I want you to know that you will always hold a special place in my heart, but I want to move on with my life now. I think you would want that, too." Robin once again picked up the black velvet box, looking for a moment at the diamond ring still resting inside, and then with an apparent and deliberate finality, snapped shut the lid, and in the process, snapping shut that chapter of her life which the object represented. She brought her fingertips to her lips, placed a gentle kiss on them, and then brought her fingers back down to rest against the brass marker. "Goodbye, David."

She wiped the remaining tears from her eyes and stood to leave, turning around abruptly. As she took her first step away from the grave, she saw them. They came up the short pathway, as they had no doubt done countless times before, and made their way solemnly over to the grave where Robin was standing. Robin froze. She hadn't expected to see them, and now, here they were, and here she was. As they approached, they looked up and saw her standing there.

"Robin, is that you?" David's mother came up to Robin and gave her a gentle hug. "How have you been, dear?"

"Alright. Thank you, Mrs. Mitchell." Robin stood awkwardly. "Mr. Mitchell, it's good to see you, sir."

"Yes, Robin, it's good to see you, too." Mr. Mitchell's voice was soft.

"We heard you've moved. Florida, isn't it?" Mrs. Mitchell seemed genuinely interested.

"Yes. I accepted an offer with a law firm in Orlando. It's a good job. I'm here for the holiday, then I'll go on back." Robin glanced at a nearby tree and spoke softly. "I wanted to visit him while I was here."

Mrs. Mitchell took Robin's hand. "Of course you did. I know he would be happy that you've continued on with your dreams. Davey was very proud of you."

Robin fought with her emotions. "I have something I wanted to give to you." She pulled out the small velvet box and looked at David's parents. "I was wondering if you would take this. I can't keep it. I mean...it's hard for me to have it. I was thinking maybe you could donate it or do something good with it. I wanted you to decide." She handed the box to David's mother. "Whatever you decide to do is okay with me."

"Are you sure, Robin?" His mother took the box and held it for a moment.

"Yes. Please, I want you to have it." Robin smiled slightly, and then focused her attention back to the brass nameplate, whispering softly. "I still miss him." She turned toward where her car was parked. "I should go now so you can visit. It was good to see you."

"Alright, dear." Mrs. Mitchell gave Robin another hug. "Please take care of yourself. Tell your parents hello for us."

"I will." Robin started walking toward the car, and when she was almost half-way there, she turned back around and watched the Mitchells from a distance. *Look at them.* Mrs. Mitchell stood stoically, while David's father stood beside her, his shoulders noticeably slumped and his head bowed. *He lost his son.* He had barely spoken a word, and Robin felt that he was still stricken with grief over the loss. She walked over to the car and got inside, then stared silently at the two figures in the distance. She rested her forehead against the steering wheel and the tears started to fall all over again. *It's my fault.*

****

Jess had returned from Tampa the previous evening, having had quite an enjoyable time with her family, and now debated with herself as to whether she should go into the office to catch up on a little work. Today was Saturday, and Jess had not heard from Robin at all since she left for Michigan. That being the case, Jess reasoned that things were most likely going okay with her. Robin was, after all, with her family. Family was important, as Jess well knew, and it was good that Robin had her family to turn to. It was all good. Very good. Jess sat on the plush sofa and began packing her briefcase and organizing her paperwork. As much as she tried to convince herself that everything was alright, her internal voice kept nagging at her just the same, until she finally gave in to the insistent niggling.

You know something's wrong, don't you?

'Don't be ridiculous. Everything's fine. Go away.' The alternate

internal voice was annoyed at the intrusion into an otherwise peaceful day.

You can feel it, though, can't you? You know when something's wrong, and something is definitely wrong.

'No, I said everything's fine. Robin promised she'd call if she needed to. She didn't call, so therefore, everything's fine.' The alternate internal voice ran the logic unconvincingly.

She told you she didn't want to go. Admit you're worried.

'What part of everything's fine don't you understand?' The alternate internal voice was now quite belligerent.

You can't ignore it.

'I can if I want.' Denial was certainly a strong suit.

But you're still a little bit worried, just the same.

'I am not worried.' The alternate internal voice became increasingly agitated. *'Okay, maybe a little worried. So what?'*

You think she's not over him.

'You're certainly blunt. She said she loves me, okay? That implies she's over him.' The alternate internal voice drew the conclusion quite well.

Then you're deluded.

'Listen, buddy, there's no need for insults. I am not deluded.'

Aren't you? There's a lot going on with her past that she hasn't come to terms with.

'She said she's handling it.' The alternate internal voice tried to reason.

You don't really believe that. You think you're competing with a ghost.

'No. She said she loves me.' The alternate internal voice sounded as though that statement alone made everything alright.

While that may be true, what if she's not over him? What if she needs to stay with her family and come to terms with her loss in her own time? What will you do, then?

The alternate internal voice became defiant and did not want to continue on with the current conversation. *'She won't stay there, she's coming back, and she's over him. End of story.'*

But you don't know that for sure. She might just be running away from the memories. Even if she does come back, she might not stay here long.

'Boy, you're persistent. She said she loves me.' The alternate internal voice reiterated. *'She'll stay here.'*

Are you sure of that?

'Yes. She said she loves me.' The alternate internal voice reiterated again, this time with a bit of uncertainty.

It might not be enough.

'It is.' The alternate internal voice then became defiant once more. *'As I've said before, she said she loves me. Do I have to spell it out for you?'*

But even if she said she loves you, it's possible it might not be enough. Just think about that.

A moment's consideration of the previous statement, as requested. *'Alright, I take your point.'* The alternate internal voice held a bit of resignation. *'It's possible it might not be enough.'*

And so you're worried.

'Okay, I'm worried.'

Because she might not be over him.

'Yes.' The alternate internal voice held a tad bit of jealousy. *'Nothing escapes you, does it?'*

And she might not stay here.

'Yes.' The alternate internal voice now answered sadly.

Even though she said she loves you.

The alternate internal voice answered even more sadly. *'Yes.'*

So, it's inevitable, then. She'll eventually leave you in the end. It's just a matter of time.

The alternate internal voice was quiet for a very long moment. *'I'd rather not think about that.'*

And that's exactly why you're deluded. You should indeed be thinking about that.

The alternate internal voice shut the door soundly on the matter. *'You don't know what you're talking about. I am very content in my thinking on this matter. As I said before, everything's fine. Now, go away and leave me alone.'*

Jess immediately got up from her position on the sofa and walked abruptly out the door, leaving at once for the office. Denial was not just a river in Egypt.

****

It was well past the dinner hour when Jess returned home that evening from the office, having buried herself in her work for the majority of the day. She entered the house, immediately remembering that Robin was due home that night. She checked her answering machine for messages. There were none. Jess, of course, took this as a sign that everything was perfectly alright and mentally reminded herself to call Robin first thing in the morning. She took a frozen dinner out of the freezer and popped it into the microwave, deciding to eat quickly, watch a little TV, and then go to bed early. Once she finished eating, she stretched herself out on the plush sofa, and flipped on the television. She had just about dozed off when the phone rang. Startled, she reached a long arm out to pick up the cordless receiver.

"Hello." Jess's mind was foggy.

"Jess?" It was Robin's voice, albeit a bit shaky.

"Robin?" Jess sat up. "Where are you?"

"I'm here. Actually, I'm at the airport. I just got in." Robin's voice still sounded a little shaky.

"Are you alright?"

There was a long silence.

"Robin?" Jess became concerned.

"I'm here."

"Are you alright?"

"Um...." Robin's voice sounded distant. "Can I come over? I don't want to go home to an empty apartment just now."

"Yes. Do you want me to pick you up?"

Robin blew out an audible breath over the phone line. "No, I have my car. I'll be there in a half an hour, okay?"

"Okay. I'll be waiting." And with that, Jess clicked off the receiver and promptly began pacing, counting the minutes as they passed tediously by. Robin had definitely sounded upset. *Jess, you're quite the idiot, aren't you?* She paced back and forth. *How could you try to convince yourself that everything was alright?* A million thoughts ran through her mind, not the least of which was imagining that Robin was going to leave, and was coming over to tell her of her decision. *Damn.* Jess paced some more, and became more and more agitated as the minutes slowly and agonizingly ticked on, letting her mind conjure up all possible and assorted scenarios, none of which were pleasant. Jess looked over again at the clock on the wall for the thousandth time. *Where is she?* After another long moment of pacing, she heard a light knock sound at the front door.

She immediately rushed into the foyer, almost tripping over her briefcase in the process, and opened the door. "Robin."

Green eyes locked onto blue as the door opened. Robin stood there, hands fidgeting slightly, and not moving one inch from the doorstep. "Hi."

Surprised by the apparent hesitation, Jess quickly motioned Robin inside and closed the door. Before Jess could turn back around completely, the petite body rushed to hers and crushed her in a fierce embrace, clinging on as if for dear life, and not letting go. Jess put her arms around the small frame, holding on just as tightly, rocking them both gently back and forth. It was such an incredible feeling, holding onto each other so desperately close, as if trying to merge themselves into one being, afraid of letting the other go.

After several minutes tucked in Jess's comforting embrace, Robin finally spoke. "I missed you so much."

Jess kissed the top of the blonde head. "I missed you, too, sweetheart." She led Robin over to the plush sofa, turned off the television with the remote control, and sat down. "How are you? How was your trip?" She held Robin's hand and gently pulled her down alongside her onto the sofa.

"I've been better." Robin sat down beside Jess and then released her hand.

"Was your flight bad? I know you sometimes have a hard time." Jess momentarily thought that this was the problem.

"No." Robin smiled. "It was okay." *I feel better just being here.* "I feel so stupid. I just didn't want to go home to my empty apartment. That's all." She lied.

That's all? Jess squinted her eyes and stared at Robin for a long moment, studying the green eyes and locking them into an intense gaze. She slowly and very deliberately shook her head. "No, that's not all. Tell me?"

Robin tore her gaze from Jess and shifted her eyes to rest on the darkened fireplace, seeing, in actuality, absolutely nothing. Tears began to make their way from Robin's eyes. "I...I can't."

Jess's heart sank. All her fears were coming true. Robin was leaving. Jess lifted a shaking hand to Robin's chin and turned Robin's face toward her own, caressing the small cheek. "Robin, please tell me." She whispered the plea bravely, already afraid of the answer, and trying desperately to keep her emotions in check.

Robin quickly wiped the straying tears from her eyes, regaining her composure somewhat, and took Jess's hand in her own and entwined their fingers together. She spoke very softly. "I don't know how to tell you about this. I'm afraid you might not understand."

Jess unconsciously clenched their joined hands tighter and stiffened, bracing herself for the inevitable. "I'm listening."

"I went to visit him."

Visit him? Jess's expression became puzzled. "Who?"

"David."

Jess sat back against the sofa, not exactly knowing what to say to that. "You went to the...."

"Cemetery." Robin finished. "You're going to think this is awful of me, but it's the first time that I ever went there." She sighed heavily. "I tried to go many other times before, but I never could make myself actually do it." She paused. "This time, I did."

Jess nodded slowly and then brushed her thumb back and forth over the inside of Robin's palm in a calming motion. "You needed to visit him, right?" Jess wasn't sure she was putting it all together correctly.

"Yes. It was hard, but it was something I had to do. There was something I had to say to him." *How much do I tell her?* "I wanted to tell him that I was sorry, and I wanted to say goodbye." Robin shook her head. "I never told him goodbye."

Jess was beginning to see the picture now, and she wasn't at all sure it was something she really wanted to see. *She's never let go*. "You needed to do that."

Robin nodded. "There's something else." She glanced at Jess to gauge her reaction. "I told him that I couldn't keep the ring. I kept it until now, but...." Her voice trailed off. "You must think it's strange that I kept it all this time. I told him I was going to send it to his parents, but when I was leaving, they came there." Now, Robin's voice broke down, and the tears came quickly as she wiped them away with a shaking hand. "They looked so sad. I gave his mother the ring and I left right away. I couldn't let them see."

Jess reached her free hand over to gently wipe a tear from Robin's cheek and whispered. "See what, honey? What didn't you want them to see?"

"How guilty I was." Robin was inconsolable.

Jess collected Robin in her arms and held her close. "Oh, honey. Shhhh. Please, Robin. We've been through this. Honey, it wasn't your fault. It was an accident, that's all. It wasn't your fault." Jess's words weren't having any effect. *This is not a surprise to you, Jess. You knew she hadn't come to terms with this.*

Jess did her best to comfort Robin, and after a very long time, Robin's sobs subsided and she rested in the quiet embrace of Jess's arms. It was strange, but for Robin, telling Jess had lightened her heart somewhat. And she felt so safe and protected wrapped in the strong embrace, that she never, ever wanted to leave. There was one more thing she wanted to say, and so she lifted her head and gazed into beautiful blue eyes and whispered. "I also told him about you."

"You did?"

"Yes. I told him that I was happy." Robin grasped Jess's hand and lightly kissed the knuckles. "And I told him that I love you."

Jess nodded absently, not knowing whether to trust what Robin was saying. *She says she loves you, Jess, but it might not be enough.* For some inexplicable reason, Jess's eyes welled up with unshed tears, and she quickly turned her head away from Robin in embarrassment.

Robin was startled by the abrupt change in demeanor. "Jess, what's wrong?"

"Nothing." Her voice broke. "I don't want to upset you more." She refused to turn back to face Robin.

"But you're upset, and that does upset me more. What is it?" Robin shifted to look at Jess, but Jess continued to avoid the gaze. "Don't shut me out." Robin pleaded.

Jess closed her eyes tightly, as if in pain, and then opened them again and turned her head to stare very sadly into confused green eyes. She sat silently for a moment before speaking. "I don't think you're over him." A teardrop fell involuntarily. "I think you need to come to terms with what happened, and when you do that, I think you will realize that I was a convenient substitute, and you will eventually leave." Jess hated to be harsh but the truth was better out in the open.

Ouch. That stung. Robin swallowed hard. "You don't believe I love you?"

"I believe you believe you do, now."

Green eyes bore into blue. "But I will change my mind and leave? That's what you think."

"Yes." Jess looked away again, unable to withstand the intensity of Robin's gaze any longer.

Robin sat silently for a moment, then got up from the sofa and stepped over to stand in front of Jess. She looked down as Jess sat there, unable to make eye contact with her once more. *This has to do with James.* Robin slowly knelt in front of Jess, and reached out to place her hands lightly on either side of Jess's waist, leaning in slightly. She looked up and patiently waited as stoic blue eyes slowly tracked back to lock onto her own. She spoke calmly and with considered gentleness. "I don't know what to say to convince you that I will always love you and that I will never willingly leave you. I'm very sorry that James hurt you like he did, but I am not James, and I will not leave you." There was no expression on Jess's face so Robin continued. "I don't deny that I have issues to deal with when it comes to David. But I never saw you as a substitute for him, convenient or otherwise, and I never will." Robin reached up and brushed her fingers back and forth across Jess's cheek. "I'm going to tell you something now which may seem rather harsh, but it is the truth, and I can't change it." She paused, trying to find the right words. "If David were here right now, and if I had to make a choice between the two of you, and I know that this is not fair, but if I had to make that choice, I know who I would choose."

Jess looked at her and solemnly spoke for the first time in a long while. "You would choose him."

Robin lightly bit her bottom lip and shook her head very slowly, almost in dismay, and then whispered. "You are not listening to me." There was no hint of reproach in her voice. She now realized the depth of the hurt James had inflicted. Robin lifted Jess's hands, kissing the palms of each tenderly and with unequivocal reverence. She then slowly brought one large palm up to her own cheek, and held it there, covering it fully with her own hand. "It's you, Jess." She whispered. "Only you." Robin closed her eyes briefly, and as she did so, a silent tear fell.

And suddenly, at last, it all became so clear, and Jess finally saw it. She now saw what it was that was tormenting Robin so much. It was the guilt. Not only about the events leading up to David's accident, but also about loving Jess more. Jess immediately lifted Robin up from where she knelt and pulled her onto the sofa, leaning her back gently against the throw pillows. She laid down next to Robin and spoke soothingly, caressing a fair cheek. "Robin, I am so sorry for doubting you." Jess stroked Robin's blonde hair. "I am so very sorry. I was so consumed with my own fears that I didn't understand what you were really saying. Will you forgive me? I do understand now, and I'll help you through it, if you'll let me." She gently placed a kiss on Robin's soft lips. "I love you, Robin."

Robin closed her eyes and took in a deep breath. "Thank you for understanding." She placed a strand of dark hair behind Jess's ear. "I think I'd like maybe to talk with somebody...professionally about some things. I think I should do that. Do you know of anyone I can call?"

Jess smiled and brought her hand up to rest on Robin's shoulder. "Yes. We'll call on Monday, okay?"

"Okay." Robin nodded, then glanced shyly at Jess. "So, would it be alright if I stayed over tonight?"

Jess now grinned. "Well, I was hoping you'd want to stay. I've grown rather fond of having you in my bed."

Robin blushed. "You are incorrigible."

"Perhaps. But it doesn't change the fact that I want to be with you."

Robin blushed further. *What, exactly, are you saying?* "When you say that you want to be with me, do you mean....?" She wasn't quite sure how to phrase the question.

Jess chuckled at Robin's awkwardness. "Well, that too."

Robin hid her face behind her hands. "I am so embarrassed."

Jess removed one of Robin's hands. "Don't be embarrassed about that." She punctuated the sentiment with a small kiss. "When or if you're ready for anything more...physically, then tell me. And I promise, I'll tell you. Deal?"

Robin gave her a warm smile and sat up. "Deal. Now let me get my bag from the car. It's good I have all my stuff with me since I didn't go home first."

Robin got up and went to her car and retrieved her bag to change into her night clothes. It was a little chilly that evening, so Robin wore a fleece night shirt. Jess selected her flannel sleep shirt with matching draw-string boxers, and they set about their nightly routines. After Jess and Robin had both finished readying themselves for bed, Jess reset the temperature on the waterbed, and they both snuggled down under the covers. They cuddled together comfortably for a few moments, until Robin suddenly became all too aware of Jess's proximity.

"I could really get used to this." Robin sighed. "I think I already am." She stroked a flannel sleeve lightly.

"Me, too."

"Um...Jess?"

"Yes."

Robin thought about how to best put into words what she wanted to say, and finally just decided to simply state it as succinctly as possible. "I'm really close."

Jess opened her eyes in slight confusion. "Um...Robin, we're cuddled here close together. Of course, you're close."

"No."

"No?"

"No. I mean that you have me in your bed and I'm really close." It was no small thing for Robin to admit.

However, Jess, it seems, could not buy a clue. "You don't want to cuddle tonight? You need space?"

"Um...no. Let me explain it to you this way." Robin reached her hand down and directed it under the edge of Jess's flannel sleep shirt until it came to rest on Jess's bare stomach. She then brushed the soft, warm skin lightly, tickling slightly.

Jess inhaled sharply at the contact and then giggled. "Look

who's incorrigible, now." She grinned at the playfulness.

Robin stilled her hand and patted the bare stomach. "Perhaps. But it doesn't change the fact that I want to be with you." She paused for effect. "And that I'm really close."

I don't get it. Jess was particularly dense that night.

Robin removed her hand from Jess's stomach and turned over onto her side. "Since you said to tell you, I just thought I would."

I still don't get it. I don't get...Oh. The light was dawning. *Oh.* The light fully dawned. *Oh boy.* Jess swallowed. "Um...Robin?"

"Yes."

"Me, too." Jess was obviously not big on words that night either.

"You, too, what?" Robin grinned in the dark, determined to make Jess say it.

"Me, too, I'm really close, and I'm telling you."

"Okay. I'm glad we have that settled." Robin reached back a gave Jess a small pat on the thigh.

"Me, too." Jess apparently did not know many other words that evening. "Goodnight."

"Goodnight, Jess."

We're really close. Oh boy.

****

Robin stirred from her slumber to a strange sensation, and not being fully awake at the time, let herself linger in the space between wakefulness and sleep as the odd sensation persisted. As she became more fully aware, she registered that she was lying on her stomach and there was a slight, but fleeting, pressure on her back. It was certainly odd because the pressure would start and stop and then start up again. She finally brought herself to full consciousness and furrowed her brows, trying to determine its source.

A green eye opened and then squinted at the bright sunlight which filtered in through the Venetian blinds, trying to adjust to the light in the room as the gentle, fleeting pressure on her back continued. Robin opened her eyes more fully now to see amused blue eyes staring back at her. Jess was happily perched up on one elbow, looking down at her with a curious grin on her face.

"Hi, sleepyhead." The amused blue eyes regarded her.

"Hi." The fleeting pressure continued and Robin furrowed her brows again. As she studied the sensation, she also noted that Jess's arm appeared to be moving in direct proportion to the pressure she felt. "Um...Jess? What are you doing?"

The sensation stopped. "Who, me?" Jess asked innocently.

A chuckle. "Yes, you. What are you doing?"

"Nothing." The sensation resumed.

"Well, I'm pretty sure it's something."

The sensation stopped again. "Nope, nothing."

Another chuckle. "Then why did I feel something on my back?"

Oh, that." The sensation resumed.

"Yes that." Robin tried unsuccessfully to suppress a grin. "So, what are you doing?"

"Drawing."

"Drawing?"

"Yep. What do you think this is?" Jess traced an image on Robin's back with her finger.

"Um...a car?" Robin guessed.

"Nope. Try again." Jess traced the image another time.

Robin took another guess. "A boat?"

"Nope again. You have to concentrate." Jess drew the image for the third time. "I'll give you a little hint." She traced several words on Robin's back, as well.

Robin processed the writing. "Choo choo?" She chuckled. "You drew a train?"

"Very good." Jess grinned proudly.

"What is it with you and trains, anyway?"

"Nothing." Jess just couldn't resist the metaphor. "It just reminded me of a particular conversation we had about trains in general and how I especially like to ring the bell loudly and enthusiastically." She could barely contain the grin as she waited for Robin's reaction.

It didn't take longer than a full second before Robin caught on, and then she quickly threw the pillow over her head. "You led me right into that one before I was fully awake." The muffled voice came from under the down filling and linen fabric. "Not fair."

Jess was busily laughing, jiggling the water in the waterbed in the process. She lifted the pillow off Robin's head and leaned down next to her. "You are so cute." She then placed a light kiss on Robin's lips, brushing the mussed blonde hair with her fingers.

Robin rolled over onto her back. "Are you sure you want to be kissing me. I have morning breath, you know." She reached up and traced Jess's lips with her thumb.

"Good, because I have morning breath, too, so we're even." Jess stretched out fully on top of Robin and traced the small lips in a similar fashion. "I don't mind, if you don't mind."

"I don't mind." Robin reached up around Jess's neck and drew her toward her, kissing her soundly. She broke the kiss, and then stared into azure eyes for a moment, before claiming the lips once again. And this time, the kiss was different. Almost as if by mutual consent, the kiss deepened, and for the first time since they shared their first kiss, their kisses became long and slow, and now deep.

After several languid kisses, Jess broke away first, a lazy smile on her face. "Wow. That was amazing."

Robin took a moment to regain her senses and nodded. "Yeah. You taste very good, even if you do have morning breath."

"You taste good, too. I think we should do that more often." Jess leaned down and nibbled across a fair jaw line.

"I think you're right." Robin reached up and claimed the lips above hers once again in a repeat performance of the previous kisses.

They broke away once more and Jess slowly rolled off of Robin and onto the bed. "Could I interest you in some breakfast?"

Robin raised an eyebrow. "Do you have to ask?" She sat up and stretched.

"I stand corrected." Jess rolled out of bed. "There is eggs and toast and coffee, but not much else, since I need to hit the grocery store again. Meet me in the kitchen." She padded out of the room.

A short while later, Robin located Jess in the kitchen, dutifully fixing a breakfast of eggs and toast. "I see you have everything under control."

"Yep." Jess turned around, and then quickly glanced down at Robin's feet, suddenly laughing quite hysterically.

Robin followed Jess's glance. "Don't start with me, Jess. My feet are cold."

Jess tried to compose herself. "I think we have to have certain rules in this house, Robin. Rule number one, no bunny slippers."

"Very funny. I still say you're jealous because you don't have any. But if you'd rather I leave, I'll just take me and my bunny slippers on home." Robin chuckled and turned to exit the kitchen.

Jess reached out and playfully grabbed the back of Robin's night shirt. "Not so fast." She grinned. "I suppose we could have an exception to the rule just this once."

"Good." Robin went to the table and poured herself a cup of coffee, then looked around for the milk, finding none. "We're definitely going to have to take you grocery shopping, young lady. It seems you've been quite lacking in that department recently."

"Well, maybe I should just hire you to take care of all my

grocery needs from now on." Jess fixed the plates of eggs and toast and set them down on the table.

"You're always trying to get me to do your grunt work for you." Robin feigned exasperation.

Jess sat down and buttered her toast. "That's because you excel at all grunt work activities."

"Flattery will get you absolutely nowhere, Jess, so give it up." Robin took a bite. "I recommend an immediate grocery shopping refresher course, starting today."

"Today?"

"Yes, today. You're coming with me to the grocery store, so when I do my grocery shopping, which by the way is one of my Sunday chores, then you can do yours." Robin wagged a reprimanding finger at Jess. "And hopefully you will get into the habit of making your grocery shopping a priority from now on."

"I have a better idea." Jess took another bite. "I'll give you a list of grocery items, and when you're doing your shopping, you just pick up mine. Sounds simple enough."

"Yeah, I do all the work. That defeats the purpose of training you to do it yourself, Jess. I think you need a little hands-on experience." Robin thought about what she had just said, and before Jess could offer a snappy retort, Robin quickly responded, pointing her finger in warning. "Do not say it, Jess. Do not say it. I'm warning you. Do not say it."

"Who, me?" Jess arched a dark eyebrow innocently. "I wouldn't dream of it." She was, in all actuality, dying to say it and sat silently for a few moments stifling her reply.

"Good."

The snappy retort came anyway. "But I've never considered my so-called hands-on experience a prerequisite for grocery shopping, Robin. How do you figure that works?" She winked.

Robin shook her head flabbergasted. "You just couldn't let it go, could you? Just this once." Robin narrowed her eyes. "You are so hopeless."

"So you keep saying." Jess teased and then smiled sweetly. "You ought to know by now that it's an endearing character trait of mine."

"The jury's still out on that one, Jess."

"And since we're on the intellectually stimulating subject of grocery shopping 101, I wanted to ask you something." Jess became more serious.

"Okay." Robin poured herself another cup of coffee.

"I was wondering if you would think about something. You already have a key here, and I kinda like having you around, and not just for your grocery shopping expertise." Jess smiled a bit shyly. "What I'm trying to say, though not very well, is that I have three extra rooms. One is the guest room, another I use as an office, and the third I don't use at all. I was wondering if you would maybe consider living here. You could have any of the rooms you wanted. We'd just move everything around. I know you have your apartment and probably have several more months on your lease, and you have all your own things. But, you could live here though, if you wanted to. If you'd rather not, then that's okay, too. Will you think about it?" It was one of the longest questions Jess had ever asked.

Robin sat quietly, patiently listening as Jess completed her rather lengthy question. Robin had to ask herself, though, whether she was ready to live with someone else. *With Jess.* It would mean being together at work and at home, and sharing everything. Sharing a life. She thought about that. *Barely two weeks ago Jess wanted to slow down, and now she wants to live together.* Robin wasn't sure at the moment how she felt about that. Not to mention the fact that it might call attention to their relationship in ways she definitely was not ready to handle. She reached across the table and gently grasped Jess's hand. "I'll think about it, Jess. Thank you for asking."

"Okay. Just let me know whatever you decide." Jess attempted to act almost nonchalant about the whole thing.

Robin sought to lighten things up a little. "Um...Jess?" She looked at Jess with a semi-bored expression. "You wouldn't just be asking me to live here so you can have your own personal grocery shopping grunt, now would you?"

"Ah. I see you found me out. Would that have any bearing on your decision?" Jess raised both eyebrows playfully.

Robin considered the question. "I guess it depends on how much hands-on experience would be involved."

"I see. As a matter of fact, there would indeed be quite a bit of hands-on experience required."

Robin nodded, deep in thought. "Then, I imagine it might just influence my decision."

"Just as long as you're informed. I believe in full disclosure."

"I am fully apprised, counselor." Robin chuckled. "On a serious note, though, I do foresee that there may be at least, one, tiny little problem."

Jess furrowed her brows. "And what might that one, tiny little problem be?"

"Guess who's coming to visit?"

Jess looked at Robin out of the corner of her eye. "Who?"

"I'll give you a hint. They're from Detroit and they're related to me." *I think.*

Jess frowned. "Oh. And when would this be?"

"Christmas. So, I think whatever happens, I should still keep my apartment at least a little while longer because it might not be such a good thing for them to think I was living here."

Jess pouted. "Right."

"Jess." Robin smiled. "I said I should keep my apartment a little while longer. I didn't say I should sleep there."

"Right." Jess's expression brightened. "Right."

"Good. Now let's get going." Robin stood up to clear the breakfast dishes. "We have quite a bit of grocery shopping to do today." She and her bunny slippers padded out of the kitchen.

Grocery shopping, parents visiting, living together. Jess, you've absolutely lost your mind.

Chapter 7

Jess came in to work early Monday morning and made her way up the elevators to the Roberts & McDaniel office suite. Unfortunately, and much to her displeasure, she had a stack of client invoices waiting for her when she first stepped foot into her own office. *Is it the beginning of the month again?* She let out an audible groan. *Damn. Don't they know I have a trial?* She set her briefcase down and powered up her computer. Somewhat preoccupied, she sat down at her desk, and took a moment to gaze out the large floor to ceiling windows, watching as the early morning sun bathed the city in golden light. This was her favorite part of the day, and quite often allowed for some meditative and contemplative thinking. Today seemed to call for such contemplation.

Her mind reflected on the events of the past weekend, and she mentally chastised herself for her impulsiveness. *Living together? What the hell were you thinking, Jess?* But, that was just it, though. She wasn't thinking. She was feeling, and that was getting her into all kinds of trouble. If she and Robin lived together, it was just a matter of time before someone else found out about their relationship, or at least became suspicious, and then...then what? Then the firm would know, and if the firm knew, then there could be serious repercussions. *You're walking a fine line, here, Jess. Watch it.* It was true that she had avoided the issue for far too long. Ignoring it was not going to make it go away. It was time for some serious thinking on the matter. The computer beeped signaling that her e-mail messages had finally loaded, and she briefly lost her train of thought. She took a moment to send Paul an e-mail reminding him to prepare a motion for her to review and sign before mid-week, and then she once again settled back into her burgundy leather chair and let her thought processes resume.

So, if the firm found out about their relationship, there could be repercussions. How serious the repercussions would be was still up in the air. Robin would be fine, though. It was Jess that stood to lose, here. *I'm the senior party. I take all the risk.* Then again, even if the firm knew, she might be able to work around their concerns. Jess thought about that. The firm's concerns would mainly revolve around the issues of favoritism and lack of objectivity. *I know that I can't be objective when it comes to Robin.* Jess picked up her pen and tapped it lightly on the cherry wood desk, mentally considering whether it all was worth it. Was her relationship with Robin worth the risk? Surprisingly, without much thought at all, Jess had her answer.

Yes.

The clang of the early morning freight train passing sixteen floors below chose that particular moment to make itself heard, and despite Jess's seemingly definitive answer to the previous question, mental alarms went off inside her mind. She lifted an eyebrow and stared out the window at the rooftop of the building next door, warring internally over a nebulous thought, as the clanging of the freight train droned incessantly on. Her mind, once again, gave in to the errant thinking.

You should be very proud of yourself.

'I thought I told you to go away.' The alternate internal voice was a bit testy this morning.

Well, it seems you've been quite the selfish one.

'I don't know what you're talking about.' The alternate internal voice initially attempted evasion.

Of course you do. You might be martyring your career. How noble of you.

'I have my moments.' The alternate internal voice became flippant.

But did you discuss all this with Robin?

'Don't need to. Robin will be fine. I'm the senior person involved. I take the risk.' The alternate internal voice pompously assumed all responsibility.

Is that so? She takes no risk? Wouldn't she feel guilty if something were to happen?

'I'll handle all that.' The alternate internal voice assured. *'It's my decision.'*

Your arrogance is not becoming. Don't you think she deserves to know what you've been keeping from her?

'Why, so she can worry? That serves no purpose.'

So, you don't think she should know the risk involved to you professionally? Is that it?

'I'm protecting her this way.' The alternate internal voice responded weakly.

That's irrelevant. You've been keeping this from her, and you've been doing so for quite some time. Why?

'Hello. Is anybody home in there? I already told you.' The alternate internal voice attempted mockery and reiterated the previous statement. *'I've been protecting her.'*

No, you've been selfish. Admit it.

'Listen, I don't have time for this. I have a trial next week. This will just have to wait. However, the alternate internal voice just couldn't resist trying to have the last word on the matter. *And I have not been selfish.'*

You aren't fooling anyone. You thought if she knew, her good heart would not permit your relationship to continue, knowing your career was at risk. So, you selfishly kept it from her.

'I have not been selfish.' The alternate internal voice protested vigorously.

You were afraid she'd end it, if she knew. You didn't want it to end.

'I was not being selfish.' The alternate internal voice was righteously indignant. '*I was protecting her.'*

If you believe that, then you are even more delusional than you were before.

'I have a headache, now. Are you happy?'

You need to come clean. Tell her everything and let her decide.

'It's turned into a full-blown migraine. I'm seeing spots.'

Tell her.

The alternate internal voice groaned. *'I'm feeling nauseous.'*

Tell her. Or do you want to persist with your selfishness?

'Is there something in the water, here? How many times do I have to tell you that I am not being selfish, I'm just protecting her?' The alternate internal voice, it seemed, simply refused to admit the obvious.

Fine. Call it what you want, but fix it, before things go any further.

'What do you mean, before things go any further?' The alternate internal voice feigned innocence.

You know perfectly well. You're getting 'really close.' Just think about what that means.

A moment's silence. *'Oh, alright.'* The alternate internal voice finally relented. *'You win. I'll tell her.'*

Good.

'Can I be sick, now?'

****

Robin sat bleary-eyed at her desk, having poured for hours over everything from financial records to deposition transcripts to calendar entries. The trial was the following week, and it seemed that she was no closer to finding what she called "the missing link," or the reason why the opposing side did not want the mystery witness to appear for deposition. *I know I'm missing something.* She swiveled in her chair almost playfully as she contemplated all known facts about the case. The opposition was accusing RSJ Industries of unfair trade practices in awarding bid contracts on new and prospective research and development initiatives for its pharmaceutical division. The opposing side, Grayson Carlton Corporation, was not awarded the bid on a particularly lucrative and experimental cancer treatment drug protocol project. Grayson Carlton was now claiming that the bids were fixed, and that RSJ virtually handed the contract to a well-known competitor in the field. Anne Carver, Grayson Carlton's comptroller, prepared the initial work-ups for the Grayson Carlton bid. RSJ, of course, denies all allegations of wrong doing. Be that as it may, Robin had the gut feeling that what she was looking for was right in front of her. The facts were the facts, but sometimes cases were won and lost on things other than the facts.

She finally put the documents aside, and stretched her arms high above her head, groaning at the stiffness the lack of activity for the better part of the day had caused. She shifted her head from side to side to shake out the cricks, and then powered down her computer, packing her briefcase with a few small items to take with her that she hadn't gotten around to during the day. She really wished that she had joined a health club when she arrived in the city so that she could work off some excess energy and help her mind to focus. But there hadn't been time for all that, so she satisfied herself that she would perhaps take a jog around the apartment complex instead, not entirely relishing the prospect. Considering that it was the first week in December, it had been exceptionally warm and rather humid. The city was preparing for the holidays, with Christmas tree vendors on practically every corner around town, and the weather, it seemed, simply refused to cooperate. *It's kind of hard to think about Christmas trees in 80 degree weather.*

Robin turned off the light to her office and made her way over toward the elevators. She intended to just get on the next elevator and head on home, but a curious yet somehow familiar magnetic pull caused her to take a slight detour mid-stride. She strode non-stop through the lobby and past the reception area, down the long hallway toward a certain office with a particular wood door partially closed. All staff had since departed and, save for the cleaning crew, most everyone had left the office. Robin knocked lightly on the door, hearing a mumbled response from inside, and then opened the door fully.

"Hi." Robin stuck her head inside the office. "Working late tonight?"

Jess looked up from her stack of client invoices and grimaced. "Unfortunately. I hate the beginning of the month." She sat back in her leather chair. "Come in for a minute."

Stepping inside the office, Robin closed the door and sat down in the chair by the window, idly noting that darkness had already enveloped the city, and mentally canceling her jogging plans. "It's been a long day."

The junior partner leaned forward, perching a slender elbow on the top of the cherry wood desk. "So, tell me how it's going. Anything yet?"

Robin could sense the slight urgency in the tone of the voice, and then blew out a breath in frustration. "Nothing." She ran her fingers through her short blonde hair. "I'm going home. I just can't look at that stuff any more tonight. Maybe tomorrow I'll have better luck." Robin fidgeted slightly. "I just feel so restless all of a sudden."

"Hey, I got some good news today." Jess changed the subject and stood up, walking over to her book shelves and pulling off a black three-ring binder.

"What is it?"

"After the trial next week, I was scheduled for another smaller trial the first week in January. I was actually going to ask you to help me with that one, as well, but I found out today that it's been continued until March. I'd still like you to help me with it, though." Jess flipped through the binder until she found the index. "This is the case binder, so after we get through this trial next week, feel free to come get this from me. I had one of the paralegals put it together. It has all the key documents, the key pleadings, the discovery responses, and the background search information. Just look it through, and then if you think there's something else we need to do, let me know. We have plenty of time, now." Jess looked at Robin apologetically. "I'm afraid I haven't paid much attention to this other case, with preparing for the current trial and all."

"No problem." Robin fidgeted again.

"Am I keeping you from something?" Jess asked concerned. "I didn't mean to keep you if you had something to do."

Robin shook her head. "No, I was going to go jog for a little while, but it's already dark outside. I wanted to get some exercise in. I guess I'll just have to plan better next time."

A dark eyebrow slowly arched. "Do you swim?"

"What?" Robin asked, quite perplexed.

"Do you swim?"

The associate considered the question. "Um...yes?"

Jess grinned decisively. "Well then, use my pool. You have the key and the alarm code. Just let yourself in."

Blonde eyebrows furrowed. "Um, Jess, it's December." She wondered if Jess hadn't been staring at client bills for just a little bit too long. "It'll be too cold, don't you think?"

"Nope." Jess looked quite pleased with herself.

"Nope? Why not?"

The junior partner now grinned smugly. "Heated pool."

"Oh." Robin appeared to be considering the idea. "You wouldn't mind?"

"Nope." Jess resumed her seat behind her desk. "Feel free to use it whenever you want. Just turn on the flood lights out back. The switch is just outside the sliding doors." She set the binder down precariously on the edge of her desk. "And Robin," she leaned forward, "if you get too chilly out there, there's a Jacuzzi inside you can use if you want." She smiled sincerely. "In other words, my house is your house, okay?"

Robin smiled. "Okay, thanks." She tilted her head to one side, appearing to contemplate something for a moment. "So, how late are you working tonight, anyway?"

Blue eyes narrowed. "Did you have something in mind?"

"Nope." Robin stood up and walked toward the door. "I'll just be swimming." She turned the door handle and then walked out of the office, quickly poking her head back around the corner a second later. "Or in the Jacuzzi." Robin winked and then disappeared around the corner again.

Oh my.

****

Jess pulled her silver Mercedes into the two-car garage and then entered the house, apparently finishing up with her billing chores in record time. A small light was on in the kitchen, and she made her way over to the sliding doors, seeing the flood of bright light shining in haphazardly through the glass. She stopped and looked out the glass doors into the screened-in enclosure to find a petite form swimming laps in the kidney-shaped pool, a blonde head rhythmically popping up and then back down under the surface of the aqua-blue water. Jess watched for a moment, then opened the door and stepped outside into the pleasant evening air. The swimmer was apparently oblivious to the watchful observer. Jess stood quietly, admiring how poised and strong the swimmer's strokes were, as they cut through the water with barely a ripple.

Robin continued with her laps for several moments before finally stopping and wiping the water from her face. She looked up through her somewhat chlorine cloudy eyes, and saw a tall figure standing in the corner by the sliding doors. "So, how long have you been watching me?" She grinned.

"Long enough," came the reply. "How long have you been at it?"

Robin swam over to the nearest edge of the pool. "I've been here about a half hour. Did you finish your work?"

"Yep. I whipped right through it. It seems I had some additional incentive to complete it rather quickly." Jess grinned and couldn't help but take notice of the sleek little aqua colored one-piece swimsuit Robin was wearing. "You seem to be an excellent swimmer."

"I took lessons since I was six." Robin splashed about a little and then swam the length of the pool underwater, coming up for air on the other side.

Jess was fixated on the one-act performance. "Show off."

"Care to join me?" Robin leaned her arms back against the edge of the pool. "The water's warm."

Jess considered the offer. "You won't try to dunk me, will you?"

A blonde eyebrow raised mischievously. "Of course not."

"And you won't try to race me or anything like that, will you?"

Robin sat on the steps. "Nope." *Since I'd win.*

"Good." Jess turned to go inside to change. "Because I'd win if you did."

Robin smirked. *We'll see.*

A few moments later, Jess stepped out of the house wearing a black one-piece swimsuit, which as far as Robin was concerned, certainly accentuated all of Jess's attributes quite nicely. Very nicely, indeed. Jess set a towel down on a nearby chair and stepped into the pool, pushing off the edge and swimming slowly in Robin's direction.

"This feels nice. I ought to try night swimming more often." Just then, Robin ducked under the water and swam down around Jess's feet, grabbing onto Jess's legs and taking them out from under her. Jess sunk under the water, then quickly reappeared, brushing the water from her eyes. She glared at Robin rather playfully. "You're dead."

Robin backed up. "Now, Jess. I was just having a little fun." She backed up some more, giggling lightly. "You were already in the water, so I just helped you along a little." Now, Robin was backed up against the side of the pool, and she had no where else to go.

Jess approached. "I'd be very worried, right now, if I were you, Robin." She put her long arms on either side of Robin and latched onto the edge of the pool with each hand, effectively trapping the younger woman. "You're in a very precarious situation." She stepped closer until Robin could feel her breath. "Because I have you just where I want you."

"Where's that?" Robin nearly croaked out the words and then swallowed, acutely aware of Jess's proximity. She could see the beads of water dripping from Jess's chin and down her neck toward other very interesting areas.

"Right there." Strong arms reached out with lightning quickness and picked Robin up, whirling her around and throwing her out toward the middle of the pool. Jess waited in amusement as Robin resurfaced.

Standing up in the center of the pool and wiping the water from her eyes, Robin shook her head defiantly, staring at Jess as if in challenge. "Just for that, I'll race ya to the stairs." She didn't wait for an answer as she took off toward the stairs. Suddenly, Robin felt one of her ankles being grabbed from behind, as she was pulled firmly backward.

Jess pushed on ahead and was the first to claim the stairs. "I won." Jess grinned and declared victory, sitting herself down on the lowest step.

"You cheated." Robin sat one step higher. "No fair." She let her toes rub against Jess's knee.

"Payback for dunking me and racing me, both of which you said you weren't gonna do." Jess turned her head to look at Robin, and then suddenly, almost as if by instinct, she pulled Robin down to straddle her lap. The lapping water reached just below their shoulders as they sat facing each other. Azure eyes stared almost hypnotically into green, as Jess lightly ran her fingertips up and then back down the sides of Robin's swimsuit under the water, memorizing every slight curve in the process. Jess finally moved her hands around to Robin's lower back, and then slid them lower still, guiding Robin closer and closer. She pressed the younger woman to her, and claimed her lips in a searing kiss.

Robin brought her arms around the strong shoulders, all at once lost in the sensual nature of the kiss and the electric touch. As they held each other close, their breasts rubbed one another's through the light fabric of their swimsuits, and Robin felt herself start to respond, gently rocking her hips as the kiss intensified and progressed. Finally, breaking away and coming up for much-needed air, she leaned forward as Jess took a delicious petite earlobe into her mouth. Robin was barely able to form a coherent thought. "Uh...um, Jess." The sensations were becoming a little too overpowering. "Jess." She pulled back slightly and tried to breathe. "We need…I need to slow down."

Jess pulled back completely, taking long, deep breaths to try to calm her racing heart. "Oh, God." She leaned forward again and rested her head against Robin's forehead, swallowing audibly. "That was really...intense."

"Yeah, very."

Jess gazed up and whispered. "I've never felt that before."

Robin regained her senses and kissed the ragged wet bangs on Jess's forehead. "Me either. I almost lost control for a moment." She smiled. "You have that effect on me."

Jess tasted a water drop on Robin's jaw. "And you definitely have that effect on me." *We need to take things slowly here.* She gently propelled herself and Robin into the middle of the pool. "So, want to play some more, or are you all pruny?"

Robin studied her hands. "Pruny, but I could still play. What did you have in mind?" She took notice of the now mischievous glint in the cerulean eyes looking back at her.

"Well," Jess set Robin down so her feet touched the bottom of the pool. "There's this little game called 'Dunk the Associate' which is really a lot of fun." A playful eyebrow shot up. "Shall we try it?"

Robin backed away slowly as Jess advanced. "No, I don't think so, Jess."

The young associate's protest was too late. Jess took one leap and pounced on Robin, taking them both underwater and then back up again. One of Jess's hands quite unintentionally grazed the length of the front of Robin's swimsuit as the taller woman sought to securely wrap her arms around the slim waist from behind. Jess had no doubt about what she felt in that split second of intimate contact, and she shuddered momentarily as her mind struggled to shake free of the electrifying sensation. *Get yourself out of the water now, Jess, before you lose control again.* She turned Robin around to face her, holding her at arm's length. "Give up?"

"I...um...I...." Robin stammered, still tingling from Jess's inadvertent touch, as she stared, somewhat dazed, into magnificent blue eyes. "I surrender."

Oh God. Get out of the water now, Jess. "Good. I always win at that game." She winked and then glanced at her own fingers. "Now, I'm the one who's getting all pruny. Are you ready to head back inside?" Jess thought she maneuvered into the question rather well.

"Yeah." Robin responded nonchalantly and swam to the side of the pool. "But next time, we play another game. It's called 'Capture the Partner.'"

"Really?" An intrigued smirk. "And how do you play that particular game?"

"Easy." Robin stepped out of the pool and wrapped her towel around her shoulders. "You make the partner swim across the pool, giving them a little head start, and then you race to catch them before they can reach the other side. It's really a lot of fun."

"I see. And if you catch the partner before they reach the other side, then what happens?" Jess climbed out the water and picked up her own towel, throwing it around herself.

"Then you've captured them and they're your prisoner." Robin smiled smugly. "And, of course, you get to interrogate them."

Interrogate them? A dark eyebrow arched above wet bangs. "Is that so? And what's involved in this...interrogation?"

Robin opened the sliding glass doors and turned to look at Jess with amused green eyes. "Well, let's just say that when you're finished interrogating them, they're in no position to offer any further resistance." She ducked inside and headed toward the guest bathroom for a quick shower, leaving Jess standing mutely.

Can I surrender now?

****

After taking quick showers, Jess and Robin ordered a pepperoni pizza for dinner, and ate the entire deep dish pizza pie. It seems that both of them had worked up quite an appetite in the pool earlier, and they were both famished. When they had finished eating their pizza, they sat cozily on the plush sofa, cuddled together. One small lamp on the opposite side of the room provided the only light, as Jess gently stoked Robin's blonde hair, and every so often tenderly kissed the light eyebrows.

"Did you enjoy your swim earlier?" Jess pushed a short strand of blonde hair behind Robin's ear.

"Yeah. Thanks for letting me use your pool." Robin played with the hem of Jess's t-shirt.

"Well, I told you that you can use it anytime you want." Jess smiled warmly. "You can come over anytime you want, you can stay over anytime you want, you can be here as often as you want. You can...." *Live here.* She suddenly caught herself. *Damn. Don't push it with her, Jess.*

"I brought a few things over from my apartment." Robin looked at Jess shyly. "I was wondering if I could keep them here. It's just a few changes of clothes, a nightshirt, and some bath items. I put them in your spare room. Is that okay?" Robin didn't want to appear too forward or give the impression that she intended to move in tomorrow.

"That's perfectly okay, unless you want to use another room. We could move things around, you know." Jess found herself curiously quite eager to have Robin there full-time. It was an uncontrollable desire, although she didn't have a clue as to why she wanted to upset the normalcy of her own life. She mentally warned herself again. *Don't push it, Jess.* "Whatever you'd like to do, Robin. It's okay. You're in charge."

"Good, because I'll just use the spare room for now." Robin replied happily. "Don't move anything around just for me." A petite hand now made its way to Jess's arm and lightly stroked the smooth skin.

Jess lost herself for a moment at the tingling sensation from Robin's touch. She then nuzzled Robin's still damp hair, taking in a deep breath. "I love the way you smell."

Robin giggled. "I'm flattered. I think."

Jess took another deep, and this time audible, breath. "You smell like raindrops."

Robin giggled some more. "It's the shampoo."

"Nope. It's definitely you." Jess sighed. "I could just hold you like this forever." She became pensive. "You know, from here on through the trial, we're going to have some very late nights. We won't get to spend any time together except work."

Robin frowned slightly. "I know. But when the trial's over, I guess we'll just have to make up for lost time then, won't we?" She mentally pondered the implications of that thought.

"Definitely." Jess ducked her head and gave Robin a lingering kiss. "Hey, I forget to ask you if you got a chance to call Dr. Richmond today."

"No." Robin fidgeted.

"Oh." *What's going on?* "I just thought that you said you wanted to talk with someone about things."

"I do, but I think I'll wait until after the trial is over so I have more time to devote to some sessions." *I don't want to think about this right now.*

Jess placed her palm against Robin's cheek and turned the blonde head toward her own, speaking gently and without admonishment. "Okay, but then you'll call, right?" *Do not let her avoid this. You'll regret it if you do.*

"Right." Robin did not sound convincing and fooled no one.

For the moment, Jess decided to let it go, and instead shifted her body to lie back lengthwise on the sofa. "Come here." She gestured toward Robin.

Robin slid down partially on top of Jess as she rested herself back against the cushions. She lightly wrapped her arm around Jess's waist and placed her head on Jess's shoulder. It was so safe this way. She didn't have to think about anything else except being surrounded by the warmth of the body next to hers. She idly traced figure eight patterns on Jess's t-shirt over her stomach, then moved her hand downward toward the hem of Jess's shirt, fingering it indecisively. "Can I...um....?" Robin didn't quite know how to phrase the question.

"Can you what?" Jess seemed confused.

Robin tilted her head up to look shyly at Jess. "Can I put my hand on your stomach?"

Jess chuckled. "Yes. As I recall, you've done that several times already. I specifically remember one morning a while back when you seemed to find my stomach quite fascinating." Her breath suddenly caught as the petite hand in question slowly slid its way underneath her t-shirt to rest on the smooth skin. "And it always feels really good."

"Your skin is so soft." Robin brushed her thumb lightly back and forth across the warm flesh.

Jess was quite distracted by the touch, but she needed to discuss something with Robin, and considering their shenanigans in the pool earlier, and where Robin's touch was leading her right now, this was probably the best time to bring the subject up. *Before things go any further.* She grimaced, knowing full well the chore ahead. "Um, Robin?"

Robin continued rubbing Jess's stomach lightly, and delighted in the feel of the silky skin under her hand. "Yes."

It was unbelievably hard to do, but Jess managed to focus her thoughts and became very serious. "I think there's something we should talk about."

Robin abruptly looked up and shifted herself up on one elbow, her free hand still maintaining contact with Jess's stomach. "What is it?" She was surprised by the serious tone.

Jess tried to approach the subject cautiously. "I...um...know we talked about keeping things quiet, just between us, and I still want to do that. I think that's the best thing." She paused, trying to order her thoughts. "And I know our concerns were based mainly on the fact that our relationship is...unconventional, for lack of a better word." She fixed her eyes on sea green and took a deep breath. "But if someone were to find out, I...um...haven't told you about all the possible consequences." She mentally braced herself for the expected reaction.

Robin raised both eyebrows in slight alarm, taking her hand from Jess's stomach and reaching up to place it firmly on Jess's chin, tilting it toward her. "What do you mean?" Robin asked the question a bit uneasily.

Shit. This is hard. My headache's coming back. "I admit I've been trying to avoid telling you this." Jess sighed. "But there is really no way around it. There is something you should know." Blue eyes quietly regarded green before continuing. "If someone at work were to find out about...us, the firm may have some concerns. They don't care about personal relationships outside of work or among peers, but when it comes to those who have supervisory responsibilities over someone else, they consider it inappropriate." Jess said the last part matter-of-factly.

"Supervisory, as between a partner and an associate." Robin drew the conclusion unhappily.

Jess stroked the blonde head and nodded with regret. "Yes. Do you understand why?"

Robin nodded back. "They think the supervisor wouldn't be able to be objective in giving evaluations." She then shook her head. "But you're not the only one who has supervisory responsibilities over me. All the partners and the Management Committee do. It wouldn't be just you." Robin tried her best to argue.

"That's true, and that would be a good argument in our favor." Jess sighed again. "But realistically, Robin, there are probably only two possible scenarios if the firm were to find out." She hesitated. "The best case is that they would most likely assign you to work with someone other than me from that point forward."

Robin closed her eyes and frowned. "Okay. And the worst

case?"

Jess took a deep breath, not really able to avoid the issue any longer. "The Management Committee could reprimand me for inappropriate conduct."

At this point, Robin's eyes grew very wide in clear anxiety. "What?" Stunned disbelief crossed her face. "And what, specifically, would they do if they reprimand you?"

Jess's voice carried no emotion. "Censure me, suspend, me or remove me from the firm." She now shifted her gaze toward the window, unable to look at Robin.

All at once, Robin felt as if the air had been sucked out of her lungs, and she felt her composure give way. "Because you love me?" Her eyes welled up, and she abruptly climbed off the sofa and backed away, as if she had been burned. She stood staring mutely at Jess for several moments before bringing herself to speak once again. "Why didn't you tell me this before?"

Jess was silent. *Why were there so many obstacles?*

"Jess, this is your career, here." Robin was mortified and her tone of voice was very agitated. "I would never have done…I would never do anything to jeopardize that for you. I would never…do this to you." Robin stared up at the popcorn ceiling and tried to think calmly, and then focused her attention back toward Jess, speaking in a shaky voice. "When we talked before about the chance that people could find out, you never said anything." She paused. "And then when we saw Harry at the restaurant and I was worried about him seeing us, you still never said anything. Why, Jess?" A tear finally fell. "I had a right to know I was putting you at risk."

Jess sat upright on the sofa but otherwise remained silent, still maintaining her gaze at the window. *You screwed up, Jess.*

"Jess?" When there still was no response, Robin began to realize that there might be something more going on. She calmed herself and went back over to the sofa, kneeling down to face Jess. Her tone of voice now softened somewhat with concern. "Jess? Will you talk to me, please?"

The dark head turned cautiously from its gaze at the window and nodded. "What do you want to know?"

"Why didn't you tell me?" Robin's voice was calm and unaccusing.

There was another long silence, and then Jess took a deep breath, before finally speaking very slowly and very quietly, the profound regret evident. "I was willing to take all the risks. I was willing to risk everything to be with you. God help me, Robin, I was." Jess swallowed. "But I didn't think you would allow that." She smiled with quiet fondness. "Your heart wouldn't let you." Now, her voice hardened somewhat. "In the back of my mind, I always thought that what we have would never last. I thought that you could never really want to stay with me. You would be gone sooner or later, and the risk really wouldn't be a factor."

Robin began to understand. "You thought all along that I would eventually leave."

"Yes." Jess felt suddenly very ashamed. "And so, I thought that if I brought all this up, you would..."

"I would leave sooner." Robin finished the thought. "I would end it."

"Yes."

"Because I wouldn't want to place you at risk."

Jess hung her head and whispered. "Yes." She then looked up at Robin with deep regret. "I was wrong."

Robin thought long and hard about all of this. It really wasn't surprising, given Jess's fears stemming from James' betrayal and his leaving her. But Robin also had to consider that, most likely, what Jess said was at least partially true. Robin probably never would have entered this relationship if she had known she was jeopardizing Jess's career, or acted on her feelings, or kissed Jess that first time after they returned from the beach. She probably never would have continued to see Jess outside of work, or carry on with their little sleepovers, or let herself...love her. *As if I even had a choice*. But none of that mattered now. The truth was that Robin did, in fact, love Jess, and they were, in fact, in a relationship for better or for worse. *For better or for worse....* "Can I ask you one more thing?" Robin's tone was even.

Jess nodded. "Yes."

"Why did you mention this now? Was it because I told you that I loved you and that I wouldn't leave you, and so you felt safe enough to tell me this?" It came out harsher than Robin intended.

Jess closed her eyes in genuine pain. "No." She turned to stare intently into sea green eyes and spoke with conviction. "I would never trap you like that, and coax a promise out of you that you would later feel guilty about."

Robin flinched. "Jess, I'm sorry. I didn't mean...."

"Shhh. It's okay." Jess interrupted softly. "Let me finish saying this, okay?" Blue eyes softened and a small smile appeared on Jess's face. "I told you now because I am very serious about you, in case you haven't guessed, and I feel that we, together, are getting very serious. I've asked you to live here, and in the pool before, we almost...." She blushed in spite of herself. “I want you to know everything. I want you to know fully what lies ahead before we...go any further. You deserve that. I didn’t want you to find out later, and then feel betrayed. I know what betrayal is, Robin, and I will not do that to you, even if....” Here, she looked firmly into those sea green eyes and took Robin’s hand in her own. “Even if you decide not to allow me to assume the risk involved in continuing our relationship.”

“Okay.” Robin nodded.

“Okay?”

Robin nodded again. “Okay. Together we assume the risk. What happens to you, happens to me.”

“But....”

“No, Jess. We do this together. We are in this together, for better or for worse.” Robin lifted Jess’s hand and brought it to her lips, kissing the knuckles gently. “I will not lose you.” The edges of Robin’s lips slowly curled in a small, shy smile. “And in case you haven’t guessed, I am very serious about you, too.”

Jess smiled warmly and took the younger woman into her arms, hugging her in a tight embrace. “You are absolutely amazing.” She pulled back and focused on Robin’s beautiful face. “But you know I will try to protect you. I won’t let you suffer if I have anything to say about it.”

“I know.” Robin replied simply.

“I love you.”

“I love you, too.” Robin checked her watch and gave a small sigh. “It’s late, and I shouldn’t stay tonight. After the trial, we can talk about my staying over more, okay?”

Jess nodded, a little dejected but knowing it was for the best. “Alright. We can’t be distracted right now.” She walked Robin to the door. “But I still wish you weren’t leaving.”

Warm green eyes regarded her for a brief moment. “I’m not leaving, Jess. I’m just going to my apartment. Just so you understand the difference.”

A nod.

“Good.” Robin gave Jess a gentle hug. “Goodnight, Jess.”

“Goodnight. I’ll see you tomorrow.” Jess closed the door, and somehow, everything seemed to fall into place. She and Robin were in this together, for better or for worse. Jess arched a dark eyebrow at the seemingly benign phrase.

For better or for worse.

****

Robin filtered through the mountain of trial exhibits, looking, for the millionth time, for any clue as to what opposing counsel was trying to hide. Finally, having no success, she got up from her desk and headed over toward the coffee maker. *Ah, chocolate macadamia nut flavor.* She poured herself a cup and made her way back toward her office, stepping around a few perennial heads in whisper mode positioned seemingly innocuously near the copy machine. As Robin rounded the corner, she unexpectedly spied Paul rushing angrily down the hallway, apparently muttering something unfit for polite conversation under his breath.

"Paul, what's the matter?" Robin caught him mid-stride.

He nearly kept on walking but stopped and grimaced most unpleasantly. "How do you stand it?"

"Huh?" The confusion on Robin's face must have shown clearly.

"How can you stand working with her? She just bit my head off for no reason." They approached Robin's office and went inside.

Robin closed the door. "Who are you talking about?" She asked the question even though she was quite sure she already knew the answer.

Paul sat down in a nearby chair. "Jessica. She can be such a…." Paul stopped abruptly. "Sorry."

There was a momentary silence, and then Robin sat down behind her desk, picking up her favorite pen and twirling it in her hand. "So, what happened?" She spoke softly.

"Jessica wanted me to prepare this motion and have her review it before filing it." He waved the motion he was referring to in his hand. "The deadline to file it is tomorrow, and she needs to look at it so I can make the changes, if necessary." He stopped and ran his fingers through his slightly graying brown hair. "So, I went to go find her because she wasn't in her office."

"We have a trial next week, and I know she's in a meeting with the client right now." Robin grimaced. "You didn't interrupt her meeting, did you?"

"I had no choice." Paul raised his voice in exasperation. "She wanted to look the motion over before it was filed." He sat back in the chair. "So, anyway, after I found her, she pulled me outside the conference room door and reamed me out in the middle of the hallway. I'm sure half the office heard it. She's the one who wanted me to prepare the motion for her to review, and then she gets all bent out of shape about it."

"She's under a lot of pressure right now." It was all Robin could think to say.

Paul sat with an incredulous look on his face. "You're not defending her are you? Come on, Robin. Surely, you must've gotten on her bad side a time or two by now. Everyone has. Ask Keith or Michelle, or especially Mark. They'll tell you."

Robin sat quietly for a moment processing the information before responding. "Um...I guess I just haven't worked with her long enough to experience that side of her." She then forced a laugh. "But I'm sure my time will come, though." Robin twirled the pen faster in her hand. It seemed that pen twirling had become a nervous and common habit of late.

"It's amazing you've lasted this long. I don't know how you could have worked with her all this time and not have been chewed out." Paul snorted. "She must like you."

Uh oh. Robin stiffened. "Uh, no." *Think.* The pen tumbled helplessly from Robin's fingers, and she leaned forward to pick it up, slightly embarrassed. "I mean, I'm sure it's just a matter of time before I do something she won't like." Robin didn't at all like the direction this conversation was taking. She set the pen down deliberately on the desk.

Paul went on with his musing, quite oblivious to her plight. "Or maybe she just knows she has to be nice to you. I mean, face it, no one likes to work with her much. She probably thinks if she doesn't get along with you, then she won't have anyone to help her with her cases." He was more or less just offering commentary on how difficult it was to work with Jess, not implying anything more.

Robin resisted the urge to pick up the pen again. "I'm probably not the best person to judge that since I haven't been here very long." She felt quite uncomfortable now and just wanted the conversation to end. "Listen, I'm meeting with Jess and the client later today. If you want, I can give her the motion for you."

Paul stood up. "Well, it's worth a try." He handed the document to Robin and proceeded out the door. "Thanks."

Not a second after Paul left her office, Robin plopped herself back down in her chair and blew out a deep breath. *What was that all about?* While it was true that Robin had never experienced Jess's full fury, she had indeed heard stories. And she certainly couldn't deny that it did seem strange that everyone else, at least once, had the occasion to be on the receiving end of that fury. This led to an uncomfortable question. Was Jess giving Robin special treatment? *I hope not.* It would only serve to raise suspicions which would not likely go unnoticed for long, considering the office gossip mill.

Robin bit her lower lip lightly and swiveled to gaze out the large windows of her office, the choppy waters of the lake below capturing her attention. A cold front was blowing in from the north, and she continued to gaze out her windows, watching the light gray clouds move rapidly across the sky. She mentally considered whether to approach Jess with this matter. After all, Jess might not consciously realize that she was perhaps treating Robin differently than everyone else. Robin frowned. *Now's not the best time. Jess is preparing for trial.* But to delay the issue any longer was probably not the best idea either. *She needs to know.* Otherwise, it would just be a matter of time before someone became suspicious, and then...well, and then it would be confirmed that the firm's concerns were true. Someone in a supervisory position could not be capable of being objective with someone with whom that person had a personal relationship. And if that happened, Jess's career could be in jeopardy. It was that simple. And that dangerous. And that unsettling to think about. *I'll talk with her after our meeting today.*

****

"So, what do you think, Phil?" Jess had spent all day meeting with Phil Jones, Vice-President of Legal Affairs for RSJ Industries, and had just presented the general concepts of her legal argument to him. "Do you think the jury will buy it?"

Phil nodded cautiously. "I think it's the best we have. We've got to keep it simple, though. No high finance talk, just the basics."

Jess turned to Robin who had joined them for their afternoon session. Robin had earlier given a presentation of the chronology of events and a brief summary of their factual exhibits. "Can you give Phil a copy of the chronology and the summary of events for him to take with him tonight to review back at the hotel?"

"Sure." Robin nodded and left the conference room to have the requested copies made.

Jess concluded the meeting. "Okay, Phil, why don't you go back to the hotel and review the documents. I'll be here late tonight. Call me if you happen think of anything else." She stood up and gathered her papers. "Tomorrow we'll prep you for your testimony."

The conference room door opened a moment later, and Robin stepped back inside with the necessary copies. "Here you are, Phil. Let me know if you want to add anything."

Phil took the proffered documents. "Thanks, I will. What time do you want me here tomorrow, Jess?"

"Let's say about 9:00, and then we can get started." Jess looked over toward Robin for a moment. "Robin will be joining us, as well."

"Alright. Goodnight, then. I'll see you tomorrow." Phil exited the conference room and made his way toward the elevators.

With considerable concentration, Jess watched him leave and then glared at Robin. "Come with me." Jess strode abruptly out the door and headed toward her office.

"Okaaay." Robin muttered half to herself and followed Jess down the hallway.

Once inside Jess's office, Robin closed the door and took a seat in the chair by the window, watching faint outlines of the twinkling of the street lights below in the dark through the reflected glass. Jess dropped her papers on the cherry wood desk and turned to stare unseeingly out of the same window. "You haven't found anything yet?" Jess's tone had a slightly hard edge to it.

"Um...I've been through the documents five times, Jess. I just don't see anything." Robin shook her head. "I was so sure I'd find something."

Damn. "Well, tomorrow we're prepping Phil, and I've got to have something to rebut their case with." Jess ran long fingers through her dark hair and sighed heavily. "Without anything else, I'd say the case has less than a fifty-fifty chance."

Robin's eyes grew very wide. *That's all?* "I won't give up, Jess. I'll keep looking."

"Yeah, well I think it's just a little too late for that now, Robin." Jess snapped. There was a momentary silence, and after a second to register the stunned look on Robin's face, Jess's expression softened. "Um...sorry." She sat down in her burgundy leather chair. "I'm just really frustrated with this case right now and I shouldn't be taking it out on you."

"Don't worry about it, Jess." Robin's voice carried an air of understanding and even a hint of sympathy.

Jess felt, rather than heard, the soothing words. *How does she make me feel better like that?* "It's amazing you put up with me sometimes."

That's just what Paul said. "Uh, there's something I wanted to discuss with you, Jess." Robin stared back across the desk. "Now is probably not the best time, but I don't think it can wait."

The leather chair Jess was sitting in slightly squeaked as she leaned forward and raised both eyebrows warily. "What is it?"

"I saw Paul earlier." It was a lame beginning, and the young associate knew it.

"And?"

"He mentioned to me about your um...discussion with him in the hallway." Robin braced herself.

"And?"

"I don't think he should have interrupted you, but your reaction did seem harsh."

"And?" Jess waved her hand in front of her. "You thought you would, what? Plead his case?"

This isn't going well. "No. I told him I'd give you the motion to look at." Robin handed the paper to Jess. "I know you want to review it before it's filed tomorrow."

Jess fished around in her desk for a paper clip to play with. "Okay, is that all?"

"No. Um...he said something to me, and I got a little worried." The associate regarded the junior partner and spoke softly. "He said that you have been a bit harsh sometimes with pretty much everyone."

A frank smile appeared on Jess's face. "That's not exactly a news flash, Robin." She unbent the paper clip.

"Well, it seems that you have been a bit harsh with everyone at one time or another. Everyone except...me." Robin released the breath she was holding.

And somewhere in the dark recesses of Jess's sometimes meandering mind, a faint light appeared. "So, what, exactly, are you saying?"

Robin responded bolder than she felt. "You might not be aware of this, but I think you're treating me differently than everyone else."

A dark eyebrow shot up. "Because I'm not so 'harsh' with you?" Jess absently jabbed the tip of the paper clip against her legal pad.

"Yes." Robin's eyes narrowed, and she gazed straight ahead into deep blue. "I expect you to treat me the same as you would anyone else. I require no special treatment. If I make a mistake, I expect you to let me have it. All of it, Jess." Robin's gaze softened again. "I don't want anyone becoming suspicious of us."

The light was already shining brightly in Jess's mind at that point, and she knew fully well what Robin was saying. "But I just snapped at you, didn't I? Doesn't that count?"

Robin gave a half smile at the crack. "No, since you immediately apologized. Did you ever apologize to anyone else?"

Jess pursed her lips in thought and then mumbled. "No."

"See my point?"

Jess nodded slowly. "I hadn't realized that."

"And some people might think it a bit strange, and then get a little suspicious. Do you know what I mean?"

Jess nodded again, and then threw her now completely unbent paper clip into the trash. "Okay. So, let me see if I understand this correctly. You want me to...let you have it more often, right?" Jess held a bit of mirth in her blue eyes.

Is she teasing me? "Yes. You should definitely let me have it, especially if I deserve it." The associate got up and walked around behind the desk and stood next to the junior partner's chair. "And I mean you better let me have it good."

"Well, it just so happens, Robin, that letting people have it is one of my better skills." Jess grinned. "I'll make sure you're not neglected in that department."

"Good." Robin stepped around the back of the chair and placed her hands on Jess's shoulders, massaging them gently. "Because I definitely hate being neglected." Petite hands then made their way to the back of Jess's neck and continued the massage, kneading tiny circles. "And I definitely expect you not to hold anything back."

The neck and shoulder massage was doing wonders for Jess, and she bent her head forward to allow more of the massage to continue. Robin's hands, it seemed, somehow knew exactly where to press to work out the kinks, as the young associate continued to knead the junior partner's shoulders and neck. The touch was gentle, and firm, and delicate, all at the same time, and Jess luxuriated in the feel of it. Reaching up, she grasped Robin's hand and gently pulled her around to sit down across her lap. Blue eyes fixed on green, as Jess brought one hand up to brush blonde bangs from Robin's forehead, trailing her fingers down to rest lightly against a fair cheek. "I promise I won't hold anything back." Jess whispered.

"Good." Robin brought both arms around Jess's shoulders and leaned into the touch, looking up and locking sea green eyes on to cool blue, suddenly and helplessly held captive by the intense gaze. She leaned in and gave Jess a light kiss. *If someone were to walk in here right now, we'd be in real trouble.* Robin slowly stood up and cleared her throat, grasping one of Jess's hands in the process. "So, we're clear on our discussion, right?"

"Right." Jess smiled. "I'm supposed to let you have it if you deserve it, and I'm definitely not supposed to hold anything back." She arched a dark eyebrow. "Have I understood you correctly?"

"Yes."

"Good." Jess stood up. "Because after the trial is over, Robin, I plan on making sure you get everything you deserve." She winked. "And then some."

Oh boy.

****

It had been a late night. Both Robin and Jess had stayed at the office preparing for the trial until the early morning hours. Robin entered the office building a little before 9:00, having gotten little sleep, and scurried up the elevators just in time for her meeting with Jess and Phil Jones. They all dutifully and tediously spent the entire morning preparing Phil for his testimony based on the case thus far and discussing trial strategy. After a brief lunch break, Jess went down the hall to check on the status of the pre-trial motion preparations, most of which Keith was handling. Robin went downstairs to the delicatessen to grab a sandwich to go, before deciding to return to her documents.

Robin entered her office, sandwich in hand, and sat down at her desk, briefly perusing the new e-mail messages she had received during the morning. Noting that her in-box was once again overflowing, she quickly leafed through its contents, managing to do so one-handed while her other hand was otherwise engaged in unwrapping her chicken salad sandwich. One particular item caught Robin's attention. *What's this?* She took a bite of her sandwich. Then another item caught her attention. She pulled out the fax papers from the pile of documents she had accumulated in her in-box and studied them intently as she ate. A large smile slowly edged its way across her face. *I got it.* The smile widened further, and in no time at all, Robin picked up the phone and had the receptionist page Jess.

The phone rang back almost immediately. "Jess? It's Robin."

Jess was still in her meeting with Keith. "What is it?"

"I found it." Robin grinned mightily to herself.

A momentary pause. "Um, you found, what?"

"It. I found it. When you're finished with Keith, stop by my office and I'll show you, okay?" Robin tapped her desk lightly in exuberance and noted the time on her watch. "Whenever you're free, just come on down," she added a bit nonchalantly.

"Okaaay." The suspense was absolutely killing Jess. She abruptly adjourned her meeting with Keith and strode purposefully down the long hallway and around the corner to Robin's office, knocking lightly on the closed door. Hearing the muffled voice indicating she should enter, Jess quickly stepped inside, closed the door, and sat down in the chair opposite Robin's desk.

"Boy, that was fast." Robin grinned, looking at her watch in slight amusement.

"You were timing me?" Jess raised both eyebrows in mild surprise. "I didn't know I was that predictable." She half mumbled to herself and arched a dark eyebrow. "So, you said you found it. Care to share with me what 'it' is?"

"Yes." Robin rummaged around on her desk. "Look at this." She presented a document to Jess for inspection. "Exhibit "A."

"Okay. This is Anne Carver's resume." Jess casually perused the document.

"Correct. Note her educational background." Robin sat back in her chair, crossed her arms in front of her.

Jess studied the document further. "Undergraduate from University of Maryland, MBA from Harvard Business School. Okay."

Robin smiled. "Right. Now, look at this." She handed another document to Jess. "Exhibit "B."

Jess studied the second document, as well. "Fax from the Office of the Registrar, University of Maryland." Instantly, Jess's eyes lit up and she glanced over the top of the paper across the desk at Robin. "You're kidding me?"

Robin now had a full grin on her face. "Nope. And it gets better." She handed Jess a third document. "Exhibit "C."

Jess took the document and studied it in similar fashion. "Fax from the Office of the Registrar, Harvard University Business School." She raised another eyebrow and looked again at Robin. "Unbelievable." She shook her head. "No wonder that weasel of an opposing counsel didn't want us to take Anne Carver's deposition. She...."

"Falsified her credentials." Robin finished. "She never graduated from either school." The blonde head shook in clear disbelief. "That's pretty bold."

Jess nodded. "Yeah, but you'd actually be surprised at how often that happens. I once found out about an expert that all the firms in town used on their various cases. He testified at dozens and dozens of trials and had an impressive list of credentials. Turns out, someone deposing him decided one day to check out his credentials, and found that absolutely none of them were real, including his published papers. Not one lawyer who had offered him up as an expert at all those trials had ever checked his credentials."

"What happened?" Robin was fascinated by the story.

"The guy got wind that someone was on to him, and ran out in the middle of the night right in the middle of a trial. The lawyers on the case went to his hotel in the morning to pick him up for court, and he was gone." Jess chuckled. "It was quite an embarrassment, to say the least, and especially so when your own expert skips out like that. The moral of the story is that you should never take anything at face value. You never want to be surprised."

"So what are we going to do about Anne Carver?"

Jess pursed her lips in thought. "First, get the registrar's offices at both of those schools to overnight to you certificates of non-attendance so we can offer them into evidence at trial."

"Okay. Then what?" Robin looked over at Jess eagerly.

The junior partner had a decidedly feral grin on her face. "Then you and I are going to sit down and write the script."

"The script?" Robin was confused.

"Yep. Whenever I prepare to cross-examine a witness, I always write a script. It's basically what I'm going to ask and what the witness is going to say, and it sets forth the order I'll ask each question." Jess grinned again. "It always works."

Robin now understood. "Ah, so that's one of the reasons you wanted Anne Carver's deposition taken. So that you would know what she was going to say and you could put it in your script." Robin furrowed her brows. "But we never took her deposition."

"Doesn't matter. We have something better." Jess held up the fax papers. "We have these." She stood up and walked over to the window to look at the sparkling lake below. "Opposing counsel was probably going to put her on the stand and just skirt around her background." She turned around to face Robin and rubbed her hands together. "Now, we've got him. He never should have tipped us off."

"So, does this improve our chances?"

"Significantly. Anne Carver is one of their major witnesses, and now we can show that she has absolutely no credibility at all. The jury will eat it up. Whatever she says can't be believed. Not only that, but she's apparently not even qualified to have prepared the initial bid for the contract." Blue eyes stared warmly at green. "I didn't mention to you to go ahead and check her credentials, but you had the instinct to do it yourself. That was good work, Robin."

Robin blushed at the praise. "Thanks. So, are you going to tell Phil?"

"You bet. Come on." Jess stepped toward the door but stopped abruptly as Robin walked closer. After checking to see that the door was still satisfactorily closed, Jess impulsively leaned down and gave

Robin a small kiss.

"What's that for?" Robin's eyes twinkled.

"That's for doing such a good job. I believe in rewarding good work."

"Oh." Green eyes fixed on blue. "Do you reward all the associates like that when they do a good job?"

"Nope. Only certain ones."

Robin reached down and grasped one of Jess's fingers and held it between her own. "And how do you determine who those certain ones are?"

"They have to meet very strict criteria, Robin. I'm quite selective." Jess leaned casually back against the desk.

Robin entwined their fingers. "And what might that very strict criteria be?"

"Well, first, they must display outstanding buttering up techniques." Jess grinned. "Second, they absolutely must insist on playing hooky from time to time. And third, and very importantly, they must be willing to give neck and shoulder massages on a moment's notice."

"I can see how that would certainly limit the field." Robin stroked her chin with her free hand, as if in deep thought. "Still, there could be several people who might fit that criteria as you've defined it."

"Oh, I forgot to mention the most important requirement."

"What's that?"

"Their name must be Robin Wilson." Jess grinned warmly.

"Well, now, that does narrow the field significantly." The young associate nodded pensively. "Has anyone ever met this criteria before?"

The junior partner shook her head. "Nope. You're the very first one to meet all the specified criteria. That's quite an accomplishment."

"Thank you. So, are there any additional rewards that I should be aware of?"

"Yes. There are very many additional rewards, Robin, but before I can officially present them to you, we must be in a more...appropriate setting."

"Ah, then I guess I should advise you that I plan on doing a good job quite often." Sea green eyes met blue. "You see, I intend on collecting all my rewards very frequently...in the appropriate setting, of course."

"Of course." Jess spoke with amusement. "I am duly advised of your intent, counselor." She smiled. "Rewards, appropriate setting, frequently. Got it."

Robin laughed gently. “You are so funny.” She smirked. “You’re also very hopeless.”

“Am I?” A perplexed look. “I don’t think you’ve ever mentioned that to me before.” Jess broke into a wide grin and shook her head. “Alright, kiddo, come on. We’ve got a client waiting to be told our good news.”

“Right.” Robin walked over to the door. “Hey, Jess. Do we get to rehearse your script when it’s finished?”

“Yes.”

“Can I yell ‘cut’ at the end?”

“No.”

****

Early Saturday morning, Jess woke and readied herself to go back to the office. Trial preparations were in full gear, and later in the day, she was scheduled to meet with several witnesses to prepare them for their trial testimony. She busily showered and changed into casual twill pants and a light sweater. As she packed her briefcase with all essential items, she heard a horn honk from the street outside. *What’s going on out there this early?* She strode through the living room and into the foyer, opening the front door curiously. What she found was a blue Miata sitting idly at the curb in front of the house, the motor still running. A slim hand waved happily from the driver’s seat toward the doorway, as Jess stood in continued stunned curiosity.

“Get in.” A voice called out from the car.

“What?” The tall figure stepped further out of the doorway and onto the front porch.

“You heard me.” Robin beckoned again. “Get in.”

“Why?” Jess hesitantly made her way down to the car. “I’ve got to go into the office today.”

“I know, so do I, but we have to eat breakfast first, and I know you didn’t eat, did you?” Robin eyed Jess suspiciously, hearing no response. “I didn’t think so. You probably have no food.” She smirked, hearing no response again. “We’re going to eat breakfast, so will you get in, please?”

Jess was helpless to resist. “Oh, alright.” She mumbled playfully. “But we won’t take too long, right?”

“Right. I will have you back here in plenty of time for you to get to the office before the witnesses arrive.” Robin placed her hand across her heart in a playful attempt at seriousness. “I promise.”

"Fine. Let me lock up and set the alarm." Jess looked back over her shoulder. "You're impossible sometimes, you know that?"

Robin grinned. "I learned from the best."

After Jess finished locking up the house and setting the alarm, she unlatched the car door and settled her long frame inside the Miata. "You know, these cars weren't made for tall people."

Robin headed down the street toward the main highway. "Jess, when I bought this car, I wasn't thinking about tall. I was thinking about me." Robin stopped her explanation abruptly. "Okay, Jess." She sighed." Just say it. Get it over with, please. I know you're dying to say it, so just go ahead."

The dark head shook vehemently. "I have absolutely no idea what you mean."

"You know exactly what I mean, and you are going to say it anyway, so stop denying it, and just get it over with." Robin stopped the car at the red light.

"No." Jess pouted slightly. "You took all the fun out of it."

"Jess...." A blonde eyebrow rose expectantly. "Say it."

"No." Jess was defiant about it and stared straight ahead. "The light's green. You can go." A beat. "Shorty."

Robin narrowed her eyes as she pulled through the intersection. "You are so mean to me. And I even knew it was coming."

Jess suppressed a chuckle. "Payback for kidnapping me...again. That makes two kidnappings for you and only one kidnapping for me. I think we need to readjust the kidnapping schedule."

"I wasn't aware that we had a kidnapping schedule." Robin pulled into the Breakfast House restaurant.

"We do. You kidnapped me last time, so it was officially my turn to kidnap you."

Robin got out of the car. "So what you're saying is this. The kidnapper cannot kidnap the kidnappee if the kidnapper did the kidnapping last."

Jess had to think about that for a moment. "Correct." *I think.* She and Robin walked inside the restaurant and waited for the hostess to seat them.

Once situated at their table, they perused the breakfast menu thoroughly, with Robin deciding on a combination of pancakes, bacon, eggs, toast, hash browns and coffee, and Jess simply deciding on Belgian waffles and sausage.

"Are you going to eat all of that?" Jess eyed Robin's plate when the food arrived.

"Yep. Why? Want some?" She pushed her plate across the table toward Jess.

Blue eyes studied the amount of food on Robin's plate. "Me and what army?"

Robin took her plate back and shook her head. "Well, I'm hungry." She poured some syrup on her pancakes.

She's the most adorable thing I've ever seen. Jess gazed for a moment across the table, almost hypnotized at the simple sight of Robin eating. It was the strangest feeling of total and complete comfort. *Comfort.* That's what it was. It was comfortable. Being with Robin was comfortable. They were comfortable...together. Could they be comfortable together forever like this? *Forever together?* Jess had never talked with Robin about the forever together part. Part of her mind mulled that thought over. *Does Robin want forever together, too? For that matter, is it really possible to have forever together?*

"Jess?" Robin glanced across the table. "Jess?"

Startled from her musings, Jess lifted a dark eyebrow. "What?"

"Your food's getting cold. Where were you?"

"Um...just thinking." Jess poured syrup on her waffle.

"I see." Robin sipped her coffee. "About anything in particular?"

About everything. "Just about what lies ahead." Jess was deliberately vague. Now was not the time to get into any serious discussions. "We have the trial, and...everything."

Everything? Green eyes reached out across the table, capturing blue with an unsurpassed warmth, as if those green eyes knew exactly what questions lay hidden beneath the azure surface staring back. "Don't worry. You and I will handle the trial and...everything together. You can always count on me."

Always. "Good." Jess smiled. "Are you sure you're going to eat all of that?"

Robin glanced down at her half-eaten breakfast. "I've just begun." She whispered to Jess conspiratorially. "I might order a second plate."

"What? How could you eat…." Jess was speechless.

"I'm a growing girl. I need my strength." Robin didn't really intend on ordering a second plate, but enjoyed teasing Jess just the same.

"Strength for what?" Jess was confused "The trial?"

"Yes, among other things." Robin suppressed a grin.

"Other things?"

Robin nodded seriously. "Right, other things."

"Such as?"

Green eyes twinkled. "Such as other things that might come after the trial, of course."

"Other things that might come after the trial." Jess furrowed her brows in thought.

"Right." Robin was enjoying the continued teasing.

"And would those other things happen to involve me in any way?" Jess took a bite of her waffle.

"Perhaps."

"What if I'm not interested in these other things."

"You'll be interested." Robin responded nonchalantly.

"You seem pretty sure of that."

"Yep." Robin sipped her coffee.

Jess sat back in her chair and regarded the younger woman. "And you're sure of this, why?"

"Because I know how interested you are in rewarding those who do good jobs."

"Right. So?"

"So, I plan on doing a good job at the trial, and after we win, I'll need to collect my reward." The blonde stated all of this matter-of-factly.

"Okaaay." *Where is this going?* "So?"

Here, Robin grinned. "So, the reward I had in mind involves...the other things." She winked playfully.

A moment of silent contemplation. *Oh.* Jess nodded and then impulsively looked around for the waitress. *Maybe I should order a second plate, too.*

Chapter 8

Trial day. After meeting at the office early Monday morning, Jess, Robin, and Phil Jones headed over to the courthouse for the first day of trial. Most of that first day was spent selecting the jury. Jess knew well that there was a definite art to jury selection, and in her experience, selecting jurors was to be taken as seriously as the presentation of the entire case itself. Everything else was ready to go. All exhibits had been organized and placed neatly into binders. Exhibit boards had been prepared, colorfully emphasizing the key issues of the case. Pre-trial briefs and motions had all been filed. Jury instructions had been agreed on, and the witnesses had all been lined up. All that remained was the selection of the six jurors and one alternate who would ultimately decide the fate of the case. So, upon arrival at the courthouse, that was exactly how the first day of trial was spent. The entire day was devoted to voir dire questioning of various jury pool members, trying to find just the right blend of backgrounds and experiences for the people who would ultimately sit on the jury.

After a long first day and after having finally agreed upon a jury, Judge Hancock swore the jury members in, and then let everyone go home for the day, planning to start fresh early the next morning. Jess, Robin, and Phil regrouped back at the office and discussed trial strategy until the early evening hours. Phil finally returned to his hotel, and even though it was getting late, Jess still had yet to review her opening statement and prepare her cross-examination of the witnesses scheduled for the next day. Jess and Robin retired to Jess's office to discuss the upcoming witness schedules.

"What do you think of the jury?" Jess closed the office door and quickly walked behind her desk, sitting down in her burgundy leather chair.

Robin considered the question. "It's not as if I have any experience with these things, but according to their voir dire answers, I think we did pretty well." She sat in the chair by the window and bit her lower lip lightly. "Except maybe for juror number three. He seemed a bit shifty-eyed to me."

"Shifty-eyed?"

Robin chuckled lightly. "Yeah. Didn't you see that nasty look he gave juror number five. I think we definitely need to watch those two."

"Alright. You're the official juror watcher." Jess handed Robin her legal pad. "Now, let's go over the scripts for tomorrow."

"When is Anne Carver scheduled?"

"They're putting her up on the stand on Wednesday to close out their case. We'll take the opportunity to discredit her, and then move right on into our case." Blue eyes twinkled. "We can rehearse her script tomorrow, okay?"

"Right, chief." Robin's stomach chose that particular moment to growl. "Um, Jess? How about we get something to eat first."

Jess couldn't help but grin. "What did you have in mind?"

"Hmm." Robin tapped her finger lightly on her chin in thought. "Pizza or Chinese. You pick."

A dark eyebrow arched. "If we get Chinese, can I have....?"

"Yes." Robin chuckled.

Jess was mildly perplexed. "You don't even know what I was gonna say."

"Yes, I do." The blonde head nodded. "And yes, you can have the shrimp with lobster sauce."

"Huh. It seems I might be a bit too predictable." Jess playfully swiveled in her chair.

"Nope. You're just you. Let me go call in the order." Robin left Jess's office and made her way down to the kitchen to retrieve a menu from the assorted menu selection. As she neared the kitchen, she unexpectedly ran into Keith who was busily working on a last minute demonstrative exhibit for the case.

"Hi, Robin." Keith ran his ran his hand through his light blonde hair. "So, how are things going so far?"

"Good." Robin stopped for a moment to casually engage Keith in conversation. "We picked the jury today, and tomorrow we do opening statements and start their case. Jess and I are just going over some of the preparation now." She started to make her way toward the kitchen again.

"Hey, Robin?" Keith stopped her progress. "Are you going to the holiday party next week?"

Whoa. 'Holiday party' was the politically correct euphemism in the modern business world for Christmas party. "Um...yes, probably." *Why?* Robin asked the next question carefully. "Are you going?"

"Yeah. Uh...will you be going with someone? I mean, I know you haven't been in town very long, and if you're not bringing someone, we could maybe go together, if you'd like." Keith seemed quite sincere in his offer.

How did I miss this? Robin smiled politely, albeit a bit awkwardly. "I'm not bringing anyone, Keith, but I'll probably not stay at the party too long. This trial is scheduled to last all week, and then I have relatives coming in from out of town, so I've really got a lot going on. I may just go for a short time." *I'm rambling.* Robin tried to let Keith down gently. "Thank you for asking, though. It was nice of you to think of me. I'm sure I'll see you there."

Keith nodded. "Okay. But let me know if you ever need an escort." He bowed in exaggerated formality. "I'm at your service."

"Thanks." Robin nodded back. *He's very sweet.* A mental sigh. *But I'm not interested.* The young associate turned and once again headed toward the kitchen, calling back over her shoulder down the long hallway. "Don't work too late tonight, Keith." She entered the kitchen and pulled the desired menu off the bulletin board, proceeding to order the requisite Chinese cuisine. Once that particular task was completed, Robin sat down in one of the vinyl kitchen chairs for a moment, shaking her head to herself in mild disbelief. It seemed that things were getting more complicated. *How should I have handled that with Keith?* She mentally pondered her available options. Should she have pretended she was indeed going to bring someone to the holiday party? For that matter, when it came to firm functions, should she attempt to put on false airs, and routinely parade endless men to various events for appearance's sake? Should she accept offers from Keith or Paul or anyone else just to keep suspicions at bay? *That seems dishonest.* Or is it okay to go to these functions alone? All the time? Or is it okay not to go at all? How would that look? An audible sigh. There were just too many questions and too many complications. *I need to talk to Jess.*

After waiting a few moments, Robin dashed out to the small Chinese restaurant down the street to quickly pick up the food. She returned in short order, and immediately made her way back up to Jess's office, food in hand. She opened the solid wood door and entered the office, setting the food containers on a corner of the otherwise paper covered desk.

"Ready to eat?" Robin stepped back and closed the door.

Jess looked up from her papers. "Sure. Let me try to clear some of this stuff out of the way."

It was as if Jess and Robin had done this particular thing a hundred times before. They efficiently set out the paper plates and utensils, and then spooned out portions of the Chinese food onto their own plates. For several moments, they ate together in silence, neither one speaking or offering any conversation.

"Is everything okay?" Jess swallowed a bite of her shrimp with lobster sauce.

Robin nibbled at her egg roll. "I had a conversation with Keith earlier. He...um...offered to escort me to the firm's holiday party next week." She wasn't sure how Jess would react to the news.

"Oh." Jess considered the situation. "Do you want to go with him?" Jess thought perhaps Robin wanted to attend the party, but not alone...for various reasons.

"No." The young associate sighed heavily and then put her chopsticks down. "But we should discuss how we appear in public, don't you think?"

"What are you saying?" Jess pushed her plate away and sat back in her leather chair.

"I...um...." Robin fumbled. "I don't know the etiquette here as far as the firm is concerned. I mean, is it okay to go to these things alone, or if one of us wants to go, should we be seen with someone?" Robin looked tentatively at Jess. "We haven't really talked about the party. What are you going to do? Are you going?"

Jess met Robin's eyes, considering how to answer. "In the past, I never really went to many of these things. Wasn't my style to stand around and chit chat all night. As for whether I'm going next week, well, quite frankly, I really haven't thought about it, considering the trial and all." She grinned, somewhat mischievously. "And I've also been a little bit preoccupied with...um...other things." A blue eye winked to make her point.

Robin blushed. "Well, do you want to go?" Green eyes cautiously queried.

"Only if you'll be there."

"I want to go, yes, but I need to know what the firm's expectations are when it comes to attendance at these type of functions, and if it's okay to go alone or not go at all sometimes." The young associate slowly resumed eating. "It just doesn't seem right to go with someone if the only purpose is to present an image...a false image." She looked seriously at Jess. "That would seem like a lie."

Jess understood Robin's point. *Where do you draw the line between keeping things quiet and creating false images for appearances sake?* "I think we may need to consider all angles of this. We don't have to decide on anything tonight, but I think we should think carefully about a few things."

"Okay." Robin was hesitant.

"First, we agreed to keep things between us quiet because of the potential concerns that the firm may have, and because our relationship is no one else's business, right?"

"Yes."

"Okay, so there are consequences with keeping things quiet. It's unavoidable, but we have to watch ourselves in public. That means firm events. I agree with you that it isn't a particularly noble thing to bring along some poor soul just to keep up appearances...that is, unless you have a prior understanding." Jess tried to give Robin an option if she chose to go with it.

"Okay. What if I want to go alone, or we both want to go alone, or we both don't want to go at all?"

"Well, to be honest, it's best to go to these things most of the time and show that you're a team player. So, I'd say it's better to go alone rather than not go at all." Jess smiled wryly. "I haven't followed that rule much." Blue eyes then stared pensively into green. "If we both go alone, eventually, after a period of time, people will start to wonder why we never bring anyone. It's only human nature to speculate and to notice things like that. The gossip mills are never lacking."

Robin blew out a frustrated breath. "So it's a catch-22 situation. We can go by ourselves and generate gossip that we never bring anyone, thereby risking that the firm could become suspicious." She sighed. "Or we can not go at all, and then risk not being seen as team players."

"Or one or both of us could go with someone...um...male of course, as long as the guy knows ahead of time that it's just a simple evening at a party and nothing more. I don't think that we should leave him with any false impressions." Jess actually appeared quite sad as she said this. The idea of Robin with anyone else bothered her more than she wanted to admit.

Robin shook her head solemnly. "I don't want to be with anyone but you. Being with someone else, even at a casual party, seems like a lie, because the whole time I was with them, I'd be thinking about how much I'd really rather be with you. Do you understand?"

"Yes." The dark head nodded slowly. "I understand. Come here for a minute." Blue eyes beckoned.

Robin stood up and stepped around the desk as Jess rose from her chair. They met half way, and Jess wrapped her arms around Robin in a gentle hug. It was meant as a reassurance, to affirm their connection to each other, and remind each of them what was real and important. They stood in the comfort of their embrace for several moments, neither noticing how much time had actually transpired.

"Why is everything so complicated?" Robin finally whispered, her voice a bit shaky.

"Robin, honey, we have each other. We know that. No matter what else, right?" A large hand rubbed the petite shoulders in a soothing motion. "We don't have to decide anything tonight. Let's just get through the trial, first. Okay?"

There was no answer.

Jess pulled back slightly, and caught a glimmer of moisture in Robin's eye before the young associate abruptly turned away. At that moment, Jess nearly lost her composure. *I don't want to hurt you.* She and Robin were definitely going to have to discuss this matter more fully later on. It was now becoming all too clear to the junior partner that the toll of keeping their relationship clandestine would likely be very great. The irony of the situation was, the toll of having their relationship found out would probably be just as great. *It's a catch-22.* "Robin, look at me, sweetheart." She waited as Robin complied. "We're in this together. You told me that, remember? We'll work this out. I promise."

Misty green eyes regarded blue. "I believe you."

"Good." Jess smiled warmly. "Now let's finish eating so we can get back to work, and maybe we can get done here at a decent hour tonight." She gave Robin quick hug and then sat back down in her leather chair, looking directly across the desk. "Are you okay?"

"Yeah." Robin resumed eating. "I just have one very important question for you."

Jess picked up her chopsticks and took a bite. "Okay."

A blonde eyebrow slowly arched. "Can I have some of your shrimp?"

****

The next day, the trial went much as expected. Each counsel gave an opening statement, and then the opposing side began presenting its case in chief. Robin observed the proceedings with avid fascination, and assisted ably in locating and presenting all the proper exhibits to be used for the day's witnesses as they testified. At one point, during a potentially critical part of Jess's cross-examination of a witness, Robin noticed that juror number three appeared to be nodding off. As improbable as it may have seemed, at that precise moment, Jess turned toward Robin, and the young associate subtly signaled out the dozing juror. The junior partner promptly requested a short recess so that the jury could take a much needed break. All day long, it seemed to go pretty much the same way. Jess and Robin worked together like a well-oiled machine, each almost instinctively taking cues from the other, as if they had done this type of thing a hundred times before. Everything just seemed to click.

And so the day ended, and several points were made in favor of both the plaintiff and the defendant. Once court had recessed late that afternoon, Jess, Robin and Phil returned to the office to review the day's events and to briefly strategize for the next day's testimony. After a small catered-in dinner, Phil finally returned to his hotel, and the two attorneys retreated to Jess's office to continue with their trial preparations.

"How do you think it went today?" Jess stood at the large window and looked out at the night sky through the reflected glass.

Robin sat down in the chair next to the same window. "You made some good points on cross-examination." She hesitated slightly.

"But…."

Robin sighed audibly. "The testimony is kind of..." She didn't quite know how to put it. "Well, Jess, it's boring." Robin grinned sheepishly. "It's not you, it's just that the technical and financial terminology is rather tedious. I think more than one juror dozed off today, and I'm not sure I blame them."

"Yeah." Jess nodded. "I was thinking that, too. I think we may need to change things up a bit." She turned from the window and regarded Robin for a moment. "Anne Carver's on tomorrow. You and I have been over her script a dozen times."

"Right."

Jess brought her hand up to her chin pensively, then stared seriously into sea green eyes. "How would you feel about taking her cross-examination?"

The young associate's mouth fell open slightly, stunned surprise at the question evident. Robin remained silent for a moment before finally speaking. "You want me to...I mean, you know I don't have any courtroom experience."

"I know. But you know the script, and you've seen me cross-examine the witnesses we've had so far." Jess leaned up against the side of her cherry wood desk. "Besides, you found a key piece of evidence. You deserve a shot at her." Jess paused. "But I don't want you to feel pressured to do this, Robin. If you'd rather not, it's not a problem."

The young associate thought seriously about Jess's offer. If truth be told, Robin was absolutely itching to have a crack at a witness. All day long, she had mentally reviewed all the angles and all the questions she would have asked, as Jess simultaneously proceeded to brilliantly cross-examine and pick apart each witness's testimony. A grin slowly edged its way across the young associate's face. *Let me have at it.* "Will you help me rehearse?"

Good going, Robin. Jess grinned rather proudly. "You betcha, kiddo. You're going to do great. The jury will trust you, and they won't think you're putting something over on them. Put that in contrast to the deception by Anne Carver, and you'll have the jury hanging on your every word."

The blonde head bowed in bashful uncertainty. "You have such confidence in me. How can you be sure it'll work?"

I know you. "I know you." Jess replied simply. "And remember, Robin, I'll be right there at the counsel table. If you get stuck or she says something you weren't expecting, you can just look at me, or you can pause and come over to confer for a moment." She grinned and arched a dark eyebrow expectantly. "So, ready to rehearse?"

Robin nodded, now quite confident herself. "Yep." She rubbed her hands together. "Let me have at her. She'll be toast when I'm done."

Jess shook her head in amusement. *Ooooh, I may have created a monster.*

****

Wednesday's proceedings went much as predicted. By mid-day, the opposition was ready to put Anne Carver on the stand as their last witness before resting their case. Jess had surmised that opposing counsel would gloss over Anne Carver's background and get right into the heart of her testimony, and that's just what he did. What Anne Carver said on direct examination was damaging, and Jess could sense that the over-all tide was favoring the other side. Of course, the jury had not yet heard Robin's cross-examination of Anne Carver, nor had Jess had a chance to put up her case. But still, the defense had to play all its cards perfectly in order to sway the jury, and Jess knew it. There was more riding on the cross-examination of Anne Carver than Jess wanted to admit, and although her confidence in Robin was solid, she wondered if she may have put too much pressure on her.

After the lunch break, Judge Hancock called the afternoon session to order, and the bailiff led the jury back into the courtroom. The proceedings were now scheduled to start with the cross-examination of Anne Carver.

"Ready?" Jess gave Robin a confident smile.

Robin nodded with equal confidence. "You bet." After brief introductory formalities and a change in court reporters, Robin got to the main line of her questioning of Anne Carver. "Ms. Carver, you mentioned in your direct examination that you have fifteen years of experience in the field of accounting. Is that correct?"

"Yes." Anne Carver appeared quite sure of herself.

"Let me hand you Plaintiff's Exhibit 32, which is your resume. I see that it notes the names of the firms at which you have worked during the past fifteen years, correct?" Robin was laying the foundation for future questions.

"Yes."

"Okay. If you would, please read for the jury what you list on your resume as your educational background."

Anne Carver remained quite confident as she read for the jury her stated educational background. Jess watched the proceedings with keen interest. The jury, at this point, was mostly asleep, but Jess noticed opposing counsel suddenly straighten up in his chair at the last question.

Robin continued her cross-examination. "Now, Ms. Carver, you just stated that you graduated with a Bachelor of Science degree from the University of Maryland in 1981, is that correct?"

"Yes." Anne Carver's self-confidence never wavered.

"Are you sure that it was 1981?"

"Yes."

"Could it have been 1980 or 1982?"

"No, it was 1981." Anne Carver's voice became uncharacteristically defensive.

"And it was the University of Maryland?"

"Yes."

Jess watched as the members of the jury perked up and shifted in their chairs to pay closer attention. So far, Robin seemed to be making a good impression. She was not disrespectful to the witness, and she projected an air of honesty and wholesomeness that made her quite likeable, especially in the jury's eyes. *You're doing great, Robin.* Opposing counsel was nervously tapping his foot lightly on the tiled floor.

"I want to remind you that you are under oath here, today, Ms. Carver. Did you graduate with a Bachelor of Science degree from the University of Maryland?"

"Yes." Anne Carver remained poised.

"Ms. Carver, let me show you a document we received a few days ago. Your Honor, I'd like to offer this document as Defendant's Exhibit 15." Robin handed copies of the exhibit to the judge's trial clerk and to opposing counsel.

Opposing counsel immediately stood up. "Objection, Your Honor. This is the first we've seen of this document. It was not disclosed to us previously."

"Your Honor, Defendant offers the document for impeachment purposes." Robin explained.

Judge Hancock took the document from his trial clerk and reviewed it. "Overruled. You may proceed, Ms. Wilson."

Robin handed the document to the witness. "Would you please read for the jury what it says at the top of Defendant's Exhibit 15?"

Anne Carver looked nervously at Plaintiff's counsel then back to the document. "University of Maryland, Office of the Registrar."

"And what does it say just under that?"

"Certificate of Non-Attendance." The witness replied flatly.

"And is that your name and social security number reflected on that document?"

A moment's hesitation. "Yes."

"Does the document say that according to the University of Maryland, Registrar's Office, there is no record of your attendance or graduation from that school in 1981 or any other year?"

"Well, that's what it says." The witness attempted slight evasion.

"It says that, but that would be incorrect?" Robin queried.

"I don't know why it says that because I graduated from there. I have my degree."

Robin arched an eyebrow. "So are you saying that the Office of the Registrar is wrong, then?"

"They are wrong, because I certainly graduated from there. I'll have to check into why they don't have me listed as graduating."

Jess watched earnestly as opposing counsel hung his head. While it was true that he certainly had questions of his own regarding Anne Carver's background, he hadn't checked her credentials thoroughly, and it was possible that this was all just a huge mistake. Or she could be lying. Ethically, he couldn't let her perjure herself if he knew she was not being truthful. But still, he didn't know for sure, so he kept quiet. Jess also noticed that the jury was now on the edge of their seats as the testimony progressed. *That's one way to wake up a jury.* She smirked. *Now, go in for the kill, Robin.*

"Okay, Ms. Carver." Robin continued. "You also stated on your resume that you graduated from Harvard Business School with an MBA in 1984. Is that correct?"

"Yes." The witness answered hesitantly.

"Once again, are you sure it was Harvard Business School?"

"Yes." The witness sensed that a trap had been set.

"Ms. Carver, let me show you another document we received a few days ago. Your Honor, I'd like to offer this document as Defendant's Exhibit 16." Robin handed copies of the exhibit to the judge's trial clerk and to opposing counsel in the same manner as she had done so before.

Opposing counsel slowly stood up and voiced his objection weakly. "Objection. This document, again, was not disclosed to us previously."

"Your Honor," Robin smiled disarmingly, "Defendant offers this document for impeachment purposes."

Judge Hancock, again, took the document in question from his trial clerk and reviewed it. "Overruled. You may continue, Ms. Wilson."

Robin handed the document to the witness. "As you did before, Ms. Carver, would you please read for the jury what it says at the top of that document?"

Anne Carver swallowed nervously and then read the document. "Harvard University Business School, Office of the Registrar."

"And what does it say just under that?"

The witness hesitated, then complied. "Certificate of Non-Attendance."

"And, once again, is that your name and social security number shown on that document?"

The witness sighed. "Yes."

"Does the document say that according to Harvard University Business School, Registrar's Office, there is no record of your attendance or graduation from that school in 1984 or any other year?"

"It says that."

"Would that be incorrect?" Robin queried.

The witness was boxed in. "Well, again, I certainly graduated from there, so I don't know why they have no record of it."

Robin offered a knowing smile. "Let me make sure I understand your testimony, Ms. Carver. You're saying that you graduated from the University of Maryland and from Harvard Business School, but both schools' registrar's offices have no record of your attendance or graduation, and you don't know why? Is that your testimony?"

"It is."

"So, both schools' registrar's offices are wrong, and they both, coincidentally, made the same error. Is that your testimony?"

"It is."

The junior partner was doing her best to hold back a beaming grin. The jury was visibly shaking their collective heads, and opposing counsel was furiously writing on his legal pad, no doubt trying to salvage his case. *Now, put the icing on the cake, Robin.*

The young associate made eye contact with Jess for a brief moment, then sought to drive the point home. "Alright, then, Ms. Carver. You have fifteen years of experience in accounting, as you've noted, once again, on your resume. Is that correct?"

"Yes, it is."

"Okay." Robin walked over and stood directly next to the jury box, forcing the witness to look into the jury's eyes. "Then, in your considered experience, Ms. Carver, if a person did not have an undergraduate degree or a master's degree in business administration or any related field, would such a person, in your experience, be qualified to render a bid on a project such as the one that is at issue in this lawsuit?"

"No." The witness answered firmly. "But I am qualified."

Robin shook her head. "No further questions, Your Honor." The young associate casually returned to the defendant's counsel table and was promptly greeted with a warm smile from Jess and a nod of approval from the client, Phil Jones. Judge Hancock took the opportunity to call a recess and let the jury take a short break before commencing with the defendant's case in chief. Immediately, Anne Carver was huddled over at the plaintiff's counsel table, an animated conversation obviously taking place.

The junior partner couldn't stop smirking. It was all turning out better than she could have hoped. The jury was now wide awake, and the plaintiff's entire case was in serious trouble. Jess was quite proud of Robin. This was Robin's first foray into courtroom litigation, and she had hit a home run. It confirmed what the junior partner had known all along. Her own instincts had been right, even from the beginning, on the decision to include Robin on her trial team. All Harry's questions and concerns not withstanding, Robin was just the person Jess needed on this case. Robin was smart, had great instincts of her own, and was a hard worker. She also got along well with Jess, which was no small thing, and she projected a wholesome and honest image, which was something the lawyering profession seriously lacked. The junior partner grinned. Things were definitely starting to look up.

The remainder of the afternoon proceeded with the presentation of the defendant's case in chief, and all throughout the day, Jess had an uncharacteristic glint in her eyes. Robin knew she'd done a good job with Anne Carver, a fact which was confirmed when during the last break of the day, Jess passed a note to the young associate which simply stated:

'Good job today, kiddo. You've earned a reward.'

Robin looked away and promptly blushed.

****

It was late in the evening when Jess had finished her last bit of preparation for the following day's witnesses and eventual closing arguments. She was tired, dead tired, but all in all, it had been an overwhelmingly productive day. *Robin did great.* She smiled briefly at the thought and turned off her computer, packing her briefcase before heading home. She was just about to leave when she heard a small and unexpected knock at the door. Robin peeked in, then slipped inside the office.

"You're still here." Robin smiled and closed the door behind her.

Jess eyed Robin suspiciously. "I thought you left hours ago."

"Nope, I was sifting through my in-box and e-mails. They really do seem to accumulate." Robin chuckled lightly to herself. "Are you leaving now?"

"Just packing up." Jess walked over to where Robin stood, warm blue eyes regarding the smaller woman fondly. "I am so proud of you. Have I told you that?"

Robin blushed and then grinned widely. "I think you might have mentioned that a time or two today. Thanks." A mischievous blonde eyebrow shot up. "So, as I recall, you promised me a reward for my good work. Care to fill me in on what it might be?"

A dark eyebrow arched in response. *She wants to play.* "Here's the deal, kiddo. You tell me what I win under your point system, and I'll tell you what your reward is." Jess figured she might as well try to finagle Robin into telling her what her point prize was going to be.

The young associate tapped a petite finger lightly against her chin in thought, then shook her head decisively. "No deal."

"No?" The junior partner feigned an exaggerated hurt expression. "How come?"

"Well, the way I see it, I've already earned my reward, and you're still working on your point totals. It's only fair that should I receive my reward now, while you will just simply have to wait." Robin playfully tugged at the cuff of Jess's suit sleeve. "You thought I'd cave in and tell you, didn't you?" She smirked.

"Well, you can't blame me for trying." Jess offered a sheepish grin, and then stepped a bit closer to Robin, locking clear blue eyes onto green. "Are you sure there's nothing I can do to persuade you to tell me?"

Robin's breathing quickened a bit. "Nope. Nothing."

"Okay, then." The junior partner turned nonchalantly and grabbed her briefcase, walking purposefully over toward the door.

"Hey, not so fast." Robin raced up to her. "You can't leave yet."

"Why not?" Jess teased.

"Because I was promised a reward and I intend to collect it." Amused green eyes danced merrily.

She is so damn cute. Jess was simply helpless to resist the game. She abruptly set her briefcase down, and in one fluid motion, gently spun Robin around against the closed solid wood door. She pressed herself against the younger woman and whispered softly into a petite ear. "We're not in the appropriate setting, Robin, but I'll give you a little hint of what I had in mind." With that, Jess nibbled the small earlobe and then proceeded to nip her way down the petite jaw line, finally placing several soft, lingering kisses on Robin's sweet lips. Jess broke away, smiling blue eyes meeting dazed sea green. "Hold that thought." She winked.

Robin swallowed several times. "Uh...yeah. I mean, I will." *How is it possible that she can make me feel this way?*

"Good. Now, let's go. We've got another long day ahead of us tomorrow." Jess opened the door and strode out toward the elevators without so much as a backward glance.

The young associate lagged behind for a moment, then scurried off after the junior partner. *I might have to rethink my decision. She can definitely be quite persuasive.*

****

A cold front blew in just in time for the wrap up of the trial activities. The sights and sounds of the holiday season infused the air, and now with the colder weather upon the city, it really seemed to feel as if Christmas was near. Robin found herself actually missing the snow and the festive winter atmosphere she had become accustomed to up North. Florida, it seemed, was somehow quite lacking in the winter department. The trial had continued on for the remainder of the week, with the defense team putting on its case, and Jess, in Robin's opinion, doing an absolutely brilliant job. And so, as the trial approached its conclusion, Robin found herself sitting at counsel table Friday morning waiting rather impatiently for closing arguments to begin. She let her mind wander briefly, quietly musing about the upcoming holidays. *Christmas. Parents. Christmas and parents. Here.* Robin frowned visibly. *This is not good.* She never understood why everything always seemed to be so complicated.

Twirling her pen lightly, Robin's mind drifted to the junior partner sitting next to her. She had really wanted to spend Christmas with Jess. They hadn't discussed it, with the trial taking precedence over almost everything else during the past couple of weeks, and for all Robin knew, Jess was planning to go to her mother's for Christmas. But now, with Robin's parents visiting, it was all but certain that she and Jess were just not going to be able to spend Christmas together this year. And that really sucked. She frowned visibly again. She pondered the situation a bit more. Perhaps she and Jess could spend some time with each other after Christmas, and then maybe celebrate New Year's together. Robin considered that thought for a moment, her disposition lightening up just a bit. *That could work.*

Her mind, quite on its own and almost on instinct, led her tangentially in a different direction. *So, what to get Jess for Christmas.* Robin considered the matter. *What do you get someone who has everything?* The fact was, she didn't just want to get Jess any old thing. She wanted whatever she picked out to be special, and meaningful, and...what? *And significant.* Robin mulled that thought over. *Significant, how?* Her concentrated musings were abruptly interrupted by Judge Hancock entering the courtroom, followed by the jury, and the bailiff announcing the commencement of the day's court proceedings. She reluctantly decided to leave her Christmas deliberations for another time.

Within moments, the proceedings were underway and closing arguments began, with each side giving its summary of the case and the evidence presented during the week-long trial. The jury, to its credit, sat and listened attentively as the attorneys for each side spoke and made their points. Robin watched closely as Jess summed up the testimony and the key points made in favor of the defendant by each witness. Jess made particular reference to Anne Carver's lack of credibility, and Robin felt a curious quiet pride fill her as Jess spoke. Jess was good, there was no denying that, and Robin recalled Harry's assessment of Jess's litigation skills when he had first assigned Robin to work with her that mid-October day. *"It's really something to see her in action."* Robin recalled his words exactly. *Yes, it most definitely is something seeing her in action.* The young associate openly admired Jess's technique of drawing the jury into the defendant's point of view, taking note in particular of Jess's stance and the body language she projected to the jury as she made her final argument. The quiet intensity in the tone of her voice absolutely captivated the audience. *She's amazing.*

Time passed quickly, and closing arguments for both parties concluded right before the lunch hour. Judge Hancock proceeded to immediately read to the jury their jury instructions, charging them on their task in their deliberations on the verdict. Once the jury instructions were completed, everyone rose as the judge and the jury exited the courtroom for the midday recess.

Jess blew out a long breath and threw her legal pad in her briefcase. "Okay. Now, we wait. Let's go on back to the office for lunch."

Robin packed up the exhibit books and files and then gathered her briefcase and laptop. "I'll arrange for someone to come and pick up all the exhibits later." She followed Jess and Phil out of the courtroom, and all three of them headed back toward the office. As they walked down the long tiled corridor, Robin gave Jess a gentle squeeze on the arm. "You were great."

The junior partner glanced quietly at Robin. "Thanks. We'll see."

When they arrived back at the Roberts & McDaniel office suite, Jess escorted Phil into the main conference room where lunch was ready and waiting for them. "So, what do you think?" Phil asked as they entered through the conference room double doors.

"It's always hard to tell with juries." The junior partner sat down, eyeing the selection of sandwiches that had been brought in, and finally deciding on ham and Swiss cheese on rye.

After a few moments, Robin entered the conference room, having secured a paralegal to pick up the trial materials at the courthouse later that afternoon. The young associate selected a turkey on whole wheat sandwich and listened intently as the conversation between Phil and Jess progressed.

"I think we've got a good shot, Phil." Jess took a bite of her sandwich, not really tasting it. "One thing to consider. If the jury's out for a long time, it probably goes against us. That generally means they've decided in favor of the plaintiff and are spending a lot of time figuring out the money damages. We obviously don't want that."

Phil selected his own sandwich and nodded. "Right. Let's hope for a quick verdict after lunch, then." He poured himself a soda. "Jessica, I wanted to take this opportunity to thank you and Robin for the great job the two of you have done, whatever the outcome is for us. I know how diligently and hard you both worked to put this case together under sometimes quite difficult circumstances. I'll be speaking with Harry soon, and I'll be sure to let him know what a terrific team he has in you two." He nodded appreciatively and then turned to face Robin. "And you, young lady, did an especially outstanding job with Anne Carver. Harry, might just have to watch out that some other law firm around town doesn't snatch you away from here." He grinned. "Thank you both for your hard work. RSJ Industries appreciates the extraordinary effort."

Jess gracefully accepted the compliment. "It's our pleasure, Phil." Blue eyes tracked over to where Robin sat quietly eating her lunch and taking everything in. The young associate looked up and silently met Jess's gaze. "I certainly wouldn't have been able to do nearly as well without Robin, here." Jess smiled warmly, a blue eye slyly winking in Robin's direction as Phil was apparently too busy eating his sandwich to take notice. "Let's just hope for the best this afternoon."

And so, for several hours that Friday afternoon, they waited. And then they waited some more. It was now becoming quite late in the day, with still no word from the jury. Jess, at first, took everything in stride, but then couldn't help but become increasingly worried that things were just taking far too long for comfort. As the afternoon crawled interminably on, she finally became resigned to the fate that the jury had probably just flat out decided against them. It was all but evident now. The jury was talking about the money, and the question was, just how much money were they going to award the plaintiff? *Damn.* And she'd had such a good feeling about this one, too. A moment later, Jess's secretary, Angie, stepped inside the junior partner's office.

"What is it, Angie?" Jess fidgeted slightly, her hands playing with the glass paperweight that usually sat on her desk.

"Judge Hancock's office called. The jury's back and he wants everyone over in his courtroom in thirty minutes." Angie waited for

Jess's reply.

An audible sigh. *Here we go.* "Alright. Would you go over to the conference room and ask Robin and Phil to meet me at the elevators in five minutes?" Angie nodded and then left the office. Jess stood up and took a deep cleansing breath, mentally bracing herself for the expected loss. She shook away her worries, put on her suit jacket, and gathered her briefcase. She took a step forward, and then paused uneasily as an errant thought crossed her mind. *I'd hate it if we lost Robin's first case.* And then she promptly chastised herself for her momentary lapse. *Winning or losing a case is not personal, Jess. Don't make it such.* She shook her head in rebuke at her own foolishness. *But still....*

The junior partner strode out the office door and onward toward the elevators, her demeanor reflecting an air of confidence she absolutely did not possess. She met up with Robin and Phil waiting nearby.

"Ready?" Jess gave a confident smile.

Phil grinned. "Ready. Let's go."

The three of them headed for the county courthouse located about two blocks away from the office building. It was a rather pleasant walk down the main avenue. The cloudless blue sky and cool winter air served to invigorate the weary trial team as they walked briskly toward the newly built and extremely modern looking tall courthouse building. The city had placed festive holiday decorations all along the main avenue, the colored garland glittering in the late afternoon sunlight, and the strings of lights swaying gently in the winter's breeze. It was apparent that the evening would bring colder air across the local area, and it now seemed that it might be a bit easier for everyone in town to get into the holiday spirit.

Once inside the massive courthouse structure, the trial team slid easily through the metal detectors and took the elevator up to Judge Hancock's courtroom. Plaintiff's counsel was already in place when the defense team arrived, and all parties took their seats and waited with veiled nervousness for the arrival of the jury.

Robin tapped Jess's hand lightly as they sat at the defendant's counsel table. "You did a good job." She whispered and smiled warmly. "Even if the jury doesn't see it our way."

Jess nodded, careful not to let her doubts show. "Thanks."

A moment later, Judge Hancock entered the courtroom, and the bailiff proceeded to lead the jury into the room and over to the jury box. Robin noted that not one member of the jury looked over at either counsel table. *Is that good, or bad?* As soon as everyone was situated, Judge Hancock fumbled for a moment before putting on his wire rimmed glasses, and then directed his attention toward the jury foreman.

"Mr. Foreman, has the jury reached a verdict?"

The jury foreman rose from his chair. "We have, Your Honor."

The bailiff retrieved the jury verdict form from the foreman and handed it to the judge for his review. Judge Hancock read the verdict silently to himself, then handed the paper back to the bailiff to return to the jury foreman.

Judge Hancock proceeded. "On Count One of the plaintiff's complaint, what says the jury?"

The foreman's voice echoed slightly in the large, vaulted ceiling courtroom as he read from the verdict form. "We, the jury in this cause, find for the Defendant on Count One of the complaint."

A collective sigh came from the defendant's table, while a muffled groan emanated from the opposite side of the room.

"Alright." Judge Hancock continued. "On the last count, Count Two of the plaintiff's complaint, Mr. Foreman, what says the jury?"

The jury foreman again read the verdict form in similar fashion. "We, the jury in this cause, find for the Defendant on Count Two of the complaint."

Wide smiles combined with relief greeted each other at the defendant's table. Defeat and distress was evident on the plaintiff's side of the room. Judge Hancock quickly thanked the jury members for their time and effort, and without further ado, gaveled the trial proceedings to a close.

Robin turned around and spoke briefly with Phil, as he again thanked her for all the hard work she and Jess had put into the case. The young associate glanced across the courtroom and spied Jess engaged in an intense conversation with one of the jury members. *Isn't that juror number five?*

The courtroom emptied out quickly, and one of the paralegals from the firm arrived in time to collect all the trial exhibits and case files and return them to the office. Robin waited patiently as Jess continued her discussion with juror number five, while Phil exited out into the hallway to call his office and inform them of the trial's successful outcome.

Jess ended her conversation and walked back over to where Robin was standing. "Where's Phil?"

"Out in the hall talking to his office. What was that all about?" Robin gestured toward the area where Jess and juror number five had stood moments ago.

"Oh, I was just talking to him about why it took them so long to reach the verdict." The junior partner chuckled lightly. "You'll never guess, but it seems our juror number three was the only hold out. He apparently wanted to give the plaintiff some money."

"Ah, the shifty-eyed one." Robin smirked.

"Right. Juror number five said that he and juror number three mixed it up a bit, and they almost came to blows a couple of times. Since it's Friday afternoon, the other jurors were finally able to convince juror number three that the plaintiff had not met its burden of proof, and he eventually ended up agreeing with everyone else to find in our favor."

Robin shook her head in amazement. "I knew we had to watch out for that guy."

"You had him pegged. From now on, I dub you the official juror watcher." Jess grinned and then shook her head in amazement. "It just goes to show you that you never can tell with juries." She lowered her voice. "I'm almost embarrassed to say that when we came in here, I was sure we had lost the case."

Robin's eyes grew wide. "Really. You hid it well." She furrowed her light brows. "But it looked to me like you had the jury pretty well convinced." The blonde head nodded in affirmation. "I knew you did a good job."

"Correction." Jess strode with Robin out through the courtroom's double doors and into the mostly empty corridor. "We did a good job. Don't leave yourself out of this." She scanned the hallway looking for Phil. "Now let's collect Phil and get back to the office so we can brag a little bit." She twitched a dark eyebrow teasingly. "I love to brag."

****

The busy week had finally concluded, and by everyone's assessment, it had been a resounding success. Phil Jones was quite pleased with the trial's results and the success, in particular, of the trial team. He made sure Harry Roberts and Gordon McDaniel knew how delighted he was with the firm's work on the case. After meeting with Harry and Gordon, Phil caught a late flight back home to New Orleans. Robin left the office shortly thereafter, mentioning something about taking care of some small errands. Jess lingered about the office awhile longer, chatting amicably with Harry about the week's trial events. She made sure to acknowledge the contributions that Robin made to the trial's favorable outcome, and Harry seemed quite pleased with the results. Finally, after almost everyone else had gone home for the weekend, Jess let herself unwind from the adrenaline rush of the day, and headed herself wearily out the office door.

She drove her silver Mercedes homeward through the city streets, the blinking of the Christmas lights on the passing lamp posts serving as a constant reminder of the holiday season. She hadn't let her mind think at all about the upcoming holidays, preferring instead to dwell on trial preparations, rather than on things that contained a fair degree of uncertainty. Now, however, as she made her way silently home, her mind absently turned to those uncertain matters.

Christmas. Robin's parents were coming down to visit. That meant, obviously, that Jess and Robin wouldn't be able to be with each other on Christmas day or even Christmas Eve. Robin would be with her family, and that was really a good thing, but Jess was more than a little bit disappointed at the unfairness of it all. *Damn.* She and Robin should be spending Christmas together, Jess reasoned, feeling a bit of self-pity in the process. Jess had idly entertained the notion of bringing Robin with her to Tampa to visit her mother, either at Christmas or some other time. *Mom would like her.* She smiled at the thought. *But shit. Christmas is definitely out.* She frowned unhappily, then considered other options. Perhaps they could both plan a trip to Tampa around New Year's. That would be good, wouldn't it? *Face it, Jess. You want to bring her home to meet your mother.* It was a quaint notion, to be sure, but it also seemed to be quite important at the moment. *Would mom understand about us? Should I even tell her?*

Jess stopped at a red light and turned on the radio, festive Christmas carols interspersing between the regular light rock music selections, all of which served to distract the junior partner momentarily from her train of thought. As the light turned green, she resumed her silent contemplation. The fact was, Robin hadn't mentioned Christmas. As far as Jess could tell, Robin was planning on spending all of her time with her parents. An uncomfortable and bothersome thought crossed Jess's mind. As much as Jess wanted Robin to meet her mother, Robin may not want Jess to meet her parents. The two of them were keeping things quiet between them, and it would stand to reason that Robin wouldn't want to advertise or acknowledge their relationship, even in a casual manner. And the more Jess considered that possibility, the more it bothered her. She shook her head, chastising herself for her own foolish thoughts. *Why such a long face, Jess? You know you're not exactly what her daddy had in mind for his little girl.*

Jess proceeded onward toward home, her disposition a little sullen, notwithstanding the big trial win and despite the otherwise festive nature of the holiday season itself. She arrived at her house and pulled the silver Mercedes into the two-car garage, her preoccupied mind completely unaware of the blue Miata parked neatly at the curb. She stepped out of the car and walked over to the door, turning off the house alarm. Proceeding through the doorway and into the house, she stopped abruptly as she glanced ahead and took in the sight before her.

Flickering candles adorned the dining room table set elegantly for two. More candles glowed from the living room, their soft light casting a soothing warmth throughout the space, while a fire danced its way in harmony within the brick fireplace. Soft jazz music filtered from the stereo in the far corner etagere, and a decidedly enticing aroma emanated from the direction of the large kitchen. The ambience was, in a word, enchanting.

Robin leaned casually against the kitchen entryway, green eyes watching with undisguised interest as Jess first walked inside the house and then absorbed the intimate setting. The younger woman was dressed in a pale blue cashmere sweater with navy blue twill pants, and she stood motionless against the wall patiently waiting for Jess to finally look over and meet her quiet gaze.

The junior partner set her briefcase down, and then glanced around the room once again before slowly tracking azure eyes to formally greet sea green. In the soft glow of the candlelight, Jess was openly mesmerized as her focus locked onto the petite form leaning quietly against the far wall. *She looks good.* The dark-haired woman slowly walked over to where Robin stood, her gaze never leaving the petite form as she silently approached. Her pace quickened somewhat, finally closing the distance between them as she rushed into the waiting embrace.

"Hi." Jess kissed Robin softly. "What did you do?"

Robin smiled. "It's just a little celebration dinner for us. I thought you might like a quiet evening together." Green eyes met blue. "It's been so long, you know."

"I know. It smells wonderful. What is it?" Jess poked her nose inside the kitchen and sniffed.

"Someone's favorite seafood with a little stuffed crab."

"I'm starving." Jess felt her resolve crumbling. Although she was very tired, her senses were now on collective overload, and had been ever since she walked through the door moments ago. Combined with the lingering adrenaline from the week-long trial, the entire scene left her simply unable to think about anything except Robin. She placed her hands on the wall on either side of Robin's head and leaned down to kiss the soft lips again. "I'm starving."

Robin smiled. "You already said that. Besides, isn't that's my line?" She patted Jess's stomach lightly. "Why don't you go and change into something casual, or take a quick shower if you want. Dinner won't be ready for about another thirty minutes."

"I suppose I could do that." Jess nodded. "But don't start without me." She winked and then proceeded down the long hallway toward the master bedroom.

Twenty minutes later, Jess returned to the living room, freshly showered and wearing dark beige twill pants with a light yellow brushed cotton button down shirt. She watched with interest as Robin entered the living room from the kitchen bearing two glasses of chilled sparkling wine.

"You got champagne?" A dark eyebrow arched in question.

Robin grinned. "Of course." She handed a glass to Jess. "You can't have a celebration without a little champagne." She raised her own glass slightly in toast. "Congratulations, counselor, on a terrific win."

Jess clinked her glass against Robin's. "Congratulations, yourself, counselor. You had a very important hand in our win today." Blue eyes held a tender warmth. "I am so very proud of you."

"Thanks." Green eyes danced. "To us, then."

"To us." Jess took a sip. "We make a great team, don't we?"

"The best." Robin took several sips of her champagne. "Are you ready to eat, now?"

"Yep. I'm starving."

Robin grinned. "There you go with my line, again. Come on. Dinner's ready." She stood up and led Jess toward the dining room.

I could definitely get used to this. And her daddy doesn't get a vote.

****

"What are you thinking about?" Jess slid down lengthwise on the plush sofa, pulling Robin along with her. Dinner had been wonderful, and quite romantic. But now, both Robin and Jess were very full. And very tired. The fire crackled in the fireplace, and there was very little light in the room, save for the flickering flames of the fire's glow and the few small candles situated on the corner end tables.

Robin nestled herself alongside the inside portion of the sofa and propped her head up lazily on one hand. "I can't believe how happy I am right now. I can't believe how happy you make me feel." She traced a dark eyebrow. "Sometimes, I think it can't be real, that I can't possibly feel the way I do about you. I don't know if you know what I mean."

"Tell me." Jess shifted almost on her side to better listen to what Robin was saying.

"It's a little embarrassing to talk about."

"It's just me." The larger hand stroked the side of Robin's cheek and then remained there briefly. "Don't be embarrassed. There's nothing, absolutely nothing, that could ever change the way I feel about you."

Robin breathed a heavy sigh. This was obviously something that had been on her mind for some time. "I...I know we joke around, and tease one another and all, but I've never actually felt these...things for a woman before." Robin was very shy as she spoke. "I've never wanted to...um...touch a woman before, and I guess I'm a little bit nervous about that."

"Do you want to touch me, Robin?"

Robin's breathing quickened, the question all at once taking her by surprise. She swallowed with considered difficulty, and then nodded her head mutely.

Jess reached out and took a petite hand into her own, bringing the palm slowly to her lips, and kissed it lightly. She then, in deliberate fashion, brought the same hand down to rest on the swell of her breast, and covered the smaller hand with her own. "Touch me, Robin," she whispered.

Oh God. Robin moved her hand tentatively back and forth over the cotton fabric of Jess's shirt, feeling each and every soft curve as she did so, her gaze never leaving Jess's face the entire length of time.

"How's that?" Jess could barely breathe. "Is that okay for you?"

Robin nodded. "Yes. You?" Robin continued the motion.

"Good." Jess closed her eyes and felt her breath catch. "I have to tell you a secret." She swallowed. "I think I'm more nervous than you are."

In response, Robin took one of Jess's larger hands and brought it up to the front her own sweater, resting it lightly against her chest. "You can touch me, too, Jess." Before she had time to think, she heard herself gasp as she felt Jess's hand brush her breast through the soft fabric of her sweater, almost whimpering at the gentle exploration.

"You feel good." Jess hand continued its journey. "Are you still doing okay?"

Robin nodded, unable to speak coherently.

"Do you want to stop?"

"No." Robin finally managed, and then resumed her own gentle explorations.

They began kissing and exploring each other fully clothed, hands seemingly everywhere, and the intensity escalating at a strikingly rapid rate. Jess placed her fingers underneath the edge of Robin's sweater to lightly stroke the bare stomach, and Robin moved her way down and kissed the soft flesh at the base of Jess's neck, heading decidedly southward. Jess suddenly pulled back, her mind screaming in silent warning. *Slow down, Jess. Slow down.* She took a second to catch her breath, willing her heart rate to slow its pace, and then tenderly stroked the blonde head in front of her. "Um...let's not rush this, sweetheart, okay?"

Robin buried her face in Jess's shoulder. "I'm sorry."

That startled Jess. *Sorry?* "Honey, what are you sorry about?" *Are you sorry we went that far?*

Robin winced. "I don't know what I'm doing, and I pushed you. I didn't mean to...."

"Shhh." Jess hugged Robin tightly then looked directly into sea green eyes. "You did not push me." She smiled fondly. "The fact is, I want to be with you more than anything, in every way imaginable." She became somewhat serious. "I know, Robin, that these physical feelings we have for each other are new for both of us, and I don't want to...I wouldn't want to...I just...oh, hell." Jess was curiously having a hard time saying what she really wanted to say, so she finally just blurted it out. "I want our first time to be special."

Robin turned her head and looked up, studying the angular features of Jess's face for several moments in the shadow of the firelight. She noted the smooth planes and fine lines barely visible in the dim light, the striking beauty almost causing Robin to lose what little composure she still had remaining. Finally, she rested her blonde head back down on the broad cotton covered shoulder, breathing deeply Jess's familiar scent. "I love you so much, Jess. I want our first time to be special, too. I admit that I'm scared...not of you, but of me. I'm afraid I won't know the right things...but yet, I want to be with you so much. I know that doesn't make sense."

Jess noticed the slight tightening of the fine muscles in Robin's jaw as she spoke, and she thought she should try to offer some reassurance to the younger woman. "It makes perfect sense to me. Let me say this again for you, so you'll know I really mean it." She spoke tenderly, but sincerely. "If all we ever do is hold each other, it will be enough. There is no pressure. Whatever we do or don't do doesn't matter, as long as we're together." She kissed Robin's light eyebrows, then grinned broadly. "But let me assure you, Robin, that you were most definitely doing all the right things."

A green eye peered up. "I was?"

"Yep. That's one reason I wanted to slow down. You were making me crazy." Jess grinned.

"I was?"

"Yep. And you could have had your way with me."

Robin giggled. "Really?"

"Yep. And I would have been absolutely helpless to resist your charms."

Robin giggled again, now feeling more at ease, and then pursed her lips in thought. "Well, then, it's a good thing that we stopped when we did. You were having the exact same effect on me."

"I see." Jess considered that statement for a moment, and its implications. "So, I guess we could say that we're both ready?"

The blonde head nodded. "I think we could say that."

Jess traced a long finger over a petite shoulder blade, an idea forming in her mind. "What are your plans this weekend?"

"Um...well, I was planning to sleep in tomorrow and catch up from the long week, since we had to work late every night. My boss is a slave-driver, you know." As if on cue, an involuntary yawn escaped Robin's mouth. "Sorry. I guess I'm more tired than I thought."

Jess thought it was rather cute. "We'll discuss your so-called slaver-driver boss another time." She kissed the top of the blonde head. "So, after you're finished sleeping in tomorrow, did you have any other plans?"

The smaller woman lifted herself up on one arm. "I had planned to spend the weekend with you, unless you need to do something."

"What about your Sunday chores?"

"They could wait." Robin shook her head, slightly bewildered. "You are definitely a bad influence on me. I seem to be putting things off." She grinned "Pretty soon, I'll be just as bad as you are when it comes to grocery shopping."

Jess gave her a crooked smile. "There are worse things, Robin." She playfully brought her index finger up to touch the tip of Robin's nose.

"You are so absolutely hopeless." Robin grasped the offending finger and kissed it. "And I absolutely adore you."

In an odd sort of way, that was one of the nicest things anyone had ever said to Jess. "Well, if you can tear yourself away from your chores, would you perhaps be interested in taking a road trip with me?"

"Road trip?" Robin was intrigued.

"Yep. I was thinking that maybe we could go up to St. Augustine tomorrow, and come back Sunday?"

"What's in St. Augustine?" Robin hadn't heard of the place.

Jess stroked her fingers through the blonde hair. "Well, it's about two hours away on the coast, and it's the oldest city in the United States. They have quite a few historical places, and a fort, and they decorate the city up for the holidays. It's very quaint, and they have some very nice bed and breakfast places to stay." She hesitated briefly, then softened her voice. "We could have a special weekend."

Green eyes locked on blue for a moment, absorbing their intent. *A special weekend.* "Yes."

"Yes?"

"Yes, I want to go to St. Augustine and have a special weekend with you." Robin said it and she meant it.

"Okay." The older woman grinned. "But this time, I'm driving." She held up a finger in warning. "No arguments."

Robin laid her head back down, resting it in the crook of Jess's neck. "Fine. No arguments." A beat. "But I'm bringing Al."

What? Who's...? Dark eyebrows furrowed. *Oh.* "Why? Do you think we'll need him?"

"Well, not necessarily for luck." Robin let her fingers travel to the top button of Jess's shirt, plucking at it lightly. "But it'll be your turn to try to find him."

Jess thought for a moment and then swallowed. *Oh.*

"And then when you do find him, I believe you'll have enough points to claim your prize."

Jess swallowed again, now audibly. *Oh.*

"And, of course, I'll expect to collect my trial reward at the same time."

Oh boy. "I see." Jess grasped the still plucking fingers. "You have yourself a deal, Robin."

"I do?"

"Yes. One trial reward in exchange for one point prize. Have I understood you correctly?"

"Yes." Robin grinned against Jess's neck. *I can't wait.*

"Good." Jess felt the velvety soft lips smile against her skin. I can't wait.

K M

Chapter 9

The seasonably cool weather had finally come to Central Florida to stay. Saturday was a picture perfect day, with a clear, cloudless blue sky and crisp winter air. The sun shone brightly, making its way steadily up the morning horizon, while flocks of black birds heading further south for the winter flew in formation from treetop to treetop, occasionally setting perch on an intervening power line. Jess and Robin rose a bit earlier than either had planned, and quickly readied themselves for the overnight trip to St. Augustine. Jess telephoned several bed and breakfast establishments in the St. Augustine area, finally securing reservations for Saturday evening at a quaint little inn that had an unexpected last minute cancellation. St. Augustine at this particular time of year was known to be a popular tourist destination, with the availability of accommodations somewhat scarce, especially on such short notice. But it appeared that fate was shining on the two attorneys that day, and everything just seemed to fall right into place.

Robin stopped over at her apartment to pick up some extra clothing and to check the answering machine for messages. As she gathered her things together, she listened as the last message played, her mother's voice filling the room with plans for their visit to Florida in just over a week's time. It was not something Robin especially wanted to think about at the current moment, preferring instead to focus her attention on the weekend at hand. There would certainly be ample time to dwell on all various and sundry things regarding her out-of-town visitors when she returned from St. Augustine. Robin finished packing and made a mental note to give her mother a call early the next week to further discuss her parents' travel plans. Until then, however, she just wanted to enjoy her time with Jess without any distracting or complicating thoughts. Vowing to do just that, she grabbed her duffel bag, locked up her apartment, and headed down to the front steps to wait for Jess.

The silver Mercedes pulled into the parking lot a few moments later, and Robin bounded down the steps at first sight, ready to greet the driver. She tossed her duffel bag into the back seat and slipped inside the car.

"Hi." Robin buckled her seatbelt.

"Hi. Got everything?" Jess began to pull out of the apartment complex, careful to dodge the incoming postman who was on his way to deliver the day's mail.

Robin grimaced. "Whoops, I forgot to check my mail. I've probably got a ton of bills piled up from the past few days. Could you pull around to the mailboxes for a minute?"

Jess complied and waited as Robin retrieved her mail. "Did you get anything good?" The older woman pulled the car out onto the main highway.

Robin thumbed through the stack of envelopes. "Just bills and some junk mail, and a few Christmas cards. Nothing…." She stopped abruptly and became very quiet.

"Robin?" Jess looked over to see Robin silently staring at an envelope, a stunned expression crossing her fair features. "Hey. Is everything okay?"

The silence, however, continued.

"Robin?"

Still more silence.

Something's wrong. Jess immediately pulled the car over onto a side street and parked at a nearby curb. "Honey, what is it?" Jess was confused and a bit concerned.

Robin hadn't opened the envelope, but rather continued to hold it lightly in her hands. She finally looked up and answered Jess's question in a quiet and barely composed voice. "I think this is a Christmas card." She fingered the return address. "From his parents."

His parents. Jess closed her eyes, the grimace she most surely felt nearly making its way clear across her face. Somehow, she managed to keep her expression neutral, having absolutely no idea how she was able to pull off that little feat. *Well, doesn't that all just suck to hell.* She was careful not to betray any one of the myriad of emotions taking hold of her at that particular moment, ranging from irrational jealously to resentment to anger, as she sat perfectly still in her seat contemplating her predicament. One thing was certain. She absolutely did not need this. Not this weekend. Not ever. *Damn. Why did I let her put off that call to Dr. Richmond?* Jess took a deep breath and tried to gain some semblance of control over her spiraling emotions. She finally succeeded in her quest, and divested herself of her own selfish thoughts, focusing her attention to where it should have been all along...back to Robin. "Um...would you like a moment to yourself to open it?" Jess really didn't know what to say.

"I wasn't expecting this. It sort of came out of the blue." Robin still made no move to open the envelope. "Maybe I should leave it for later."

Jess reached over and covered Robin's hand. "If you wait to open it, you'll be thinking about it. Are you sure you want to do that?"

Robin looked into concerned blue eyes, knowing that Jess was probably right. She watched as the dark-haired woman opened the car door and stepped outside, allowing her a bit more privacy. Robin gingerly opened the envelope and pulled out the Christmas card, reading the religious holiday message inscribed on the front. Loose inside was a separate letter, which fluttered out as she opened the card wide. She picked up the engraved stationery and read the letter to herself, fighting the increasingly insistent tears that threatened to escape as she did so. The letter spoke of the holidays and wished her well. That was all very nice, but then the letter also went on to explain what David's parents had done with the ring. *The ring.* They had donated it to a local children's home, which in turn had sold it and used the proceeds to buy the children new clothes, a new group television, some Christmas gifts, and books for the children's library. The letter also made a point of noting that the books all carried a special inscription acknowledging the donors as David Mitchell and Robin Wilson. It was upon reading this last part that Robin lost whatever tenuous composure she had remaining, and just simply let the tears fall unhindered.

Jess walked alongside the desolate street. She was far enough away to afford Robin her privacy, but yet close enough to see that Robin was becoming upset. Everything inside the older woman told her to go back to the car and comfort Robin, but a part of her still demanded that she stay put and not intrude on the private matter. *Let her deal with this her own way.* She stood by helplessly and looked down the length of road between herself and the Mercedes, watching the now quietly weeping form in the front seat. *Let her deal with it her own way.* She stared uncomfortably at her feet, and then looked back down the street and through the windshield of the silver car, sensing and almost feeling the building distress. *Let her deal with it.* And even as her mind kept saying it over and over again, Jess's feet rapidly picked up beneath her, entirely of their own accord. She ran at lightening pace toward the parked car, gaining unstoppable momentum until she finally closed the distance. She quickly opened the passenger door and gathered the smaller woman into a strong and comforting embrace.

"Shhh, honey. It's alright." Jess soothed. "I've got you, sweetheart."

Robin's tears slowed and then stopped. It was strange, but not really so, that the comfort of Jess's embrace would ease her sorrow. The younger woman pulled back, slightly embarrassed at the display of her own uncontrolled emotion. "I'm sorry."

A large hand brushed through the golden bangs. "No. Don't be." Jess kissed Robin's forehead. "Anytime you need to let it out, it's okay. You can't hold it inside."

Robin offered a timid smile. "Thank you for understanding."

"Are you alright now, or would you like to go back home?"

Home? Robin grasped Jess's fingers. "When I'm with you, Jess, I am home. I want to go with you, like we planned." She suddenly had an uneasy thought. *Does she think I'm still not over him?* "Unless...you don't want to go anymore."

"I just...." Jess wasn't sure what to say.

"Go around and get back in the car, okay? I want to show you something."

Jess was a bit confused but complied, getting into the car and settling herself snuggly into the driver's seat. "Robin, you don't have to...."

"I want to." Robin handed her the letter from the Mitchells. "I would like it if you read this." Green eyes implored. "Please, Jess, will you read it?"

The dark head nodded reluctantly. "Alright." Several silent moments elapsed, as Jess first took the letter from Robin, and then quietly read its contents. Once she was finished, she understood what had touched Robin's heart so deeply, although she didn't dare speak openly to Robin about something that was obviously so personal.

Reserved green eyes met compassionate azure, and Robin suddenly felt a need to explain why she had become so emotional. "It's good to know something good came from everything. I feel better, almost like a heavy weight's been lifted from me. I can breathe again. I suddenly felt such relief." Robin sighed and then lowered her gaze to her fingertips. "But I'll understand if you don't want to be with me right now."

Jess was quiet for a very long moment, considering how to best respond. She definitely wanted to be with Robin this weekend, but at the same time, she didn't want to intrude on what was an extremely personal matter. She surmised that Robin was really asking for some reassurance, something to indicate that Jess wasn't going to up and run away every time David's name was mentioned. Jess thought about that some more. It was true that the thought of David made her crazy, on many, many levels. And she'd never even met the guy. But Robin needed to know that Jess accepted the burden Robin carried as if it were her own. *For better or for worse.* Finally deciding on the appropriate course of action, Jess looked over and gave Robin the sweetest crooked grin. "Robin, there is absolutely no way you can possibly get rid of me. I'm like crazy glue."

Green eyes blinked, a bit confused. "You're like what?"

"Crazy glue." Jess started the car again and fastened her seat belt. "You're stuck with me."

"I'm stuck with you?"

"Yes. And I'm very sticky." The silver Mercedes pulled out onto the main highway.

It's amazing how she can make me feel better. "I see. So there's no way to get unstuck from your stickiness?"

"Nope. Once you're stuck, it's quite permanent." The older woman grinned. "So, how about it? Feel like getting stuck with me in St. Augustine this weekend?"

Robin smiled. "I think being stuck with you in St. Augustine would definitely be on my top ten list of things to do."

"Is that so?" A dark eyebrow raised. "Care to fill me in on the other nine?"

"How about we discuss the other nine this weekend. Being stuck with you might just cause me to alter my opinion." Robin chuckled.

"Well, I intend to make sure that being stuck with me makes it all the way to number one on your list. And number two, and number three…."

"So, you want to be my whole top ten list?"

"And number four, and number five, and number six...." Jess playfully continued.

"I'll consider it."

"And number seven, and number eight, and number nine...."

"You've made your point, Jess." Robin grinned. "You can stop now."

"And number ten. Okay, I'll stop. I just wanted to make sure that we're clear on the matter." Jess glanced over at Robin. "And for the record, you're already my whole top ten list." She winked and then focused back on the road.

"You are very sweet." Robin chuckled. "Hopeless, but very sweet."

"You don't say." Jess quipped.

There was a long silence as Robin watched the passing trees rush by the side window. "Thank you."

"For what?"

"For knowing just what to say to make me feel better. I don't know what I'd do without you."

"I told you, I'm like crazy glue."

Robin gave Jess the most adoring smile. "And I'm stuck with you."

"Yes." *Forever? Do you want forever, Robin?* "I'm glad you understand that."

"I do." *I absolutely do.*

****

Later that morning, Jess and Robin arrived in St. Augustine and drove down the old city streets, finally locating the little bed and breakfast inn where they had reservations for Saturday evening. They parked the car and then entered the old Spanish-style house made of coquina shells and stucco. Inside, the Spanish architectural flair was evident, the inn boasting of a history dating back to the mid-1700s. The décor was tastefully appointed with lace curtains and wrought-iron and wood furnishings, lending a feel for the historical ancestry of the house itself. A main sitting room prominently held a versatile fireplace, together with comfortable sofas and chairs. Rounded archways depicted the Spanish architectural influence so common of the era. The entire living space and stair banisters were highlighted with tasteful holiday decorations, and strands of small white lights adorned an eight foot tall Frasier fir tree which served as the focal point in the inn's great room. The decidedly sweet scent of the fir tree permeated throughout the entirety of the first floor of the house.

Robin and Jess were shown to their room, a fairly large area complete with private bath and a separate fireplace. The room itself contained a small sitting area near the cozy hearth, a table and two chairs set near the street-side window, and a four-poster queen-sized bed covered with a lovely handmade quilt bedspread. Hardwood floors and tasteful throw rugs completed the ensemble.

Robin marveled at the sight. "This is really nice, Jess, don't you think?" She took a seat in one of the chairs near the window and continued her survey of the room.

"Yeah." Jess put the duffel bags on the bed. "I didn't know we'd have a fireplace." She peered into the brick and mortar structure and noticed the fire logs neatly stacked next to the hearth. "It appears well stocked." She grinned thoughtfully. "We can make use of it tonight since it'll be kinda cool out."

"Cold, Jess. It'll be cold out tonight. I heard the weather report before we left." Green eyes playfully teased.

"Remind me, Robin, never to discuss the weather with you. It seems that you and I are simply unable to agree on the precise definition of cold."

"Fine. We'll just have to refer to it as 'not hot,' then." Robin stood up and wandered into the private bath. "Oooh, look, Jess. There's a whirlpool tub in here."

A dark eyebrow shot up. *Whirlpool.* "Is that so?" Jess quickly followed Robin into the bathroom. "Hmm. Maybe we could try it out later. What do you think?"

Robin nodded, feeling a little shy at the thought. "Yeah, maybe we could do that."

"Good." The older woman walked back into the main room and began unpacking some of her things. "Want to head out and explore the city some this afternoon. There's a mission, the old bridge, and a huge fort we could go to, if you want."

"Sounds good to me." Robin unpacked her duffel bag of the few items she'd brought. "Um...Jess?"

"Yeah?" The dark-haired woman looked up from her unpacking.

"Could we…."

"Eat lunch first." Jess finished for Robin, the corners of her mouth smirking as she did so.

Robin smirked back. "You think you're so funny."

"Nope." Jess replied innocently. "I know I'm so funny." She quirked a grin. "And you love it."

"You are so goofy." Robin completed the last of her unpacking and pulled out a lightweight jacket to bring with her. "So, can we go eat?"

"You betcha, kiddo." Jess grinned happily. "I must keep your stomach happy." She eased up behind Robin and wrapped her long arms around the small body, whispering softly into the petite ear. "Besides, you need to keep up your strength. I have big plans for you and your stomach later on."

Robin felt herself blush. "I think I'm counting on that." She turned around and gave Jess a quick kiss on the chin. "Now, come on.

Let's find someplace to have lunch. I'm starving."

Jess followed the younger woman out the door, an almost giddy expression crossing her dark features as she trailed slightly behind. *I definitely have big plans.*

****

Jess and Robin meandered down the brick paved streets looking for a place to eat, finally settling on a small sandwich shop with a beautiful view overlooking Matanzas Bay. Several sailboats were cruising out on the choppy waters, the swift breeze providing more than ample sailing conditions. The midday sunlight sparkled brightly off the waves, while several white caps were visible from the shoreline. It was a perfect day for walking around and about the old city, sight-seeing and enjoying the quaint charm the old town provided. The cool, crisp winter breeze carried a hint of hickory smoke from several nearby chimneys, infusing the brisk air with the wonderful scents of the winter season.

After a brief lunch, the two women made their way to the Castillo de San Marcos, a massive fortress built by the Spanish several hundred years ago in order to defend the St. Augustine coastline. The entire historic fort and its surrounding area had been declared a national monument now operated by the National Park Service. The symmetrically laid out compound constructed of coquina brick consisted of powder magazines, storage rooms, sentry towers, a large courtyard complete with cannonball stockpiles, a parapet lined with cannons, and what was once a formidable moat encircling the stronghold. An experienced park service guide gave a narration of the history of the Spanish fortification, and each area of the fort contained labeled placards detailing the purpose and significance of the rooms visited. The views afforded from the sentry towers overlooking the bay and the city proper were particularly breathtaking in their magnificence, and the defenses provided by the moat itself had yielded ample protection against invading pirates and British, alike.

Robin stood near the corner sentry tower looking across Matanzas Bay toward the old Bridge of Lions. It was hard to imagine that the coquina fort was nearly four hundred years old, and yet from her position near the sentry point, she could almost place herself in that period of time. It was a fleeting, but eerie, sense of displacement, and it felt very odd.

"Hey." Jess ducked her tall frame into the sentry tower for a quick peek inside, and then retreated to where Robin was standing.

"Whatcha looking at?"

"Just watching the sailboats. It's really beautiful up here." Robin leaned herself nearly half way over the ledge of the parapet wall to peak at the moat below, and then continued to dip her body still further over the edge to gain a closer look at the fort's exterior walls.

The dark-haired woman watched as Robin dangled herself precariously over the side of the fort, a petite foot now boosting the small frame high above the ledge. Jess stood by nervously for a moment, observing silently, before a sudden wave of panic overtook her. *Don't fall.* She instinctively rushed forward and abruptly grabbed Robin's waist from behind, swiftly lifting her up and away from the perceived peril. As she did so, an odd sense of déjà vu passed over her.

"Hey." The younger woman protested.

"Hey nothing. Get down." Strong arms released Robin from their protective grasp. "The sign says not to stand up there. You could've fallen." Anxious blue eyes suddenly met green. *We've done this before, haven't we?*

"I wasn't going to fall, silly. I just wanted to look at the outside of the fort. I wanted to see if there were any bullet holes." Robin hadn't picked up on the apparent similarity in events.

This is weird. Jess uncharacteristically fell mute, and turned to gaze in silent fashion across the choppy waters, her thoughts attempting to process the obvious but curious coincidence.

"Jess?" A small hand came to rest on the older woman's upper arm. "What is it?"

Azure eyes cast out across the crystal bay. "I...um...just had the strangest feeling when I pulled you off the ledge, like I'd done that before."

The comparison suddenly came to Robin. "You did, in New Orleans, remember? You saved me from falling overboard off the riverboat." She grinned thoughtfully. "Although I wasn't really going to fall."

The dark head nodded. "Yeah, I thought of that, and you're right. It was just like that, except...I don't know." Jess let go a small sigh. "It was also something else. I can't describe it, only to say that I feel like I've done that several times. It was almost as though, if I didn't catch you, you were definitely going to fall. It's strange, and I can't explain it, but I feel like you fell once, and I couldn't catch you." She shook her head helplessly at Robin. "It's weird, and it's probably just my bizarre mind making stuff up."

It is kinda weird. Robin didn't know what to say. She, herself, had gotten an eerie feeling as she looked out across the bay just moments before Jess had arrived. Unexplainably needing some sense of contact with the taller woman, Robin cautiously peered around the sentry area to assess the location of the other tourists. Seeing no one else nearby, she closed the distance between herself and Jess, and wrapped her petite arms around the older woman's waist in a brief hug. "I think it's wonderful that you care about me and want to protect me." Sea green eyes locked onto cool blue. "I treasure that in you." Robin was absolutely serious.

Jess simply nodded, trying to shake off the disquieting feeling that had previously settled upon her. She broke away and stepped over to the stairs that led down into the open courtyard. "So, where to next, kiddo?" An eyebrow lifted. "You're the boss, you know."

"I'll remember that." Robin quirked a grin. "Let's wander around the fort for a few more minutes, and then watch the Spanish infantry musket demonstration. After it's over, we can make our way down to the old bridge."

"Fine by me. Lead the way, senorita." Jess winked.

Robin slid on her sunglasses and then led them both down toward the open courtyard area for a little additional exploration. Her mind, however, continued to ponder the previous events. What Jess had said earlier had affected her. *Had we really done that before?* It didn't seem possible, and yet the odd sense of displacement she had felt near the sentry tower came back to her. A flood of other thoughts came back, as well. Thoughts of the undeniable connection she and Jess had shared from the very beginning, and how it seemed that some inexplicable force had drawn them both together. Of how Robin initially had the feeling that Jess seemed somehow familiar, and how, as impossible as it might have been, Robin had sensed that she indeed had known her. *Weird. Very weird.* And then there were those blue eyes...those irresistible blue eyes the color of the sky that seemed to reach out and grab her, capturing her heart in their penetrating gaze. Robin used her sunglasses as cover, and watched secretly as Jess walked beside her, studying the tall profile unseen as they made their way quietly down the courtyard steps. Her subconscious mind quickly made the unerring conclusion, one which her consciousness was, as of yet, unable to recognize. *It's you.*

****

Jess and Robin strolled down to the old Bridge of Lions, enjoying the crisp, late-afternoon air and waning sunlight as they leisurely walked along the brick paved streets. When they reached the bay, they stopped at the foot of the old bridge and surveyed their surroundings. Horse-drawn carriages carried passengers along the carriage route and could be seen loading and unloading their riders from the area adjacent to the Castillo de San Marcos fortress.

"I wonder why they call it the Bridge of Lions." Robin studied the expanse of bridge.

"Do you see those marble lion statutes guarding the bridge? They were put there when the bridge was built in the early part of the 1900s connecting the mainland to Anastasia Island. It was part of a revitalization of the city. I heard recently that some people want to renovate the bridge to allow for more traffic flow, but there is also a preservation movement that's started up to save the bridge." The dark-haired woman studied the architecture of the bridge with its tiled roof towers and graceful archways.

The blonde head nodded pensively. "It's hard to think people would want to destroy a part of history like that." Robin stood and admired the bridge for another moment, then looked around the bayfront area in panoramic fashion, suddenly spying with interest the horse-drawn buggies. "Hey, Jess. They have carriage rides over there..." Green eyes sparkled, leaving the thought deliberately unfinished.

"Yep." Jess remarked, seemingly uninterested.

"They probably ride by all the historic sites." Robin continued the line of thinking.

Blue eyes focused their attention lazily across the bay. "Yep."

"So, maybe we could take a ride."

Jess continued her perusal of the water, fully aware of Robin's keen interest in taking the carriage ride, but curiously not uttering a single sound.

Blonde eyebrows knit together at the apparent indifference. "Jess, are you even listening to me?"

The corner of Jess's mouth quirked ever so slightly, betraying her teasing intentions. "Um...I'm sorry, did you say something?"

So, she wants to play, does she? "Nope. Didn't say a thing." Robin abruptly turned and headed down the street toward the carriage coach stand.

Oh shit. Jess stood for a second, slightly stunned, and then raced to catch up with the rapidly retreating form. "Robin?" She finally reached the younger woman. "Hey, I'm sorry. I was just teasing." *Jess, you're a complete idiot.*

Robin didn't slow her pace until Jess stepped out in front of her and blocked her path. The older woman appeared so absolutely remorseful that Robin couldn't stand to keep up the charade any longer. She cocked her head to one side and broke into a devilish grin, mirroring Jess's previous words to her. "I'm sorry, did you say something?"

Jess stood there speechlessly, her mouth slightly open, as she considered the surprising response. Finally realizing the joke, she shook her head and offered a wry grin. "Well, that'll teach me."

Green eyes danced merrily. "Darn right, it will." Robin resumed walking, wagging a petite finger toward Jess in mock reprimand. "Don't mess with me, Bucko."

A playful pout. "But, I was just playing around." Jess followed Robin along the sidewalk toward the waiting carriages.

She is so absolutely gorgeous. Robin was thoroughly taken by the sight. "You are very cute when you pout, do you know that?"

"I'll have you know that I'm an expert pouter, Robin." Jess grinned rather proudly at her own accomplishment. "I could pout some more if it would help me get some more points under your point system." She eyed Robin hopefully.

Light brows knit together. "Don't bet the farm on that."

"If that doesn't work, how about this?" Jess produced two vouchers for the horse-drawn carriages and handed them to Robin.

"You got...." The blonde head shook in amazement. "When did you get these?"

"Before." Came the brief reply.

Robin nearly squealed in delight. "I can't believe you." A decidedly curious eyebrow arched above golden bangs. "Hmm. You seem suspiciously eager to accumulate points." Robin stepped up to the coach stand. "Any particular reason?"

Jess scanned the surrounding crowd, then lowered her voice a notch to make clear the intended point. "I don't think you really want me to answer that question at this particular moment, Robin." A blue eye winked, acknowledging the throng of people nearby. She then leaned in very close to Robin's ear. "At least, not in specific detail."

"Two, please." Robin handed the vouchers to the carriage driver, nearly croaking out the request as she did so. *Has it gotten rather warm all of a sudden?*

****

"You know what this reminds me of?" Robin sat back leisurely in the carriage seat. "Remember when we were in New Orleans and we took the buggy ride there?"

Jess glanced at Robin out of the corner of her eye, and drawled in her best southern accent imitation. "Why yes, Miss Scarlet."

A giggle. "That was a lot of fun, wasn't it?" The horses began their journey along the carriage route.

"That was a document review, Robin. Didn't you get the memo?" Blue eyes twinkled. "Document reviews are not supposed to be fun." Jess furrowed her brows. "It seems my indoctrination techniques may have failed."

Another giggle. "Well, I think the fun part had something to do with who I was with, not necessarily the actual document reviewing itself." The horses' hooves clip-clopped their way down the Avenida Menendez.

"I see. So, are you saying then, if you had gone with someone else, you wouldn't have had so much fun?" Jess relaxed as the driver started to give his guide speech.

"Well, it would have depended on whether the person showed me a good time or not." Robin smirked.

Both dark eyebrows shot up in unison at the remark, and Jess's jaw dropped slightly as she sat in the carriage seat entirely astounded.

Green eyes took note of the dumbfounded expression. "Close your mouth, Jess. People are starting to stare." Robin patted Jess lightly on the arm.

The dark-haired woman leaned over, not particularly caring at the moment who was or who was not staring, and whispered in the petite ear. "I better be the only one showing you a good time, Robin."

Robin suppressed a grin and gave Jess's arm another playful pat. "We can talk more about that later on. Let's listen to the driver now, okay?" She deliberately ignored the still wary look on Jess's face, and proceeded to cross one leg loosely over the other as she settled into the carriage seat. With her leg now serving as a convenient cover, Robin placed a hand on the seat between herself and Jess. She let her fingertips gently grasp the long fingers already resting in the tiny space between them.

Jess felt the tender contact and simply melted at the touch, the sensation quite exquisite. *She has me so unbelievably hooked.* The feeling the simple gesture invoked was indescribable, and Jess relished it throughout the remainder of the ride. After a one-hour tour of the historic district, the carriage rounded its last corner and Matanzas Bay came into view once again. She felt Robin release her fingers, and immediately found herself wishing that they could continue holding hands. But such wishes ignored reality. She shifted her attention back to that reality. “So, did you enjoy the ride, kiddo?” They both stepped out of the carriage.

“Yeah, I thought it was very interesting.” The younger woman peered at the horizon and noticed a slight chill in the approaching evening air. “The sun’s setting.”

Jess nodded absently. “I have one more thing we could do, if you’re interested. Well...actually two.”

“I’m game. What’d you have in mind?”

In what was becoming common fashion, Jess produced two more tickets. “Here.”

Robin was truly baffled. “When do you have time to get these things without me seeing you?” She grinned and eagerly took the tickets from Jess, reading them silently to herself. “They have a riverboat here, too?”

Jess looked down at her feet, suddenly feeling uncharacteristically shy. “Yeah. It’s a paddle wheel boat that goes around the bay and Matanzas River.” She met Robin’s gentle gaze. “At twilight, you can see all the lights that they put up along the waterfront this time of year. It’s really very pretty, all lit up like that.” Jess continued to focus on sea green eyes, speaking very softly and with a hint of quiet sincerity. “Will you go with me?”

Robin’s breath caught. There was something about that particular moment that moved her far more than words could say, and the revelation took her quite by surprise. She suddenly realized that Jess had arranged, to a certain extent, to parallel the events the two of them had shared in New Orleans. *That was our first time together.* The significance of the sentiment was not lost on Robin. *This is our first time together.* She abruptly averted her eyes and blinked back the tears that threatened to fall.

“Robin?” Jess closed the distance between them, suddenly concerned. “Honey? What is it?”

Robin’s voice was thick with emotion. “You are absolutely the sweetest person I have ever known.” She took a deep breath in an attempt to regain some of her composure. “And I would absolutely love to go on the riverboat with you tonight.”

A beaming smile graced the taller woman’s face. “Good. And afterward, I know this great Italian restaurant we can go to for dinner...that is, if you think you’d be hungry.” Blue eyes held a hint of mirth.

That drew an immediate grin. “Like there’d be any doubt.”

“Just checking.” Jess led them both toward the municipal marina where they were scheduled to board the riverboat. After walking silently for a few moments, the dark-haired woman glanced over at Robin. "Is everything okay?"

Robin nodded and cast a warm smile in Jess's direction. "Everything is very okay."

And it was.

****

The cool night air and surprisingly gentle breeze enveloped the passengers as the paddle wheel riverboat cast off from its berth at the municipal marina and headed steadily out into the Matanzas River. Its ultimate journey would plot a course along the shoreline, under the old bridge, and around the perimeter of the adjacent Matanzas Bay. As predicted, sunset brought the first glimpse of at least a million decorative white lights strung along like pearls up and down the glittering waterfront.

Jess and Robin stood out on the upper deck of the riverboat, leaning against the railing and admiring the brilliant view of the shore, as the boat cruised its way near the Bridge of Lions. The breeze had picked up slightly as they headed farther out into the bay, and the night chill began to settle its way upon the old city as the sun completed its descent into the horizon. Robin took the opportunity to don her lightweight jacket, shivering slightly in the cool breeze.

"Cold?" Jess stood next to Robin, their shoulders touching and their forearms braced on the ledge of the rail.

"A little." Robin looked across the shimmering water at the shoreline. "It's really very beautiful." She gazed up at Jess, suddenly awestruck as the now brisk breeze blew strands of dark hair haphazardly about the older woman's face. Jess's profile stood in stark relief against the twilight sky and the backdrop of endless white lights, and Robin surreptitiously took the opportunity to admire the remarkable and stunning features of the beautiful face before her. She noticed with considerable interest the way the dark hair framed intense azure eyes, and the way the strong cheekbones and well-defined jaw lines accentuated the gentle elegance in perfect symmetry. She was openly fascinated at the way the entire portrait exuded an incomparable quiet majesty and strength befitting the most noblest of royalty. It nearly took Robin's breath away, and she could not, for the life of her, take her eyes from the captivating sight.

Blue eyes found green. "You seem quiet tonight." Waves gently lapped against the side of the boat as the paddle wheel propelled them steadily forward.

"I guess I'm just a bit...overwhelmed." It was the truth.

Jess smiled. "Me, too."

The smaller woman leaned slightly over the railing, peering in a curious manner at the water below. There was no bottom rung to prop her feet on, so she tried to be content with simply looking over the top ledge.

"Don't even think about it." A long finger pointed at Robin in strict warning.

The younger woman reacted in innocent fashion. "What?"

"You know perfectly well what, and I'm not saving you from falling twice in one day"

Robin giggled. "I'm not going to fall. I just want to look at the paddles down there." She bent over the top rail as far as she could, which wasn't very far. "Um...Jess? Could you give me a boost?"

Blue eyes narrowed considerably, and Jess tried in vain to suppress a small grin. "I will do no such thing."

"Come on." Robin playfully whined. "I won't fall in. I promise."

"No."

Robin glanced toward the back portion of the deck. "Maybe that guy down there will give me a boost." She started to make her way toward the stern of the boat.

With lightening quickness, a long arm shot out and pulled Robin back, a low voice resonating in a petite ear. "I don't think so, Robin." Jess immediately encircled Robin's waist from behind, lifting her up and against the railing to better view the waters below and the large paddle wheel turning in constant rhythm. Long arms held on tightly. "Now, you've seen it, okay?" She gently put Robin down on the deck. "Happy now?"

With your arms around me, I'm happy. "Yes." Robin looked back over her shoulder at the older woman. "Could you do it again?" Green eyes twinkled in the moonlight.

This time, Jess couldn't contain the grin. "Absolutely not. People will stare."

"So, let them."

"How about if I just do this?" Jess pressed herself against Robin's back and placed her arms on either side of the petite body, grasping the forward ledge of the railing with each hand. She whispered softly into Robin's ear. "Will this work?"

It was the most complete and profound sensation of being snuggly wrapped in a cocoon of warmth that Robin had ever experienced. Jess's breath tickled the back of the younger woman's neck, causing her to momentarily forget the question. “Um...yeah.” She reveled in the sensation a moment longer. “Is anyone staring?”

“Nope.”

Robin sank back further into the circle of warmth. “Jess?”

“Yeah.”

“Earlier today, at the fort, I...um....” Robin whispered. “Felt it, too.”

“You felt it?” Jess wasn’t quite sure she understood exactly what Robin meant.

The blonde head nodded. “Just before you came over to the sentry, it was strange, but I felt like I’d been there before. I know it’s weird.”

Jess tried for a logical explanation. “Sometimes the mind can imagine things that seem real. Maybe that’s what happened to both of us today.” Not entirely comfortable with the nature of the conversation, Jess shifted to Robin’s side and deftly changed the subject. “We’re almost back. Can I interest you in dinner?” She already knew the answer.

“Of course you can, but only if you let me buy.” Robin insisted.

“Not necessary. I invited you here, remember?”

“I know, but you’ve paid for everything else.” Robin’s hand gestured widely in front of her. “Let me pay for something.”

It was apparent that Robin felt a need to contribute to their weekend, even if in a small way, so Jess acquiesced. “Alright. You win. You’re buying.” Jess grinned. “And it just so happens that I’m starving.”

“You keep stealing my lines, Jess.” Robin teased. “You’re going to have to come up with your own.”

“Fine. How about if I just say I’ve suddenly developed a voracious appetite.” Jess spoke the last part a bit seductively.

Robin swallowed. *Are we still talking about food?* Green eyes fixed on cool blue. “Then I guess I would say we’re pretty evenly matched, appetite wise.”

A dark eyebrow arched at the thought. *Maybe we should skip dinner.*

****

The Italian restaurant was quietly nestled in a cozy section of the old city overlooking the bay, the large windows providing a perfect view of the strands of white lights dotting the coastline. Jess and Robin sipped leisurely on their glasses of Chianti and admired the glittering decorations in the distance, as the tabletop candle flickered and cast a soft glow around them. It provided a decidedly intimate ambiance which they both found quite to their liking, and gave them an opportunity to wind down from the rather hectic pace of the day. They relaxed in companionable silence as they awaited their meal.

Robin spoke first. “This weekend is really wonderful, Jess. Thank you.”

“I’m glad you’re enjoying it. I hope everything meets your expectations.” Blue eyes hid slightly behind dark bangs.

There was something in the way Jess said the last part that caused Robin to take pause. *Expectations.* The full meaning of the word became clear. She looked down at the tablecloth and fingered the decorative lace patterns stitched in the fabric. “I have no expectations, Jess.” She responded softly. “Everything about this weekend is a bonus to me.”

Jess nodded, grateful for the sentiment. “Me too.” Any additional words seemed redundant.

Trying to lighten the mood a little, Robin leaned forward and rested her forearms on the table, green eyes now twinkling. “So, tell me, what does a junior partner like you want for Christmas, anyway?”

That drew a deep chuckle. “Well, there’s nothing I really want that I don’t already have. You don’t need to go and buy me anything.”

“Oh, come on, Jess. Surely, there’s something.” Light eyebrows knit together. “Do we need to take another trip to the mall?”

Jess shook her head vehemently. “I don’t think that will be necessary, Robin. Besides, I can only stand to have so much fun once in a great while.” A dark eyebrow lifted in careful consideration. “Unless, of course, I get to ride the train again.” She smirked happily, and then decided turnabout is fair play. “What about you, kiddo? What does an up-and-coming young associate like yourself want for Christmas?”

Robin’s wide smile met her eyes. “Well, you see, there’s this really great sporty looking BMW that I’ve had my eye on.”

The older woman’s jaw dropped. “You want a car?”

“It’s not just any car, Jess. It’s really cool. Besides, it has a back seat, and room enough for even the tallest person to fit comfortably without complaining.” Robin gave the older woman a sarcastic grin.

Jess really had no response to that statement.

“So, other than that, which I’m saving up for myself, I guess I really can’t think of anything I’d really want for Christmas.” Robin took note of the waiter heading their way with the main course. “We’ll have to continue this conversation later.” She grinned. “The food’s here, and I'm starving."

"Imagine that." Jess retorted. "It may interest you to know that my voracious appetite has also kicked in."

Robin brought her hand up to shield her face, a faint blush crossing her features. *I can't believe she did it to me again.*

****

Upon finishing their dinner, the two women made the short walk back to the bed and breakfast inn located only a few blocks away from the restaurant. It was still fairly early in the evening, and the city continued to bustle with holiday sight-seers. They approached the inn and went inside, immediately surrounded by the quaint furnishings and the cozy warmth of the fire blazing in the great room's fireplace. The sweet scent of the Frasier fir tree filled the area, and the tiny white tree lights gently twinkled from amidst the glittering garland. Robin and Jess paused for a moment to admire the enchanting sight, and then headed up the stairs toward their room, entering it quietly.

"Are you tired?" Jess wasn't quite sure why she asked the question.

"No, not really." Robin hung up her jacket. "I need to wash up for a minute. Would you make a fire? It's kinda cold in here." She caught herself in her minor faux pas and amended her statement. "I mean, it's kinda 'not hot' in here. She grinned and entered the bathroom.

Cerulean eyes twinkled in amusement as Jess complied with her request, proceeding to arrange the previously furnished wood neatly in the fireplace and light the firelog. "All ready." The dark-haired woman proudly proclaimed as Robin returned. The nicely roaring blaze of the fire provided immediate warmth throughout the room. "You get all warm and cozy. My turn to wash up."

Several minutes later, Jess stepped back into the dimly lit room. The fire continued its steady blaze, as the crackling of the wood echoed slightly, and haphazard shadows danced lazily against the stucco walls. Robin sat in one of the chairs next to the fireplace, absorbing the warmth as the flames flickered. A small lamp stood on the weathered wood table by the window, providing the only other light in the small, but cozy space.

Jess walked up behind the chair where Robin was seated and leaned down, speaking succinctly into a delicate ear. "Where is he?"

Startled by the question, Robin jerked her head around and looked at Jess, extremely confused. "What?"

The older woman straightened up. “You heard me. Where is he?”

A perplexed look. “Um...who?”

“You know perfectly well, who.”

Still perplexed, Robin countered. “Jess, there’s no one here but us.”

“Don’t play innocent with me, Robin. I know he’s here.” With disbelief clearly evident, Jess walked over to window. “Is he out there on the roof?” She opened the window to look at the rooftop above the first floor of the inn, and then closed the window again, frowning slightly.

Robin watched in utter amazement.

“Is he under the bed?” Jess proceeded to kneel on the hardwood floor and check underneath the queen-sized bed, finding nothing. “Or how about inside this closet?” Jess walked across the room and opened the closet door, immediately shutting it again. “He can’t hide forever, Robin.”

By now, Robin was getting a little worried. “Jess, I...I don’t know what you’re talking about.”

“Of course you do.” The dark-haired woman strode purposefully back over to the fireplace where Robin was sitting. “You specifically told me he would be here.” Blue eyes bore steadily into green.

A sudden smirk crossed Robin’s face. “So I did.”

“So tell me where he is.” Jess demanded.

“No.” Green eyes narrowed in defiance. “You have to find him yourself.”

At this, Jess considered her options, tapping her chin lightly. “Could you maybe give me a little hint?”

“No.”

“How about if I walk around the room and you tell me if I’m warm or cold?”

Robin feigned exasperation. “Oh, very well.” She relented. “Start walking.”

“Alright.” Jess rubbed her hands together and walked over to the front door. “Here?”

“Cold.”

“Hmm.” Jess next went over to the table and chairs. “Here?”

“Colder.”

A frown. Jess crossed over to the bathroom doorway. “Here?”

“Warmer.” The younger woman watched in amusement.

An excited look from Jess. She stepped over next to the fireplace. "Here?"

"Very warm."

Blue eyes twinkled in anticipation. Jess slowly walked over to the chair and stood directly in front of Robin. "How about here?"

Robin stood up. "Hot." She whispered and then leaned into Jess, feeling an almost magnetic pull.

Jess's heart was racing. She bent down and gave Robin a lingering kiss, then pulled back, her voice but a breathless whisper as she studied sea green eyes. "So, where is he, Robin?"

Robin, herself, could barely speak, but managed to issue the soft command. "Find him."

The dark-haired woman encircled the petite body in a tender embrace and whispered gently. "Come over here with me." She led Robin over to sit on the edge of the bed, and knelt on the floor in front of her. "Would he be in your shoes?" Jess slowly unlaced the shoes Robin wore, and removed them one after the other, looking inside each thoroughly as she did so. "No, he's not in there." She paused. "How about in your socks?" Jess proceeded to remove and check each sock in similar fashion. "Hmm. Not in there, either." She gently caressed Robin's feet and leaned down and placed soft delicate kisses on the top of each dainty foot. "Where is he?"

Robin's breathing quickened as the light caresses continued. Her eyes fluttered briefly at the loving kisses bestowed on her feet and ankles. "Keep looking."

"Is he in your pockets?" Jess raised up on her knees and reached out to lightly examine each of Robin's pants pockets, probing inside until she was sufficiently satisfied. "No, he's not there either."

The anticipation was steadily building. "You'll have to look harder, then." Green eyes lock on to blue.

Jess brought her hands to Robin's waist and glided her hands just underneath the edge of the knit sweater, trailing her long fingers gently across the smooth stomach. "How about here?" She lifted the sweater slightly, inspecting the area, then leaned down and bestowed the same fluttering kisses to the bare skin of Robin's stomach. "I still don't see him." She whispered.

Robin couldn't think. All she could feel were the moist, soft kisses covering her skin. "Look some more." She whispered back.

Complying, Jess slipped her hands fully under the soft fabric and brushed her thumbs in circling motions over the bare skin for a brief moment, before proceeding further. She looked up and into sea green eyes shaded by the dim light, and then grasped the edge of Robin's sweater, pulling it up swiftly over the blonde head. Her eyes sparkled as she finally found what she'd been looking for all along. "Ah, there he is." Jess grinned. Her hand took hold of the small good luck charm dangling from around the younger woman's neck. "I win."

"Yes, you win." Robin tenderly brushed the dark bangs.

Blue eyes fixed steadily on green. "Can I claim my point prize?"

"Yes." Robin stroked a soft cheek with her fingertips. "Can I receive my trial reward?"

Jess nodded. "Yes." She felt Robin's fingers reach down, and with deliberate purpose, tug her sweater up and over her head. Jess wrapped her arms around Robin's bare shoulders, kissing the base of the petite neck, and then quickly glided up to plant several kisses on the soft lips. She moved her hands around to unfasten Robin's bra, removing it with ease, and then effortlessly climbed up on the bed and laid Robin back against the pillows. Jess lifted the small charm from around Robin's neck and set it on the nightstand, before easing her own body down slightly on top of the smaller woman. They were both breathing heavily by now, as their kisses intensified, and Jess felt the smaller hands reach tentatively around her back. "It...um...unhooks in the front."

Robin made quick work in that area, and then threaded her fingers through the long dark hair. "Jess, I don't...." The younger woman fell silent, a somewhat hesitant expression crossing her features. It wasn't as if Robin hadn't thought about this before, but here they both were, and she had absolutely no idea what to expect. She looked into the blue eyes positioned just above her own, and whispered softy. "Do you know what to do?"

Jess smiled in gentle reassurance. "I think I have a pretty good idea." She lavished Robin with tender kisses and then whispered softly into the nearest ear. "How about if I do some things, and you tell me if they're okay, and we'll see if it works? Is that alright?" Jess nibbled a delicious earlobe.

"Um...yeah." Robin was quickly losing all coherent thought. She whimpered as the large hand trailed down her neck and briefly brushed and then explored her breast on its journey southward. The hand then moved to unfasten the button on Robin's twill pants and slowly lowered the zipper. Robin whimpered again, and before she knew it, the pants and everything else had been whisked away. The tall, warm body quickly closed upon hers.

"Is this okay?" Jess found a particularly sensitive area and proceeded with her nibbling.

Oh God. Robin had never felt anything like it before, and her senses were definitely on another plane altogether. "Um...um...yeah." It was the most coherent thing she could manage. She was somehow rational enough, though, to return the previous favor and swiftly divest Jess of all remaining clothing items.

For Jess, there was something just so instinctive about it all, as if she had known all along what to do and how to do it. That in and of itself was interesting because she, like Robin, had absolutely no experience in this particular area. "Is this still okay?" Jess continued the relentless nibbling.

Robin nodded but couldn't speak, the pressure building rather quickly. She felt long fingers trail down the outside of her thigh and then move to the inside, tracing back up and sending shivers throughout her body. Robin stifled a moan and clutched her fingers tighter through the long dark hair, all intelligent thought having temporarily escaped her. Long fingers gently touched and stroked and massaged seemingly all the right places, as the pressure finally reached its precipice. Her release came quickly, as she cried out and wrapped her arms tightly around the strong body next to hers, and just held on.

Jess whispered tenderly. "I love you, Robin. Hold on to me, sweetheart." The older woman pressed herself against Robin for several moments until she felt the petite body finally relax. She leaned down and gently kissed the soft lips once again as a lingering shudder passed through the smaller frame. Jess smiled and regarded Robin almost shyly. "Did it work?"

Green eyes blinked and then focused on blue. The glow of the fire highlighted Jess's beautiful face, leaving Robin almost mesmerized. "Yes." She touched her fingers to the shadowed cheek and smiled. "It definitely worked."

"Was it like you thought?" Jess whispered softly.

"Better." Robin turned on her side and pushed herself up on one arm. "It was absolutely and totally amazing." She leaned in and gave the older woman a delicate kiss. "I want you to feel it, too, Jess." She locked her gaze on the deep blue eyes in front of her. "Can I...see if it works for you?"

Large hands captured the blonde head, and the older woman brought Robin's sweet lips down to meet her own. "Yes." Jess spoke softly. "Try doing what I did, and we'll see if it works."

The blonde head ducked and began kissing Jess in ardent fashion, her hands touching and stroking in much the same way Jess had done. She tenderly nipped and tasted the slightly salty skin of Jess's neck and then trailed even lower, stopping to linger at certain intriguing places. Robin added a few interesting things of her own, which she curiously and somehow instinctively knew, as she brought the dark-haired woman toward an intense and spiraling release. She braced herself as Jess finally arched and clutched to her body, the older woman exploding and rapidly cascading over the same precipice Robin had visited just moments before. “I love you, Jess.” Robin repeated softly. “I love you.” She felt Jess’s heart beat wildly beneath her, and then finally calm its rhythm as they both remained very still for several moments more. *It’s funny how I knew what to do.* “So, did it work?” Robin asked lazily into a nearby ear, already knowing the answer.

Jess grinned lazily back. “It more than worked. It was....” She took a moment to find the proper word. “Incredible.” Long fingers reached to entwine with Robin’s, and Jess slowly and deliberately brought their joined hands up to meet her own lips. She kissed the petite knuckles repeatedly. “You’re incredible.”

“So are you.” Tender kisses met the dark eyebrows.

“So....” Those same dark eyebrows waggled a bit. “Want to check out the whirlpool tub in there?”

Robin couldn’t help but grin. “Oooh, that sounds...interesting.” A blonde eyebrow arched. “Would you wash my back?”

Blue eyes sparkled in the waning firelight. “Well, now, that would depend. Would I be required to wash just your back, or are there other areas that need washing, too?”

“I think all areas pretty much need washing.” There was somewhat of an anticipatory hitch in Robin’s voice.

“I see. There is one condition, though.”

“And that would be?” A petite finger traced the strong jaw.

“I would have to be awarded many, many points for my back washing skills.”

Robin chuckled and then considered the request. “Deal. But don’t forget about all the other areas, too.”

Jess smiled, then leaned over and kissed Robin soundly. “I can guarantee you, Robin, that I will definitely not forget about the other areas.”

“Good.” The younger woman appeared to contemplate something for a brief moment. “And, of course, after you’re finished, it will be my turn to wash your back.”

Oh. “Okay.”

“It’s only fair, after all, that I return the favor.”

Oh. Jess swallowed. “Right.”

Robin cocked her head and fought hard to suppress a teasing grin. "So, should I simply wash your back, Jess, or are there other areas that need washing, too?"

Jess grasped the covers and pulled them up and over her head in mock surrender. *I am definitely in so much trouble.*

****

Brilliant rays of sunlight streamed in through the lace curtains and cast warm shadows against the wall of the inn's quaint bedroom, as the morning sun rose high above the old city's horizon. Both Robin and Jess had slept in just a little, whether from an inclination to catch up on much-needed sleep or simply due to the comfort of their being together. The small body stirred and a sleepy green eye opened to find a still slumbering form curled up snuggly to her side. A long arm was wrapped protectively around her waist.

Robin took a moment to silently contemplate the situation further. They had spent part of the night in the whirlpool tub, making sure they were both thoroughly clean, before finally crawling back into bed and falling asleep snuggled against each other. Robin felt herself blush at the memory of the prior evening's events. It amazed her even this morning how wonderful it all had felt. It just seemed so comfortable and so completely natural to be with Jess in that way. *Natural.* She shook her head at the thought. Robin wasn't sure if she, herself, would consider their relationship natural, even though it certainly felt that way. She mentally recalled the previous evening, and chuckled lightly under her breath as several scenes played out in vivid fashion in her mind.

"I heard that." A low voice raspy with sleep piped up.

"You're awake."

"Yep. Have been."

Robin peered up at the still closed eyes. "For how long?"

"Long enough to catch you snoring." A slow grin edged its way across Jess's face.

"I do not snore."

"You never heard yourself. Believe me when I tell you that you definitely do snore." Blue eyes were now fully open wide.

"I don't believe you. How come you never mentioned this before?"

Jess bit her lower lip lightly. "You got me there, kiddo. Alright, you don't exactly snore, it's more like a small squeak, and it's really quite adorable." She gave Robin light kiss on the temple. "That's why I like waking up first and watching you sleep. I find you very cute."

This little admission made Robin blush all over again. She shifted slightly and an unexpected realization suddenly took hold of her. She cautiously lifted the covers and peered underneath them. "Um...Jess?" Robin let the covers return to their previous position, her blush deepening severely. "We're um...."

Dark brows knit together in thought. Jess lifted the covers slightly and surveyed the situation, before letting the linen fabric gently flutter back down to its original location. "Not wearing anything?"

"Um...yeah." Robin didn't understand why she suddenly felt so self-conscious. It was silly, really, considering everything she and Jess had shared the previous evening.

"Does that bother you?" Jess asked quietly.

How do I answer this? "I have to admit it's different for me. I guess I'm just used to waking up wearing something."

Jess lifted one hand and turned Robin's face toward her own. "Listen to me, honey. I don't ever want you to feel uncomfortable. If something doesn't feel right for you, please don't be afraid to tell me. I think we have to talk to each other about what we think and how we feel."

The blonde head nodded cautiously. "Alright." Robin took a deep breath and then released it. "Jess, I feel better wearing something when I sleep."

"Okay."

"But Jess, I don't want to...."

Jess stopped her mid-sentence. "No. This is important. Let's agree that if one of us isn't comfortable with something, anything at all, we won't do it. Period. And we have to promise to tell each other if we're not comfortable with something. Deal?"

Sea green eyes gauged gentle azure, reading their open sincerity. "Deal." Robin snuggled against Jess's side. "Can I say one more thing?"

"Yes."

"Waking up this way does have its benefits." Robin smiled against the bare skin of Jess's collarbone.

A dark eyebrow shot up. "Such as?"

"Your skin feels really, really good next to mine."

That drew a low chuckle. "I aim to please."

Robin giggled. "That reminds me." She propped herself up on one elbow. "Last night...um...how did you know what to do, if you hadn't...?" She left the thought deliberately unfinished.

"Well..." Jess drawled. "I said I'd never been with a woman before. I never said I was naïve." She had what could only be described as a self-satisfied smirk on her face.

"Oh."

"And how about you?" Both eyebrows lifted behind dark bangs as a wide grin eased its way across the angular face. "You certainly seemed as if you knew what you were doing."

Robin promptly turned an adorable shade of pink, and then buried her face in Jess's shoulder. *I just knew.* "I just knew." She mumbled.

Jess's smile softened and warmed at the admission. "Me too. I just knew." They snuggled together for a moment longer until a blue eye peered over at Robin. "Want to...um...try it again?"

As if on cue, Robin's stomach rumbled. Loudly. "Well, now, it seems I have quite a dilemma, here." She grinned and considered her options studiously, weighing them with careful deliberation. "Breakfast...Jess. Breakfast...Jess." Green eyes danced. "Hmm. What shall I do?"

Jess watched in near disbelief. *She's not really considering going down to breakfast, is she?* "If you want to go downstairs to breakfast, Robin, it's okay. We can go." Jess tried unsuccessfully to keep from pouting.

I can't take my eyes off of her this morning. "Alright. I've made my decision." Robin grinned happily. "Breakfast can wait."

"But your stomach's growling." *Did I just say that?*

Robin chuckled. "That's true, but I do remember you promising to take care of me and my stomach this weekend. Something about big plans, as I recall." She lifted a blonde eyebrow. "As I see it, taking care of my stomach is definitely your job, Jess, and should be the number one priority. I expect the works."

The works? "Now, there's an invitation I simply can't refuse." Jess gave the stomach in question a gentle squeeze, then proceeded to dip down and brush her lips lightly against its silky soft skin. "So tell me, Robin, are you sure you wouldn't rather go downstairs to breakfast?" Soft, moist lips kept up their assault.

"Um...no." It was becoming difficult to think.

"Because we can just get dressed and go." Fingers trailed lazy patterns on the bare skin, causing goosebumps in their wake.

"Um...no." Coherent thought was but a memory.

"It's really no problem if you want to head downstairs, now." Jess smiled against Robin's abdomen, the long, slender fingers continuing their sensual onslaught. "It's up to you."

"Um...um...." Robin forgot the question.

Tender lips resumed their expedition. "Or not."

Oh God. Robin finally found her voice again, albeit with tremendous difficulty. "Or not."

****

Later that morning, after a delayed breakfast, Robin and Jess headed out to wander the Spanish Quarter. They proceeded onward through the famous city gates still standing guard after nearly five centuries. They strolled up and down St. George Street looking at the old historic buildings and window shopping in the many quaint little shops that lined the city's oldest street. At one point, a confectionery caught Robin's eye, and they absolutely had to go inside and sample the sweet treats. Chocolate, of course.

As they meandered down near the main plaza, the church bell of the Cathedral-Basilica of St. Augustine began its harmonic chime. The cathedral, itself, was situated adjacent to the plaza square and well within Jess and Robin's immediate view.

The older woman watched silently as the throngs of people made their way inside. "Today's Sunday." Jess mused out loud. "It's time for noon Mass."

A curious expression crossed Robin's face, one which Jess couldn't read. "Yeah." Robin leaned against a nearby lamppost, as an errant thought came to her. "Are you Catholic, Jess?"

The dark-haired woman's face held a bit of regret. "Not practicing. Used to be." She kicked the ground uncomfortably. "You?"

Robin studied the length of the old bell tower as the chiming continued. "Same."

Jess silently took in this bit of information. *Same?* "How long has it been?"

"Not long, just since...." Robin closed her eyes briefly in a vain attempt to conceal her lingering sorrow, and whispered. "Since David died." She abruptly averted her gaze away from the cathedral.

That soon? Jess watched the play of emotions cross the younger woman's face. "Oh." She really didn't know what to say.

Robin looked blankly ahead. "I just can't forgive Him."

"You can't forgive who?" Jess wasn't sure she understood.

"God."

Jess's eyes betrayed her shock at the admission. It was quite disturbing on many levels. "You can't forgive…."

"God." Robin supplied again, and then blew out a long breath. "I really don't want to talk about this right now, Jess. Not this weekend, okay?" Green eyes pleaded with the older woman just to let it go.

But we need to talk about this. Jess knew the whole issue would likely come back at them later on, but she relented, totally against her better judgment. "Alright." She hesitated. "But, will you call Dr. Richmond tomorrow?"

Robin's shoulders slumped. "If I have time, I will."

Not good enough. Jess moved in front of the smaller woman and ducked her head, looking her squarely in the eyes. "Promise me, Robin, you'll call."

Their eyes remained locked. "I promise I'll call and make an appointment, but it'll be after the holidays." *Don't push me on this, Jess, please.*

The dark-haired woman sighed and then, quite reluctantly, acquiesced. "Okay. After the holidays, then." *Wasn't it 'after the trial,' Jess? Now it's 'after the holidays.' Something's just not right.* Jess tucked the issue away for later, determined not to let anything unpleasant spoil their weekend together.

"Thank you." Robin smiled gratefully and quickly changed the subject. "So, what do you want to do next?"

The Spanish mission's definitely out. Jess led them back in the direction of the quaint St. George Street with its myriad of little shops. "Well, let's see. We've done just about everything except the winery and the lighthouse."

"And lunch." Robin cheerfully reminded.

Jess feigned surprise. "Lunch? We just had breakfast."

"That's true." Robin turned thoughtful. "But I worked up an appetite this morning."

"From window shopping?" Sometimes Jess was quite clueless.

Robin blushed slightly and barely suppressed a grin, finding a nearby crack in the pavement suddenly very interesting. "Um...right. From window shopping."

Window shopping. The taller woman stopped and stared at Robin. who was, by now, grinning rather sheepishly. *Oh.* Amused blue eyes twinkled. "I see."

"So you understand why it's important for me to keep up my strength."

"Absolutely." Jess quipped. "So you can do more window shopping."

"Exactly." Robin turned into the nearby pizza parlor. "I'm so glad you understand the dynamics involved."

I most certainly do.

****

After a leisurely lunch and another stroll down by the bayfront, Jess and Robin headed over to the San Sebastian winery for a quick tour. It was absolutely fascinating to Robin that there was wine made exclusively from Florida grapes. She was quite surprised that grapes even grew in Florida, let alone the fact that there were several active wineries and vineyards throughout the state. The winery tour provided a comprehensive overview of the art of grape-growing, focusing specifically on the grape varieties indigenous to the state of Florida. These included the popular Muscatine grape and its various hybrids. The tour also demonstrated the process for fermenting the grapes, aging the wine, and then bottling the finished product. Jess and Robin decided that they couldn't possibly leave without purchasing several bottles of the vintage wine made exclusively from Florida grapes.

"That was fun." Robin grinned as she opened the car door and slid into the passenger seat.

"Glad you enjoyed it." Jess placed the newly acquired bottles of wine in the back seat and climbed into the car. "So, where to next, kiddo?" She started up the ignition. "You're the boss."

"I'm glad you realize that." Robin chuckled. "Saves me from having to always remind you."

Jess narrowed her eyes. "Wise guy."

"And don't you forget it, either." Robin fiddled with the radio, trying to locate a light rock music station. "How about if we go to the lighthouse and then head on back home?"

"Sounds like a plan, Stan" Jess pulled out onto the main highway.

"Stan? Is that a new name or just a term of affection?"

"You don't need to be coy, Roy."

Robin stared at Jess in utter disbelief. "I'm trapped in a car with a nut."

"Like I told you before, I resemble that remark. You could always hop on the bus, Gus."

Robin was completely dumbfounded. "You're impossible. Give me the key, Lee."

"What?" Jess knew the tables had been turned.

"I'm driving. Pull over."

"But I...."

Robin shook her head. "Nope. If I didn't know better, I'd say you had a little bit too much wine back there, but I know neither of us had more than a sip."

"I was just saying the words to the song." Jess playfully protested.

Robin gave her a frank look. "Jess, think about the title of the song."

"Fifty Ways to Leave...oh." Jess sheepishly replied. "Sorry."

Robin chuckled. "It's alright, and I suppose you can keep on driving. But let's just listen to the songs on the radio, okay there, Bucko?"

"That's the second time you've called me Bucko. Is that a...term of affection?" A blue eye peered expectantly over at Robin.

The blonde woman hesitated, then smirked. "No comment." At Jess's overly chagrined expression, Robin broke out into a fit of giggles. It was really quite charming, the gentle teasing and light banter that she and Jess so naturally shared, and it warmed her up in the most delightful way just thinking about it. She finally regained her composure and cast a wide smile at Jess. "You are so much fun. I absolutely love being with you."

Jess glanced over at Robin fondly. "Same here, kiddo."

"Um...Jess?" Robin sobered somewhat. "I want to thank you again."

"For this weekend? Not necessary."

"Well, yes, for this weekend, but also for sticking with me earlier and not pressing me too much." Robin fingered the seatbelt buckle. "I know it must have been very difficult for you." Her tone was guarded.

Jess sensed that Robin was referring to her continuing emotional issues concerning David, especially the incident at the cathedral, and most likely her receipt of the Mitchells' Christmas card. "Like I said before, I'm like...."

"Crazy glue." Robin supplied.

"Correct."

"And you're very sticky."

"Correct."

"And I'm stuck with you."

"Absolutely correct." Jess gave Robin a very tender smile. "We're stuck with each other."

Robin nodded. "We're stuck with each other."

"For better or for worse."

Robin nodded again. "For better or for worse."

"Good." Jess focused on the road. "Because I quite like being stuck with you."

"Crazy glue and all?"

"Yep." Jess winked. "Crazy glue and all."

Chapter 10

If there was ever a way to jolt oneself back into reality, a Monday morning litigation breakfast was the sure-fire way to go about it. The quarterly litigation department meetings served very little purpose, in Jess's opinion, save for providing a forum for some of the more verbose members of the firm to have their say on matters which ordinarily no one would find interesting in the least. That being the case, the only real accomplishment of the meetings was that nearly every litigation attorney spent several hours of precious billable time cooped up in a conference room fending off complete boredom. The cheese danish, on the other hand, was not bad.

The meeting was interminable, and with at least another hour to go, it became increasingly clear that Jess was simply not able to concentrate. Far too many distractions occupied her mind. For instance, only twelve days remained until Christmas, a major appellate brief needed to be filed, and Robin sat at the opposite end of the conference table. Enough said. Instead of focusing her attention on the immediate agenda item, something which purportedly dealt with garnishment law revisions, Jess allowed her distracted internal thought processes take control of her wandering mind once again.

My, you've certainly been the busy bee.

'Yeah? So what? And why are you here, anyway?' The alternate internal voice was a bit cranky this morning.

You know exactly why I'm here. Something's bothering you.

A lapse into the usual modus operandi of initially denying the obvious. *'Nope. You're wrong. Nothing's bothering me. Everything's fine.'*

Is it?

'Absolutely, positively.' The alternate internal voice happily replied.

Then why aren't you paying attention to the new garnishment law requirements?

'Because, buddy, I'm practically dying of boredom, here. Give me a break.' An exaggerated internal sigh. *'Alright. Fine. You've made your point. Can we get on with this?'*

Certainly. So, you think things are going rather well for you right now, don't you?

'Yep.' The alternate internal voice seemed quite pleased with the recent turn of events.

You and Robin are getting along terrifically, you've just had a fabulous weekend together, and Christmas is coming up. All in all, things couldn't be better. Agreed?

'Yep, again.' The alternate internal voice was now buoyant. *'You get bonus points for your stellar powers of perception.'*

And that's exactly why I'm here. You need to take a hard look at some things.

A mental groan. *'Listen, buddy, I'm in a good mood. Let's not spoil it, okay?'*

Sorry. No can do. Shall we begin?

'Do I have a choice?'

No. First item on your voices agenda: Robin's procrastination on calling Dr. Richmond. Something's going on there.

'She said she'd call after the holidays.' The alternate internal voice explained matter-of-factly.

And you believe her.

The alternate internal voice brimmed with confidence. *'Yes.'*

Yes?

A little less confident. *'Okay, maybe not.'*

She's avoiding it. Why do think that is?

'How should I know?' The alternate internal voice became somewhat agitated. *I'm not Sigmund Freud.'*

But you think you know, don't you? You think she's avoiding it because she's afraid of what she might find out. Specifically, you think she's afraid that when she comes to terms with David's death, she might realize that you were right all along. She'll see that you were indeed a convenient substitute for him, and she won't be able to handle that.

'No.' The alternate internal voice vigorously defended. *'Robin assured me she never thought of me that way.'*

And you believe her.

'Yes.' The alternate internal voice was quite adamant.

Yes?

Slight hesitation. *'Yes. She said she loves me. I believe that. We spent the weekend together.'*

You went a little further than merely spending the weekend together, didn't you?

'I won't apologize for that. What's your point?'

You've made no commitment.

'We love each other.' The alternate internal voice resolutely responded.

I repeat, you've made no commitment.

'And I repeat, we love each other.' The alternate internal voice made a valiant attempt to rationalize the situation with legalese. *'A commitment is implied therein.'*

Is it? Don't add to your delusion, counselor. Consider this. If you move along blissfully without a commitment, you're just as guilty as Robin is in her procrastination at seeing the therapist. You're both guilty of failing to confront the same reality.

'And what same reality might that be?'

The possibility that her feelings for you might not be what she thought they were. Without making a commitment, she is conveniently free to leave, and you are conveniently free to let her go. You spent the weekend together, you say you love each other, but you've made no commitment. You want forever but you have no idea if Robin wants it, too. Face the facts. Without a commitment, she's free to leave you, especially if she thinks it's for the best.

The alternate internal became indignant at the implication *'She will not leave me.'*

Are you sure?

A lengthy silence. *'I can't listen to this. The garnishment laws have changed. I need to pay attention, here.'*

You can't ignore it. She's avoiding something. If not this, then what?

The alternate internal voice blithely tuned out the mental dialogue.

It will come back at you when you least expect it.

Said tuning out continued.

Wake up. You know you have to deal with it.

'Oh, were you saying something?' The alternate internal voice feigned innocence. *'Did you know that the garnishor now has to inform the judgment debtor of his options before garnishment can proceed?*

It's absolutely fascinating.'

Facetiousness serves no purpose here. You refuse to deal with it, so let's move on. Second item on your voices agenda: Christmas. Or more specifically, Robin's parents and Christmas.

'What of it?' The alternate internal voice grew cautious.

What's going on?

'Nothing. They're coming down from Michigan and she's spending Christmas with them. End of story.'

Is that your final answer?

'Cute.' The alternate internal voice turned flippant *'That is my final answer.'*

Sorry to disturb the little delusion thing you've got going on, but you're wrong. Think about it. She's not said one word to you about when they're coming down or how long they're staying. You don't even know what their intentions are once they get here.

'Their intentions are to visit.'

Perhaps. But they certainly may be worried about her. Their intentions could be to convince her to go back to Michigan.

'She won't go.' The alternate internal voice responded definitively. *'She won't.'*

Okay. But the fact is, she hasn't indicated that she wants to you meet them.

A moment's reflection. *'True, but it's really too soon for her to discuss our relationship with them. Meeting me will bring up questions. After all, I'm not exactly what her daddy had in mind for her.'*

Be that as it may, it hurts, doesn't it, that she's not clued you in on any of her plans?

The alternate internal voice tried the noble approach. *'I understand.'*

But it hurts just the same, doesn't it?

'Okay, yes.' The alternate internal voice reluctantly acknowledged. *'It hurts just the same.'*

Then you and Robin had better discuss it. At the very least, find out when the two of you can spend some time together during Christmas week.

'That's probably a good idea.'

And then you'll know the real reason why she's not mentioned any of this to you. She could be avoiding her parents, or maybe she just doesn't want to involve you in her plans.

The alternate internal voice suddenly became apprehensive. *'And if she doesn't want to involve me in her plans?'*

Then she's afraid to acknowledge your relationship, and she'll have to figure out why that is. It could be because she doesn't want to deal with it with her parents, or it could be because she subconsciously knows that her feelings for you might not be what she thought they were. Either way, she'll probably need Dr. Richmond to help her figure it out.

The alternate internal voice turned somber as the realization suddenly became clear. *'I could lose her.'*

It's possible. You could lose her. You need to be prepared for that.

'I'll never be prepared for that.' The alternate internal voice sounded broken-hearted.

Look at the bright side. Once she comes to terms with everything, the weight of this matter will be gone forever.

The alternate internal voice reverted to sarcasm once again. *Well, you're quite the philosopher. Socrates and Aristotle have nothing on you. Not to mention Plato. I think I'd much rather stay in my blissful ignorance and contemplate how many days the garnishee has to answer the writ of garnishment, thank you very much.'*

Fine. Delusion suits you. Let's move on to the third item on your voices agenda: Christmas gift for Robin. By the way, do you see a trend here?

'Okay, I'll bite. What's the so-called trend?'

Every single one of your voices agenda items has to do with Robin.

'So?' It was easier for the alternate internal voice to play stupid, than to face the truth.

Just an observation. We'll discuss addictions later. Back to agenda item number three. What are you getting Robin for Christmas?

'Don't know. She wants a car.'

You're not getting her a car, are you?

An internal laugh. *'Of course not. She was trying to make a joke about my complaining that her car is too small. She's probably saving up for one, though.'*

So, then, what are you getting her?

'You seem awfully nosy about it.' The alternate internal voice was a bit annoyed. *'Listen, I really don't know, okay? Unless you, the all knowing voice of...whatever, have something in mind?'*

Just some advice. Want to hear it?

An internal grumble. *'As if I could stop you.'*

Give her your heart.

'What?'

Just what I said. Give her your heart. If things are meant to be, she'll hold your heart and take care of it. If not, then you gave it to her freely, and that's all anyone could ever have done. Think about it.

'Alright, I'll think about it.' The alternate internal voice needed time for serious contemplation. *'Are we finished, now?'*

Yes, except for the pop quiz. How many days does a garnishee have to answer a writ of garnishment?

'Twenty.'

Very good. Now, go get another cheese danish.

'Gee, thanks.' The alternate internal voice muttered. *'Then you can beam me up.'*

****

Robin sat at the far end of the conference table sipping her Irish Crème flavored coffee and paying rapt attention to the current topic of discussion. She smiled to herself when she felt, rather than saw, familiar blue eyes settle their gaze upon her. She snuck a quick peak, and was barely able to contain the grin which unconsciously edged its way across her face. She finally succumbed to the distraction, losing all semblance of concentration on the immediate agenda item, and let her mind take her to other places. *Christmas.* She pondered the issue for a moment. It was time to call her mother and discuss her parents' plans. Fine, she could do that, although she still felt uneasy about their coming to visit. She suspected there may be another reason behind it. *What's Jess doing for Christmas?* It was true, she and Jess hadn't discussed their respective plans, and now, with less than two weeks to go until the holidays, they really needed to decide when they could both spend some time together.

The young associate doodled a bit on her legal pad as she continued to contemplate the upcoming holidays. Okay, so her parents wanted to see that she was doing all right. That was understandable considering everything that had happened. *Should they meet Jess?* Robin let the question hang out there unanswered, the implications plain and the ramifications uncertain. But why not? She was going to be living with Jess. They'd come to know that sooner or later. *I could tell them we're roommates.* Robin smirked to herself. *Right. Roommates.* Leaving the final decision for another time, she returned her attention to the loquacious speaker up front. *The garnishor has to inform the judgment debtor of his options before garnishment can proceed. I'll have to remember that.*

An hour later, the meeting finally concluded, albeit a bit later than usual, and Robin set about tackling her overflowing in-box and waiting e-mails. She was continually amazed how fast it all seemed to accumulate. With most of the morning having been spent in the litigation meeting, she was barely able to finish wading through all her various messages and paperwork before the noon hour arrived. Almost as if on cue, her stomach grumbled, signaling that now would be an excellent time to take a lunch break. Her pen twirled unconsciously in her fingers as she contemplated and then discarded various lunch options. Green eyes lit up, and Robin smiled as an appealing idea came to her. She quickly opened a new e-mail message and typed in the simple request.

J,
Free for lunch?
R

She clicked the send button, then sat back in her chair, swiveling lightly. *Hope she's in.* Robin shifted her gaze to stare out the large window, idly noting the somewhat choppy waters of the lake below. The overcast day did nothing to dampen her mood, the memories of the past weekend in St. Augustine still lingering in her mind. It had really been quite special. She smiled to herself. *Special.* Even the prospect of her parents' visit wasn't enough to take away the euphoria she now felt. Her wayward, though pleasant, musings were suddenly interrupted by a familiar beep from her computer, indicating new mail had arrived. Robin glanced at the sender, and then quickly opened the message.

R,
Lunch? Now, there's a surprise. Meet you at the elevators in five.
J

Robin grinned as she read the message, and then considered how only a few words from Jess could make her feel so happy and so very much alive. It was simply amazing, and she made a mental note to ponder the effect more at another time. She grabbed her purse and quickly strode off, heading toward the elevators and one waiting junior partner in particular.

****

"Do you have to work late tonight?" Robin sat down at a corner table in the small delicatessen.

A dark eyebrow arched suspiciously. "Why?"

"Well...." Robin drawled as she tapped the side of her finger lightly against the tabletop. "I was thinking we could go out tonight and get a Christmas tree." She gave the junior partner opposite her a hopeful glance.

"A Christmas tree? For your apartment?"

"Um...actually, no. A Christmas tree for The Ranch." Robin took a bite of her chicken salad sandwich, then had a sudden thought. "You don't have a fake one stashed somewhere, do you?"

"Nope. No fake tree stash." Jess munched a dill pickle. "So, now, let me see if I understand you correctly. You want to go out and get a Christmas tree and put it up at the house?"

"Yes." The blonde head nodded. "I was thinking we could go tonight and pick one out." Robin noted the particularly odd expression on the junior partner's face. "Don't you usually get a Christmas tree, Jess?"

Jess considered the question. "Well, no, I haven't actually gotten a tree before. Wasn't any reason to. It was just me, and it seemed kinda pointless to put up a bunch of decorations if no one was gonna see them." She took a bite of her turkey sandwich. "Besides, I usually go to my mother's for Christmas, and she has a tree every year. I get my tree fill there."

The young associate cocked her head, her light brows furrowing in downright disbelief. "Are you saying you've never had a Christmas tree?"

"Robin, it's not a horrible thing, it's just a tree, and like I said, I get my tree fill at my mom's."

The look of disbelief persisted. "Tree fill." Robin contemplated the phrase. "What is that?"

Jess grinned. "Tree fill. You know, seeing a Christmas tree long enough to last until next year. I don't need to have one of my own to get my tree fill."

Robin's mouth fell open as she tried to fathom the explanation. She shook her head, obviously failing to grasp the concept, and then resolutely set her half-eaten chicken salad sandwich down on her plate. "Alright." She dusted her hands together in determined fashion. "This simply cannot continue. We have to remedy the situation immediately." Robin picked up her pickle and waved it purposefully at Jess. "For your information, there is absolutely no such thing as tree fill, and you are definitely coming with me tonight to pick out a Christmas tree." She jabbed the pickle in Jess's direction to further her point. "Then you and I going to put it up at The Ranch and decorate it."

Jess was secretly amused. "Number one, Robin, there most certainly is such a thing as tree fill. Number two, there really isn't any room in my living room to put this tree that we're supposedly going to get. Number three, I have no decorations to decorate this supposed tree with."

"Are you finished?" The young associate resumed eating.

"No. Number four, I don't necessarily need a tree. Number five, you could get one and put it up at your apartment for when your folks come visit. And number six, I already have a wreath that I put on my door which is decoration enough for my house."

Robin took a sip of her soda. "Are you finished, now?"

"Yes."

"Good. I'll pick you up at seven."

"Fine."

****

Jess and Robin spent the better part of the evening searching for the perfect tree, or as better stated, searching for Robin's idea of the perfect tree. Jess, on the other hand, thought all the trees looked nice. Three tree lots and one all-night superstore later, Jess and Robin finally trekked back to The Ranch with their painstakingly selected and perfectly proportioned Christmas tree securely in tow. Of course, trying to fit said tree into Robin's Miata was another story altogether. They ended up setting the netted tree in the trunk of the car, half-way sticking out, and then tying it down with twine. Jess was designated as the tree look-out, a very important job position charged with ensuring that said tree did, in fact, stay put in said trunk for the duration of said drive home. Once at The Ranch, Jess and Robin hauled the nearly seven foot tall Frasier fir tree inside the house, trying valiantly not to trail too many tree needles in their pathway. It didn't work. Needles scattered across the floor unhindered from foyer to living room.

"Okay. Where are we putting it?" Jess set the tree down in its stand.

Robin surveyed the entire living room, considering each potential location with a critical eye. "We could put it in the corner between the sliding doors and the fireplace. What do you think?"

"The etagere's there."

"Then we'll have to move it" It wasn't much of an obstacle in Robin's opinion.

"Fine, but then where are we going to put the etagere?"

Robin pursed her lips in thought, tapping a petite finger lightly against her chin. "We could move it into the spare bedroom."

Jess considered the idea. "Are you sure it won't be in your way in there?"

"Jess, I just have my clothes in that room now." Robin looked up a bit sheepishly. "It's not like I sleep in there, you know."

Good point. The dark-haired woman had to agree. "True."

"Especially, since there is no bed."

Let's keep it that way. Jess smirked. "Alright. Let's move the etagere in there." They went about moving the etagere, which was rather heavy, into the spare room, careful to place it out of the way of Robin's things. The younger woman had moved quite a few items from her apartment over to The Ranch, finding it easier to keep a healthy supply of clothing and personal effects close at hand. This was especially true considering the amount of time she was now spending there. Once the little chore of moving the etagere was accomplished, Jess placed the tree into the previously designated corner by the fireplace. "How does it look?"

"Turn it to the left just a bit." Robin directed.

Jess complied. "Now?"

"No, turn it back a little."

Jess complied again. "Okay, now?" She eyed Robin hopefully.

"Um...." The younger woman walked from side to side, studying the view from all possible angles. "Move it to the right just a little more."

Jess narrowed her eyes and moved the tree as instructed. "Now?"

"Well...maybe move it forward just a teensy weensy bit."

Jess blew out a breath in minor exasperation, then complied one more time. "Okay?" She arched an eyebrow at Robin in a playful dare to ask her to move it again.

"Perfect." Robin happily proclaimed.

"Are you sure? Because we're not moving it after it's decorated."

"Yes, I'm sure." The younger woman grinned eagerly. "Okay, now we have to put on the lights, and the ornaments, and then the tinsel." Robin retrieved the packages of decorations they'd bought earlier in the evening. "Here, take these and put them on the tree." She handed Jess a box of Christmas tree lights.

Jess dutifully strung the old-fashioned style colored lights around the tree, making sure they were evenly spaced between the branches. Next, Robin and Jess proceeded to decorate the tree with ornaments of varying shapes and colors. There was an impressive variety, consisting of shiny ball-shaped ornaments, tiny pine cones, gold-colored musical instruments, red and gold drums, wooden painted toy soldiers, and striped candy canes. With the colored lights all lit up and ornaments hanging from every branch, the tree really did look quite stunning.

"I almost forgot." Robin dug into another bag. "Do you want to put a star on top or an angel?"

"You mean we have a choice?" Jess watched as Robin pulled both treetop ornaments from the bag.

"Well, I wasn't sure at the time, and you were over looking at the miniature trains." Robin playfully smirked at the reference to trains.

Jess grinned. "I love trains."

"I'm sure I didn't know that." Robin quipped.

"I got to ring the bell."

The younger woman tried, but failed, to suppress a small grin. "That confirms it. You are absolutely hopeless."

"Listen," Jess wagged a playful finger at Robin. "I am not the one who made all those guys at all those tree lots open up each and every single six to seven foot tree they had, just to determine which specific tree had the straightest trunk and the fullest branches. One guy opened up so many, he got his workout for the month."

"You would have picked the very first one they showed us."

Jess recalled the Virginia Pine they first looked at. "It was a perfectly lovely tree."

"The branches were all smashed on one side. Honestly, Jess, you have to look very closely at all the angles. See, the one we got is completely symmetrical."

Jess patiently waited for Robin to finish. "Are you done?"

"Yes."

"Good. Come over here for a minute." Mischievous blue eyes twinkled.

Robin cautiously approached the older woman. "What?" They were both standing in the entryway to the kitchen.

"Look." A long finger pointed upward.

Mistletoe? Robin smiled. "When did you get that?"

"When I was over by the trains. I was listening to the bells and whistles, and I naturally thought about kissing you. Then I saw the mistletoe. It was divine providence. I had to buy it."

"You are very sweet." Robin leaned underneath the hanging mistletoe, meeting Jess's lips in a tender, lingering kiss. After several moments, the younger woman broke away, breathing a bit heavily. "I'm hearing bells and whistles, too. I believe you're right. It's definitely from kissing you."

Jess ducked in for several more kisses. "Yep. Bells and whistles. And here I thought it was the trains all along. Silly me." She grinned, then paused. "Angel."

"Angel?"

"Did you want the star?"

"Oh. No, the angel's perfect. Can you put it on top of the tree?" Green eyes twinkled a bit. "I can't reach."

As soon as Robin said it, long arms grasped her from behind and guided her toward the tree, pausing at the treetop ornaments lying on the oak coffee table. Jess picked up the white and gold angel and handed it to Robin. "Here." She boosted the petite body up level with the treetop. "Put it on."

Robin positioned the angel on top of the tree and plugged it in with the rest of the tree lights. As the strong arms set her down, Robin took a moment to gaze up a the brilliantly lit Christmas tree. "It's beautiful."

"Yeah." Azure eyes tracked from the tree to Robin. *Beautiful.*

"There's still one more thing." The younger woman rummaged through another bag, finding a box of shiny tinsel. She divided up the tinsel and handed Jess half. "Here, take some of this and put it over on that side of the tree."

"Alright." Jess took the shiny strands and watched intently as Robin started hanging her half of the tinsel on various tree branches. The dark-haired woman proceeded to do the same thing on her side of the tree, finishing in short order. "Okay, I'm done."

Robin peaked up at Jess, her mouth open slightly. "You can't be done."

"Yep." Jess raised her hands, palms open. "See, all done."

Robin stepped around to view Jess's handiwork. The younger woman was, quite frankly, a bit flabbergasted. "Um...Jess, have you ever put tinsel on a tree before?"

Dark brows knit together. "No." Jess regarded her side of the tree. "Is there a problem?"

How do I put this delicately? "Jess, honey, when you put tinsel on a tree, you generally hang it from the branches. You don't usually throw it on in clumps."

Jess continued to study the tinsel she'd placed on the tree. "It's faster that way. And it still sparkles."

Robin shook her head gently. "No, honey. Here, let me show

you." She took several of the clumps of tinsel from the tree and proceeded to place one strand at a time over the branches. "See? This way, the tinsel hangs down and looks like rain or icicles." She picked off some of the other clumps and handed them to Jess. "I'll help you, okay?"

The older woman took the tinsel from Robin and began placing it, as instructed, on the upper branches of the tree, while Robin busily worked on the lower branches. Of course, in Jess's considered opinion, this method of tinsel hanging was rather boring, so she decided to amuse herself in another way. She hung one strand of tinsel on an upper branch, then placed a second strand over Robin's head. Since Robin appeared not to notice, she tried it again, placing one strand on the tree, and then another on Robin's head. This process worked out so well that Jess performed the same ritual several more times, making sure that the blonde head was sufficiently and thoroughly covered with shiny tinsel.

Robin diligently placed her portion of the tinsel on the bottom half of the tree, filling in the gaps between the branches then strategically covering the tree light wires. Something tickled her nose, and a green eye watched with sudden interest as a wayward strand of tinsel fluttered downward. She bent her head and watched another strand fall. "Jess...is there something you want to tell me?"

"No." Jess hid a smirk.

"I think there is." Robin straightened up. "Let me help you. Tinsel goes on the tree, not on me. Are we clear?"

Blue eyes twinkled. "But it looks really good on you." Jess studied the blonde head a bit more. "I quite like it."

Green eyes narrowed. "Just you wait, Bucko. I'll get you back when you least expect it."

"Yeah, yeah. I've heard it all before." Jess waved a dismissive hand.

"Hey, Jess. Can you give me a boost up so I can put a little more tinsel on the top?" Robin pointed up near where the angel was positioned.

"How about if I get you a chair to stand on?"

Robin shook her head. "Nope. Just give me a boost. It'll only take a second."

The older woman complied, kneeling down with one leg bent at the knee to give Robin a place to step. "Okay, but my leg isn't going to hold out forever."

Robin placed one foot on Jess's knee and then lifted herself up level with the angel on the treetop. She leaned against a broad shoulder to brace herself, as Jess steadied her legs with her hands. The younger woman placed the shiny strands on all exposed upper branches until they were sufficiently covered, then turned slightly and proceeded to dump the remaining unused tinsel on top of Jess's head. Robin dusted her hands together, then jumped down, grinning satisfactorily. "I think I'm finished now."

Jess cautiously stood up, glittering pieces of tinsel strewn haphazardly about her head and hanging in front of her eyes. She was silent for a very long moment, and then slowly and deliberately pulled all offending strands of tinsel from her hair. "Was absolutely that necessary?"

"Yes." Robin appeared quite pleased with herself. "I think we're even now."

I can't believe I fell for that trick. "We most certainly are not even. I put a few pieces of tinsel on you. You dumped a whole handful on me. That is not even." Jess fixed Robin with a steady glare. "I would be very afraid right now if I were you, Robin."

"Now, Jess." Robin backed away. "That was the only way I could get you back. You're taller than I am, so I had to improvise." She took several more steps backward toward the kitchen.

"Is that so?" The dark-haired woman closed in on Robin, taking slow, exaggerated steps. Suddenly, with lightning quickness, Jess grasped the younger woman around the waist and spun her underneath the hanging mistletoe. A low voice rumbled in a petite ear. "If we get into improvisation, Robin, I promise you, I will win." She leaned down and kissed Robin soundly.

Robin leaned back against the nearby wall, a bit dazed. "Um...it seems I may have greatly underestimated your improvisational skills." Sea green eyes fixed on cool blue. "Care to demonstrate that again?"

Jess willingly complied with the request, then stood for a moment and gazed back into the living room. "The tree really looks nice." She offered a somewhat wry smile. "Tree fill has nothing on this."

That sent Robin into a fit of giggles. "And don't you forget it, either." She looked down at her hands and forearms, inspecting them for a moment. "I'm covered with tree sap, and this stuff's really hard to get off, even with soap. I need to go get cleaned up."

"I have a better idea." The taller woman made a cursory review of her own hands and arms, finding them just as sap-covered. "Want to hit the Jacuzzi?"

A blonde eyebrow slowly lifted. "Ooooh. That sounds...decadent."

You have absolutely no idea. "How about if you finish up in here, and I'll get the Jacuzzi ready. Sound like a plan, Stan?"

Robin grinned and pointed a playful finger at Jess. "Let's not start that again. And for the record, the name of that song is 'Fifty Ways to Leave Your Lover,' and it doesn't exist in my book."

There was something implied in that statement, and it made Jess pause and take notice. *She means no leaving?* "So, there's no slipping out the back, Jack?

Robin shook her head. "No."

"No making a new plan, Stan?"

"No." The blonde head shook again.

"How about being coy, Roy?"

"No." It was a definite statement.

"I see." Jess continued. "So, there would be no hopping on the bus, Gus?"

"Definitely not."

"What about dropping off the key, Lee?"

"No." Green eyes locked onto soft blue. "No one leaves."

I want to believe that. Jess stroked Robin's cheek. "No one leaves." She gently guided Robin back underneath the mistletoe for another lingering kiss.

"You know," a green eye peered up at the mistletoe. "We really should put that stuff somewhere more...convenient."

"I'll see what I can do." Jess grinned. "Alright, kiddo, let me get the Jacuzzi going. Why don't you go ahead and clean up in here."

Robin nodded, then began industriously clearing the empty ornament boxes and shopping bags from the living area. Jess took a step forward, then suddenly stopped her progress and turned back around, quietly regarding the sight before her. The Christmas tree stood in the corner of the room, brightly lit and decorated beautifully with colored lights and ornaments. The white and gold angel shone down from its perch on the treetop, its wings outstretched, as if somehow serving as a guardian of the home. The taller woman silently watched as Robin walked about the room busily removing the empty boxes and bags and taking out the cordless hand vacuum to clean up all loose tree needles and unused tinsel. Jess continued her observation in quiet fascination, the domesticity of it all suddenly striking her. She swallowed back a curious lump in her throat, as the unfamiliar feeling surrounded and then enveloped her completely, quite unwilling to let go.

I want this forever.

****

"Ooooh, this feels nice." Robin relaxed against the front portion of the roman tub as the Jacuzzi jets bubbled hot water in soothing waves around her. The low incandescent lights from the track lighting shone indirectly along the bathroom walls, as scented candles flickered gently from the imported marble countertops and around the edges of the large oval-shaped tub.

"Yeah." Jess leaned back against the opposite edge. "I usually unwind by taking a long, hot bath." A sudden thought popped into her mind. "I have a confession to make."

A curious blonde eyebrow arched. "Spill it."

"It was shortly after I met you, and I had a really bad day at work. I came home and decided to take a hot bath to relax." Jess offered a sheepish grin. "I turned on the Jacuzzi jets and almost drifted off, and when I shook myself out of it, I realized that I was thinking about you being in here with me."

"That was before we…."

"Yes."

"Oh." Robin considered the confession. "How did you feel about that?"

Jess's hands played with the water. "I told myself that I was just tired, and that I really wasn't thinking clearly."

The blonde head nodded pensively. "I have a confession, too."

"Okay."

Robin stared down at the foaming bubbles. "When we were in New Orleans, and we stayed in the hotel room together, the next morning you were in the shower and I had just woken up. You came out of the bathroom to get something, and you were wearing only a towel. I couldn't help it. I stared at you." Robin blushed even now at the memory, then shook her head slightly. "I didn't know why I did that."

"We both should have figured things out sooner, huh?"

"Yeah." Robin smiled. "Hey, Jess, will you wash my back?"

"Sure. Hand me that wash mitt, will ya?" Jess pointed to the terrycloth mitt folded neatly on the side of the tub.

Robin reached for the requested item, then suddenly burst into giggles. "Um...Jess?" The younger woman held the object up in front of her, inspecting it more closely. "What is this?"

Dark brows furrowed. "What do you mean, 'what is this'? It's a wash mitt."

Robin giggled again. "It has a smiley face on it."

"Your point?"

"Nothing." Robin continued to contemplate the mitt in question. "Did you...um...buy this yourself?" She tried, but failed, to suppress yet another giggle.

"For your information, Robin, my nephews left it here the last time they came to visit. I absolutely, positively, and most certainly did not buy it." Jess tried to sound indignant.

"Right." The younger woman grinned. "But you kept it."

Point made. "Okay, I kept it. Happy now?"

"Yes." Robin handed the mitt to Jess, green eyes holding a bit of mirth. "And Jess, not one more word about my bunny slippers, okay?" A blonde eyebrow arched to further her point. "Not even a tiny quip."

"Nope. No can do. One smiley face wash mitt does not equal two floppy-eared bunny slippers, no matter how you look at it. Sorry, kiddo." Jess savored her momentary victory. "Now, go ahead and turn around so I can get your back." She lathered up the wash mitt. "Did you get all the tree sap off?"

"Most of it." Robin shifted so Jess could easily reach her back and shoulders, letting the gentle rubbing and massaging further relax her muscles. After a moment, the younger woman chuckled lightly under her breath.

"What's so funny?"

"The mental image of a smiley face against my back just made me laugh." Robin chuckled again, then suddenly gasped as the smiley face mitt in question was replaced by genuine smiling lips trailing and kissing their way lazily from shoulder blade to shoulder blade. Sea green eyes fluttered closed, as Robin felt those same lips move to the base of her neck.

"So, where do you still have tree sap?" The alto voice spoke softly into a conveniently placed ear.

"Um...mostly on my hands." Green eyes opened and watched in rapt fascination as Jess reached forward and thoroughly cleansed one hand after the other of all visible traces of tree sap.

"Anywhere else?" Smiling lips journeyed along the top of a petite shoulder, as the wash mitt moved its way around to a particularly sensitive area.

"I don't think there's any tree sap there." Robin tried unsuccessfully to remain focused.

"Pretend there is." Came the low reply.

"Okay." It was the last coherent thought Robin had that evening.

****

As far as most weeks went, this particular week moved along at an unusually slow pace. Whether it was from the excitement of the approaching holidays, or just a natural end-of-the-year lull in what otherwise was a typically heavy workload, the week seemed to drag along interminably. Robin completed her legal research for the day and stretched her hands high above her head, swiveling lightly in her chair. The twilight sky outside signaled the fast approaching evening, and Robin gazed with interest out the large glass window and down to the lake below, as masses of people gathered for an evening of Christmas caroling.

Her mind brought her back to earlier in the day, when a group of children from a local boys' academy had visited the firm and entertained the entire staff with festive Christmas carols. The children were absolutely adorable, especially the one little boy of about six years old who tapped his hand-held drum to the tune of "The Little Drummer Boy." The corners of Robin's mouth curled into a smile as she recalled the event, then a curious wave of something else surfaced, barely registering in her conscious mind. It was a quiet longing, one that she hadn't allowed herself to consider lately, but one which nevertheless had far reaching implications. *I want children.* She shook her head slightly, bringing her out of her wayward musings, and set her mind back on the present day. *Okay, what are we doing about the holiday party?*

Deciding the matter needed to be settled once and for all, Robin stood up and strode out into the hallway, making her way quickly through the empty reception area and past the elevators toward an exceedingly familiar office. The younger woman stood silently for a moment before knocking on the closed wood door, then opened it slightly. "Busy?"

Jess glanced up from her computer. "A little. What's up?"

The young associate stepped inside and closed the door. "Can we talk about the holiday party? It's tomorrow, and I think we should discuss it." She took a seat in the chair by the window.

"Alright." The junior partner shifted in her burgundy leather chair to face Robin. "Do you want to go?"

"Yes." The golden head nodded.

"Okay, then go."

"You're not helping, here, Jess." Robin frowned. "Are you going?"

Jess tapped her fingers lightly on the cherry wood desk. "You know I don't like those things, Robin. You go, and if you don't want to go alone, maybe Keith will still escort you."

Robin shot up from her chair. "That is not an option and you know it." She stepped forward, and then knelt in front of the junior partner. "Jess, I think we both should put in an appearance, but I don't want you to go if you'd really rather not."

Blue eyes softened. "Alright. How about if we do this. You and I can go separately for just a little while. We'll put in an appearance and then leave separately." Jess sighed somewhat audibly. "People will probably notice we're both alone, but they'll get over it." She had a brief thought, then looked at Robin through long, dark bangs. "You know, you can go with someone else, Robin. I'm okay with that."

Green eyes flashed. "Well, I'm not okay with it. Why are you?" Robin seemed genuinely hurt.

Damn. "No, honey." Jess rushed to clarify. "I'm not okay with you being with someone else. But I am okay with you protecting yourself. Do you understand?"

The young associate nodded, then relaxed. "I'm going to go alone, Jess."

The junior partner grasped Robin's hand and brushed her fingers back and forth over the smooth skin. "Alright. I'll go alone, also. We'll let the chips fall where they may." *I hope I don't regret this.*

"Thanks." Robin stood up and smiled. "See you back at The Ranch later?"

"You betcha, kiddo." Jess winked. "Keep a spot warm for me on my favorite sofa."

Robin started to turn the doorknob, then threw a look back over her shoulder at Jess. "I'll be keeping other things warm for you, too." She gave Jess a wink of her own, then walked swiftly out of the office without a second glance.

Jess stared at the closed door. *Oh boy.*

****

"The tree really looks nice." Jess reclined on the plush sofa and admired the newly decorated and brightly lit Frasier fir tree. A fire flickered in the fireplace, the wood crackling and hissing, as orange flames cast dancing shadows across the far wall. Except for the tree lights and the fire, and one bayberry scented candle, there was no other light in the living room. Soft Christmas music filtered in from the stereo situated in an adjacent corner. "It smells really good, too."

Robin took up her favorite position, sliding down on the sofa so she was nestled against the cushions, with her head resting on Jess's shoulder. "Yeah, I could stay here for days and just look at it." A green eye peered up at the taller woman. "Are you sure this beats tree fill?"

"Absolutely." Jess chuckled. "Like I said, tree fill has nothing on this." She grinned, then turned a bit serious. "You know, I never realized the things I was missing until I met you. I thought I had everything I wanted or needed." She tucked an errant strand of blonde hair behind a petite ear. "I was wrong."

"How so?" Robin was intently curious.

Dark brows knit together in slight concentration. "It's like this. Every year, I contented myself to go over to my mother's house for Christmas and spend a couple of days getting my tree fill. That would be enough to last me until the next year, when I'd do it all over again." Jess was having a rare moment of insight. "Now that I have my own personal Christmas tree in my living room, I see that tree fill is a mere crumb compared to the real thing. You showed me that." She placed several gentle kisses on top of the blonde head. "It's the same way now for everything, from 102 flavors of ice cream to grocery shopping. It's more real when I'm with you."

Robin really did understand the somewhat awkward explanation, and the genuine sentiment behind it. She smiled in contentment, and then wrapped an arm tightly around the older woman's waist. "You say the sweetest things."

Jess grinned, then spent a few moments relaxing next to Robin, quietly enjoying the view of the brightly lit tree and the sound of soft Christmas melodies in the background. "Um...Robin?" Jess knew she needed to have a particular conversation with Robin, one that she'd been putting off for the past few days. "Can we talk about something kinda important?"

The blonde head tilted upward. "What's on your mind?"

"I wanted to talk about Christmas." Jess began cautiously. "I was wondering…." She took a deep breath. "What's happening? You haven't mentioned anything, and I know your parents are coming in."

Robin blinked, and then shifted up on one arm so she was looking directly at Jess. "You seem a little upset."

The older woman shook her head almost in disbelief. *Is she in denial about this?* Jess kept her tone even. "I'm not upset, I just...I wanted to spend time with you. I don't know what your plans are, and I thought perhaps you might be spending all your time with your folks." Jess cast her gaze over toward the flickering fire. "Then we wouldn't be able to be together at all for Christmas."

What's she really saying? Robin watched the play of emotions cross the chiseled features, and the slight tensing of the fine muscles beneath the surface of a tightened jaw. She recognized the tell-tale signs that Jess was indeed upset by the fact that the older woman avoided looking at her directly. Petite fingers turned the angular face back meet her own. "You're upset because we haven't discussed my plans?"

Jess couldn't bite back the flippant retort that followed. "If you don't want to spend any time together during Christmas, Robin, just tell me. I'm a big girl. I can take it."

Robin flinched. It was never her intention to cut Jess out of her plans. It was just that Robin had avoided the issue for so long, that she, herself, had only recently learned of the details of her parents' visit. "No, Jess." She responded firmly. "That's not it."

Jess stayed silent, the invitation to continue clear.

"If I could have my choice, my parents would stay in Michigan. But my mother is quite stubborn, and when I told her I didn't want to go back up there for Christmas, she went full-steam ahead and made plans to come down here." Robin frowned slightly. "They worry about me because of everything that's happened. They're insisting I move back up there with them."

The dark head abruptly turned toward Robin, ice blue eyes penetrating sea green. Jess's heart rate suddenly sped up, and her whole body tensed reflexively, as she felt the air being sucked from her lungs. She instinctively averted her gaze back toward the fireplace, closing her eyes tightly to the sudden stab of pain that cut deeper than anything she ever could have imagined. She took a shuddering breath, and then spoke very slowly and very deliberately, her steady voice belying her inner turmoil. "I see." She swallowed. "They're coming to take you back with them."

What? Robin felt the body beneath hers tremble slightly, and her eyes grew wide as she realized the impression she'd left, and its magnitude. She rushed to correct the misperception, practically shouting the forceful denial that followed. "No." She swiftly reached for Jess's face and turned it back toward her own, fixing her gaze solidly on the now guarded azure eyes. "No." It was only then that she saw the wet trail marks of fresh tears tracking away from the long, dark lashes. Robin's heart nearly broke, and her own composure was shaky, at best. "Oh, Jess, no." She brushed away the tears. "Honey, please. I'm not going back with them. I'm not." *She's so fragile about this. Damn it, James. You did this to her.* The younger woman now came to realize how deeply Jess had been hurt. It was a hurt so profound that constant reassurances and unconditional love might never be enough to completely heal the still open wounds or alleviate the underlying fear. Robin, for her part, tried anyhow. Sincere green eyes found blue. "Listen to me, Jess. I promised you, remember? No one leaves. I meant that." She tucked the older woman's head against her chest, and stroked the dark hair soothingly, whispering softly. "I love you, Jess, so much. I won't leave."

Jess curled up into the circle of Robin's arms, welcoming the comfort. She melted into the embrace, as if that one place was the safest in all the world. And at that particular moment, it was. The sudden and intense wave of emotion seemed to come out of nowhere, and had taken over her with unsettling force. She hadn't felt anything like that before. *Not even when James left.* She took several deep and even breaths in an attempt to regain her composure, then finally spoke, slightly embarrassed by the unexpected loss of control. "I'm sorry. I don't know where all that insecurity came from."

I do. Robin brushed her thumb back and forth against Jess's cheek. "It's alright, Jess. It was very insensitive of me to worry you like I did. Will you let me explain?" At Jess's nod, the younger woman continued. "Ever since I found out my parents were coming down to visit, I've avoided the issue. You see, they don't want me to be here alone, and they'd rather I'd move back to Michigan. I'm not going to move back up there, and I don't want to fight with them about it." She grasped the long fingers and gently kissed them. "It wasn't until this week that I finally talked to my mother and found out their exact plans. I just didn't want to deal with it before." Green eyes closed in sincere regret. "But by not dealing with it, I worried you. I'm so sorry for that."

Jess found herself sighing in relief. *She was avoiding her parents, nothing more.* She reached a long finger up to trace a delicate jaw. "It's true, I was worried. I had convinced myself that you were beginning to realize that your feelings for me weren't what you thought they were. You seemed as if you had changed your mind about calling Dr. Richmond, and when you didn't mention your plans for Christmas, I thought you might want some time away from me to sort things out while your parents were here." Jess suddenly felt ashamed. "I thought you might want out."

Robin shook her head. "No. Please listen to me, Jess. I've said this before, and I absolutely, positively, without a doubt mean it. I will never, ever willingly leave you, and I won't ever change my mind about loving you." *I have to keep reassuring her.* Robin's voice became very quiet and held somewhat of a serene quality as she spoke her next words. "Jess, you are the best thing in my life. You saved me when I wasn't sure I could move forward. You're my best friend." A tear drop fell unimpeded, as green eyes solidly locked on blue. "Our weekend together was the most beautiful thing I have ever experienced. I did not take it lightly. I would never have...been with you that way if I wasn't sure." Another tear fell as Robin tried her best to find something, anything, to help her say what she sensed Jess needed to hear. "Let me say it this way. You know that I've been with only one other person, and we were going to be married. It's a very serious thing for me to be with someone that way." She grasped Jess's hand and intertwined their fingers, bringing them to her heart. "I'm with you, Jess, because I want to be with you, in every possible way, totally, unquestionably and undeniably, with all my heart. It's a very serious thing for me." She gave Jess a heartfelt smile. "How could I ever leave that?"

Jess was silent, absorbing the words Robin had spoken and letting them wash over her in gentle, calming waves. She blinked back a tear of her own, then paused, giving the younger woman the most adorable crooked smile. "Sometimes you just have to hit me over the head."

Robin let go a relieved laugh, as she hugged the older woman tightly to her. "Where's a frying pan when I need one?" She laughed again, grateful for a break in the tension, then let a few silent moments pass by so they both could collect their thoughts. Robin gazed quietly at the colorfully lit tree, then propped herself up again on one elbow. "So, let's talk Christmas. What do you say?"

Jess grinned. "What a great idea. You go first. Tell me your plans."

"Alright. My parents are coming down two days before Christmas and then leaving the day after."

"Where are they staying?"

"My place. They can have my room. I'll sleep on the sofa while they're here."

Jess became a bit introspective. "I'll miss you."

"Yeah. Me, too. It'll be strange waking up without you. I've almost forgotten what that's like."

The older woman nodded, then regarded the Christmas tree. "Are you sure you don't want to put a tree up at your place? I would help you." She looked at Robin out of the corner of her eye. "I could do the tinsel."

That brought a chuckle. "No, Jess. No tree, and definitely no tinsel from you. Anyway, my apartment's a little too small for a tree. I'll put up some decorations so it looks more like Christmas, and then I have a snow village I can put up. It'll look nice." Robin scooted down a little and positioned her head so it rested once again on Jess's shoulder. "So what about you? What are your plans for Christmas?"

Jess shrugged. "I'll go to my mom's on Christmas Eve, and then come back the day after Christmas." This was said in an almost off-handed way.

Robin considered her next question carefully. "I want to ask you something, but I don't want you to feel obligated to agree."

"Okay."

Robin suddenly had trouble phrasing what she wanted to say. "Um...if you're going to be here during the day on Christmas Eve, would you like to join me and my parents for brunch? My dad's taking us out."

The older woman smiled a little to herself. *She wants you to meet her folks, Jess. You're an absolute idiot for ever doubting her.* Jess reached down and tilted the blonde head up. "Are you sure that's what you want?" There was another implied meaning to the question. Having Robin's parents meet her would almost certainly invite inevitable scrutiny. The impact might not be felt right away, but it likely would make its presence known at some undetermined point in the future.

Robin nodded. "Yes, I'm sure, Jess. I want them to know you." She looked down a bit awkwardly, her voice barely a whisper. "I...um...don't want to tell them about us, though. I'd like them to get to know you first." Petite fingers brushed against the soft skin of Jess's forearm. "I want to tell them that you're my friend, and that you know about everything that's happened." She took a deep breath, then released it. "I also want to tell them that I'm moving in with you."

Blue eyes grew wide in surprise. "Are you comfortable with that?"

Robin nodded. "I've thought about this. I can tell them that we'll be roommates. Technically, that's true. Besides, they're going to find out sooner or later." Robin reached for Jess's hand and intertwined their fingers. "I want them to get to know you, Jess, and I want them to know that you're important to me, but I'm not ready to tell them about us." She sighed. "Please understand."

Jess gave her a warm smile. "I do understand, and I'd love to join you and your parents for brunch on Christmas Eve day." She gave Robin a gentle kiss. "Now, what would you say to coming to Tampa with me on New Year's Day? I'd really like for you to meet my mom."

"Yes." There was absolutely no hesitation.

"Good." Jess smiled. "Glad that's settled." She traced a long finger along a petite shoulder blade. "Now that we've gotten everyone else squared away, let's talk about our Christmas time together, yours and mine. We could maybe celebrate it after your parents leave."

"I'd like that." Robin snuggled into the crook of Jess's neck, breathing in the decidedly familiar scent. She suddenly giggled a bit. "So, tell me, Jess, what'd you get me?"

"Excuse me." The low voice answered dryly.

"You did get me something, didn't you?"

Dark brows furrowed. "If I did get you something, Robin, and I'm not saying I did, but if I did, I certainly wouldn't tell you."

"Did I mention that I saw this really great car, and it has...."

"Enough room so even the tallest person couldn't complain." Jess finished. "Yeah, yeah. I think you might have mentioned a little something about that." She rapped her knuckles lightly on the blonde head. "I wouldn't count on it, though, kiddo." *I have something else in mind.* The taller woman snuck a peak at the silently grinning face. "I have a much, much better idea. How about you tell me what you got me." She raised her eyebrows hopefully.

A small giggle. "I'm sure I have no idea what you're talking about."

"Hmm. What if I bribe you?"

"Nope. Won't work. If you won't tell me, then I'm not telling you."

"Alright, then." Jess relented. "I guess we'll both just have to be surprised."

"Yep." *I hope you like what I got you, Jess.* Robin gazed up at the angel perched on the treetop, its wings outstretched and a candle glowing in each hand. Her mind flashed back to a time a short while ago, and the vision she'd had while admittedly feverish with the flu. *You're my angel, Jess. You always have been.* "Jess?"

"Yeah."

"I already have my gift." Robin truly meant the sentiment.

Jess tenderly kissed Robin's forehead. "Me, too, sweetheart."

****

The country club ballroom was elegantly apportioned with tasteful holiday decorations in silver, gold, red, and green, while small white lights set loosely amidst pine branches adorned the serving tables. Favorite Christmas melodies furnished by a brass and string band filtered throughout the room, and a wooden planked dance floor served as center stage for entertainment later that evening. Four separate buffet tables were positioned neatly in the corners of the spacious ballroom, complimented by two open bar areas located on opposite sides of the dance floor. The guests arrived in semi-formal attire, the evening chill forcing many to don additional outerwear, while a coat attendant efficiently checked assorted hats and coats into the adjoining cloak room.

Robin entered the ballroom and immediately noticed that Jess had not yet arrived. Paul and a woman whom Robin presumed to be his date chatted near the shrimp buffet. Keith and Michelle stood with their dates next to one of the open bar areas, appearing to listen to the band. Several secretarial and support staff members milled about the various buffet tables, while others positioned themselves strategically near the doorways, surreptitiously observing the comings and goings of other staff personnel and their respective dates and escorts.

Robin quietly took in the scene, and was startled a bit as someone tapped her on the shoulder from behind. She turned to find Jess's secretary, Angie, and Angie's husband standing beside her. "Hello, Angie."

"Robin, I'd like you to meet my husband, Doug. Have you seen Jess this evening?" Angie glanced around the room, seemingly searching for her boss. "Is she here yet?"

If Robin had thought about it, she would have realized the set-up when she heard it. "I don't know. I just got here myself."

"Well, we'll keep looking for her. Did you bring someone with you tonight?"

Robin mentally cringed. "No, I'm not staying long. I have company coming in from out of town, and I have a lot to do to get ready."

Angie spotted a friend near the pasta bar. "There's Betty. Doug, let's go say hello." She turned to leave. "Have a good evening, Robin."

"You, too." The young associate watched as Angie and Doug strode off toward the opposite end of the ballroom. Robin headed over to one of the drink bars, ordering a glass of Chardonnay, and stood silently watching the mingling crowd.

"Fancy meeting you here." The low voice came from behind, its owner stepping to one side and ordering a vodka tonic. "Been here long?" Jess received her drink and gazed around the ballroom.

"A few minutes. Can we find a table? I want to get some food."

The junior partner started to offer a snappy remark, but then thought the better of it given the setting. "How about we sit with Harry and Barbara over there?" She pointed toward the center of the room, then led Robin over to Harry's table. "Mind if we join you two?"

Harry stood up, welcoming them in delighted fashion. "Hello, there. Glad you both could make it. Jess, I see you've finally come to one of our little soirees."

"Well, there's a first time for everything, Harry." Jess grinned and took a seat. "Nice seeing you again, Barbara."

Barbara nodded. "It's good to see you, too. And you, as well, Robin."

"Thank you. It's nice to see you." The young associate smiled politely and took a seat next to Jess.

Once everyone was seated, Harry picked up his drink and turned to his wife. "Dear, did I tell you that Jess and Robin recently won a major trial for us. It was simply outstanding work." He beamed.

"Well, isn't that wonderful." Barbara enthused. "The firm is certainly lucky to have such a talented team on board." She watched the subtle interaction between the two women, then turned toward Harry. "Isn't that right, dear."

"Absolutely." Harry very happily agreed, not aware of his wife's full intent at the comment. He turned to Jess and Robin. "You ladies must try the shrimp and pasta buffets. The fettuccini with the Alfredo sauce is outstanding."

That was all that needed to be said. Several shrimp plates, pasta courses, and meat buffet trips later, Robin finally decided that she was full. Jess, for her part, went back for seconds on the shrimp cocktail and bacon-wrapped shrimp hors d'oeuvres. No particular newsflashes on either front. The evening's conversation with Harry and Barbara was exceedingly enjoyable, with Harry engaged in recounting old "war" stories of trial glory days past. Robin found the tales quite fascinating and very entertaining.

Meanwhile, Paul and Keith, along with their respective dates, were gathered over near one of the open drink bars. Michelle Richards, a third-year associate with the firm, approached the group, along with her date for the evening. She surveyed the room, finally settling her gaze on the center table. "Well, Keith, it seems that Robin made it."

Keith ordered another beer from the bar. "Yeah. It looks like she's here alone."

Michelle continued to watch the Roberts table. *Perhaps.* "Nice of Jessica to finally put in an appearance." The remark was casually sardonic and was made to no one in particular.

Paul, mostly out of curiosity, silently followed Michelle's gaze. He was not usually one for casual observation. Most men aren't. But as he studied the Roberts table, there was something that struck even him, as he watched Robin quietly steal a quick glance at Jess. *Curious.* He continued observing the pair for another moment, until his date beckoned him over to the pasta buffet.

Across the room, Angie stood near the doorway with Betty, watching the mingling crowd. "I see Paul has a date tonight."

"I thought he was all ga-ga over Robin. What's up with that?" Betty scanned the room for her boss, Harry Roberts.

"She axed him. Poor guy was quite depressed about it." Angie smirked. "I guess not for too long, though. Did you get a look at his date tonight?"

"Where?" Betty finally spied Paul and his date over by the pasta buffet. "Oh, I see what you mean." She scanned the room further. "Look, there's Robin over with my boss and his wife." She stared intently at the center table. "Well, wonder of wonders. Isn't that Jessica Harrison? This is what, the first holiday party she's been to?"

"Yep. And neither she nor Robin brought anyone tonight." Angie cocked her head "You know, Robin's the only one who seems to be able to work with my boss."

Betty laughed. "It's a good thing, too. Otherwise, you'd be stuck with a lot more paperwork."

"Still, there's something about that. I can't put my finger on it, but where my boss is, Robin is, and vice-versa." Angie studied the Roberts table pensively. "They eat lunch together a lot, they're in each other's offices a lot, Jessica's got Robin working on all her cases."

"Well, Jessica's got to get someone to help her. She is quite temperamental, you know."

Angie rolled her eyes. "You're telling me."

"Maybe they're friends." It was an offhanded remark.

"Maybe." Angie considered the statement. "I think there's something else going on."

"Ooooh, do tell."

Angie shook her head. "Don't know yet. It's just that no one gets along with my boss as well as Robin does, and that's saying a lot. I'll figure it out, though. Give me some time." She scanned the room in an attempt to locate her husband. "Where did Doug run off to?"

The band began playing the Christmas Waltz, and the gentle melody floated throughout the spacious ballroom. Harry turned to his wife. "Would you like to dance, dear?" He glanced at Jess and Robin. "Will you ladies excuse us?"

"Of course." Jess nodded appropriately. "Have yourselves a good time out there. I'll be calling it an evening, myself."

Robin offered a plausible scenario of her own. "I'll stay a while and mingle a bit, then I'll need to get going, also."

"Well, it was very nice chatting with both of you tonight." Harry stood up and took his wife's hand.

"Yes, it certainly was a lovely evening." Barbara Roberts smiled as she rose from her chair. "I hope we see each other again soon."

Robin nodded politely. "That would be nice. Goodnight." As she watched the couple head out onto the dance floor, her mind quite irrationally wondered what it would be like to dance with the person she loved. *Just not in public.* She sighed, then turned to Jess. "Did Angie find you?"

The junior partner seemed confused. "Angie?"

"Yeah. She was looking for you earlier. Did she find you?" The young associate sipped her wine.

"No." Jess seemed a bit unsettled. "How do you know she was looking for me?"

"Well, she came up to me before you got here and asked me if you were here yet."

Jess suddenly became pale. *Oh shit.* "She asked you if I was here yet?"

"Yes." *What's the big deal?* Robin didn't get it. "Jess, what is it?"

Don't panic. Jess swallowed uneasily. "I need to get some air. Meet me in the parking lot in ten minutes." The older woman abruptly rose from her chair and headed out the doorway, right past Angie and Betty who were dutifully observing the happenings with great interest.

Ten long minutes later, Robin found Jess in the parking lot next to the silver Mercedes. "Will you tell me what's going on?"

Jess paced. "What exactly did Angie say?"

"She asked if I'd seen you this evening, and whether you were here yet." Robin still didn't get it. "What's the matter?"

Jess stopped her pacing, sighing heavily. "Robin, Angie has been my secretary for nearly seven years. She knows full well that I never go to these things."

"So?" The younger woman shook her head slightly. "I'm sorry, Jess, I'm not following you."

"Robin, she asked you if I was here yet. I never told her I was planning on going tonight. She should have assumed I wouldn't be here, just like all the other times. She had absolutely no reason to ask you that."

"Then why..." Robin braced herself against the car, a sickening thought nearly causing her stomach to rebel.

"She was baiting you, Robin."

"Baiting me?" *This was bad.* "What do you mean?"

"She wanted to know what your answer would be." Jess looked

grim. "When she asked you if I was here yet, what did you tell her?"

"I told her that I didn't know, that I'd just gotten here." Green eyes closed tightly. "How bad is this?"

Jess took a moment to think, pacing again lightly. "Okay, it's not actually too bad." She took a few more paces. "Angie was fishing. If you had definitively said either that I was or I was not going to be here, it would have given her something to chew on. She certainly would have wondered why you knew so much about my plans, and she probably would have found it interesting had you said that you were definitely expecting me, especially since I don't normally show up at these things." The taller woman relaxed somewhat. "But, you said you didn't know, so she got nothing."

"But she suspects."

"Not necessarily. She's curious and looking for a little gossip. She has nothing." *I hope.* "We're going to have to be much more careful from now on, Robin. People are watching us."

"That's creepy." Robin felt her queasiness return.

The junior partner sighed, her unease at the situation evident. "I know."

As Jess and Robin were talking in the parking lot, Paul and his date exited the country club and waited for the valet to retrieve their car. Paul quite casually glanced over toward the parking area, catching a glimpse of the two attorneys standing near the silver Mercedes. It was clear, even to his considerably untrained eye, that their rather animated discussion appeared not to be business oriented. *Interesting.* He arched an eyebrow, continuing to observe the scene until the valet finally returned with his car.

Jess unlocked the Mercedes' car door and then turned toward Robin. "Meet me back at the house, okay?"

The young associate was clearly agitated, her stomach doing flip-flops as she tried in vain to remain calm. "Yeah. See you there." She made her way uneasily over toward the blue Miata parked a few spaces away.

Jess quickly slid into her silver Mercedes and started up the ignition. As she did so, she spied Paul standing at the country club's main entrance, his gaze squarely fixed on the parking lot. *Damn.* She pulled out of the main drive, then turned onto a nearby side street, stopping the car and resting her forearms heavily against the steering wheel.

Now might be a very good time to panic.

Undeniable

Chapter 11

A sleepy green eye opened, then squinted, as it adjusted to the mid-morning sunlight filtering in through the Venetian blinds. The first thing the petite form noted was that a very warm body completely enveloped her own, a familiar large hand situated underneath her nightshirt and wrapped securely around her waist. The smaller figure snuggled further into the cozy cocoon, as a lazy, but contented, smile made its way across her fair features. *This is nice.* The current sleeping arrangement seemed to be her companion's favorite position, and the petite form had to admit that it was indeed quite comfortable. The small frame turned slightly and stretched a bit, reveling in the surrounding warmth, then looked over to find smiling blue eyes quietly regarding her.

"Good morning, sleepyhead." The low voice whispered.

A smile. "Good morning. You always wake up before me."

A sideways glance. "That's because you snore and wake me up."

Still sleepy green eyes narrowed. "You are so mean to me. I thought we decided that I definitely do not snore."

Jess pursed her lips. "As I recall, we decided that you squeak when you sleep, and that you are also very cute."

Robin fully turned in Jess's embrace, contentedly closing her sleepy green eyes again. "I'm on to you now, Bucko. You say something against me, then you follow it up with something really nice so that I can't complain."

The older woman shook her head vehemently. "No, I don't."

"Don't even bother denying it. I'm on to your tactics." A lazy smile followed. "You forgot something, though."

Dark eyebrows furrowed. "I did?"

"Yes." Robin opened her eyes and raised herself slightly up on one elbow. "This." She leaned in and gave Jess a lingering good morning kiss.

"Oh. Right. Sorry." A crooked grin appeared, then an eyebrow slightly raised. "Can we do that again?"

"Yes." Robin leaned in and repeated the procedure, then laid back down on her side facing the older woman. "Jess, can we talk about something?"

Jess turned to fully face Robin. "Okay. What's on your mind?"

"I know we talked about the party last night, and we agreed that we shouldn't panic, but I'm still a little worried. I mean, this is your career, and I don't want to do anything to jeopardize that."

A long finger stroked the nearby cheek. "Listen, we don't need to worry. Angie's curious, yes. Paul did see us in the parking lot, but he doesn't know anything. Besides, right now, people are busy with the holidays, and then things will die down after the first of the year. Like I said, we've just got to be more careful."

The blonde head nodded. "I was just thinking about when I move in here full-time. People might notice that we're living together." Robin glanced at Jess a bit tentatively. "Do you think I should wait a while? I could renew my lease for another few months."

Jess felt her pulse quicken and her heart rate curiously speed up as she rushed to answer. "No. There's absolutely nothing wrong with us living in the same house." *You're fooling yourself, Jess. People will notice.* "I want you here with me, Robin." She grasped a petite hand and brought it to her lips, placing a tender kiss on the knuckles. "Let me be clear. No matter who knows, no matter what anyone finds out, no matter what anyone thinks, no matter what happens to me, I want to be with you. You're more important than all of that."

Robin stroked her thumb against the determined jaw. "I never want to do anything to put you at risk. Don't you understand that? I'd resign first."

"Absolutely not, Robin." The dark head shook solemnly. "If people question our living arrangements, we'll deal with it. But we'll deal with it together. That was our agreement, remember?"

"I remember."

"Good." Jess offered a small smile, then an uneasy thought came to her. "Unless, you'd rather not...live here." *You're an idiot, Jess. You're just thinking about yourself. It never even occurred to you that she might be afraid of what people will think.* "I mean, if the questions made you uncomfortable, I wouldn't want that."

"No, Jess. I can handle the questions, and I do want to live here." *I just worry about you.*

Jess nodded, then took the petite hand in her own and intertwined their fingers together. "It's really going to be okay, I promise. We'll be careful at work and we'll address our living arrangements, if we need to, by explaining that we're roommates. People at the firm have shared houses together before, and no one's ever batted an eye."

"Alright." Robin sighed, then snuggled further against Jess's chest, letting her eyes flutter closed once again. "You've convinced me." A moment passed, then a green eye peered upward. "Jess, do you suppose we could possibly get some breakfast, now?"

A very large grin edged across the older woman's face. "Are you sure you wouldn't rather go back to sleep?"

Robin considered the question a little longer than necessary, then nodded decisively. "It's a tough decision, I agree. But, I think I'm more hungry than sleepy."

"Okay. I'll go fix breakfast." Jess started to get up.

"Nope." A petite hand tugged at the back of the Calvin sleep shirt. "It's my turn. Let me get it."

The older woman arched an eyebrow, then contemplated the offer. "You wouldn't, by any chance, be trying to butter me up again, would you?"

"Of course." It was said matter-of-factly. "As I recall, it worked very well before. Are you still susceptible to my buttering up techniques?"

"Well, Robin, I think I've adequately demonstrated how susceptible I am to your buttering up techniques. You can butter me anytime." Jess grinned and touched a finger to Robin's nose. "Okay, kiddo. You go get breakfast while I make a couple of phone calls. I'll meet you in the kitchen in a few minutes."

"Right, chief." Robin got up and padded over toward the bathroom while Jess made her way down the long hallway to her home office located on the opposite side of the house.

Once her phone calls were made, Jess strode into the kitchen and watched as Robin stood at the stove preparing a breakfast of pancakes and sausage. "Smells good." Jess came up behind the younger woman and peered over her shoulder. "Maybe I should hire you full-time."

"Very funny." Robin threw back a frank look, then narrowed her eyes. "Jess, is there something you want to tell me?"

Dark brows furrowed. "Um...no."

"Are you sure?"

"Yep." Jess sat down at the kitchen table.

"Look at my feet."

"What?"

"You heard me. Look at my feet." A blue plastic spatula pointed down at the feet in question.

Jess complied with the unusual request. "Okaaay. I see your feet."

"What's on them?"

"Um...socks?" Jess replied a bit too innocently.

"Right. Socks." The blue spatula waved purposefully. "So, give them back."

Silence.

"Did you hear me, Jess? I said give them back."

The dark head shook in vehement denial. "I have absolutely, positively no idea what you're talking about."

"You absolutely, positively do so know what I'm talking about." Robin jabbed the spatula in a pseudo menacing fashion in Jess's direction. "Last night, I put them exactly where I always do. This morning, I get up and they're not there. I know you have them. Give them back."

Jess tried to hide her guilt. "If you lost them, Robin, it's your own fault, not mine."

"Ahaa." Robin stepped over to the table and put the spatula to Jess's throat in a mock threat. "So you admit you know what happened to them."

A very bored look. "I admit nothing."

"It will go easier on you if you cooperate."

Now, an aggrieved sigh. "Must you resort to theatrics?"

Green eyes narrowed. "You have absolutely no right to hold them hostage." Robin pressed the spatula lightly against the older woman's neck, and spoke in a very determined tone. "Give. Them. Back."

"You know the house rules, Robin." A playful smirk appeared. "Rule number one specifically states, no bunny slippers."

The blonde woman stepped back for a moment and carefully flipped the pancakes, then quickly replaced the lethal spatula in its previous position against Jess's neck. "Let me be perfectly clear. My feet are cold. I need my slippers. If you don't give them back, I will be forced to take drastic measures."

Drastic measures? "Um...what exactly do you mean by that?"

"Someone, and it won't be me, will be sleeping in the guest room."

"But…."

"Nope." Robin shook her head and extended her hand, beckoning with her fingers. "Give."

A defeated look, then a very long, exaggerated sigh. "Oh, alright. Fine." Jess got up and exited the kitchen, only to return shortly with the two floppy-eared bunny slippers in question. "Here. Happy now?"

The younger woman put on her slippers. "Yes."

"Rule number two, Robin. No spatula violence allowed."

Green eyes narrowed considerably. "I can assure you, Jess, you have not yet seen spatula violence. I wouldn't push it if I were you." She waved the blue plastic spatula a bit for emphasis. "Now, go sit down. Breakfast is ready."

"Thank God."

"I'll pretend I didn't hear that." Robin began fixing the plates. "Could you get the coffee?"

Jess retrieved the coffee pot and set it on the kitchen table. "This discussion isn't over." The older woman simply couldn't resist having the last word on the matter. "Rule number three, no one except a guest sleeps in the guest room."

Robin grinned and walked up to Jess, giving her a quick kiss on the cheek. "Okay, I'll give you that one." She set down the plate of pancakes and sausage in front of Jess. "Now go ahead and eat before I change my mind."

The dark-haired woman nodded, grateful for her small victory, then poured syrup on her pancakes. "So, when do you think you'll give up your apartment?"

Robin sat down with her own plate of pancakes and sausage. "I've already spoken to the apartment manager and given my notice for next month." Even though Robin knew the issue had been settled, she wanted to give Jess one more time to reconsider. "I could still renew."

A slender eyebrow shot up. "I thought we already decided this. You're not renewing, right?"

Robin nodded. "I just wanted to make sure." She sipped her coffee thoughtfully. "How much rent do you want?"

That drew an utterly perplexed look. "Rent?"

"Yes. How much do you want?"

Jess was a bit surprised at the suggestion that Robin would be a mere tenant. "Robin, there is no rent. You'll live here, like I live here. No rent is necessary."

"Well, Jess, we're going to have to come to some arrangement regarding finances. I insist on paying my way."

The older woman took a bite of her pancake. "Robin, as far as the mortgage is concerned, I'm going to pay that like I always do. After all, it's my mortgage and my responsibility. I didn't ask you to move in here to take on my responsibilities." She poured herself another cup of coffee. "The only other expenses are the normal household expenses, like utilities and food."

"Fine." Robin contemplated the situation. "I'll give you money for those things."

The dark head shook decisively. "No."

The younger woman stopped eating. "Jess." She ducked her head to meet clear blue eyes. "If I'm going to be part of this household, I intend to do my part. It's only fair."

Jess sighed audibly, then finally acquiesced. "Alright. What if we open up a joint checking account for household expenses, and then both of us deposit money in it every month? Then we can draw from that account for the household things."

Robin considered the offer. "That'll work." She bit a sausage link, then suddenly frowned. "You're holding out on me."

"What?"

"I'm on to you." Robin poked her sausage in Jess's direction. "What about the pool service, the lawn service, and the housekeeping service? Who would be paying for those?"

Jess suddenly found her coffee cup very interesting and mumbled. "Me."

The blonde head shook defiantly. "No. It comes out of the joint account, too."

"But that's a lot more than you're used to paying." Jess protested. "You're saving for a car, remember?"

"I make a very good salary, thanks to your law firm. I can pay my share. I'm not poor." Robin bent her head and sighed, then set her sausage link down. She wiped her hands on her napkin and looked across at Jess, speaking in a very sincere, yet gentle tone. "Jess, I can't let you pay for everything. It's not right. Besides, we're a team. I consider us partners. Don't you?"

Jess stopped mid-chew and considered the phrase. *Partners.* They were partners, after all, a team, at work and outside of work. *Partners for life? Forever?* She nodded in agreement. "Yes. We're partners." The older woman set her fork down in deliberate fashion, coming to a conclusion. "Alright. This is my final offer. Everything except the mortgage comes out of the joint account. Agreed?"

Robin grinned happily in her minor triumph. "Agreed." She finished her last bite of pancake. "Um...Jess? How much is your mortgage, anyway?"

Jess pushed the sausage around on her plate. "Do you know how much your rent is?"

"Yes." The younger woman casually took a sip of her coffee.

"Five times that."

Robin coughed, nearly choking on the coffee in her mouth. She cleared her throat, then spoke, truly incredulous at the thought. "How do you manage that?"

Blue eyes fixed on green. "I have some money."

"From the firm?"

"Yes. And other places."

Robin stared at Jess for a lingering moment, then simply nodded. She didn't want to pry, and Jess seemed reluctant to offer very much information. "Okay."

Jess changed the subject. "So, what do you have planned today?"

"It's Sunday."

A momentary blank look, then Jess nodded. "Need any help?"

The younger woman finished her coffee and smiled. "I'd love it. I've got to get ready for my parents' visit, and I've also got a lot of grocery shopping to do." Light brows furrowed. "Come to think of it, you could certainly use some more food in this house, yourself."

"I'll get by."

"Nope." Robin shook her head, having already decided on the appropriate course of action. "We'll do our grocery shopping together." Green eyes looked up mischievously. "You remember how, don't you?"

That question just begged for a snappy retort, so Jess, without hesitation, provided one. "What I remember, Robin, is that it requires a certain amount of hands-on experience." She winked a bit suggestively. "Would you say that I'm qualified in that regard?"

The blush from Robin's face traveled all the way to her ears. *She got me again.* "That's not what I meant and you know it."

"We were talking about grocery shopping, weren't we?" Jess looked up entirely too innocently, then cocked her head. "Or was it...window shopping?" Blue eyes twinkled.

Window shopping? Robin's mind flashed back to her own joke the previous week in St. Augustine. She burst into giggles. "You are absolutely incorrigible."

Jess stood up and cleared away the breakfast dishes. "That's why you love me, kiddo."

"Right." The younger woman cleared her throat teasingly, then went over and began putting the dishes in the dishwasher. "So, are you sure you can play hooky today?"

"Yep. You have my undivided hooky attention." The taller woman strode out of the kitchen, throwing a look back over her shoulder. "And Robin, lose the bunny slippers, will ya?"

Robin smirked to herself. *As if.*

****

"Bananas."

"What?" Jess furrowed her brows as she followed Robin down the next aisle.

"I said we need to get some bananas."

"Oh. Right. For a moment, I thought you were referring to my state of mind, in which case you would be correct."

Robin chuckled. "You're in rare form today, even for you." She maneuvered her shopping cart between two stock clerks. "So, what do you want to have for dinner tonight?"

No answer.

"Jess?" Robin turned around slightly, not finding the taller woman behind her. *Where did she run off to?* She diligently searched the immediate area, then finally spied Jess over near the seafood department. *Figures.* Robin came up beside her. "Is there something you wanted to get?"

Jess longingly eyed the rock shrimp. "No."

Robin smiled. "You can, you know."

"No. It's okay." Jess was like a little kid afraid to ask for a treat.

Robin beckoned the clerk over. "Two pounds of the rock shrimp, please."

Jess gave the smaller woman a sideways glance. "Thanks."

"You're welcome." Robin smiled. " Now, come on. Let's get those bananas." She took the package of shrimp from the clerk and placed it in the shopping cart. "I think we should get some strawberries, too."

"And chocolate sauce." Jess piped up.

"Chocolate sauce for the strawberries?" Robin headed for the produce section.

"Um…." Jess stopped and cocked her head, then grinned. "That too."

The smaller woman selected a bunch of nearly ripe bananas. "If you weren't thinking of the chocolate sauce for the strawberries, what did you want it for?"

Jess leaned down and whispered into a petite ear. "I really don't think you want to have this discussion right now, Robin."

Green eyes met blue. "Why not?" She noted a not too subtle raised eyebrow, then suddenly realized the implied intent of Jess's comment. Robin swallowed, trying unsuccessfully to stop an adorable blush from crossing her fair features. "I see." She pointed a playful finger at Jess. "You need to behave."

"Where's the fun in that?" Jess pouted.

"Oh, alright. Fine." The blonde head shook at the playful antics. "We'll get some chocolate sauce. But first, I want to get some tea, and then some honey."

"Honey for the tea?" As soon as Jess said it, she knew she'd walked right into that one.

Robin stopped, then cocked her head to one side, amused green eyes unabashedly twinkling. "That too."

Touché.

****

All Sunday chores having finally been completed, Jess and Robin returned to The Ranch for a quiet dinner. They ate a simple meal of grilled shrimp and pasta, with a small green salad on the side, then set about clearing the dinner dishes and preparing the after-dinner coffee. Robin had previously ordered several additional cans of the Café du Monde New Orleans chicory coffee and kept a stash at The Ranch. Once the dishes were cleaned up and the coffee was made, they retired to the living room to relax and enjoy the brightly lit Christmas tree and the happily blazing fire.

"Thanks for helping me today." Robin sipped her coffee and kicked her stocking feet up on top of the oak coffee table. "I think everything's ready now for when my parents get here."

"No problem. Your snow village is really nice, by the way. I like the way it lights up and has that little ice skating pond in the middle."

Robin chuckled. "I'll be sure to set it up here next year so you can look at it."

Next year. Jess became introspective. *How about every year from now on?* "I'd like that." She scanned the living room. "But where would we put it?"

Robin considered the matter. "Well, we could move the chess set and put it on the table over there."

Jess shook her head. "Nope. The chess set stays."

Blonde eyebrows furrowed in slight confusion. "Why?"

This was something Jess wasn't sure she could adequately explain, but she gave it a shot, nevertheless. "Someone very special gave it to me, and every time I look at it, it reminds me of this special person." She looked fondly at Robin. "When this person isn't with me, I can still feel that person's presence when I see it." Jess got up from the sofa and walked over to where the chess set lay. She picked up an onyx chess piece, rubbing the smooth, sleek surface back and forth between her fingers, then continued. "And when I'm missing this person very much, and my heart aches because I can't be with this person, I pick up one of these pieces and then I feel better. That's why it has to be here where I can see it. So I can be near this person always."

Robin sat very still on the sofa. To say she was truly speechless would be an understatement. She hadn't realized just how profound an effect her gift had indeed had, and it genuinely moved her beyond words. She took a deep breath, then held out her hand. "Come sit with me."

Jess walked back to the sofa and sat down next to Robin, still clutching the onyx chess piece. The older woman examined the piece, seemingly completely fascinated by it, and then fingered the intricate carvings. "It's silly of me, I know."

All Robin could do was shake her head gently. "No, Jess, it's not silly. It's one of the sweetest things I've ever heard." She gave Jess a tender, heartfelt kiss, then rested her head against a broad shoulder. "And you are definitely the sweetest person I have ever known."

Jess kissed the top of the blonde head, then peered down at Robin. "I bet you say that to all your bosses."

Robin giggled lightly. "Absolutely." She closed her eyes and breathed in the familiar scent. "What am I ever going to do with you?"

A dark eyebrow raised in a playful question. "Anything you want?"

Robin smiled "Count on it." She placed her coffee mug down on the coffee table. "Let's look at the tree for awhile, okay? Unless you're tired."

Jess stretched her long frame out on the plush sofa and pulled Robin down alongside her. "No, I'm not tired." For some as yet unexplained reason, Jess felt an unexpected wave of emotion hit her. She was acutely aware of Robin curled up neatly beside her, together with the fire blazing in the fireplace and the beautifully lit Christmas tree in the corner with the white and gold angel gracing the treetop. "Robin?"

Robin snuggled next to the tall body, her head resting in the crook of Jess's neck and her hand loosely positioned so it rested over Jess's heart. "Yeah?"

Jess was silent for a long moment, then proceeded. "I don't know why or how, but what I'm feeling right now...it's very intense."

Robin felt the insistent beat of Jess's heart beneath her hand speed up slightly, and curious green eyes tracked up to meet blue. "What do you mean?"

Jess sighed nervously and tried to order her thoughts. "I've never been this close to anyone before, not even James, and the way it feels, it's so…." She paused, searching for the right word. "Strong."

The smaller woman reached up and brushed the dark bangs. "I think I understand. It's like we're a part of each other."

Jess simply nodded.

Robin lightly trailed her petite fingers down to rest against Jess's cheek and whispered. "It's like no matter what I do...." She moved those same fingers to the base of Jess's neck and stroked the soft skin. "No matter how much I try to show you physically that I love you...." She gently kissed the pulse point, then trailed her hand to the top button of Jess's shirt. "And no matter how many times I say the words…." She undid that button and then the next. "It can never be enough to fully express everything I feel for you." She traced lazy patterns on the exposed flesh. "It goes beyond that."

Jess nodded again mutely, then closed her eyes, the intense feelings becoming even more intense as the emotion of the moment overwhelmed her. She felt the small fingers undo the remaining buttons, then pull her shirt aside, as soft lips kissed their way across her now sensitized skin. Her breathing became labored, the sensual touch almost too much to bear, as the gentle caresses continued. Small hands brushed her breasts, then journeyed further southward, unfastening the button on her jeans and slowly sliding the zipper downward. Jess nearly whimpered in spite of herself, as she felt her clothing being slowly removed piece by piece, only to be replaced by soft lips and warm hands. Shaded blue eyes captured sea green, then held the gaze, before long arms reached out and lifted Robin's sweater up and over her head in one swift motion. Large hands removed each and every additional article of clothing in deliberate fashion, then settled the smaller body beside her own, allowing their skin unhindered contact. The resulting sensation was electrifying, the intensity more powerful than either had previously experienced.

The pace quickened almost frantically, hands and lips kissing and stroking in near unison, until they simultaneously reached their crescendo, and cried out against the intense, ensuing waves. They clung tightly to each other and let the tremors subside, as their heartbeats slowly returned to normal. Neither had any particular inclination to speak, preferring instead to immerse themselves in their unspoken connection. Jess reached up and pulled the light blue afghan blanket from the back of the sofa and gently covered them both with it. They rested comfortably for several moments, nestled together in each other's arms, not wanting to move for fear of breaking the semi-hypnotic spell.

Finally, Robin leaned up and kissed a strong jaw, whispering softly. "I love you." It was a simple statement.

"And I love you." Jess gently stroked the blonde hair.

Sea green eyes fluttered closed. "That was really intense, Jess."

Jess nodded, then an odd expression crossed her angular features. "But it's not enough."

The younger woman was a bit confused. "Not enough?"

Jess tilted Robin's face up to meet her own, and repeated Robin's earlier sentiment. "It's like no matter what I do, no matter how much I try to show you physically that I love you, no matter how many times I say the words, it can never be enough to fully express everything I feel for you." Jess felt a lump suddenly form in the back of her throat, surprised, herself, at the emotion her own words provided. "It goes beyond that."

Robin nodded, studying the face she loved for a long moment, then rested her head on Jess's chest. "Even though it's not enough, I say we should keep trying."

That drew a smile. "Okay. We'll keep trying."

"Often?"

The smile widened. "Yes." Jess drew Robin up even with her and lavished her with tender kisses, then whispered. "But it goes beyond that for me. Just so you know that."

Green eyes locked on blue. "It goes beyond that for me, too." Robin kissed Jess lightly, then grinned. "But I still want to keep trying."

A chuckle. "Now who's incorrigible?"

"I learned from the best."

"Thank you."

****

The mall was crowded, jam-packed as a matter of fact, with holiday shoppers scurrying about from shop to shop trying to complete their last minute gift buying. The food court played center stage to long lines of small children anxious to see Santa Claus and present him with their carefully prepared Christmas lists. Festive decorations of oversized wrapped gift boxes and ornaments hung from the two story vaulted ceiling, while piped in Christmas carols sounded in the background throughout the open areas. Christmas, it seemed, had inevitably become a commercialized endeavor.

It was mid-morning when Jess entered the mall after finally finding a parking space for her silver Mercedes in a far corner of the crowded parking garage. The waves of people milling around the center areas of the mall nearly made her claustrophobic, as she single-mindedly made her way down the escalator toward the mall's largest jewelry store. The lack of convenient parking spaces made it necessary that she travel through the food court area, past Santa Claus and the long, winding lines of waiting children, in order to finally arrive at her ultimate destination.

She stood in front of the jewelry shop and took in a deep breath. For some inexplicable reason, she hesitated outside the store. One would not have thought it would be such a difficult thing to step inside, but Jess knew that her next actions would have far-reaching significance, and perhaps, unimaginable complications. Abruptly, she turned around and proceeded back into the center of the mall, deciding instead that a cup of cappuccino at the coffee bar and some much-needed confidence building was in order. She ordered her cappuccino and sat down at a suddenly vacant table, contemplating with considerable deliberation her next course of action.

Jewelry. That was a big step. Jess had an idea of what she wanted to buy, having thought about it almost constantly during the past week, but the proverbial cold feet kept getting in the way. She noted that her internal voice chose that precise moment to register once again. *Give her your heart.* Jess sighed to herself. *But would it be appropriate?* No easy answer came to her, and so the question remained. Jewelry was a personal thing, and could have considerable significance depending how a particular item was perceived. It was possible that Robin could think that what Jess had in mind was too forward or even pretentious. The dark-haired woman sipped her cappuccino, considering her options. It was a risk, to be sure, and there were many reasons to forget the idea entirely. She took another sip. *But still....*

Jess debated the matter for several more moments, then tossed her empty coffee cup in the trash and made her way in more confident fashion back to the jewelry store. This time, she walked briskly inside without hesitation, and was immediately surrounded by sparkling diamonds and glittering gold. The incandescent lighting gave the various pieces of jewelry an incredibly dazzling quality that nearly took her breath away. She scanned the rows of jewelry cases, then quickly stepped toward the back of the store where numerous diamond necklaces were displayed. She searched a large case, then found what she was looking for. There, in the very front, were several heart-shaped diamond pendant necklaces, none more than an inch in diameter. Several were tasteful and dainty, about three quarters of an inch or less in width, hollow in the center and surrounded by a perimeter of clustered or cut diamonds. One in particular caught her eye.

A salesman sidled his way over to the jewelry display case, noting Jess's interest in the diamond pendants, and spoke in a slight British accent. "May I help you with something?"

Jess looked up and then pointed to an item. "Yes. Could I see that one there?" She watched with interest as the salesman removed the necklace from the case and laid it out on the velvet display cloth. Jess took an apprising look at the piece. It was even more stunning up close. The heart-shaped pendant necklace was trimmed in a fourteen carat gold channel band around the perimeter, with cut diamonds inlaid within the band. The center of the heart was open, giving the piece a tasteful, yet elegant appearance. It was simply perfect, in Jess's opinion, and conveyed just the right sentiment. The necklace did not boast of possessiveness, or attachment, or convey any type of presumption. Robin could wear it as a simple piece of jewelry, and yet it would still have a certain significance. Jess listened politely as the salesman adequately described the quality of the cut diamonds and their solid gold setting. She particularly noted the way the diamonds sparkled brilliantly in the incandescent lighting.

"This is a very fine piece." The salesman continued to boast.

Jess fingered the necklace, then looked at the price. For all practical purposes, price wasn't an issue. The piece cost a fair amount, but it barely registered in Jess's mind as she continued to contemplate the purchase. The faintest smile appeared on the edge of her lips as she made the final decision. "I'll take it."

"Excellent choice." The salesman clasped his hands together in approval, and then retrieved a velvet box in which to lay the necklace. "Will there be anything else today?"

Jess quickly handed him her credit card, and was about to respond in the negative, when, in a purely reflexive motion, she turned toward the adjacent display case. And that one spontaneous action was her undoing. Her cool blue gaze settled upon the sparkling items inside. *Rings.* She couldn't resist the temptation, and stepped forward to take a closer look. Her mind spun uncontrollably in a million different directions, as if she had been fighting this very notion all along. And, in truth, she had. Rings were too presumptuous. They conveyed possessiveness, boasted of attachment, and implied a certain understanding of a long-term commitment that she and Robin had simply not discussed. *Forever.* She contemplated the idea, then discarded it. It was just not a good idea to indulge in such fantasy. It was absurdly foolish to even consider it. She continued to gaze at the rings wistfully. *But still....*

The hopeful salesman rushed around the display case to accommodate any additional requests. Even as Jess canvassed the wide selection, she mentally chastised herself for her wayward thoughts, this time more forcefully. *What the hell are you thinking? Are you insane?* It was true, this was absolutely ridiculous, ludicrous, even. She and Robin needed to discuss things first before entertaining such a move. Not to mention the fact that wearing a ring publicly would invite the inevitable scrutiny. Jess scanned the case another time, letting her eyes linger on its contents a bit longer than necessary. *But still....*

She took a deep breath, and even as her mind dismissed the notion outright, she found herself pointing to one dainty ring inquisitively, beckoning the salesman to bring it forth from the glass case for further inspection. He eagerly complied, setting it upon the velvet cloth. And suddenly, it was right in front of her. A ring that would convey everything from attachment to commitment and more. *Forever.* Jess picked up the piece and held it to the light, studying the glittering diamonds as if transfixed. The salesman droned on about the solid gold setting, the color and clarity of the diamond solitaire, the small diamond clusters on either side, and the total carat weight. One and a half carats to be exact. Jess set the ring back down and blew out a small breath, wrestling with her inner self. Everything she had thought before was still true. Every reason not to get the ring still remained. Every reservation she had ever had passed through her mind with startling clarity. It was pure folly, and it was absolutely, positively, and without a doubt, insanity to even consider it. She picked up the ring and studied it again. *But still....*

Jess closed her eyes, and listened to her heart for once, ignoring the bothersome internal niggling that so often got her in trouble.

Despite the voice's persistence, her heart finally won out. "I'll take this, too." She indicated toward the ring, not even looking at the price. "Could you engrave something on the inside for me?"

The salesman was truly delighted. "Absolutely." He handed her a blank sheet of paper and pen. "Just write down what you'd like engraved."

Jess complied, scribbling something, then folded the paper and handed it back to him. "When will it be ready?"

"I'll prepare both of your purchases and have them for you in thirty minutes."

Jess nodded. "Thank you." She completed her transaction and then headed back into the mall to wait, finding herself wandering aimlessly throughout the food court area. Once she had time to think about it, she realized how impulsive she'd been. Robin's Christmas present was set. The diamond pendant necklace was her gift. The ring...well, that was another matter, altogether. It was way, way too presumptuous. *Correct.* After much internal deliberation and not too subtle self-berating, she decided to put the ring away for another time...that is, another time if and when it became appropriate to consider giving it to Robin. Now, however, was definitely not that time. With her mind seemingly made up, she proceeded to collect her day's purchases and then exit the mall, homeward bound.

After fighting the unusually heavy holiday traffic, Jess arrived back at The Ranch, noticing that Robin's blue Miata was not there. After pulling her silver Mercedes into the garage, she turned off the alarm to the house and stepped inside, immediately noticing an odd sound reverberating from the direction of the living room. *What the...?* To Jess, the foreign sound resembled a soft, monotonous clattering. Curious, she walked further inside the house and around to the living area to investigate. She proceeded, then suddenly stopped in front of the solid oak coffee table. There, around the base of the Christmas tree, she found a small train chugging its way along a circular track. Jess couldn't help but smile. *Robin.* She stepped forward and watched, nearly hypnotized, as the train traveled its continuous path. As the train approached her again, she saw a piece of paper stuck inside the back of the caboose. She bent down and picked it up, the words "Read Me" written in bold letters across the front. Jess flipped open the note.

J,

A gift for you in advance. Went to meet my parents at the airport. Call you tonight about brunch tomorrow. I'll miss being with you on Christmas.

Choo choo.

I love you.

R

Jess stared at the note for another moment, then a wide grin slowly edged its way across her face.

A train. She knows me so well.

****

It was impossibly chaotic. The airport was swarming with holiday travelers making their way in every direction to family and friends. Some, judging by their mouse ears attire, had just departed the Magic Kingdom in Walt Disney World. Others no doubt were on their way to spend the holidays at the same place. It was a well-known fact in Central Florida that most travelers passing through the Orlando airport were traditionally headed for the Florida attractions. Today was no exception.

Robin made her way through the crowded main terminal. She checked the arriving flights board, then boarded the monorail shuttle to the airside gates. An automated voice came across the on-board speakers as the shuttle departed for the airside terminal, expressing the city's thanks for visiting Orlando. *Interesting.* Robin recalled that when she returned home to Orlando from Detroit at Thanksgiving, the automated voice expressed the city's hope for an enjoyable visit. She shook her head at the anomaly. *They certainly do cater to the tourists.* Upon arrival at the airside terminal, Robin made her way to the designated gate area to greet her parents' flight. She checked the arrival time, and found to her slight annoyance that the flight had been slightly delayed. *Great.* Having nothing to do but wait for the next thirty minutes, she took a seat in a nearby corner and watched the throngs of people scurrying to catch their flights.

Her mind took a detour amid the chaos, and Robin idly wondered what Jess was doing and whether she had returned home to find her gift. *She loves trains.* Robin grinned, thinking about Jess's reaction, then grew serious as she watched the passing crowds. She swung her feet impatiently back and forth, noting with interest that the arrival time had just been pushed back another ten minutes. This produced a very weary sigh, and Robin let her mind wander further.

She had gotten several Christmas gifts for Jess, but one in particular occupied her thoughts the most. She dipped into her purse and pulled out a square flat box, momentarily considering it strange for her to have actually brought it with her today. For some unexplained reason, having the gift in her possession made her feel closer to Jess, even though they were apart. *I'm the hopeless one.* She fingered the outside of the box, then proceeded to open it, peering inside the enclosed velvet case just as she'd done countless times before.

Inside, rested a beautiful white and blue sapphire encrusted gold bangle bracelet, elegantly designed and delicately etched. The jewels sparkled, an s-link pattern alternating blue and white sapphires around a gold band. Robin regarded the bracelet almost reverently. Sapphires, blue especially, were her favorite stone, and seemed to fit Jess perfectly. As a matter of fact, Robin's favorite color was blue, as evidenced by her car, and many of her clothing items. *Blue.* She sat back and idly thought about the azure eyes she knew so well, considering it somehow fitting that they were also an incredible shade of blue. Another thought came to her, and gave her significant pause. As improbable as it seemed, she wondered whether it was more than just mere coincidence that her favorite color happened to match the color of the eyes she loved. *Weird.* Robin thought about that some more. Everything about her relationship with Jess seemed predestined, as if almost inevitable, and she wondered if it was really random at all. She glanced down at the bracelet and fingered the inscription she'd had engraved inside. It was simple, yet still conveyed everything she wanted to say, and everything she wanted Jess to know.

Robin snapped the velvet case shut and replaced it in her purse. Her mind flashed to another smaller box she'd left at home, one that held the other piece of jewelry she'd bought, and one that contained something she wasn't sure she'd ever give to Jess but bought anyway. Her sentiment was real, but her courage was another thing, altogether. And timing. It just wasn't the right time. Too many issues were still left hanging, most notably a promised visit to a therapist Robin wasn't sure she wanted to keep. She sighed, not really quite in the frame of mind to dwell on that little matter at the moment. She was abruptly jarred from her musings as she heard the gate agent announce the arrival of her parents' flight. *Okay, let's get this show on the road.*

She stood up and waited as the passengers disembarked the plane, and then searched for the expected familiar faces. She didn't have to wait long. Her parents exited the jet way, and Robin stepped up to greet them.

"Hi. How was the flight?" Robin hugged her mother, then her father.

"Hello, dear." Colette Wilson barely broke stride as she headed toward the baggage claim area. "Sorry we were delayed."

Thomas Wilson followed with the carry on bags. "Hi, honey. How are you doing?"

"Good, Dad." As they proceeded toward the shuttle, Robin took a few moments to catch up with her parents on some hometown gossip. Upon their arrival at the main terminal, she noted the increasing crowds. "Did you reserve a rental car, Dad?"

"Yes. All taken care of." Her father stopped in front of the baggage claim area to await their luggage. "Why don't you go ahead and get your car and meet us at the rental car lot. Then we'll follow you to your apartment."

Robin nodded, then headed in the opposite direction toward the parking garage and her blue Miata. She arrived at the car, pulled out her keys and unlocked the car door, sliding into the passenger seat. She braced her arms against the steering wheel and took a deep breath.

Okay, here we go.

****

As it turned out, much of the day was occupied with situating Robin's parents back at the apartment. Once settled, they decided to take an afternoon drive downtown to visit Robin's law firm, and then spent a little time driving around the city. Robin's parents had been to Orlando many years ago when Robin was about eight-years-old, and they had all spent a long weekend at Walt Disney World. During the nearly four months that Robin had now lived in Orlando, she hadn't ventured out to the various attractions, although the thought had crossed her mind more than once. She made a mental note that trips to the Magic Kingdom and Epcot, and perhaps Universal Studios, were definitely in order. That is, of course, if she could persuade a certain junior partner to go along with her.

After returning home, the Wilson family finished dinner, then relaxed in the small living room of Robin's apartment. Colette leisurely sipped her coffee and admired the modest holiday decorations. "No tree this year, Robin?"

Robin sat on the fluffy sofa. "It's really too small in here for a tree, so I just put up the snow village and a few other things."

Colette quickly got to the point of her intended conversation. "Your father and I wanted to discuss something with you." She set down her empty coffee cup. "We were hoping that you might consider returning to Michigan. We hate the thought of you being here all alone."

Here it comes. Robin took a deep breath. "Mom, we've had this discussion before. I want to stay here in Florida. I have a job and friends here. I like it."

"But dear, your father has spoken with one of his business associates who is in charge of recruiting for a large law firm in Detroit. This man has agreed to meet with you for an interview."

The blonde head shook vehemently. "I really wish both of you would listen to me. I want to stay here. I'm doing all right. I don't want to go back to Michigan."

Thomas Wilson leaned forward in his seat. "Honey, we just want you to think about it."

Green eyes focused on him intently. "I appreciate your efforts, but I've made my decision. I want to stay." Robin glanced at her mother. "There's actually something I wanted to tell you. I'm going to give up my apartment next month and move into a house with a friend of mine from work."

"Who is this friend?" Colette asked cautiously.

"Her name is Jessica Harrison, and she's a partner with the firm where I work. She has a huge house and currently lives there by herself. I work on many cases with her, and we recently completed a major trial, which we won, by the way." Robin grinned widely. "She's been a very good friend to me, and she knows about everything that's happened. She's offered and I've accepted."

Robin's parents were silent for a moment, then Colette spoke again. "How large is this house?"

"It has four bedrooms, a living room, dining room, eat-in kitchen, front porch, back patio with screened-in pool, utility room, security alarm, two-car garage, fireplace...." Robin looked up. "Shall I go on?"

Robin's father ran his hand through his sandy blonde hair. "Why does your friend want to take on a housemate?"

"Dad, she has a big house and plenty of room. Like I said, she knows about everything that's happened and is a good friend to me. This way, neither one of us will be alone. It also helps that we work together." Robin thought her explanation was going rather well. It seemed the perfect time to broach the next subject. "If it's okay, I've invited Jess to go to brunch with us tomorrow. You would be able to meet her then."

Colette's pale green eyes lit up. "That's a splendid idea. We'd like to meet her." She wasn't totally in agreement with Robin's decision to stay in Orlando, but was willing to at least meet this friend before making an issue of it. To be sure, Colette still believed it was in her daughter's best interest to return to Detroit. "What do you think, Tom?"

"Robin, your friend is welcome to join us for brunch." Thomas Wilson sighed heavily. "Honey, we want you to be happy, but we also know how difficult things have been for you. Just say the word, and we'll get you moved back home. We'll have a law position available for you, as well." He sat up a bit straighter. "Now, I want to ask you something, and I'm hoping you'll give us an honest answer."

Robin raised both eyebrows cautiously. "Okay."

"How are you really doing? Have you talked with anyone professionally? The reason I ask is that the entire situation was very tragic, and you were under a lot of stress at the time, as I'm sure you still are. So, again, honestly, how are you really doing?"

Robin thought about the question carefully, and how to best respond. "I admit that some days are hard. But most of the time, I'm doing really well. I like my job and the people I work with, and I've made some new friends." She looked him squarely in the eyes. "And yes, I've agreed to see a therapist beginning after the holidays to talk about some things. It was actually my friend, Jess, who first suggested that I do that."

Thomas was reflective of the answer. "Your friend seems as though she cares about you."

"She does." It was a simple statement but absolutely the truth.

"Alright." Her father smiled, clearly not wanting to proceed further with the subject at the current time. "Now, let's go see if we can scrounge up some ice cream." He winked, then got up from his chair and ushered Robin into the kitchen.

A voice called out from the living room. "Don't forget to bring me some while you're at it."

Robin grinned and shook her head to herself. *That went surprisingly well.* She hesitated for just a second as an uneasy feeling came over her. *Or did it?*

****

The phone rang twice, then a familiar voice answered. "Hello?"

A calm settled over Robin. "Hey, Jess."

"Hey there, kiddo. So, how's it going with your folks?"

"Alright." There was a unrecognizable clattering sound coming through the phone line. "Jess, what's that noise?"

"Um...." A brief pause. "Oh, that. Just playing with my new toy." The older woman grinned into the phone. "I love trains."

A giggle. "I know that, silly. Do you like it?"

"You bet. By the way, thanks."

"You're welcome." Robin cleared her throat, then turned a bit serious. "Um...so, brunch is set. I told my parents about you and that I planned to move into your house next month."

"How did they react?" Jess's low, rich voice filtered through the phone line.

A long very weary sigh. "Pretty well, I think. They're anxious to meet you."

"Am I on trial?"

That question was unexpected. "No, Jess, don't think of it like that. I think they just want to satisfy themselves that I have a friend who cares about me. They don't want me to be alone."

Jess's tone softened. "You're not alone."

Robin swallowed, a slight tightening in the back of her throat causing her voice to rasp. "I know." It was all she could say at the moment.

Jess noted the shaky response. "Are you okay?"

"Yes. Just missing you."

"Me, too, kiddo. It's not the same looking at my Christmas tree on my favorite sofa without you."

Robin smiled at the sentiment, sensing a bit of a pout on the other end of the phone line. "Just save my spot."

"You bet." Jess attempted to lighten things up a bit. "At least I have my train to keep me company."

That brought a grin. "I'm glad you like the train, Jess, but surely that train can't keep you warm at night."

The sultry voice came from the other end of the line. "You'd be surprised."

"I won't even go there." Green eyes twinkled in amusement.

"Um...Robin, you're not within earshot of your parents, are you?"

"No, why?"

"Just checking. Our conversation was getting a little personal and I was hoping they weren't near enough to overhear."

"Don't worry. I'm in my room with the door closed." Robin sighed, wishing she could prolong the conversation, but her mother wanted to retire early, and her parents were staying in her room. "I need to go, Jess. I just wanted to let you know about brunch. Can you meet us tomorrow morning at 10:00 at Chez Pierre on Park Avenue?"

"I'm there, kiddo." There was short silence, almost as if more needed to be said.

"Is everything alright, Jess?"

"Yeah. I just hate being apart."

Robin took a steadying breath. "Me, too. I'll see you tomorrow, okay?"

"Okay. Goodnight, sweetheart."

The warmth of Jess's voice seemed to reach right across the phone line and wrap snuggly around Robin. "Goodnight, Jess."

"Choo choo." The line softly clicked off.

Choo choo? Robin found herself both smiling and curiously feeling a bit melancholy at the same time.

Dear God, please get me through the next few days.

****

The Park Avenue restaurant was elegantly decorated in holiday themes. Robin and her parents sat at a front table awaiting Jess's arrival. A nearby window allowed a clear view of the rows of quaint little shops lining the length of Park Avenue, shoppers leisurely passing by and ducking in and out of the various storefronts along the way. Robin scanned the restaurant's entrance area several times, hoping to spot her friend as soon as she arrived. She checked her watch nervously, noting that Jess was about ten minutes late. *She'll be here.* Green eyes anxiously searched the main entranceway again, then finally spied the dark-haired woman as she stepped inside the restaurant. Robin let out a relieved breath, then caught the older woman's glance, waving her over.

Jess approached the table. "Hi. Sorry I'm a bit late. I had trouble finding a parking spot."

"No problem." Robin smiled, then made her introductions. "Jess, I'd like you to meet my parents, Thomas and Colette Wilson. Mom and Dad, this is my friend Jessica Harrison."

"Mr. and Mrs. Wilson, so nice to meet you." Jess politely extended her hand before taking a seat next to Robin.

Colette nodded. "Jessica, we've heard so much about you from Robin. It's a pleasure to meet you."

"Thank you. And please call me Jess, if you'd like."

"Alright." Colette continued, her demeanor courteous, yet reserved. "So, Jess, Robin tells us that you are a partner at the law firm where she works."

Jess took a sip of water, suddenly thirsty. "Yes, actually, I just became a partner this year." She tried to steer the conversation away from herself. "Since Robin's joined us, I've worked with her extensively. She's been a terrific addition to our firm. In fact, she was a major part of a recent trial victory we had." Blue eyes beamed proudly.

"That's wonderful of you to say." Colette, undeterred, led the conversation back in its previous direction. "Robin also tells us that you've graciously offered to take her on as a housemate."

Jess required another sip of water. *I am definitely on trial, here.* "Yes, that's right. I have a rather large house where I live by myself, and I have plenty of room. It will be nice, I think, for both of us. I'd certainly enjoy the company."

"Robin, honey, are you going to be able to handle your share of the living expenses with such a big house?" Colette inquired, a pensive look crossing her features.

Her daughter nodded. "Jess and I have discussed all that, and we've worked it out. Besides, I make a very nice salary from the firm."

Jess studied the situation and sensed a slight unease from Robin's mother. She decided to make an offer she hoped might help. "Once we're finished here, you're all very welcome to come by the house and take the grand tour, if you'd like."

Colette seemed very pleased with the overture. "That would be lovely."

Robin's face went suddenly pale. *No, Jess. My stuff's all over the place.*

Out of the corner of her eye, Jess caught Robin's panicked look. "I had a little time to clean up the place a bit before I left the house this morning." She grinned confidently.

Robin let go an almost audible sigh. *Thank you, Jess.*

Thomas Wilson cleared his throat and finally spoke up, changing the direction of the conversation. "Jessica, I'm very happy to know that Robin has a friend here in Orlando. I think you know that she's had a very difficult year."

Jess glanced at Robin, noting that the younger woman was staring out the window and idly fingering her napkin. "Yes, Robin's told me about everything that's happened."

Thomas continued. "We're concerned about her, as you can imagine."

Blue eyes fixed decidedly on his. “I understand what she’s been through, and I’ll help her in any way I can.”

Colette didn’t miss Jess’s subtle glance in Robin’s direction, and discerned a certain sincerity in her statement. “It’s good to know she can count on you.”

By now, Robin had just about had enough of the blatant cross-examination going on around her, and abruptly picked up her menu. “Could we go ahead and order, now?”

“Good idea.” Thomas waved the waiter over. “Let’s eat, then we can continue our conversation.”

And so it went. They ordered the usual brunch fare, and then ate in casual fashion, engaging in idle chit chat on topics ranging from the weather to sports to the business climate in Central Florida. All conversation was focused on things deliberately general in nature, and in that regard, it was quite pleasant and very polite. After finishing their meals, the four adults lingered at the restaurant for another round of coffee, the discussion turning once again to more serious matters.

Thomas Wilson began. “Jessica, I want you to know that we are very pleased to meet you, and we are grateful for your friendship toward our daughter. She also seems to enjoy working at your law firm.”

Jess swallowed. She could almost feel the next part coming. *But....*

“But, we’ve told Robin that she can come back to Michigan, if she wishes, and we will have a law position waiting for her there.”

Not very subtle. “Whatever Robin decides, Mr. Wilson, I’m with her one hundred percent.”

Colette smiled. “Thank you, Jess.”

I know she may eventually leave me. I have to accept that. Jess stiffened ever so slightly.

By now, Robin knew Jess all too well, and recognized the sudden tense posture for what it was. *I’m not leaving.* Petite fingers discreetly slid their way underneath the table and gently brushed against Jess’s hand in calming, soothing circles. “I’ve explained to my parents, though, that I like it here and I have no wish to leave.” She offered a small smile.

Thomas glanced up from his coffee cup and rested his hands neatly in front of him, creating a steeple with his fingers in a deliberative manner. “Very well, then.”

Both Robin and Jess had the same thought.

This isn’t over.

****

Jess drove her silver Mercedes down the Interstate 4 corridor en route from Orlando to Tampa. She flipped on the radio and kept one ear tuned to the local soft rock station, as thirty-six hours of Christmas music had just begun its play rotation. Her mind reflected on the day's earlier events. *Brunch.* What to make of it? Okay, so Robin's parents were very polite and cordial. No problem there. They were also very concerned about Robin's well-being. Again, no problem. They made no secret of the fact that they thought Robin would be better off back with them in Michigan. That, definitely was a problem. How far would they push it? Jess thought about that. Perhaps once they saw that Robin was doing fine, they'd ease up. Maybe. She lifted an eyebrow slightly. Or, maybe not. Even though Robin appeared to be doing quite well right now, and the Wilsons surely saw this, they still persisted in their belief that Robin should move back to Michigan. It seemed as if they may never be completely satisfied. Jess sighed. *Damn.*

The traffic slowed almost to a stop as she passed through the Disney area, no doubt due the high volume of cars on the roadway. Either that or a wreck. Jess suspected the holiday traffic was the true culprit. Her mother always worried when she was late, and stuck in traffic was not exactly Jess's idea of a fun time. *Damn.* Her mind went back to her previous line of thinking. So, what to make of the grand tour of the house. Well, Robin's mother seemed impressed, quiet pleased with the alarm system, the swimming pool and the well-manicured upscale neighborhood. *Just like a mother.* Mrs. Wilson appeared to approve of whole idea of Robin living there. Still, Jess sensed a bit of reluctance, but perhaps it was due to Robin's decision to stay in Florida. Mr. Wilson, on the other hand, was a bit harder to read. Although he was very accommodating of Robin's plans, he had undisguised concerns about her well-being, emotionally. The more Jess thought about that, the more she realized that he was not totally unjustified in his thinking. Robin has emotional issues, and God-willing, would start her appointments with Dr. Richmond soon. Jess swallowed hard as an unsettling thought came over her. If Robin refuses to see the therapist, her father may insist on moving her back to Michigan. *Damn.* It was a popular word today. *I have a splitting headache, now.*

The traffic jam finally eased, and Jess was on her way again. Before long, the dark-haired woman pulled her silver Mercedes into the driveway of her mother's townhouse near the nature preserve. She retrieved her Christmas packages from the car and rounded the sidewalk to the front door. As she did so, a tiny, pint-sized cherubic face greeted her.

"Nana, Jessie's here!" The little voice squealed in delight.

"Jeremy, you little rat." Jess picked up her four-year-old nephew and gave him a big hug. "Where's your brother, kiddo?"

"Here is!" A small blue eye peeked around the door frame, the small voice giggling lightly. "Jessie! Jessie!"

Jess playfully rushed up to the door and corralled the two year old. "Hey, big guy." She lifted the laughing child high in the air. "Are ya ready for Santa tonight?"

A tall, slender built man appeared in the doorway. His neatly cropped jet black hair framed a handsomely chiseled face. "Michael, let your aunt come inside the house." He stepped back and held the door while the giggling trio trekked inside.

"Hi ya, Peter. How ya doing?" Jess knelt down and set her gifts underneath the Christmas tree in the living room. "Where's Mom?"

"In the kitchen. She's gone all out this year. First Christmas Eve, then Christmas tomorrow. We can't possibly eat all the food she's cooking." Peter grinned widely.

Once the presents were sufficiently situated, Jess straightened up and dusted her hands together. "Well, then, I guess I'll just have to help her out. And, of course, sample the fare." She winked, then made her way into the large eat-in kitchen where she found her mother dicing bread in preparation for the turkey stuffing. "Hi." Jess leaned casually against the door frame.

Elaine Harrison looked up. "Jessie. I was worried about you. You said you'd be here an hour ago." She wiped her hands on a dish towel and stepped over and gave her daughter a hug.

"Yeah, well you know how the holiday traffic is. Next time I'm gonna tell you I'll be here an hour later than I intend, so if I'm late, it won't matter. I'll be on time and you won't worry." Jess chuckled, proud of herself for finding the perfect solution.

"Come sit down. Tell me how you've been." Elaine sat her medium-built frame down at the kitchen table and picked up another loaf of Italian bread.

Jess followed. "Here, let me help you with that." She grasped a knife and a cutting board and took a seat. "Things are good, Mom. Work is great. I had a trial a couple of weeks ago." She glanced up and grinned a bit cockily. "We won."

"That's wonderful." Elaine Harrison began trimming the crust. "What else is new?"

Jess sighed thoughtfully. She considered how to broach the topic, then finally decided on the direct approach. “I’m taking a housemate next month.” There, she said it.

Elaine sliced off several pieces of bread and began dicing. “I didn’t know you needed to take on a tenant.”

“I don’t. It’s a friend of mine from the firm. She’s one of our associates. We work together a lot. Her name’s Robin.” *Succinct and to the point.* For some reason, saying just that much took a lot of energy. To provide herself with a much needed distraction, Jess began chopping the celery.

Her mother looked up from her dicing, her voice very gentle. “That’s nice, Jessie. But you didn’t answer my question. Why are you taking on a tenant?”

Jess stopped her celery chopping. “Robin’s not a tenant.” She focused her gaze out the kitchen window at the neatly arranged flower garden. “We’re friends.”

Elaine set her knife down on the cutting board and studied her daughter’s demeanor. “Does Robin not have her own place?”

“She has an apartment, but she’s letting it go at the end of the month.” This was getting more difficult by the minute.

“Is she unable to afford her own place?” Her mother was genuinely not trying to be obtuse.

“No, Mom.” Jess let go a breath in exasperation. “We want to live together.” Blue eyes closed tightly as she realized what she’d just said, and her body posture stiffened appreciably.

“Okay.” Elaine resumed dicing the bread. “It’s just that you’ve never taken a housemate before. What makes this different?”

Jess didn’t answer.

Elaine glanced at her daughter. She set her knife down once again, and pushed the cutting board away. “Jessie? What’s going on, honey?”

Jess felt her heart rate speed up. She knew she’d proceeded too far to escape making the final admission. “Robin and I are….” She mentally braced herself for the anticipated reaction. “Together.”

“Together?”

“Yes.”

Elaine furrowed her brows and considered the statement. “In what way?”

Jess swallowed. “In every way.”

Now, it was Elaine’s turn to swallow. Hard. “I see.” She took a moment to process the information, then spoke softly. “I didn’t know you...preferred women.”

"I don't."

Elaine was confused. "Then...?"

"I prefer Robin. Just Robin." It didn't make much sense, even to Jess. She looked at her mother, then took a deep breath and tried to explain. "I don't know how it happened, or why. I just know that Robin touches a part of my heart that I never knew existed." Jess closed her eyes, trying valiantly to keep her emotions under control, even as she felt her composure slowly melting away. "She's shown me how to love someone again."

"You love her." It was a statement, not a question.

"Yes." Jess was shaking now. "I love her very much." She felt the sting of tears against her eyes. "I want to be with her forever."

Elaine got up from her chair and went over to Jess. She wrapped her arms tightly around her daughter and whispered. "It's okay, Jessie. If you're happy, honey, then I'm happy for you." She smiled tenderly. "You know that I love you, and nothing will ever change that, right?"

"Yes."

"Good. And you are happy?"

Jess cleared her throat. "Yes, I'm very happy." Her eyes lit up as she continued. "Robin makes me laugh, and she's so cute, and so sweet. We get along so well." Jess stopped and became a bit pensive. "But we do have some things to work through. She recently lost her boyfriend right before they were to be engaged, and she has some lingering guilt over his death."

"That's very sad." Elaine sat back down. "Where is Robin today?"

"She's with her parents. They came down to visit her from Michigan where they live. I actually had brunch with them this morning." Jess stared out the window again. "They worry about her because of what happened with her boyfriend. She hasn't mentioned anything to them about us."

"I take it Robin's feelings for you are a new experience for her, then?"

Jess smiled at her mother's tact. "Yes, Mom. Neither one of us has had this experience before. It was as much of a surprise to her as it was to me."

"And Robin feels as strongly for you as you do for her?"

Jess started to answer, then hesitated. She wanted to believe it was so. She wanted to believe that Robin would never leave. But...as much as she tried, she still, still, even today still, even after all of Robin's assurances still, still was afraid that Robin would eventually leave. *Damn.* Jess closed her eyes, ashamed at her own continuing doubts. "Robin loves me, I know that. She needs to come to terms with her boyfriend's death, I think, before she can move forward. She's going to talk to someone about that."

"I don't want to see you hurt again. That's why I asked."

"It's worth the risk. Robin's worth the risk."

Elaine stood up and spread the diced bread in a shallow pan. "She must be very special for you to love her so much."

Jess gave her mother a truly radiant smile. "She is. I've invited her to come back with me next weekend for New Year's Day. Is that okay?"

"Of course. I'd love to meet someone who obviously means so much to you." The older woman put the pan of bread in the oven to toast. "Now, you hurry up and finish with that celery so I can sauté it for the stuffing, okay?" She winked at her daughter. "I need to go and check on the kids for a minute, including your brother."

Jess watched as her mother left the kitchen, then stared down at the partially chopped celery, letting out a relieved breath. *Thank you, Mom, for understanding.*

****

The mid-morning sun steadily made its ascent up the horizon, as bright beams of sunlight cut through the vertical blinds in the upstairs townhouse bedroom, bathing the room in a warm yellow-orange glow. Jess picked up the cordless telephone and dialed a very familiar number.

"Hello?" Robin's sweet voice filtered through the phone line.

"Merry Christmas, sweetheart."

"Jess." The quiet voice responded with a slight hint of relief. "Let me go into the other room." A brief pause. "Okay, I'm by myself, now. Merry Christmas, Jess."

"Are you having a good day today?" The older woman sat on the corner of the bed.

"It's fine." There was a definite lack of enthusiasm. "I miss you, though."

"Me, too, kiddo." Jess focused out the far window at a nearby maple tree. "I just wanted to take a moment to call you and hear your voice."

"I'm glad you did. How's your Christmas going?"

"Well, things are gonna get really crazy around here very soon once my nephews come back over. We've got so many gifts under the tree downstairs that I can barely walk through the living room." The older woman chuckled.

"I'm so glad you're enjoying your visit with your family, Jess. I know how important that is to you."

There was an undercurrent of something Jess couldn't quite decipher in Robin's tone of voice. "Are you doing all right? Have your parents been pressuring you?"

Robin made an effort to sound cheerful. "I'm fine, Jess, and no, my parents haven't pressured me at all. My mom's busy fixing a turkey, and my dad and I were just watching TV." She lowered her voice. "The Christmas parade's on, now. They were just getting to the Snoopy float when you called."

The Snoopy float? "Is there a significance to the Snoopy float?"

"Just that Snoopy is my favorite character. I love his legal beagle shtick."

"Well, then, I'm sorry I interrupted." Jess quipped.

A giggle. "Since you made me miss him, you'll just have to make it up to me."

"Is that so?" Jess arched an eyebrow. "Well, I suppose I could show you my own personal legal beagle impression." She spoke a bit seductively. "If I do, will you...scratch behind my ears?"

"Yes."

"Will you...rub my tummy?"

"Yes."

"Will you...give me a treat if I beg?"

"Absolutely." Robin giggled.

"Okay, then, it's settled. Consider me your very own legal beagle." Jess grinned into the phone, then sighed a bit wistfully. "And your legal beagle loves you very much, sweetheart, and misses you more every second."

"Jess." Robin's voice cracked with emotion. "You are the sweetest person."

"Puppy." Jess corrected.

That drew a laugh. "Okay. Let me rephrase that. You are a sweet, but very hopeless, puppy." Robin's voice became soft once again, and very sincere. "And I love you, too, my legal beagle."

Several long seconds elapsed as Jess simply took comfort in the gentle breathing on the other end of the phone line. *God, I miss her.* Even though they were a hundred miles apart, she could still feel the powerful connection between herself and Robin. "Well, everyone will be here soon, kiddo. I think I should go. I'll be back home tomorrow afternoon, okay?"

"Yeah. Then we can celebrate our own Christmas."

"You bet."

Robin's voice took on playful tone. "So, what'd you get me?"

"Never mind, but don't think for one minute I got you that car."

"Rats."

Jess chuckled. "Alright, kiddo. I'll see you tomorrow."

"Okay. See you tomorrow, Jess. Drive safely."

And for the second time in a many days, Jess and Robin each had the same thought.

I can't wait until tomorrow.

Chapter 12

Robin busied herself tidying up the house and making sure that everything was in perfect order for Jess's arrival home from Tampa later that afternoon. She placed the remainder of the presents under the Christmas tree, careful not to disturb the miniature train which circled its way around the base. Once everything was situated to her satisfaction, Robin sat down on the plush sofa and admired once again the beautifully decorated Frasier fir tree. Her mind flashed back to when she and Jess had put it up, and her eyes crinkled a bit as she remembered what was now affectionately known as "the tinsel incident." She laughed gently to herself. *She is so hopeless.* She curled her petite body up against the length of the familiar sofa and drew the light blue afghan blanket from the top of cushions down around her, snuggling lightly. She took a deep breath and filled her lungs with the distinctive and decidedly familiar scent that lingered, strangely comforted by it.

It was true, Robin was definitely glad to finally be back at The Ranch after so many days at her apartment. Her parents' visit was surprisingly nice, but taxing just the same, and now she couldn't help the melancholy that settled over her as she thought about missing Christmas day with Jess. She mentally shook her head, slightly annoyed at herself. *I need to get over it.* Robin tracked her eyes up toward the angel on the treetop, thoughts of the sapphire bracelet she'd gotten Jess entering the forefront of her mind. She sighed, suddenly not quite sure the gift was at all adequate. Her goal all along had been to give Jess something that had meaning, and Robin thought she'd found that perfect gift in the bracelet. The added bonus was that Jess could wear it and not have to answer an onslaught of probing questions. For some unexplained reason, the petite woman now had doubts that her gift was enough, especially in light of the other little present she had bought and had tucked away for a later time. She frowned. That other little item would almost certainly lead to questions, probing and otherwise, and that would definitely not be a good thing. Robin tugged the blanket further around her as she pictured the other gift in her mind. Tucked away in her apartment was a simple, yet elegant, diamond cluster ring with what could only be described as a stunning eighteen carat gold setting. The piece also cost a fair amount, not that Robin minded one bit, but she was pretty sure Jess would have never agreed to its extravagance.

So, what exactly was it that made her purchase the ring in the first place? More importantly, would she ever give it to Jess? The simple truth was, Robin absolutely could not imagine her life without the older woman. The only real question was whether it would conceivably be possible for the two of them to have a life together. She pondered that some more. All the public complications aside, would sharing their lives be something Jess wanted, too? And if so, how could they possibly keep their relationship concealed. That one thought both angered and terrified Robin. A part of her resented that they should have to hide their relationship at all, and another part knew that revealing it could cost Jess, and possibly herself, their livelihoods, not to mention their family and friends. *It just wouldn't work.* Reluctantly, and after considered thought, the younger woman came to the conclusion that the ring was nothing more than a naïve fantasy, plain and simple. She had foolishly allowed herself to indulge in it, but it was apparent now that such a move would likely cause more problems than she ever intended. Neither she nor Jess was ready to handle the complications just yet, and that simple fact would be true even if Jess were to feel the same way as she did about a future together.

A long, unhappy sigh escaped her lips and she got up from the sofa, suddenly feeling very much alone. Her gaze found and then rested upon the onyx chess set sitting on the table in the opposite corner of the room, and her feet, quite on their own accord, stepped over toward it. She picked up one of the carved pieces and fingered its smooth surface, noticing with curiosity the strange comfort it provided. *Jess was right.* It was almost as if the tangible object somehow provided an unseen connection that defied any rational explanation. With the onyx chess piece clutched securely in hand, Robin walked back over to the sofa and resumed her position beneath the afghan blanket. Within minutes, her eyelids grew heavy, drawing her ever nearer to sleep's embrace, even as something in the back of her mind tried valiantly to make its way to the forefront. As she finally drifted off, whatever it was silently slipped away, although her subconscious mind was quick to supply the now elusive answer. *A part of me is missing.*

****

Jess arrived home and walked through the door leading from the garage. She stepped into the living room, immediately spying the peacefully sleeping form on the plush sofa. It was really a sweet sight, with Robin curled up on her side and the afghan blanket wrapped loosely around her waist. *I missed you, sweetheart.* She stepped noiselessly over to the foot of the sofa and silently watched as Robin slept, then set her package down on the solid oak coffee table. Grasping the edges of the blanket, she gently pulled it up to Robin's shoulders. It was only then, as she gingerly tucked the blanket around the younger woman, that she noticed the onyx chess piece clutched in a petite hand. Jess's mind did a double take, and her mouth slightly opened as she realized the significance of the gesture, remembering her own explanation of the chess set to Robin just a few days earlier. She sighed almost audibly. *Damn. Robin, honey, I'm so sorry we had to be apart.* She decided not to wake the smaller woman and instead headed back into the master bedroom to unpack her things. Completing that task in relatively short order, she proceeded down the long hallway to her home office to work a bit on a legal brief which was due after the first of the year.

About an hour or so later, Robin awoke from her nap, a bit groggy but nonetheless feeling refreshed. She glanced lazily around the room to get her bearings, idly noting that it was already late afternoon, and was about to return the chess figure she'd been holding to its proper location when something caught her eye. There, perched on the edge of the coffee table, was an adorable plush stuffed animal staring right back at her. Green eyes blinked to focus, then blinked again. *Snoopy?* The corners of her mouth twitched to a grin as she picked up the plush toy. *Jess is home.* Robin stood up, and after giving her petite frame a quick stretch, made her way down the long hallway, first checking the master bedroom, then wandering over to the other side of the house to Jess's office. The door was slightly ajar, and Robin stealthily opened it a bit more, regarding the older woman unseen for a brief moment. She silently leaned a shoulder against the wood doorframe, while clutching the Snoopy stuffed animal to her, and watched as Jess diligently worked at her computer. Suddenly, surprised blue eyes tracked over to meet her own.

"Well, someone's finally awake." Jess grinned.

"Hi." Robin smiled affectionately, then walked over to the desk. "You didn't wake me up. How long have you been home?" The younger woman knelt down in front of Jess's chair and interlaced the larger fingers with her own.

"Not long, but you looked so cute sleeping. I thought I'd let you get some rest while I got caught up on some work in here." Jess spoke very softly. "I missed you, kiddo."

Robin set the Snoopy down on the floor. "Me, too." She leaned forward and wrapped her arms tightly around the older woman, irrationally afraid that if she let go, Jess would somehow disappear again. "I'm so glad you're back."

Jess returned the hug with equal intensity, then kissed the blonde head. She released Robin and sat back, stroking a fair cheek with her finger. "So, did it help?"

Light brows furrowed in slight uncertainty. "Um...did what help?"

Blue eyes glanced up shyly. "The chess piece." It was said with a gentle understanding.

"Oh." Robin laid her head to rest on Jess's lap. "I didn't mean for you to see that, but yes, surprisingly, it did help."

Long fingers stroked the short blonde hair. "I'm sorry we couldn't be together."

Green eyes fluttered closed. "We're together now. That's all that counts." Robin reached down and picked up the Snoopy. "Thanks for this."

A wide grin appeared. "You're welcome." Jess closed out her computer program and set the screen saver. "How about we go out by the tree?"

The younger woman nodded and stood up. "It's a deal." She held out her hand. "Come on, Snoopy. We've got some presents to open."

A dark eyebrow arched. "Snoopy?"

"You're my legal beagle, aren't you?"

I did say that. "I am." Jess smiled, then allowed the younger woman to help her up.

"Good. Then, let's go, Snoopy." Robin walked out into the hall. "And if you're really, really good, I'll give you a treat."

With that, Jess's eyes lit up. "Ooooh, a treat. What kind?"

Robin arched an eyebrow of her own. "A chocolate covered treat, of course." She winked, then quickly retreated down the long hallway, leaving Jess to ponder that rather bold statement.

Oh my.

****

A hearty fire burned brightly in the fireplace, the evening dusk settling upon the city and providing precious little natural lighting inside the spacious house. The Christmas tree stood in the corner of the living room, its colorful lights illuminating the tinsel and hanging ornaments in twinkling fashion, while the angel on the treetop glowed resplendently from on high. Familiar holiday carols played softly in the background, as Jess and Robin sat on the oriental rug in front of the fireplace sipping spiked eggnog and opening the many gifts situated around the tree.

"You know, somehow when I left for Tampa, I could swear there weren't so many presents underneath this tree. Then, when I got back, I could barely walk in here." Jess shot Robin a look out of the corner of her eye. "What happened?"

Green eyes twinkled. "I guess I just got carried away." Robin gave the older woman a frank look. "So, sue me."

"You know what they say, Robin. You can sue a ham sandwich."

"Very funny." The younger woman grinned. "Now, open up your presents."

"Okay, okay." For several moments thereafter, both Jess and Robin opened their gifts. Most were clothing items and an few small trinkets each thought the other would like. Of specific note was a shrimp-shaped key chain meant for one junior partner in particular. Jess held up the item and examined it. "I must say, you have excellent taste."

"Thank you." Came the pleased reply.

A long sideways glance. "I was talking to the shrimp." Jess quipped, then tuned and pointed to the last gift under the tree. "Hey, you forgot one."

Robin stifled her giggles and picked up the medium-sized rectangular box, shaking it a bit. "What is it?"

"Just open it." The older woman smiled, her blue eyes sparkling somewhat mischievously.

"Okay." Robin quickly unwrapped the gift, then looked at the front of the box, her light eyebrows furrowing in moderate disbelief. "Um...Jess?

A blue eye peeked beneath the dark bangs. "What?"

"It's not gonna work."

"What's not gonna work?" Jess inquired all too innocently.

"I know you. You think that by getting me these, I'll wear them instead."

Jess again feigned innocence once again. "You don't like them?"

"They're lovely. But it's still not gonna work."

Rats. The older woman attempted to salvage the situation. "I just thought that if you ever lose yours again, you'd have these as a back-up."

Robin couldn't help it. She tried, but failed, to suppress a huge grin. "As I recall, I did not lose them. You took them."

"But, I gave them back." A dark eyebrow lifted playfully. "Besides, you can't ignore the house rules, Robin."

The golden head shook. "Let me be clear. I object to that house rule, I never agreed to that house rule, and I appeal that house rule."

"Appeal denied." The junior partner smirked, sure she had gained the upper hand. She was, however, quite wrong, and an apparent stalemate ensued.

"Jess." Green eyes twinkled in defiance, a grin hinting at the very edges of Robin's lips in the process. "I will wear my bunny slippers if I want." A full grin now appeared. "But, thank you. They're very nice, and if, and I mean if, I ever need a second pair of slippers, I will be sure to wear these."

It was the best the older woman could hope for. "Alright." She pointed toward the gift. "So, do you at least like the color?"

"Yes. Blue is my favorite color." Robin paused as a thought occurred to her. "Jess, what's your favorite color?"

"Green." *Sea green.*

"Oh." That required further consideration, so Robin turned her attention to the base of the tree. "Did we miss any other gifts?"

"Just one." The older woman pulled a smaller box from behind her. "I saved the best for last." She handed it to Robin.

Petite hands took the gift from Jess and unwrapped the shiny gold paper, revealing a rectangular burgundy-colored velvet case inside. The younger woman hesitated for just a second, then slowly lifted the lid. Her breath caught as she stared in awe at the elegant diamond pendant necklace inside. "Jess…."

Jess rushed to explain. "It's my heart." She had originally prepared a speech, but for some explained reason couldn't find the right words at the moment.

Robin lightly fingered the delicate diamonds along the edge of the heart-shaped pendant. "It's beautiful."

Jess moved over and sat very close to Robin. She reached down and gently grasped one of the smaller hands and brought it up to rest over her own beating heart. She took a moment to order her thoughts, then almost shyly met the sea green eyes in front of her own. "Robin, I'm giving you my heart. It's yours, only yours, and I will never, ever ask for it back. This diamond necklace is a symbol for you to know that. And when you wear it, if you want to wear it, you'll know that my heart is always with you."

The younger woman listened, quite captivated as the sincerity of the words struck her, even as she felt the insistent beating of Jess's heart beneath her hand. She knew how hard it was for Jess to trust someone with the deepest part of herself, and she knew how fragile Jess still was over the constant fear that one day Robin would leave. It was this last thought that struck Robin the most. Jess loved her so much that she was leaving herself completely and undeniably vulnerable to her greatest and deepest fear. *I will not leave you.* Robin set the velvet case down and immediately wrapped her arms around the older woman. She clung on tightly, as if one hug could express all she felt at that very moment. "Thank you." She whispered softly, her voice breaking. "Your heart means everything to me, Jess. I promise I will take very good care of it."

Jess pulled back and met Robin's gaze, noting in the firelight the light tears glittering from the green eyes in front of her. She wiped the tears away with her thumb, then gave Robin a delicate kiss. "I know you will, sweetheart."

Robin picked up the velvet case once again and fingered the diamonds. "Will you put it on me?"

Wordlessly, Jess removed the necklace from its case and placed it around the younger woman's neck, fastening the clasp. The pendant hung just a couple of inches below the juncture of Robin's collar bone and was quite stunning, indeed. "How's that?"

Robin nodded. "Good." She brought her hand up to rest on Jess's cheek. "You are an amazing woman."

Jess kissed the petite palm. "So are you." A very broad smile followed. "So, I take it you like it?"

Robin almost giggled. "I love it, but we have one other little matter to take care of." She pulled out a small square box that had been hiding under the tree skirt. "This is for you." She handed it to Jess, watching nearly transfixed as the older woman slowly and very methodically unwrapped the gift as she tried not to tear the wrapping paper in the process. Robin sighed with unrestrained impatience, then gently prodded. "Don't worry about the paper, Jess. Just open it."

"Okay, okay." Jess grinned, then finally unwrapped the last of the paper to uncover a square gray velvet case. She opened the case with deliberate purpose, slightly taken with the how the firelight glinted magnificently off the white and blue sapphires as the bracelet came into full view. Blue eyes regarded it for several seconds, then the older woman lifted the bracelet out of its slot. "Robin, this is…." The proper word escaped her.

"They're sapphires." Robin began rambling nervously. "I know you don't wear much jewelry, but I thought it would look nice on you if you wanted to wear it, or you don't have to wear it if you don't want to, but if you wanted to wear it, it's not too formal or anything. It's completely up to you, so…."

"Robin." Jess gently stopped her. "It's beautiful, and yes, I do want to wear it. After all, it's from you, right?" She grinned, noting Robin's rather shy smile. "Here, let me put it on so we can see how it looks." She unfastened the clasp and began to slip the bracelet over her wrist, then suddenly hesitated. The combined light of the tree lights and the fire glittered off the inside of the gold band to reveal an inscription inside. Jess held the bracelet up to the faint light, squinting her eyes slightly to make out the small engraving. It contained one word. Only one word. That was all. But that one word, to Jess, held more meaning than a thousand other words. Her hands started to shake slightly as she read what was written, and she felt herself go a bit weak as she continued to stare mutely at the inside of the bracelet.

Robin watched all this closely, at first with curiosity, then with a bit of concern. "Jess?" The younger woman sensed an increasing build-up of emotion, and rushed to place both hands over Jess's larger ones, trying desperately to still them. "Jess?"

Jess said nothing for a very long moment, her unsure blue eyes tracking slowly to Robin's gentle green. She whispered the inscribed word, almost as if she needed verbal confirmation of what she'd just read. "Forever?" The reverent question hung almost palpably in the air between them, and Jess held her breath for a seeming eternity as she awaited the affirming response.

The fire's glow settled behind them, casting their profiles in dim silhouette. Robin inched her way directly in front of Jess and ducked her sea green eyes to lock fully upon the shaded blue. "Yes." She gently took the bracelet from the older woman's hands and placed it around the larger wrist, snapping the clasp closed. "Forever."

Forever. Jess could barely breathe. *Robin wants forever.* She was caught entirely in the emotion of the moment, desperately needing to hug the younger woman close to her. "Come here." She opened her arms.

Robin fell into the wonderful embrace, feeling the strong arms completely envelope her. She turned her head and kissed Jess's cheek, then pulled back and searched the azure eyes now in front of her own. "Is it all right?"

Jess brought her lips to Robin's and gave her a tender kiss. "It's more than all right. It's the most beautiful gift I've ever received. Thank you."

The younger woman couldn't contain the wide smile that followed. "I really like the blue sapphires. I thought they'd look nice on you, almost as if they were meant for you." She fingered the bracelet on Jess's wrist, then looked up a bit shyly. "What I wrote inside, I…."

"I know." Jess nodded sincerely. "Me, too." She shifted her position on the oriental rug, shaking out a kink in her leg. "Let's go over to the sofa where it's more comfortable." She got up and pulled the smaller woman with her.

Robin sat down on the plush sofa, then quickly stretched out to lie lengthwise, propping her knees up over Jess's lap. "I really love the gifts you got me, Jess."

The longer body shifted and nestled up against the petite frame. "You do?" A dark eyebrow arched in a bit of a challenge. "Even the slippers?"

Green eyes narrowed playfully. "Don't push it, Jess." Robin grinned, then pursed in her lips as a thought came to her. "Except, I didn't get my car."

"Excuse me." Came the low reply.

"I thought I was quite clear on the matter. BMW, really sporty looking, room enough for the tallest person, etcetera, etcetera." Robin waved her hand in a circling motion.

A bemused expression. "I thought you were saving for that yourself."

"True, but you can't blame me for trying." A green eye peered over at Jess. "You know, my birthday's next month."

"And?"

"Nothing. Just thought I'd let you know."

Jess rested her forehead against Robin's. "For your information, Robin, I already know."

A smile. "Good." Robin snuggled closer to Jess. "Can we just stay here awhile and look at the tree and listen to the music?"

A long arm wrapped itself contentedly around the smaller body. "I'd like that." Jess breathed in Robin's sweet scent, one which she could only characterize as spring rain. "So, tell me, how did it go the past few days with your folks."

"It went okay. They didn't say anything more about my going back to Detroit. I guess they're hoping I'll think about it." Robin frowned. "I don't think they're giving up, though."

Jess considered the statement. "Otherwise, no problems?"

There was a long sigh, but no answer to the question.

"Robin?"

"Um...there was one issue." Robin closed her eyes. "I don't really want to talk about it."

Uh oh. "Honey, please talk to me."

There was silence for several seconds as Robin contemplated what to tell Jess. "The issue was Christmas Mass. I didn't want to go, but in order to keep the peace, I went anyway. They know my feelings, but they don't accept it."

Jess took a deep breath. *We shouldn't avoid this any longer.* She decided to bring up the subject she'd put off for far too long. Sure, it would be difficult, but ignoring the problem wouldn't make it go away. She had to ask. The question had been circling around in her mind, niggling at her almost at every turn. Bracing for the response, Jess spoke in the gentlest of voices. "Have you completely given up God, Robin?"

Robin furrowed her brows, her attempt to dismiss the matter evident. "I don't want to talk about that."

Jess's expression was very sympathetic. "I think we should, sweetheart." She tapped her finger lightly on the side of Robin's head and whispered. "What's going on in there?"

I really don't want to get into this. The smaller woman shifted, then acquiesced to the request. "All right. To answer your question, yes, I have given up God."

Jess proceeded cautiously. "Because David died?"

Robin's features took on a hard expression. "Not entirely. I believe God abandoned me first."

Abandoned? "What do you mean?"

"I'm afraid you won't understand."

"I won't judge you."

Robin hesitated, then nodded her assent. "Okay." Soft eyelids closed tight in an as yet unresolved pain. "The night that...it happened, I had just completed law school. David came over. He said he wanted to talk about our future. He said he had changed his mind about what he wanted, and before we went through with the engagement, he wanted to make sure we both agreed. Instead of my starting my law career, he said he realized that what he really wanted was a more traditional family life. He didn't think I should work. Ever." Robin paused and took a breath.

Jess listened quietly. Robin hadn't spoken about the details of the evening of the accident, and she was sure the younger woman had taken great efforts to avoid thinking about it. But at what cost? Surely, it was better to talk about it. Sometimes things can be put in perspective that way. Or put behind you. *That's what you want, Jess. You want all of it behind her, so it won't come between you...so you won't have to compete with it.*

Robin swallowed, then continued. "I overreacted to what he said. I had just had a grueling week, and I didn't need to hear what he was saying. I couldn't understand why he had changed his mind. That wasn't at all what we had planned. I was so upset that I didn't want to listen to him anymore." She bit her bottom lip lightly. "I told him that he was selfish, and I didn't want to see him anymore if that's what he wanted. I told him to go away to never to come back." Robin started crying. "And he didn't."

Oh God. Jess held Robin tightly. "Shhh. Robin, honey, shhh." Gentle fingers wiped away the tears from the younger woman's face. "You were angry, honey. It wasn't literal. You know that."

The soft crying continued for another moment, then Robin sniffled and began again. "When his father called me to tell me that David had been in an accident, they said they were going to the hospital and for me to meet them there. As I drove the way to the hospital, I prayed that David would be all right. I prayed that I would be able tell him that I didn't mean any of the things that I said, and that my hateful words wouldn't be the last ones he heard." The tears came harder this time. "But when we got to the hospital, David had already died. God took him away, and I didn't have the chance to make it right. David never knew that I didn't mean what I said. I asked God for the chance to make it right, and He didn't listen." Robin abruptly wiped the tears from her eyes and hardened her features. "He abandoned me, and David, and I can't forgive Him."

"Come here, sweetheart." Jess held Robin very tightly. She kissed Robin's forehead and spoke in gentle, soothing tones. "Honey, you know I love you, and you know that I will never judge you. I will tell you this, though. God knows your heart, and He knows you didn't mean what you said. I believe David, in his heart, knew that, as well."

"You don't understand."

"What don't I understand?" Jess whispered.

A petite hand reached over and traced the strong jaw. "Because I said what I said, David died. Because David died, I came to Florida." She stroked her thumb against the side of Jess's cheek. "Because I came to Florida, I met you. And because I met you, I'm happier than I deserve to be. It's a chain of events."

What's she getting at? "We can't always know what lies ahead for us."

Robin closed her eyes again, the guilt at this point almost too much to bear. "Don't you see? God knows what I did. My actions brought about everything that has happened so far. It's only because David died that I'm with you at all, and that only happened because David and I fought that night." She opened her eyes and stared at Jess with startling sadness. "By my anger, I sacrificed him to ultimately be with you."

What the...? Sacrificed? The shock of hearing what Robin had just said surely registered on Jess's face. It was quite worrisome, indeed. The guilt had consumed Robin to the point that she couldn't see the inherent fallacy in her own logic. Jess took a breath, then spoke very firmly. "You listen to me. You did absolutely no such thing." Her tone was almost harsh, then softened a bit. "Honey, you didn't know. You had no control over what happened, and you certainly shouldn't feel that your being with me is at the expense of David. That simply is not true."

"Well, Jess, it started when I got angry, and it ended with you. It seems pretty clear to me. I set the chain of events in motion. I made it happen."

"No, you didn't. Look at me, sweetheart." Jess tilted Robin's head up to meet her own gaze. "I'm not a trained counselor, but I do know that this guilt you have is misplaced. Please, honey, for me, call Dr. Richmond." Jess studied the green eyes in front of her and noted the blank expression on the younger woman's face. *She still doesn't get it.* The older woman feared she was losing the battle. *Think.* Jess tried another approach. "Let me tell you something. I love you, Robin, but, as much as you may want to think so, you had absolutely nothing to do with that, other than be who you are. No one made it happen. It just did. And even if you had wanted to make it happen, if I didn't already love you, no matter what you did, you could never have made it so."

The blonde head rested heavily against Jess's shoulder. Robin didn't speak for several moments as she considered all of what Jess had said. Maybe some of that was true. Maybe nothing that happened was foreseeable. Maybe it wasn't all connected after all. On the other hand, maybe it was. Finally, Robin spoke, her voice almost forlorn. "I'm afraid."

That, and the way Robin said it, nearly broke Jess's heart. "What are you afraid of, honey?"

"I'm afraid that Dr. Richmond will make me see that it's all my fault, and that I shouldn't be with you because I don't deserve to be." Robin shuddered slightly, then spoke in a barely audible voice. "I couldn't bear that."

"Honey." Jess hugged Robin to her with all her might, then smoothed the ragged bangs on Robin's forehead. "That will never, ever happen. I promise you. You, of all people, deserve as much happiness as possible. I've said this before. I'm no great prize, Robin. I know that. Sometimes, I don't know why you want to be with me. But if you're happy, that's all that really matters." Jess placed a delicate kiss on Robin's lips. "And I promise you, I promise you, that I will do everything I possibly can to make sure you are happy." She gently touched her finger to Robin's nose. "You absolutely do deserve that."

Robin clung to Jess, unwilling to let go. "Okay."

"Okay?"

"I will see Dr. Richmond."

Jess blew out a very relieved breath, then offered a small smile. "Good."

Several moments passed as they both reflected on their conversation. Finally, green eyes looked up at Jess. "Are you sure there wouldn't have been anything I could've done?" She paused. "To make you love me, I mean."

"Nope." Jess smiled. "I loved you because you were already you. It absolutely had nothing to do with what you wanted." The smile widened. "I was already a goner."

Robin smiled back, feeling a bit better. "That's very sweet." Her brow creased a bit. "I think." She snuggled further against Jess. "Thank you for my necklace, Jess. I really love it."

"And thank you for my bracelet, sweetheart." *And the inscription.* "It means more than you know."

****

The office seemed nearly deserted. The week in-between Christmas and New Year's almost always was the slow point in the litigation department, save for one year when a labor trial was set to begin on January 2. That particular year, nearly everyone had been asked to work throughout the holidays to prepare. It was Jess's first case as second chair, and she took to the rigors of trial work like a fish to water. It had consumed her, and she found that she very much liked it that way. It had succeeded in allowing her less time to dwell on certain recent unpleasant memories...specifically, those of James. From that very point forward, Jess made it nearly her life's mission to immerse herself completely and fully in her work, and she was very good at what she did.

Robin sat at her desk and waded through her in-box. Mail doesn't take much of a holiday, she mused. It just piles up. She procrastinated a bit more, then stared blankly at her telephone, her mind flashing back to the previous evening. *I need to do this.* She flipped through the phone book, fingering through to the appropriate page, then dialed the number she'd been putting off calling. It barely took a minute. An appointment with a certain therapist was made for the following week and the task was completed. Robin set the receiver in the cradle. *Why was that so hard?* She was about to return her full attention to her mail when a light knock sounded at the partially closed office door.

The tall figure stood in the doorway, a bit hesitant to intrude. "Busy?"

"Jess?" Robin whispered almost surreptitiously. What are you doing here?"

That remark was unexpected. "Um...I work here."

Robin shook her head. "Come in and close the door." She waited for the junior partner to comply. "You know what I mean. We're supposed to be more careful, right?"

A scowl appeared. "Yes. I thought that's what we were doing." Jess sat down in the chair in front of the desk. "Are you saying that I can't come to your office anymore?" A look of absolute frustration spread across the angular features.

The young associate stood up and walked over to Jess, leaning her weight slightly against the front edge of the desk. "I don't know." She sighed. "I think we need to keep our distance at work."

The junior partner fiddled with the fabric on the arm of the chair. "Well, I don't see how we can do that totally. After all, we do work on the same cases." She flashed a wide smile. "Especially since you do all my grunt work."

Green eyes twinkled. "Ahaa. I knew it. You just want me around to do your grunt work for you." She pointed a finger playfully at Jess. "I'm on to you, now."

The junior partner's lips twitched to a grin. *She is so damn cute.* She wanted to slide her arms around the young associate right then and there, but the rational part of her mind realized that Robin was right. They needed to be careful. "My reason for coming over here, just so you know, is that I wanted to give you this case notebook." She handed a black binder to Robin. "Remember, you were going to help me with my trial in March?"

"Right." Light eyebrows furrowed. "So how can we be careful if we're going to see each other all the time at work?"

Jess thought about that, deciding on a course of action. "Here's the deal. We eat lunch separately, and then when we have to work together, we keep the office door open." She glanced deliberately at Robin's closed door.

The young associate's mouth fell wide open as the realization hit her. She nearly raced over to the door, opening it wide. "Okay." She situated herself back at her desk and spoke a little louder than necessary. "About that case notebook, what would you like me do?"

A blue eye winked. "Go through the pleadings and discovery responses. See if we need to depose anyone else or prepare supplemental requests for documents or another set of interrogatories. Also, see if we need to do any third party subpoenas. This is a fairly small case, so there won't be too many documents to go through." The junior partner stood up, a tiny smirk playing across her lips. "I know how much you love document reviews, Robin. I hope you're not too disappointed."

The young associate tried to keep a straight face at the last remark. *Not hardly.* "I'll have you know that document reviews have their benefits."

"Is that so?" Jess strode over toward the door and flipped a look back at Robin. "Then, I proclaim you document queen. Every single document review I have from now until further notice is all yours." A mischievous grin. "And I mean every single one of them, Robin. You're going to have so much fun." Another quick wink, then a prudent exit out the open office door.

Robin stared at the now vacant doorway, her green eyes narrowing at no one in particular. *I swear she baited me into that one.*

****

"Ooooh, that feels really good." Jess was spread out on the waterbed, lying on her stomach, her eyes completely closed in pure pleasure. "Where did you learn how to do that?"

"I have magic fingers." Robin grinned as she sat on top of the older woman, massaging the bare upper back and shoulders. "You do seem rather tense. What did you do today that caused this?"

"Hmmm." Jess was fading fast under the gentle assault. "Nothing. It just must be from sitting in that chair all day long and catching up on my work." A crystal blue eye opened. "I did have one unexpected surprise today."

"Really? What was that?" Robin kneaded the space between Jess's shoulder blades.

"There I was, busily working on my appellate brief, when Sam from the file room marched into my office and unceremoniously deposited a brown paper bag right on top of my desk." A hint of a grin played at the edges of the junior partner's mouth.

"Is that so?" Robin seemed unaffected.

"Yes, and when I opened the bag, much to my surprise, do you know what I found?"

Small hands worked a stubborn kink in Jess's lower back. "Can't imagine."

The taller woman snuck a peak back at Robin, noting a mischievous twinkle in the green eyes focused intently on the task at hand. "What I found, Robin, was lunch." She let go a soft, relaxed groan as Robin continued to probe her lower back. "It was very strange. I hadn't ordered lunch, and Angie hadn't ordered any lunch for me. I wonder where it came from."

"Hmmm. Well, now that is very strange." Skillful fingers pressed up and down the older woman's spine. "Didn't Sam know where it came from?"

"Nope. Just that it was left at the front desk for me." Jess let out another low groan. "God, that feels so good." She nearly drifted off, then remembered that she was in the middle of an interrogation. "You wouldn't happen to know anything about that, would you?"

The associate placed a small kiss on the junior partner's left shoulder blade. "About what?"

"Um...." Jess had trouble thinking. "About my mysterious lunch."

Robin moved over to the right shoulder blade and repeated the process. "Oh, that." Soft lips trailed up to Jess's neck and continued the assault. "Since we decided not to have lunch together anymore, and I knew you probably wouldn't eat, I happened to order some lunch for you when I ordered mine." Those same lips traveled to a nearby earlobe and nibbled happily. "Do you object?"

Jess swallowed, lost in the delicious sensation, then croaked out. "What was the question?"

Warm, moist breath caressed the ear below as the associate

spoke again. "Do you object?"

With surprising alertness, Jess turned herself and flipped Robin over in one fluid motion, landing fully on top of her. "I absolutely, positively do not object, Robin. I have a voracious appetite, remember?" She peered down into sea green eyes, then hungrily devoured the sweet lips in front of her. After a moment, Jess came up for air, murmuring softly. "You drive me absolutely crazy."

That's the idea. "Just because I bought you lunch?" Robin brushed her fingers back and forth against Jess's bare chest.

"Yes." Large hands deftly slid underneath Robin's flannel nightshirt and stroked the smooth skin. "My stomach is quite happy, thank you. Now, how about yours?" She lifted the nightshirt and placed several delicate kisses across the stomach in question. "Is it happy?"

Robin closed her eyes, thoroughly enjoying the light, sensual touches. "Um...yes, it's very happy." She laced her fingers through the dark hair and guided Jess to other areas. "All of me is quite happy right now, Jess."

"Good." Long arms pulled the nightshirt up and over Robin's head. "I aim to please." Jess resumed her position on top of the younger woman, and trailed her fingertips teasingly all the way from Robin's shoulders to her toes, stopping to linger at certain areas to explore them more fully. "Am I doing okay?"

"Yes." Robin gasped at the touch, then aided in removing Jess's Calvin boxers. She began kissing every inch of exposed flesh, finally making her way up to capture the soft lips once again. Green eyes fixed on blue. "I'm buying you lunch every day." Velvet lips kissed Jess's jaw, then ran back down her neck.

"And I'll see that you're stomach is happy every day." Jess began rocking her hips. "Deal?"

Robin's breathing became labored. "Deal." And as she spiraled slowly and uncontrollably toward release, it occurred to her that their entire conversation had, in fact, been in a sort of code. The deal of happy stomachs and lunch every day was in reality a disguised reference to something much, much deeper. She closed her eyes and allowed the impending waves cascade over her, while the translation rang out clearly in her conscious mind.

Forever.

What Robin didn't know was that Jess, as she followed the younger woman over that now familiar precipice, had the entirely same translated thought.

****

Later, Jess curled around Robin's petite form and breathed in deeply, Robin's sweet scent filling her lungs. It was very quiet in the darkened room, save for Robin's gentle breathing. Having studied the younger woman's sleeping patterns for several months now, Jess knew that Robin was still awake.

"How are you?" Jess stroked a pale eyebrow.

"Good. You?"

"Good." A large hand fumbled for a moment, then grasped the loose flannel nightshirt at the foot of the waterbed. "Here." Jess watched as Robin took the nightshirt from her and put it on. "Are you sure everything's okay?" The taller woman located and put on her own Calvin Klein sleep shirt and boxers.

Robin cuddled against Jess, snuggling within the warm embrace. "Yes."

Something's going on. "You remember our deal, right?"

The blonde head tilted upward, eyes narrowing slightly. "Which one?"

That brought a genuine smile which then turned serious. "The one where we agreed to tell each other if something makes us uncomfortable. If something makes either one of us uncomfortable, we're not going to do it. Remember?"

"I remember." The answer was short.

Jess asked the question again. "So, is everything okay?"

Robin burrowed her head further into Jess's chest. "Yes. I just surprised myself."

"How so?" Jess ran her fingers through Robin's soft hair.

The younger woman wasn't sure she could explain it properly. "Every time I think I have everything figured out, something happens and I realize something else." She furrowed her brows unseen, finally deciding to make the admission once and for all. "Jess, I think I'm addicted to you."

A low chuckle rumbled from Jess's chest.

"You're laughing." Robin couldn't help letting go a muffled laugh herself. "Cut it out." Her light giggles continued. "I'm serious here."

"Okay." Jess put on a straight face. "You're serious. You're addicted to me?"

"Yes."

A very wide grin. "I'll have you know, Robin, that I've been addicted to you for a very long time."

Robin propped herself up on one elbow. "Really?"

"Yes. It's quite hopeless."

Robin grinned. "See, I had you pegged all along." She ducked her head and gave Jess a tender kiss. "You are very hopeless.

"Damn right." Jess drew Robin tightly to her. "So, tell me, is it a bad thing being addicted to each other?"

"I don't think so." Robin pillowed her head on Jess's shoulder. "It just surprised me, and maybe scared me a little, to realize that I was so emotionally dependent on someone. I knew that I loved you, and that I felt very close to you, but I didn't associate that with actually needing you." Her fingers idly played with the hem of the Calvin Klein sleep shirt. "I guess it actually hit me over Christmas, but I didn't recognize it then. When we were apart, even though it was only for a few days, I felt like a part of me was missing. Now that we're together, I feel so…."

"Whole?"

The younger woman reflected on that. "Yeah, I feel whole again. I know it seems weird." Small fingers continued to fiddle with the hem of the sleep shirt.

Robin didn't see it, but Jess discreetly reached up and brushed a bit of moisture from the corner of her eye, then swallowed back the lump which had unsuspectingly formed in her throat. "No, it's not weird. I feel it too, sweetheart." She quickly gathered her composure, then brought up something which had been on her mind. "Do you still want to go to Tampa with me on New Year's?" There was a slight hesitancy in her voice.

Green eyes peered up, a bit confused. "Of course I do, unless you think there might be a problem."

"No. No problem. My mom would love to meet you." Now was as good a time as any to confess. "I...um...told her about us."

Robin abruptly stilled her fingers on the sleep shirt hem, then spoke softly. "What did she say?"

"She wants me to be happy, and she can't wait to meet you." A small, reflective smile played at the edges of Jess's mouth. "I have to say, though, that I was a little nervous about telling her. I should have known that she'd understand." Robin was very quiet. Too quiet. "Does it bother you that I told her?"

A very long sigh. "Well, I would never tell you not to tell your mom anything you wanted to tell her. It's just that I'm not real comfortable with anyone knowing. I certainly don't know when or if I'll tell my parents." *I seem to be very good at avoiding things.* Another long sigh. "I guess I just wish we had discussed it first."

The older woman mentally kicked herself. *Damn. You're an idiot, Jess. You're not the only one in this relationship.* "I'm sorry, honey. It was wrong of me not to talk to you first." Jess rubbed Robin's back soothingly. "To tell you the truth, I didn't know until right beforehand that I was going to tell her. It just came out. I shouldn't have done that, though."

Robin shook her head against the broad shoulder. "No, it's okay. You should be able to talk to your mom about whatever you want. I'm just being silly." A small finger traced indistinct patterns on the Calvin Klein covered stomach, a bit of insecurity now making its presence known. "What if your mom doesn't like me?"

That earned her a soft chuckle and a very strong hug. "She will love you. I guarantee it." Jess kissed the golden head. "And I love you. So don't you worry, okay?"

A muffled acknowledgment was the only reply, the sleepy green eyes now fully closed.

Jess watched for several moments as Robin's breathing evened out in slumber, then reflected on their light pillow talk. *Addicted to each other. How about that?* She wondered if it was really possible for them to have a life together forever. Her own eyelids grew heavy, and she began to drift off as one last thought meandered its way in an almost casual fashion throughout her consciousness.

I feel whole again.

****

New Year's Eve arrived. Several people from the office had planned a few parties, but neither Jess nor Robin felt inclined to make an appearance, opting instead for a quiet evening at The Ranch. Robin had picked up some ribs and was in the process of preparing dinner when Jess arrived home. Robin's not so secret rib recipe called for boiling the ribs in beer prior to barbecuing. This required, of course, that she drink the extra beer while awaiting the completion of the boiling process.

The dark-haired woman strode into the kitchen, her nose twitching at the enticing aroma. "Whatcha fixing?"

Robin twirled around, beer can in hand. "Oh good, you're home. Could you start the grill? We're having ribs tonight." She finished the near-empty can of beer.

An expressive eyebrow arched. "I see you've started the New Year's Eve celebration without me."

Green eyes squinted in concentration. "You mean this?" She held up the now empty beer can. "I'll have you know that I was just finishing the leftover beer from the ribs."

"Right." A blue eye winked. "That's your story and you're sticking to it."

"Goofball." Robin grinned playfully. "Want one?" She handed Jess a beer, then went back to her cooking.

"Thanks." Jess popped the top and took a sip. "Are you sure you don't want to go anywhere tonight?"

"Nope." Petite arms ushered the older woman out of the kitchen. "Now, go get the grill going or we'll never eat." Robin watched as the retreating form exited onto the patio, then checked on the status of the side dishes. A few moments later, she heard Jess come up behind her. "Is the grill ready?"

"Yep." The older woman wrapped her arms around Robin from behind and softly began humming, then singing, the words to an old familiar holiday favorite.

Maybe it's much too early in the game
Ah, but I thought I'd ask you just the same
What are you doing New Year's, New Year's Eve?

Robin closed her eyes and rested her hands on top of the strong arms wrapped snuggly around her.

I wonder whose arms will hold you good and tight
When it's exactly twelve o'clock that night
Welcoming in the New Year, New Year's Eve.

They both started swaying to the imaginary music.

Maybe I'm crazy to suppose
I'd ever be the one you chose
Out of a thousand invitations
You'd receive.

Jess spun Robin around in her arms, blue eyes locking steadily onto green.

Ah, but in case I'd stand one little chance
Here comes the jackpot question in advance
What are you doing New Year's, New Year's Eve?

Robin leaned in a gave Jess a sweet kiss. "You're very romantic." She grinned contently. "You sing well, too."

"Thank you." Jess gave Robin another light kiss, then raised a hopeful eyebrow. "So?"

"Um...so?"

"So, what are you doing New Year's Eve?"

"Oh." A chuckle. "Spending it with you, silly." Robin turned around and carefully placed the beer-cooked ribs on a plate. "I was thinking that we'd stay up late, have a little popcorn, and watch the ball drop in Times Square on TV. What do you say?"

"An absolutely fantastic idea. Can I be in charge of the champagne?"

A giggle. "Hmmm. Popcorn and champagne. That's an interesting combination." The smaller woman pushed the plate of ribs and some barbecue sauce into Jess's hands. "I suppose it would be okay. That is, of course, if you know how to open the champagne without spraying it all over the place."

Jess started to turn around, but stopped as a snappy retort came to mind. "Are you asking me if I know how to pop the cork?"

Robin's mouth opened as the phrase registered. *I can't believe she got me again.* The smaller woman turned Jess fully around and pushed her out of the kitchen for the second time that night. "You're incorrigible. Now, go on and put those ribs on the grill."

Jess chuckled on her way out the door. *That was too easy.*

****

After a tasty dinner, Robin and Jess retired to the living room with their coffee to watch a few old-time reruns before the New Year's Eve festivities on TV began. As midnight drew near, Robin got up from the sofa and put some popcorn in the microwave while Jess took the chilled champagne from the refrigerator.

"Need help?" Robin watched as Jess started to twist off the wire from the lid.

"Nope."

"How about if I put a dish towel over the top in case it sprays?"

"Nope."

"How about if you stand over the sink just to be safe." Robin backed away from both Jess and the champagne, not trusting the situation for one minute.

"Nope."

"Are you sure?"

The older woman gave Robin a frank look and began to ease the cork from the bottle. "I'm in charge of the champagne, remember? You go tend to your popcorn."

"Fine." Robin grabbed a bowl for the popcorn. "But don't say I didn't warn you."

"Yeah, yeah."

"And point it in that direction, will ya?" Robin indicated the pass-through opening on the opposite side of the kitchen. Just then, she heard a vacuum pop as the cork sailed through the pass-through and into the dining room. The younger woman turned around and gave the older woman an "I told you so" look.

Jess rushed to the sink, then glanced at Robin, both eyebrows raised innocently. "What?"

"So, how much of it spilled?"

A sheepish grin. "Hardly anything. For your information, Robin, I have everything perfectly under control."

"Right." Robin smirked. "We'll be looking for that cork for days."

Jess opened the cabinet and pulled down two champagne glasses. "I have a snappy remark to that, but I think I'll save it."

The smaller woman shuffled out of the kitchen, patting Jess's stomach in the process. "That would be very wise."

Upon preparation of all necessary popcorn and champagne, Jess and Robin situated themselves back on the plush sofa in the living room, popcorn bowl placed neatly in between them and champagne glasses sufficiently filled. They flipped the television to the correct station and awaited the final New Year's Eve countdown.

"It's starting." Robin's eyes lit up as the count began. "You know, they change that ball every year."

"Really? I hadn't noticed." Jess munched her popcorn. "It looks really cold up there."

"And it's only cool, here. Right, Jess?

That earned Robin a piece of popcorn to the head. Then another.

"Hey." A petite finger pointed at Jess. "Be good. I'm trying to listen to this." Another piece of popcorn flew by. "I'll pretend I didn't see that. It's ten seconds, Jess." More popcorn sailed. "It's five, four, three, two...." Robin was completely cut off as non-stop popcorn rained down from on high. She stared at the older woman dumbfounded, then shook the excess popcorn from her head. "Was that necessary?"

"Yes." Jess grinned happily. "It's my popcorn confetti." She dropped another piece of popcorn on top of Robin to make her point. "Happy New Year."

"Happy New Year, goofy." Robin leaned over and gave the older woman a lingering kiss, then picked up the champagne glasses from the coffee table and handed one to Jess. "A toast." She held up her glass. "To our new year together."

A very warm smile. “To our new year together.” Jess clinked her glass against Robin’s, then took a sip of champagne. “The first of many?”

Sea green eyes locked intently onto crystal blue. “Yes.” Robin finished her champagne, then set both glasses back down on the coffee table. “The first of very many, Jess.”

“Good.” Jess whispered, then pulled Robin in for an achingly tender kiss, one which held a hint of a promise mere words simply could not express. She pulled away, the devotion evident on her face. “Happy New Year, sweetheart.”

Robin rested her head against Jess’s forehead. “Happy New Year, Jess.”

****

“So fill me in on the who’s who of your family.” Robin sat back in the passenger seat of the silver Mercedes as they headed down the stretch of Interstate 4 to Tampa.

“Okay, first, there’s my mother, Elaine. Then, there’s my older brother, Peter, his wife, Peggy, and their kids, Jeremy and Michael.” Jess kept one hand on the steering wheel as she fetched her wallet from her purse. “Here. I have some pictures in there.”

Robin took the proffered wallet and opened it to view the referenced photographs. “Who’s the little one?”

“Michael. He’s two. Jeremy is four.”

“They’re adorable.” Green eyes studied the recent snapshots. “I can see the family resemblance.”

“You can?”

Robin flipped to a family photo. “Yes.”

“Then following your logic, I take it you mean I’m adorable, too.” Jess gave Robin a sideways glance.

Robin looked at the older woman in near disbelief. “My, we do have a high opinion of ourselves, don’t we?”

“Just repeating your own words, Robin.” The cross-examination began. “Did you or did you not say that my nephews were adorable? Yes or no?”

I’ll play. “Yes.”

“And did you or did you not then state that you could see the family resemblance?”

“I....”

The dark head shook. “Just yes or no, please.”

An aggrieved sigh. “Yes.”

“There you have it, ladies and gentlemen.” A triumphant look. “I’m ready to rule on the matter, now, Robin. The opinion of the Court is clear and unambiguous. I am adorable.”

“You are hopeless.” The associate muttered under her breath.

“Did you say something?” Jess inquired. “You’re my star witness, Robin. If you have something you want the Court to consider, speak up.”

“I said you’re hopeless.”

“Immaterial. I can be hopeless and still be adorable.” The junior partner smiled confidently. “So, then what you’re really saying is that I’m hopelessly adorable.”

Oh brother. “Pull over.”

Jess ‘s mouth fell open. “How come?”

“Because I’m convinced you’ve been sipping at the left-over champagne.”

“For your information, Robin, there was no left-over champagne. You finished it last night right before you started crawling around underneath the dining room table.”

“I was looking for the cork that practically sailed into the next county after somebody, who shall remain nameless but who is very hopeless, attempted to open said champagne in a correct manner but obviously failed to do so.” A small smirk. “If this particular person, who purportedly was in charge of the champagne, had listened to the person who was in charge of the popcorn, then perhaps the person in charge of the popcorn wouldn’t have had to crawl underneath that table to begin with.”

A quick roll of the driver’s blue eyes, but otherwise no comment.

“And another thing, if the person in charge of the champagne had listened to the person in charge of the popcorn, maybe some of said champagne would not have spilled onto the kitchen floor.”

A very bored look. “Are you finished, now?”

“Yes.”

“Good, because number one, Robin, I cleaned up the two drops of champagne that spilled on the kitchen floor. Number two, we will eventually find the cork. And number three, and most importantly, we still did not get all that popcorn out of the sofa.”

Robin was indignant. “Wait a minute, Bucko. I was not the one who decided to use the popcorn as confetti.”

“Oh. Right.” The junior partner contemplated her rebuttal. “It still doesn’t matter, Robin, because the person who was in charge of the popcorn still had the ultimate responsibility for everything pertaining to said popcorn. Don't blame me for your failure to adequately perform your responsibilities in the popcorn department." The older woman was quite satisfied with her argument.

Green eyes narrowed considerably. "You're impossible."

"I'm hopeless." Jess corrected.

"Finally." Robin gestured with her hands. "Something we agree on."

"Right. Hopeless." A blue eye peered over at the younger woman. "And adorable?"

That absolutely did it for Robin. She broke down in uncontrollable giggles, then reached over and took Jess's hand in her own, rubbing her thumb lightly over the knuckles. "Yes, Jess, you're hopelessly adorable."

Jess gave the smaller hand a gentle squeeze, then beamed in total victory. "See, I knew you'd see it my way."

The younger woman stared at Jess for a moment as the realization hit her, then shook her head. *It's amazing how she got me to admit that.* "You planned that very well. I'm quite impressed."

"Thank you." The junior partner grinned proudly. "It just takes a little practice. Do I get any points for my effort?"

Robin chuckled, then pondered the question carefully. "You certainly have excellent powers of persuasion, I'll give you that, especially since the subject doesn't know you're persuading him or her until it's too late." She considered the matter further. "Since I'm the judge of all things point-related, and I was very impressed with your persuasive skills, as opposed to your so-called champagne opening skills, I say yes, you definitely get points for your efforts."

"Good. Let me know when I have enough." Jess focused on the road.

"Enough?"

"Points."

"Oh." A blonde eyebrow arched. "Don't worry, Jess. You'll know."

I'm counting on that.

****

The silver Mercedes pulled into the driveway of the modern townhouse well before noon and well before its scheduled arrival time. Robin slid out the passenger seat and joined Jess for the walk up the sidewalk to the front door. All was very quiet, and Jess used her house key to enter the residence. Inside, the blue spruce Christmas tree was lit beautifully with colored lights, while an attractive fire glowed softly in the living room fireplace. Several stockings were hung on the mantel bearing the names of all members of the Harrison family.

Robin took in the scene with interest, the warmth of the family gathering room evident from just a moment's presence inside. She mused to herself that it was somehow reminiscent of a seasonal postcard setting, and all that was truly missing was the view of snow-covered trees and hillsides outside. To complete the setting, green garland, together with evenly spaced mauve colored bows, adorned the banister. Robin's nose twitched as she detected a faint cinnamon scent permeating its way throughout the house. It was entirely comfortable, and to be honest, Robin had never experienced this type of feeling before. Her own holidays from years past were very nice, but rather formal in nature. Her mother had a way of making everything very precise and proper, but not terribly original. She walked further into the room and admired the fireplace, examining with amused green eyes the stockings still hung at the mantel. She stifled a small giggle.

Blue eyes shifted in her direction, then an accompanying dark eyebrow shot up. "Something you find funny?"

Robin pointed to one stocking in particular. "Would that one be yours?"

Jess hesitated, then drawled. "Yes."

"It's very nice...Jessie." Another louder giggle.

A long finger wagged playfully. "It's a family nickname, Robin, and I don't want to hear another word about it." Blue eyes narrowed in mock threat. "You got that?"

Robin made an exaggerated show of zipping her lips shut, then turned to admire the Christmas tree. "Your mother did a great job of decorating the house. It's no wonder you get your tree fill every year here. I love the old fashioned ornaments."

Just then, an older woman stepped out from the kitchen, dusting her hands on her apron in front of her. "Oh, Jessie, you're here. I wasn't expecting you for another hour." She walked over to where Robin and Jess were standing.

"All part of my plan, Mom. See? You didn't worry, and we had plenty of time in case we hit traffic." It really was a terrific plan, Jess had to admit. She gave her mother a hug then introduced Robin. "Mom, I'd like you to meet Robin." Jess practically beamed as she said made the introduction.

"Robin, how nice to meet you. Jessie has spoken so wonderfully of you." Elaine Harrison grasped Robin's hand warmly. "I'm so happy you could join us today."

Green eyes lit up. Robin liked Jess's mother already. *I don't know why I was worried.* "Mrs. Harrison, it's nice to meet you, too. Thank you for inviting me."

"Come on, girls, let's sit down." Elaine led them over to the sofa and took a seat in the opposite chair. "Jessie, how was your week?"

Jess caught Robin's amused glance and leaned over to whisper something in her mother's ear, then sat back. "Slow week, really, but everything's great."

"That's good, Jess." Elaine enunciated the last word quite deliberately, enjoying Robin's not too subtle grin as she did so. "So, Robin, tell me how you're finding Florida."

"Other than missing the change of seasons, I really like it. I'll have to wait, though, until I experience the summer months before I give my full opinion."

"Most of the year is summer, Robin." Jess quipped.

The younger woman gave a Jess frank look. "As I recall, we had a few cold days not too long ago."

"Cool days." Jess corrected.

A playful smirk. "Right."

Elaine watched the gentle teasing with an interested eye, thinking how comfortable her daughter seemed to be in the presence of Robin. Her daughter did indeed appear happy, the relaxed demeanor a cue to how the younger woman had effectively washed away an underlying pain that Jess seemed to always carry with her. "Well girls, Peter and the boys will be over shortly so I need to get going with dinner. We'll be eating early so you girls won't have to drive back to Orlando in the dark." She got up and made her way toward the kitchen. "We're having ham today."

"Hey, Mom, are you making...?"

"Of course." Elaine smiled warmly and stepped into the next room.

Golden eyebrows furrowed. "Is she making what?"

"Nothing." Jess nonchalantly dismissed the question.

"You know I'm gonna find out. Just tell me."

The dark-haired woman seemed almost embarrassed. "She makes me a special side dish."

Robin's eyes twinkled and her nose crinkled up in a very cute fashion. "The main ingredient in that side dish wouldn't happen to be...say...shrimp, would it?"

"Maybe."

Robin chuckled a bit uncontrollably. "You are so hopeless."

"I thought we already decided that I was hopelessly adorable." A blue eye winked.

"Right." Robin contemplated the current situation, her green eyes holding a bit of mirth. "This is quite serious, you know. Even I hadn't realized the extent of your shrimp fetish until now."

"It is not a fetish." Jess insisted.

Robin patted Jess's arm indulgently. "Whatever you say."

The front door opened and two small, rambunctious rugrats raced inside, followed by two more subdued adults.

"Jessie!" Jeremy ran over to the sofa, with his brother in tow.

"Hey there, kiddos." Jess gave both boys a huge hug, wrapping an arm around each, then glanced up as Peter and Peggy entered the room. Peggy was a slightly taller than average woman with light blonde hair, and at the moment, a very frazzled demeanor. "Hi, Peter, Peg. Happy New Year."

"Happy New Year." Peggy crashed on the nearby loveseat.

Peter followed. "Hi, Sis. Happy New Year."

Jess began her second round of introductions. "Peter, Peg, I'd like you to meet my friend, Robin. She works with me at the firm."

Peggy extended her hand. "Hello, Robin. Good to meet you." She heard one of her children making a bit too much noise in the other room and turned to her husband. "Honey, could you check on the boys? I'm afraid they're bothering your mother in there."

"Sure." Peter stood up. "Nice to meet you, Robin." He turned and left the room, leaving the three women alone.

Jess watched as her brother retreated into the kitchen. "Kids a bit much today, Peg?"

A soft laugh escaped Peggy's lips. "You could say that. It's barely noon and I feel like I've run a marathon."

Jess thought for a moment, then shifted slightly. It occurred to her that her posture may appear a bit too cozy near Robin. After all, she hadn't disclosed their relationship to her brother, and thereby, his wife. Peggy was a very nice person, very friendly and easy to talk with. Still, Jess wasn't sure how her sister-in-law would react to the revelation. As a matter of fact, Peggy was a religious person and made sure the family attended Mass every week. She had even made arrangements to have her children attend the parochial school when they were old enough, a spot for each of them already reserved on future school rolls. As for Peter, to be honest, Jess wasn't sure what her brother would think about her relationship with Robin. That brought up another whole aspect to the situation. Would their relationship become a religious issue? Although Jess didn't often attend Mass, she did still believe many of the things she'd learned in Catholic school, even if she no longer practiced all aspects of the faith. She was brought from her momentary musing by a light tap on her forearm.

"Jess, do you think your Mom needs any help?" Green eyes studied the now pensive features.

"Let me go check." Jess made a hasty retreat and entered the kitchen, finding her mother preparing the glaze for the ham. "Hi. Where are the boys? I thought they'd be in here."

"Oh, they're out back with Peter running off some of that energy." Elaine turned the spice rack several times until she found the dry mustard. "I wonder what's got them so wound up today." She pulled the brown sugar down from the cupboard. "Is everything going all right out there with Robin and Peg?"

"Yeah." Jess hesitated for just a second, then finally spit it out. "Listen, Mom, I was wondering if we could keep my relationship with Robin quiet just for now?"

Elaine stopped, sensing a certain anxiety from her daughter. "Honey, of course. It's up to you when and how much you want to tell anyone." She picked up a small knife and began neatly scoring the ham, then offered a simple, yet sincere, comment. "She's lovely."

Jess visibly melted. "She is, isn't she?" A small, self-deprecating chuckle followed. "Sometimes, I can't imagine why she'd want to be with me."

Elaine added the cloves. "She loves you." There was really no further explanation needed.

Jess nodded. *She loves me.* It was indeed amazing. A small smile graced her lips as she pondered that statement a moment more. *Amazing.* "Here, Mom, let me start the sweet potatoes while you finish with the ham."

Finally, the meal preparations were completed and later that afternoon dinner was served. The boys ate most of their dinners and behaved well enough, save for one minor crying spell over the almond string beans. For Robin's part, she absolutely soaked it all up. The family atmosphere and warmth infused her spirit, something which until this very day she hadn't known she was missing. It was a beautiful family, loving and caring and accepting. Robin considered that thought a bit more. Elaine knew about her relationship with Jess, but not once did she appear awkward or uncomfortable. In fact, she seemed as if everything was perfectly normal. She even seemed...pleased, if that was the right word. It was an incredible feeling, and amazing at the same time. In just one small visit, Robin felt as though she belonged, and that, itself, felt very good.

After dinner, the adults gathered in the living room while the children went out into the backyard to play. The boys kicked the soccer ball around a little, and although Michael was barely two years old, he attempted an admirable job. Robin watched through the sliding glass doors with amusement, finally giving in to the urge to join them at their game. The boys did, after all, need a goalie.

As the younger woman ran and played with the boys, Jess watched from inside with considerable interest. *She's very good with them.* She watched further as Robin picked up Michael and gave him a big hug before lining up the ball for him to kick. *Does she want children?* Blue eyes focused on the younger woman's gentle manner. *She'd be a good mother.* Robin next lined up the ball for Jeremy and pretended to guard the imaginary goal. *She'd be a great mother.* A light touch on the shoulder brought Jess from her thoughts.

"Go on outside and play with them, Jessie. I'm sure the boys are running Robin ragged by now." Elaine winked conspicuously.

"I suppose I should try to rescue her from being overrun." Jess grinned, then joined Robin in the backyard just in time to see both boys pounce on the younger woman in fits of laughter.

Inside, Peggy kept a watchful eye on her children, mainly to make sure the little ones didn't overwhelm Jess's guest. It was in this context that she picked up on the unmistakable affection between her sister-in-law and Robin. Although she couldn't pinpoint anything in particular, Peggy got the sense that there was more going on than appeared at first glance. She had to admit that Jess's friend had quite a way with her kids, who definitely would have driven anyone crazy by now. That certainly was a very good thing and earned Robin high marks as far as Peggy was concerned.

After an eventful day, Jess and Robin reluctantly decided that it was time to head back to Orlando. If they left right away, they wouldn't have to make the hour and a half trip primarily in the dark. It was Elaine who worried the most about the trip back and forth from Orlando, especially when traveling alone at night. The two women bid their goodbyes, then set off for home.

Jess slid into the driver's seat and buckled her seatbelt. "Ready, kiddo?"

Robin smiled. "Yeah." A very thoughtful sigh followed.

"Something on your mind?" The older woman backed out of the driveway and headed out past the security guardhouse.

"It's funny, but I miss them already. Your family, I mean."

Jess smiled fondly. "Me, too, kiddo. But, we'll come back and visit again soon."

"Promise?"

"I absolutely promise." Long fingers reached over to grasp Robin's. "You can count on that."

I am.

****

"Hey, Jess?" Robin cuddled up tight against the older woman's chest. The still and dark of the late night surrounded them in lazy comfort.

"Yeah?" Jess wrapped her arms snuggly around the petite form.

"I had a wonderful time today. Thank you for inviting me." Robin felt a soft kiss against her forehead. "I really love your family."

"See, there was nothing to worry about." Jess traced tiny patterns with her finger on Robin's back. "And I know for a fact that they loved you."

"You do?"

"Yes." A low whisper. "My mom told me so."

"Really?" A small finger brushed the satin of Jess's pajama top, feeling its silky smooth surface.

"Yes. And I always believe what my mother tells me." Large hands rubbed back and forth in assurance against the cotton flannel nightshirt Robin wore. "You know what they say." Jess grinned in the dark. "Mother knows best."

A small giggle, then a contented sigh. "I love you."

"And I love you, more than I could ever say." Jess stroked the side of Robin's cheek tenderly. "You're the best thing that's ever happened to me and the best thing in my life. I'm very much looking forward to spending the new year with you."

Robin swallowed, then whispered. "I'm looking forward to that, too." There was a hint of uncertainty as she spoke her next words. "I'm also looking forward to spending many new years with you, Jess, if you still want that."

Yes. Azure eyes fluttered closed. "Yes." Jess ducked her head and kissed Robin lips ever so lightly. "That sounds very good to me." She hugged the smaller woman close.

"So, it's a deal, then?

Jess smiled unseen. "Yes. It's a deal."

"Good." Robin interlaced her fingers with Jess's larger ones.

"Good." Jess drew their joined hands up and underneath her

chin.

Peaceful sleep's embrace came quickly that evening as the two slumbering forms nestled snuggly against each other in quiet contentment, the dark and gentle stillness of the night surrounding them with a promise for the future both dearly hoped for and neither could live without.

The End

About the Author

KM lives and works in Orlando, Florida, although she is not originally a native of the Sunshine State. Born in New Jersey, she and her family moved to Florida when she was only six years old. The warm Florida sunshine proved to be a lure her family simply couldn't resist.

A graduate of Florida State University with a Bachelor of Arts degree in Psychology and Criminology, she went on to attend a paralegal school in Atlanta, Georgia before living in Birmingham, Alabama for several years. Thereafter, she returned to Florida in order to be nearer to her family.

A paralegal by profession, KM always sought more enjoyment from her personal life rather than her working career. She enjoys music and playing the guitar, having been a contract musician for the local navy base before it closed and then volunteering to provide music and voice vocals at local retreats, conferences, and other services. She also enjoys traveling and hopes to explore more of the many fascinating places the world has to offer.

KM is new to writing, having only recently attempted to tap the muse. The mixture and range of emotion she puts into her writing, from sorrow to humor, is often more a reflection of her own personality than of anything else. Her stories are written as a part of herself, and she hopes to continue on with the journey.

Order These Great Books Directly From Limitless, Dare 2 Dream Publishing		
The Amazon Queen by L M Townsend	20.00	
Define Destiny by J M Dragon	20.00	The one that started it all…
Desert Hawk,revised by Katherine E. Standelll	18.00	Many new scenes
Golden Gate by Erin Jennifer Mar	18.00	
The Brass Ring **By Mavis Applewater**	18.00	HOT
Haunting Shadows by J M Dragon	18.00	
Spirit Harvest by Trish Shields	15.00	
PWP: Plot? What Plot? by Mavis Applewater	18.00	HOT
Journeys **By Anne Azel**	18.00	NEW
Memories Kill By S. B. Zarben	20.00	
Up The River, revised **By Sam Ruskin**	18.00	Many new scenes
	Total	

South Carolina residents add 5% sales tax.
Domestic shipping is $3.50 per book

Visit our website at: http://limitlessd2d.net

Please mail your orders with credit card info, check or money order to:

Limitless, Dare 2 Dream Publishing
100 Pin Oak Ct.
Lexington, SC 29073-7911

Please make checks or money orders payable to: Limitless.

Order More Great Books Directly From Limitless, Dare 2 Dream Publishing		
Daughters of Artemis by L M Townsend	18.00	
Connecting Hearts By Val Brown and MJ Walker	18.00	
Mysti: Mistress of Dreams **By Sam Ruskin**	18.00	HOT
Family Connections **By Val Brown & MJ Walker**	18.00	Sequel to Connecting Hearts
A Thousand Shades of Feeling **by Carolyn McBride**	18.00	
The Amazon Nation **By Carla Osborne**	18.00	Great for research
Poetry from the Featherbed **By pinfeather**	18.00	If you think you hate poetry you haven't read this
None So Blind, 3rd Edition By LJ Maas	16.00	NEW
A Saving Solace **By DS Bauden**	18.00	NEW
Return of the Warrior By Katherine E. Standell	20.00	Sequel to Desert Hawk
Journey's End **By LJ Maas**	18.00	NEW
	Total	

South Carolina residents add 5% sales tax.
Domestic shipping is $3.50 per book

Please mail your orders with credit card info, check or money order to:
Limitless, Dare 2 Dream Publishing
100 Pin Oak Ct.
Lexington, SC 29073-7911

Please make checks or money orders payable to: Limitless.

Introducing...
Art By Joy

By JoyArgento

Hi, allow me to introduce myself. My name is Joy Argento and I am the artist on all of these pieces. I have been doing artwork since I was a small child. That gives me about 35 years of experience. I majored in art in high school and took a few college art courses. Most of my work is done in either pencil or airbrush mixed with color pencils. I have recently added designing and creating artwork on the computer. Some of the work featured on these pages were created and "painted" on the computer. I am self taught in this as well as in the use of the airbrush.

I have been selling my art for the last 15 years and have had my work featured on trading cards, prints and in magazines. I have sold in galleries and to private collectors from all around the world.

I live in Western New York with my three kids, four cats, one dog and the love of my life. It is definitely a full house. I appreciate you taking the time to check out my artwork. Please feel free to email me with your thoughts or questions. Custom orders are always welcomed too.

Contact me at ArtByJoy@aol.com . I look forward to hearing from you.

Motorcycle Women

Joy Argento

Check out her work at LimitlessD2D or at her website.

Remember: ArtByJoy@aol.com !

Printed in the United States
68482LVS00011B/61

9 780975 492253